DOUBLE WIDE

DOUBLE WIDE

LEO W. BANKS

BRASH
BOOKS

The characters and events portrayed in this book are fictitious. Any similarity to real persons, living or dead, is coincidental and not intended by the author.

ISBN: 0997832347
ISBN-13: 9780997832341

Published by Brash Books, LLC
12120 State Line #253
Leawood, KS 66209

www.brash-books.com

ONE

I got home at dusk and saw the shoe box on the steps of my Airstream. It wasn't there when I left. The hackles went up on my neck. I didn't even know I had hackles, but there they were. My trailer park sits on empty desert with nothing but jackrabbits and saguaros for miles around. Nobody lands at Double Wide by accident, unless they're lost or on the run.

The box was a message.

Opal Sanchez hustled up to the driver's window and gripped my forearm with two iron hands. "I've been waiting for you, Mr. Whip," she said. "You're late coming home."

Opal had been my tenant for six months. She showed up on foot, walked straight off the Tohono O'odham Indian Reservation. She wouldn't tell me why she was hoofing through the desert alone, anything about her family, or what went wrong at her village. All I knew was that she was seventeen and needed a place.

"What do you mean late? I just went to town for groceries."

She studied the dangerous sky. Hanging black clouds took the tops off the mountains, and a wind had kicked up. Monsoon. That was good news. It had been the hottest day of the summer so far, and a storm would cool things down.

Opal said, "It's going to rain. Hard, hard. It suu-ure is."

"Don't you know better than to stand outside in a storm? Is something wrong?"

Her face looked like the devil had just paid a visit. Her eyes shifted to the box, back to me, and then to the box again.

I said, "Yeah, I'm getting the same vibe," and sat there thinking things over.

The feeling hit that if I knew what was good for me, I'd throw the Bronco into reverse and gun it, leaving Double Wide forever. But lousy decisions had become my trademark. I had to be coming up on the record, and it seemed a shame to stop.

"Tell you what," I said. "I'm going to go eat and not worry about whatever's in that box. Pretend it isn't there. If I don't open it, it can sit there forever, right? Does that work for you?"

Opal nodded, mouth hanging open, eyes bulging.

Supper was leftover steak and refried beans with a bottle of Tecate. I took my time eating and tried not to think about the box. You can guess how that worked out. Every few minutes I got up and peered out the door.

The rain had started, fat drops angling down, popping onto rooftops. Opal was still standing out there. I hollered for her to get inside, but I don't think she heard me over the swirling wind.

Maybe that wind would carry the box off to hell, and I could get on with my life.

The storm roared like a monster. It whipped trailer doors open and shut, rattled the railings on my corral, and generally made it sound like the end of the world had arrived.

With my lights blinking on and off, I sat at the kitchen table sipping my beer. I made a game of it. In the darkness, a sip, and in the light, the bottle went back to the table.

Waiting, waiting. Then the lights flipped off again, and I stole another sip.

They say people don't know how to have fun anymore.

A desert monsoon changes everything. That far-off time before the clouds gathered, all of an hour before, is gone, washed away like a bad memory. Your troubles from the fire of midday have been cleared from the register, and in the liberating cool of the evening, life is completely different.

Your second chance has arrived. That's the West for you, the home of second chances.

When the lights came back on for good, I walked outside breathing in as much of that glorious wet air as my lungs could hold. The box was still there, and I'd grown curious.

What could be heavy enough to hold it down against the wind?

See what I mean about mistakes?

A rock kept the lid in place. I tossed it away. Bundle, one of my black Labs, peered out from underneath Opal's trailer, turned his face to the sky, and howled. Opal stood behind me, hair matted from the rain, clothes soaked, a specter in the post-storm light.

The object inside was wrinkled and beginning to darken with decay, from canvas colored to blood purple. My first thought was a fish, but we don't get many of those in the desert, and fish don't have fingers.

A glove? That was more hope than reality. I stared a moment longer to confirm that I was looking at a human hand.

That wasn't the worst of it. I recognized the former owner, if that's the correct term. Letters on the back of each of the four fingers of the right hand, between the second and third knuckles, spelled out M-A-R-Y. Between the thumb and forefinger was a small, sharply drawn tattoo of the Blessed Virgin's face.

Years before, at the ridiculous age of seventeen, I signed a contract to play professional baseball. I could throw a BB through a keyhole at a hundred yards. My catcher was Rolando Molina. We worked together beautifully, became close friends.

I last saw Rolando two years ago at the front door of a rehab center in Malibu. Two smiling brutes in lab coats escorted him inside to begin treatment for a serious cocaine problem.

I looked down at his rotting hand, thinking, I don't want the trouble that's coming. I don't want to go back out into the world. I want to stay at Double Wide with my dogs, my tenants who don't pay, and my bygone dreams.

But if you live by the known rules of life, the right and wrong of things, some decisions are made for you. Cutting off my friend's hand and stuffing it into a shoe box was all the way wrong. I had to find out what happened to Rolando Molina.

TWO

I slipped the hand into a clear plastic bag and put it into my storage freezer behind the Airstream. My hands shook so hard I could barely hold it. I covered the freezer lid in a heavy canvas and went back around to the front.

Opal was sitting behind the wheel of the Bronco. I got in on the shotgun side and asked if she knew what was in the box. She stared straight ahead. I took that as a yes.

She said, "Are you gonna call the cops? I sure wouldn't."

That made me suspicious. "Is there something you want to tell me?"

"Course not." Pause. "Well, okay. There might be some people looking for me, is all."

"What people?"

"From the Rez. Busybodies that go peeking around, finding out what everybody's doing."

"Sounds like cops."

"No, duh. Who do you think it is?"

"I'm not even going to ask. Jesus."

Opal held her hand out for me to drop the keys into it, which I did. "Want to tell me where we're going?"

She pointed out the windshield. Paradise Mountain loomed two miles south, an indistinct darkness against the sky. At the peak sat a town that grew up around a gold mine that hadn't been worked since the late 1800s. The old buildings stood empty, but drug smugglers used them as a pass-through point and rest stop.

Their route led off the mountain and through the wash right behind the Airstream.

Sometimes at night I could hear them down there talking things over. I kept a nine-millimeter Glock under my mattress in case they came out looking for a cup of coffee. The gun gave me options. Without it, all I could do was ask if they took cream.

Opal flipped on the high beams. "Check it out." She motioned to the dirt in front of the Bronco. "That loose ground holds on to tracks real good."

I got out and looked. The rain had washed the ground clean except for two curving ruts, probably where a vehicle had turned around and sped away toward the mountain.

Back in the Bronco, I said, "Deep tread and diamond grooves. I'm not much of a detective, but I'd say those tracks were made by a heavy truck. Had to be four-wheel drive. Nobody's going to tackle that mountain in a Ford Focus."

"A big red truck. Maybe an F-350."

"Let me take a stab at this. You were watching from your window, and somebody drove off the mountain, left the shoebox on my stoop, pulled a U-ey, and hauled ass back up there. And we're going to chase him. We're like a posse. Like those guys riding after Butch and Sundance."

She glanced over at me, confused. Opal had perfect, caramel skin, a jutting mouth, a wide flat nose, and brown eyes that hid nothing. Her body was round, and there was plenty of it. Her black hair was parted in the middle and flowed off her shoulders and all the way down her back. Straight, not a curl in it. The rain had left it gleaming.

I said, "You don't know Butch and Sundance?"

"Sure, I do. I seen them on YouTube. They do karaoke, right?"

"I can't see anything going wrong here. Really, I think we're good. Hold on a minute."

I ran inside and grabbed the Glock. Opal started the engine and revved it. At the familiar sound, Bundle came running and jumped into the back.

"Better hold on tight," Opal said.

She mashed the accelerator and banged across the open desert like somebody was chasing us. I reached up to grip the roll bar. Opal looked through the space between the wheel and the horn, her tongue showing between her lips.

The road was more of a two track. She could've stayed far to the right, keeping the wheels on the grassy hump between the ruts. But she made sure to drive into every cavernous puddle, spraying water far from our doors. We could only see to the end of the headlights, a tunnel-like stretch of sand, rock, and creosote bush cutting through the darkness.

As the road climbed, the jostling worsened. Opal tried putting the Bronco into four-wheel drive, but it kept dropping out of gear. Frustrated, she jammed the brakes and got out, leaving the motor running and the headlights on.

The rain had become a light drizzle. I grabbed my flashlight from the glove and flipped the dashboard switch on the four 120-watt day-lighter lamps rigged to the roll bar.

Opal walked ahead. When she reached the end of the beams, she stopped on her toes and windmilled her arms as if on a high cliff, and one more step would send her over the edge.

She spun and hoofed back to me. She had that ghostly face again. "You shouldn't go up there. Nope, nope. Better stay away."

"What's up there?"

"The breath of the Gila monster will set you on fire!"

"Knock off the crazy talk."

"That's serious business, Mr. Whip! Don't you do it!"

"Just wait here. I'll be right back."

I picked up the tire tracks again, and they matched, the same diamond tread. I whistled for Bundle. Doing his best warrior imitation, he darted into the darkness ahead, and I followed.

We hadn't gone a hundred yards past the headlights when he started barking. It began like normal backyard yapping and quickly accelerated, becoming the continuous, jaw-snapping growl of a frightened animal.

Running to the commotion, I lost my footing on the slick ground and pitched into a depression. My jaw smacked against something hard that wasn't the ground. The blow obliterated a few seconds of time, and when I returned to full consciousness, Bundle was jumping in circles and making the racket of a dozen mad hounds.

Trying to get up, I planted my palms on the chest of a dead man.

Rolando. I've found Rolando.

I'd seen bodies before, but none had ever looked deader. In the beam of my flashlight, the eyes were like a doll's, wide open, fixed, and big as hubcaps. The color had left them. There was nothing real about those eyes, no sense they'd ever seen anything at all. They were bottomless holes in a bloodless cardboard face.

I stared, waiting for my mind to kick in and confirm, yes, this is my old friend.

Can't you tell? It's Rolando. Look closely.

Nothing came to me.

His hands! See if he has hands!

His left arm lay exposed at my feet, the hand in place. The right arm was trapped beneath his body. I bent over the corpse, dug my shoes into the ground, and pushed the body up far enough to lean my shoulder against it.

It was hard work, like trying to roll a dead horse. My breath came and went fast, mixed with spit and fear.

Holding him in place, I pulled his right arm free and held it in the air like a corner man celebrating with his boxer. With sweat and drizzle blurring my vision, I had to hold it right in front of my eyes to see it clearly.

The hand was there, attached to the arm.

THREE

The dead man was shirtless and looked athletic. His upper body and arms were well muscled. His head was nothing but skin all the way around, the hair razored off. He had a black beard of a few days' growth, and his mouth was a tight grimace along porcelain lips. Mexican, maybe late twenties. I fished through his pockets for identification and found nothing.

I saw no obvious sign of trauma on his chest or stomach. But blood had pooled in the dirt under his head, a small circle black in the darkness. I gritted my teeth, raised his head, and felt around. The tips of my fingers found two small holes behind his left ear.

The double tap is a cartel signature.

Something else about the dead man caught my attention.

His jeans were unbuckled and his belt gone. If the killer had stolen it, that said a lot. Not only was he able to kill up close, but after doing the deed, he had the stomach to wrestle the corpse for an article of clothing.

Opal was waiting in the passenger seat when I got back to the Bronco. I told her about falling—but not what I'd landed on—and started driving back to Double Wide.

I said, "Okay, we've got a red truck, possibly an F-350, right?"

"That's it." Opal sat with her legs folded underneath her. Her back was erect and her chin raised, an attitude that, seen in tight profile, might've appeared to project pride. But she was trying to see over the dash.

I said, "The guy that left the box, describe him."

"Full moon."

"Full moon. What's that mean?"

"His head. It looked like the full moon."

"That's all you can give me?"

"How about you describe him? You seen him yourself, all dead up there."

"How'd you know that? And don't give me any more business about giant lizards."

"I got ears."

"Shot three times, right?"

"Twice. But nice try." Opal grinned, enjoying her little victory. "If the wind's right, you can hear a long way out here." She had a typical teenager's voice, cool, sweet, singsong, and loaded with drama when she needed it. She grew up speaking Tohono O'odham and you could hear its echo in the way she pronounced each word separately, a staggered sound with hard stops at the ends.

I asked if the driver was alone. She said there was something black next to him, maybe a passenger, maybe a jacket on the hook between the seats.

"If it was a man, he was teeny tiny," she said.

"Look, I'm keeping the hand. We're not saying anything to the cops about the hand."

"You don't need cops. I keep telling you."

"I can't leave that guy lying dead on the mountain."

"Ever heard of coyotes, Mr. Whip? Like, excuse me? Two days and he never existed."

"I've got enough trouble sleeping."

"You're such a saintly guy, a saint of the church. Like, seriously."

"That's me. A saint with a severed hand in his freezer. Remember, nothing about the hand. A strange truck came through, and we followed it up the mountain. That's it."

"Easy peasy." Opal flipped her wrist like it was a cinch. "I lie to white people all the time."

We bumped along the trail. The Bronco had no roof. It blew off a while back, and I hadn't gotten around to replacing it. My jaw felt like a block of granite that someone pounded with a jackhammer every five seconds.

Double Wide sat in dim light at the bottom of the mountain. There wasn't much to the place, seven trailers along both sides of a dirt road lined with white-painted rocks. Those rocks had been my first community-improvement project.

After that I dug a hole outside the Airstream and installed a forty-foot flagpole with the American flag at the top. Cashmere Miller, one of my tenants, a veteran of Iraq and Afghanistan, put up his own pole flying the marine corps flag.

I have a windmill to pump water, a corral with no horses, and out on the county road, next to the steer skulls hanging on the barbwire fence, I stood up a cardboard sign painted in red: *Welcome to Double Wide, Arizona, Population Six.*

As I pulled up outside the Airstream, I had my cell stuck to my ear talking to the 911 dispatcher. The sheriff would need forty minutes to drive over the mountain. I went inside, and Opal came with me.

My other black Lab, Chico, was lying on his side under my kitchen table. He didn't get up when he saw me but gave the floor a good hammering with his tail.

I filled his food bowl. He rolled upright and ate with the bowl between his paws, the tail sweeping the floor as he chewed. Without asking, Opal handed me a glass of milk, and I stepped outside again and sat at my midnight table to do some thinking.

What were you into, Rolando? Last I heard, the rehab had worked, and you were living happily in Mexico. How'd you wind up dismembered in a part of the world owned by drug smugglers?

There's lots of terrain between using and smuggling, and I couldn't believe he'd crossed that line. Something else had brought him to Paradise Mountain.

After a while, Opal came outside and handed me a rolled-up washcloth. "You need to ice up that jaw."

"I can get my own ice."

"Yeah, but you won't. You'll just sit there and take it."

"Good night, Opal."

"You're trying to get rid of me, aren't you?"

"Absolutely."

"I have stuff to do too, you know. I'm gonna make my noodles and watch TV."

Her trailer was directly across from mine. I watched her go.

Sitting there, I wondered if keeping Rolando's hand was a mistake. But I couldn't stand to see it stashed in some police freezer in downtown Tucson. At least behind the Airstream, he was with me. It might not be home, but it was as close as he was ever going to get again.

Almost 9:00 p.m. and the drizzle had stopped. Nothing fell on Double Wide now but starlight. I sipped my milk and waited to see the cop headlights streaming over the pass.

FOUR

'd never been around a homicide detective. But I grew up reading crime novels and had an idea what to expect. It turned out
those books hadn't made me as smart as I thought.

Benny Diaz from the Pima County Sheriff's Department
didn't fit the picture at all. He lacked the hard edge, the mean,
suspicious eyes. He was young and earnest and didn't know
that he was supposed to be an exhausted bellyacher in sweaty
clothes.

Diaz had a pleasing face and short black hair trimmed to
perfection. He wore a white short-sleeved pullover shirt. His
black slacks were beautifully pressed, his service weapon hooked
to his belt. He wore brown shoes with tassels.

I'd seen men wearing tassel shoes before, and all of them sat
in baseball offices nursing pulled muscles from moving piles of
paper.

He was fit but not athletic, with a gym rat's body. His arms
swelled inside his shirt sleeves, the veins bulging down to his
wrists. That told me he had time on his hands and was unmar-
ried. He was somewhere around thirty and probably hadn't
worked more than two or three homicides.

He introduced himself at the Airstream before driving up
the mountain to look over the crime scene, and when he came
back ready to talk, I was sitting outside smoking a cigar. By then,
cop cars were streaming up the mountain.

Diaz said, "I checked your name before coming out here. Prospero Stark. You're Whip Stark, right?"

"That's right."

"I read about that unbelievable game you pitched at Hi Corbett. That was some performance."

Hi Corbett was Hi Corbett Field in Tucson, home of the AAA Tucson Thunder. When I pitched for the Thunder, the whole baseball world knew me. Cover of this, cover of that, ESPN. That's where "Whip" came from. A sportswriter gave me the nickname on the idea that I threw the ball so hard that hitters got whiplash trying to follow it.

On the night in question, I struck out twenty, still the record for that ballpark.

Diaz sat opposite me. He leaned forward with his arms on his thighs and gave me his working smile. "I checked your stats. You rewrote the Pacific Coast League record book."

"I call it the family album. Those records still stand."

"You were a lock to become a big league superstar. They called you the Phenom."

"They called me a lot of things, Detective."

"If you don't mind my asking, whatever happened to you?"

I got that question at least three times a week and had perfected my answer to a single word. "Shoulder," I said with finality, eliminating the need for further inquiry. I waved my cigar at the trailers of Double Wide. "I'm a landlord now. As you can see, things turned out fine."

He didn't know what to say to that and nodded absently. A breeze blew down Main Street. It carried the animal smell of the desert after a rain.

Diaz said, "Now, the name Prospero, that comes from Shakespeare, correct? *The Tempest* was his last play."

"A homicide detective who reads. I'm impressed."

"I know that because of your father, Mr. Stark."

"Everybody calls me Whip. You know Sam?"

"I took his Shakespeare class at Arizona State. Best class I ever had. I was dismayed to read about his current trouble and very sorry."

Dismayed? Did I call the cops or the country club? "Nice of you, thanks. But I had all the Shakespeare I could handle growing up."

"You're not a fan?"

"My taste ran to the hard-boiled stuff. Cain, Cornell Woolrich, Jim Thompson."

"I'll bet that didn't sit well with Professor Sam."

"Did you know he kept a bottle of Glenlivet in his desk at school?" I was happy talking about Sam and Shakespeare as long as he wanted. I figured he'd used the drive over the mountain to work out how he wanted to play this and he'd get around to business in time.

I sipped my milk and continued. "My father delivered drunken soliloquies from the podium and came home to deliver drunken soliloquies from the dinner table. When I couldn't take it anymore, I went to my room to read about men murdering each other with belly guns."

"You enjoyed that?"

I puffed my cigar and blew. "Helped me sleep."

"Well, detective stories are still quite popular."

"They move, and they have endings. Nobody comes to terms with anything."

After a pause, and a glance to make sure the sky was still there, he said, "It's so unusual, isn't it?"

I motioned with the cigar for him to go on.

Diaz said, "The son of a renowned literary scholar prefers action-packed stories to Shakespeare and goes on to succeed in a physical profession like baseball."

"Fathers and sons. I'm still his biggest supporter."

"Blood loyalty. I'd expect that." He shifted in his chair and fussed through several expressions meant to convey heavy thought. Finally: "Like it or not, my profession makes a thinker out of me, Whip."

"Sounds exhausting."

Diaz tapped his temple. "I make connections between things. I'll give you an example. A heroin-addicted professor named Sam Houston Stark allegedly carves up his prostitute, and I'm sent out to investigate a murder near a major cross border heroin trail, below which lives the very same professor's son. Who himself did time in Mexico for cocaine possession."

That did it for chitchat. Diaz had officially arrived at work. We stared at each other for a moment.

"My father didn't carve up anybody. He's innocent, and the trial will show that. As for the Mexico trouble, I'll tell you whatever you want to know."

Diaz gave me his sympathetic face. "You understand my position, Whip. I've got to throw everything into the soup."

"Don't go too wide, Detective. You have a body on a smuggling trail, two eyes in the back of his head. It's a drug hit."

"You're sure about that?"

"Every night the gang that owns this trail runs loads through here. I thought it was marijuana, you say heroin. Okay, they've expanded operations. But it's every night."

"You don't call the law?"

"Out here, civic pride can get you killed."

"You understand we rely on the public's participation."

Those words gave me a chill. I think he believed them. "Let me tell you the rules of living on a smuggling trail. Never touch the loads. That's number one. Number two, let the *narcos* do their business, and you do yours and hope the two don't meet. That means losing your peripheral vision. See only what you need to see. Lose your telephone, too, because you're on your own."

"But you called us anyway?"

I pointed at the mountain, now shining with police lights. "That fellow up there, he needed a wagon to come pick him up. Everybody deserves that much at the end."

Diaz sat watching me with a figuring expression. "I don't get it. You were a star athlete, a really big name. You must've made a few million bucks in your career, but you live in the middle of nowhere on a drug trail twenty-five miles from the Mexican border?"

"I like the views."

"With tenants of questionable character."

That didn't sit well, but I let it go. Diaz fetched a pair of black glasses from the pocket of his slacks and put them on. They angled off the tip of his nose. From the same pocket, he retrieved a notebook and flipped it open to the page he wanted. He said, "There's a fellow here I'd like to speak to. Charles Hearn O'Shea."

"Yeah, Charlie." I motioned to the trailer sitting across the southern end of Main Street. It was held up by stacked cinder blocks at the four corners, but the top block underneath one corner had shattered, likely in the storm winds. "What do you want with Charlie?"

"Earlier today, we got a call about a knife attack at Woody's Lounge on South Sixth Avenue."

"Charlie left here a few days ago on vacation. That's what he calls it when he goes to town and drinks for a week. He's a housepainter."

"He witnessed the attack, and deputies talked to him at the scene. But he disappeared before we could do a follow-up." Diaz studied his notebook and peered at me over his glasses. "How about Cashmere Miller? Where can I find Mr. Miller?"

"Cash has put his life back together, I can attest to that. He's a veteran." After Iraq and Afghanistan, Cash went to work for his brother, who happened to run a truck-theft ring. When the cops moved in, Cash sang about everyone but his brother and got probation.

"I'll need to have a word with him," Diaz said.

"Look, I've got five tenants, and none of them are involved in the trade. If they were, I'd run them off. I hate drugs and everybody involved in drugs and won't tolerate it here. I make that clear the first day."

"It's routine. I assure you."

"Looks to me like you're harassing my people for no reason." I took a last puff of my cigar and threw it away.

Diaz held the notebook between his knees and watched me with cool eyes. I understood his position. The chief of detectives sent him out to investigate a body on a remote mountain trail with no expectation that he'd find a thing. They rarely do.

In the viciousness of the drug war, the desert sprouts bodies like beer cans, and there's nothing to go on. Death by gunshot, perp gone, no murder weapon, no decent forensics, motive unclear. Close the drawer and move on to the next one.

But Benny Diaz wasn't the type to walk away. He was going to look under every bed, and I might even help him if it got me closer to finding out what happened to Rolando. I just needed to make sure he stayed away from that freezer.

When Diaz got around to the body on the trail, I gave him the sanitized story, and he walked over to Opal's trailer. Hers was the biggest of the seven, four bedrooms with a lime green exterior except where side panels had fallen off, leaving rectangles of black tar paper.

There were no steps to get inside, and Diaz might've stood five foot seven on the Phoenix phone book. Opal's front stoop came to his belt buckle. She kept an upturned paint bucket on the ground below the door.

Diaz studied his predicament, planted a tasseled shoe on the bucket, and reached forward with backward-turned hands to grab the jamb on both sides and pull himself inside.

FIVE

I dug through a drawer to get a phone number for Rolando's family. Finding it was the second worst part of my day. Now I had to call and say whatever I was going to say.

How do you tell parents you have their kid's hand in your freezer? And do you tell them? I didn't know where the rest of him was and that was the first question they'd ask. The next question was how did I happen to possess the hand?

Well, you see, someone in a red truck put it in a shoe box and left it on my steps, but that person got bushwhacked on a drug trail.

What do the police say? They don't know about Rolando or the hand in my freezer because I didn't tell them.

The answers got worse the further along I went.

I had met Rolando's parents once before, back when we were making our way through the minor leagues together. They came to watch us play in Vegas, against the Las Vegas Stars. His dad, Oscar, owned a cattle ranch, and his mom, Natty, looked after the brothers and sisters.

We gave them a tour of the locker room, they watched us play, and afterward we had dinner and showed them the town. They were great people, delighted to be part of their son's world. It was one of those nights you don't forget.

I killed the remaining hours before midnight with my cell in hand, but my muscles weren't cooperating with punching in the number.

Why not wait until morning? The police were still on the mountain, and maybe they'd come back with information to fill out the story. They might even find Rolando's body.

I settled into bed around 1:00 a.m. and fought the mattress until dawn, when I got up and let Chico out. I waited to make sure he got down the steps all right. Chico had three working legs. He came back from the desert one day with a bullet in his left hind leg, leaving it a useless husk dangling off his hip.

When he was safely outside, I went back and sat on the edge of my bed. Waiting wasn't going to make talking to the Molinas any easier. I punched in the number and felt relieved when their zombie message kicked on. I left an urgent request for a call back.

After showering and dressing, I got busy cooking breakfast. I'd recently finished a complete renovation of the Airstream that included a new three-burner stove that cooked as well as any house stove.

I was using a fork to wrangle the bacon in the pan when the door opened and Opal walked in. No knock. She'd just rolled out of bed and looked like it in loose-fitting black paisley-print pajamas. She shouldered past me. "Scooch. I need OJ."

"I hope I'm not in your way."

She yawned and scratched her head. "No, you're fine."

She poured herself a glass and sat at the kitchen table. It was to the right of the door as you entered and hugged the rounded back window. A three-section bench seated five, as long as every-one kept their elbows close, and folded out into a bed if necessary.

I'd rigged a small TV to the ceiling above the table. Opal sipped her juice and watched CNN. I asked what she was doing up so early.

"I need to get to town to work. Can I hitch with you? I'm, like, totally out of money."

"After I get a call. How'd it go with Diaz?"

"I didn't think he'd be so handsome."

"The truck, Opal. Did he press you about the truck?"

"Not too bad. I told him like we said."

A few minutes later, Chico came back and settled under the kitchen table, his favorite place since the shooting. Cashmere Miller wasn't far behind.

"I got back late last night, missed the excitement," Cash said. "Big transmission job."

"They killed a guy," Opal said, without taking her eyes off the TV.

"All them lights, man, I thought the mountain was on fire," Cash said.

He was pale and thin with a long neck, narrow sloping shoulders, wide-stepping feet, and spindly legs. He had a runway for a forehead and curly-wire hair that topped his head like a broccoli crown. He wore a blue flannel shirt with the sleeves torn off, leaving long threads dangling against the dagger tattoos along both biceps.

He poured himself coffee and sat opposite Opal, cupping his mug with grease-stained hands. "Do we know who it was, the dead guy?"

"Nope." I was stirring scrambled eggs in the frying pan.

"Drug stuff?"

"What else?"

"Them mooks, they'll shoot anybody. Uh-huh, uh-huh." As he spoke, Cash swung his head back and forth in a pendulum motion. His owl eyes moved in sync with his head, never settling directly on the listener.

I filled the plates at the kitchen counter and set them down on the table, and we ate. A sheriff's car roared down the entrance road that leads into Double Wide, turned in front of the Airstream, and continued toward the crime scene on Paradise Mountain. The sound of it in the quiet morning had us all leaning down and looking out the open door as it passed.

I said to Cash, "I noticed that rig you were driving last night."

"My brother's Dodge Dart. What about it?"

"That trouble of yours with the stolen trucks. Is that it, or is there anything else I need to know about?"

"Got into some shit in the marines, but that don't count."

"The detective working this murder is Benny Diaz. He wants to talk to you."

"Uh-huh, uh-huh." That was Cash's all-purpose conversation mover. Anything he wanted to communicate could be done with a double "Uh-huh."

"You're sure that's it?"

"Ain't done nothing but go to town and fix cars in my brother's driveway. Sweat."

A car stopped outside, and Diaz came up the front steps. He flattened a palm on either side of the door and poked his head inside. "I'm looking for Cashmere Miller."

"Copy that," Cash said.

"We need to talk outside, if you don't mind."

Cash said, "Thanks for the grub, Mr. Mayor," and walked out the door.

Diaz raised his eyebrows at me. "Mr. Mayor?"

"It was a by-God landslide."

When Diaz was gone, Opal said, "If I knew he was that handsome, I so would've done my toenails."

SIX

I cleaned the kitchen and made an appointment with a curator at the Arizona Historical Society in Tucson. The call came just after 10:00 a.m.

"Mr. Stark, I'm Alice Menendez, Rolando's cousin." Panic ran along the edge of her voice. "Rolando's missing! Do you know where Rolando's at?"

The words landed on me like a sofa and I almost blurted it out: he's in my freezer, at least part of him. Alice went on talking, or I might've done it.

"Everyone's so upset," she said. "He was helping his brother, and he just disappeared."

"Helping his brother how?"

"In baseball. Fausto pitches in Monterrey, for the Sultans in Monterrey." The Sultans were a franchise of the AAA Mexican summer league. It looked like Fausto was following Rolando's lead in the game. I asked how long he'd been gone.

"Two weeks. He told Fausto he needed to take care of some business, and that was the last we heard from him. Nobody knows where he went to, and his phone goes right to voice mail. He wouldn't just go away like this. Something's happened."

I didn't want to tell Alice what I knew. His parents deserved to hear it first.

"Did he have any business up here?"

"I was hoping you'd know," Alice said. "We called everyone. Nobody knows nothing!"

"All right, where's Oscar? Is Oscar there?"

"Oscar's out working. We sent somebody to find him."

"You mean at the ranch?"

"No, he lost the ranch, Mr. Stark. Things were bad, money and everything."

"Sorry to hear it. I know how much he loved that place."

"He does mining now. He goes for days, and sometimes there's no signal out there. We're trying to find him. This is so terrible. Oh, it's so terrible!"

"What about Natty?"

"She's here, Mr. Stark. But she can't talk. She's too upset."

I heard anguished voices in the background and Alice Menendez trying to quiet them.

I said, "Was Rolando in any trouble that you know of?"

"No, no, no, everything was fine."

"I'm talking about cocaine, Alice. Was he backsliding?"

She let a long time pass before answering. "I don't know. We never talked about that. Maybe he did it a little bit, but I don't think so. No, no, I'm sure he was clean."

Alice sounded young, likely a teenager. She talked as if she knew me, and that probably came from family stories. I let her go on because she needed to unload. I was a friendly voice, a well-known American, and she thought I could help.

She said Rolando had gone to Monterrey in April to help Fausto train in advance of the Sultans' opening game and stayed on. She gave me Fausto's contact information. I heard Natty wailing in the background and Alice trying to calm her.

Alice kept saying, "Stop it, Natty! You're being so crazy today! *Que lastima!*" Then to me: "I have to go!"

"Alice, are you still there?"

"Yes, yes...Natty, please...don't be that way! Yes, I'm here, Mr. Stark."

"Have Oscar call me. Soon as he comes back, he needs to call me."

Alice said okay. Then: "Mr. Stark, please, help us find Rolando? Promise you'll help us find Rolando?"

"Yes. I promise."

I felt like the world's biggest heel. They deserved to know. But I was counting on the problem working itself out in a hurry. They'd find Oscar, he'd call me, and I could reveal the terrible truth—the part of it I knew, anyway.

SEVEN

As soon as I hung up with Alice, I left a message with Fausto. At 11:00 a.m., I started the Bronco and hit the horn and Opal hurried out her front door carrying her easel and a small gear bag. She did pencil sketches on the sidewalk in downtown Tucson. She wore a floppy white sunhat with a plastic red rose tucked under the black band.

The trip was sixteen miles. The first five crossed empty desert before climbing into the Tucson Mountains. The road was steep and winding. The mountain slopes were covered with massive multiarmed saguaros, the tallest ones marking the sky.

In the tightness of the pass, with the saguaros crowding both doors, it felt like driving through an alternate world populated by staring, spiny green monsters.

After the peak, the view opened to the city itself, a panorama of glaring sunlight, dust, asphalt, and sprawl. What a strange sight: a million people mashed into a valley of sand and scorpions, a flat, scorching-hot, slow-moving college town of flip-flops, palm trees, drifters begging from street corners, the look of easy southwestern charm, the world's unquestioned leader in back-in parking.

Throughout its history, Tucson has never had water, money, jobs, or shade, but that hasn't stopped the people from coming and the bulldozers from roaring. And when nobody was looking, the drug goons slipped into town.

The city sits along a cartel distribution network that moves every drug you can name through its streets and to every city and town in the country. But some of it stays behind, and that means shootouts over missing shipments, deliveries not made, promised payments that get lost or diverted, and retribution must be taken.

Those are matters of profit and loss, matters of real substance, although the trouble doesn't need to stem from substance. It can be as pointless as a sidelong glance at a south-side traffic light, one gang member bracing a rival. It gets messy. A lot of blood gets spilled. You can read all about it in the gang graffiti written across the bridges and buildings of the city.

The drug trade has burned a hole through Tucson's innocent heart.

I drove east into town on Speedway Boulevard. Opal's best work spot was outside the convention center, where she could hit up downtown workers, and whatever visitors happened to be around in July.

She sold her portraits for $20 apiece. On good days she left with $200, assuming she didn't give away money. If someone walked by with a weepy story, she'd peel off a $20 bill and hand it over.

Pulling up to the curb, I said, "Don't be giving away your cash, understand?"

"I'm gonna make money, not give it away."

"I'll pick you up. Say around five."

"Ten-four, Mr. Whip." She had trouble getting out of the Bronco. She juggled her sketch gear and somehow got wedged in the door. She was built like a fullback with broad shoulders and plank legs.

Just as she got one foot on the ground, a gust of wind nearly stole her hat. She squealed, got it back, set her duck feet onto the pavement, stumbled against the curb, and mashed her free hand down on the hat before it flew away again.

She yelped, "I meant to do that!" Then she yanked her pants out of her crack and scooted down the sidewalk.

EIGHT

I drove east of downtown to the edge of the University of Arizona campus and parked outside the Marriott Hotel. The parking meters give you fifteen minutes for twenty-five cents. I coughed up four quarters, figuring that should be enough to get what I needed from Tork Mortenson at the Historical Society.

The building, catty corner to the hotel, looks like a mausoleum from the street and gets worse inside. Mortenson waited in the basement, which was part storage area and part office space. His particular hole in the wall was dusty, echoing, and freezing cold in contrast to the outside air. The air conditioner bellowed nearby.

When I appeared in his doorway, Mortenson came around his desk with a hearty greeting. "I hope you didn't have trouble finding me."

"Not at all," I said. "You give good directions."

"Some people get lost coming down here. Not the state budget cutters. They know right where to go." He motioned to a chair opposite his desk. "Have a seat, have a seat."

Mortenson looked to be near retirement. He was thin, wiry, and academic, born to sit in a cluttered office wearing corduroy and soft shoes. He had a fuzzy white mustache that wanted to crawl into his mouth. He moved with vitality and clearly loved what he did, which was talking about the past.

He held up a book, *The Fever: Discovering Gold in Arizona Territory, 1863–1895*. The cover image was a period black-and-white of a grizzled miner holding a gold nugget over his head.

"You indicated you were interested in learning more about gold mining at Paradise." He held up the book. "I wrote this underappreciated epic twenty-two years ago and had to dig it out to refresh my memory. It's remarkable what you forget over time. Are you a writer, Mr. Stark?"

"Of record books."

He gave me a blank stare. Mortenson had no idea who I was, and that was refreshing. I didn't have to go back through any stories or explain what I'd been doing since I fell off the earth.

"Well, I can tell you there were two major claims up there, the Katharine Anne and Glory Town." Mortenson opened his book and looked at me. "Don't you love the names?"

"By glory, I'm guessing they mean money."

"The commonality through time, yes." Mortenson flipped to the page he wanted and dragged his finger down as he read, his nose almost against the paper. "I wish I could give you figures, exact dollar amounts. It's difficult to estimate, and of course most of the official reports were exaggerated for investment purposes. Well, for swindle purposes."

"But they were paying mines?"

"Indeed. The yield on that mountain was substantial."

Mortenson kept reading. He mumbled along with the words. With one hand, he shielded his eyes against the overhead light. "Hmm, certainly an interesting history. Lots of violence, I'm afraid. They had issues with bandits, and that area being so remote, why, law enforcement was ineffective. Just getting out there took hours."

He looked at his text again. "I see here the first three owners were murdered outright, and several successors simply disappeared."

"When did the loads play out?"

"The main veins were plundered to nothing by the early twentieth century or thereabouts. But even today you can still find gold up there, assuming you know how to retrieve it."

"The dream never dies," I said.

"The awesome power of gold. It's made fools of men through history and continues to do so. I'm told there's a new bunch working up there now. They've started a digging of some sort. They're not welcoming to visitors either."

"You've been up there?"

"Some friends have, and they got a frosty reception," Mortenson said. "They were approached by men wearing hip artillery, as they say, and the message was, 'Get lost.' I'm part of a group called the Rich Hill Gang. We travel to old mines and make a day of it. Have a nice lunch, tell stories. We've been concentrating on the borderlands recently, but I didn't make that particular trip."

Mortenson got a dreamy look and folded his hands behind his head. "What a marvelous piece of history. Are you familiar with the story of Rich Hill?"

"As a matter of fact, I am. I read a lot."

"Cheers to you. There aren't many of us left."

Rich Hill was in the mountains near Wickenburg, west of Phoenix. In 1863, when Arizona was open frontier, the mountain man Pauline Weaver led an exploration party into that country. In a basin at the top of what came to be called Rich Hill, the men found chunks of gold lying on the ground. News of the find spread and attracted adventurers to the Territory.

I said, "They called that basin the potato patch. Lincoln wanted Arizona's gold to help save the Union."

"The Paradise story is similar," Mortenson said. "There's an old wagon road that comes up from the Mexican border, crosses Highway 86 around Three Points, and keeps going north to

Paradise. The first settlers reported finding nuggets lying out in the sun along that last section of road. They called it the Glory Road. All they had to do was pick them up, and it was fast horses and choice beef to the end of their days."

That sounded like my kind of work.

Mortenson spread a map across his desk. "The nuggets were gone quickly, of course. You'll still find drifts and shafts up there, and I'm sure you know the difference. A shaft goes down into the ground and a drift sideways, usually into a mountain slope. There are buildings at the summit as well, a town if you will."

He nosed the map. It showed most of southern Arizona. Tucson and its environs took up the largest portion, with Nogales on the border sixty miles south.

He used a finger to find Highway 86, also known as Ajo Way. It began on Tucson's south side and ran due west, away from the city's last homes. He pinpointed the start of the wagon road from the border up to Paradise Mountain.

On the map, it showed as a series of staggered blue dashes, meaning "stay away unless you have four-wheel drive." There were no markings to note the intersection of Highway 86 and Glory Road as it proceeded north.

But the map was laid out in square-mile sections. I counted twenty-five from Tucson's city limits to the intersection.

I asked Mortenson the names of his friends who were hustled off the mountain.

"What say I give them a call first, if that's okay. Protocol, you know."

"I should tell you that the men your friends met up there might've been part of a smuggling operation." I told him about the mountain being taken over by *narcos* and the body on the trail.

He shot back in his chair with saucer eyes. "Did you say murder?"

"Afraid so. Up close. A hit."

"Well, well. It appears the Old West is making a comeback up there."

"Something like that."

"Names, names, yes. I'll do it right now." He grabbed his cell, brought up his contact list, and pushed a button to make the call. While he waited, he dropped the phone to his shoulder and said confidentially, "They were shaken up for sure, but I think they'll talk to you."

He made two calls and left two messages, after which he grabbed a pair of glasses, put them on, and immediately pulled them off and tossed them back onto the desk. "I have to admit, this is quite exciting. I'm tickled to have an actual blood mystery to unravel."

I had to get out of there before Mortenson had a stroke. He let me borrow his book and promised to call as soon as he heard anything.

NINE

It was still early, a few minutes past 2:00 p.m. I wanted to give Opal more time to make money, and that was partly self-interest. She owed me two months' rent.

I went upstairs to the research library, a silent, dusty room with long tables and chairs, old-fashioned card catalogues, and computers. The librarians wait behind the main desk, and when you tell them what you want via the required form, they disappear into the cavernous rooms in back to retrieve it. They serve it to you like a box lunch.

I was curious about Gila monsters and Opal's remark that their breath would set you on fire. I like legends and folklore and had time to kill. The Gila monster is a venomous orange-and-black lizard that can grow to twenty inches in length. I doubt any inhabitant of Arizona's natural world has been the subject of more crazy stories.

The librarian's folder swelled with them, random newspaper clippings from the nineteenth century to the present.

I looked for something that might explain Opal's fire-breathing claim, and there it was. The story likely stemmed from the common superstition that the Gila monster's breath was searing hot, foul, and routed through its anus.

Reading that, I let out an involuntary yip of laughter that broke the library's church-like silence. The people around me stared with squinty-eyed disapproval. I considered explaining but thought better of it. Talking about a lizard's blazing rear end was unlikely to calm anyone.

Some of the material in the folder cited more contemporary scientific sources, and was in fact true. Gila monsters inject their venom by taking hold of the part they object to—say, your prying hand—and grinding on it with their teeth. The best way to loosen the grip is to stick a pen in its mouth. If you don't have a pen, I guess it's not your day.

But the odds of having to take such action are slim. In recorded history, human deaths from Gila monster bites number a handful or two. They're fundamentally polite creatures that retreat when anyone comes around, only getting aggressive if bothered in some way.

I could relate to that.

Closing the folder, I returned it to the ghostly librarian. "I think Gila monsters are underappreciated."

She raised a feeble fist. "Hear, hear!"

I still had time before meeting Opal and decided to take a stab at finding Charlie O'Shea. He bounced between two or three of the same bars, and one of them was fifteen minutes from the Historical Society.

Hoping to get lucky, I drove east on Speedway to midtown and found him at a joint called the Bunker.

Seven regulars sat at the bar. I knew they were regulars because when I pushed open the door, they cussed and shielded their eyes against the assault of sunlight and good breathing air.

I had to tap Charlie's shoulder three times to get his attention. He shot off the seat like he was on fire, and tried to stand perfectly still.

The more he tried, the faster he wiggled.

"Oh, good evening, Mr. Mayor."

"It's afternoon."

"To what do I owe this…" He stopped to let his brain buffer. Then, squeezing his chin in thought: "Lordy, where was I?"

Charlie had a pleasant face, crinkly blue eyes, and a neck that widened under his ears. He had skinny arms and girlish legs that weren't exactly white, more a curdled cream. He wore a short-sleeved pool-party shirt with palm trees on it. His hanging belly beneath the untucked shirt made it look like he was hauling overseas cargo.

In the summer he wore Bermuda shorts, a different color each day. Red, yellow, money green. Today was heavenly purple.

I asked him about the knife attack.

"Saw the whole thing. A bloody mess for a Tuesday." He chuckled, dimpling his cheeks.

"A cop named Diaz wants to talk to you about it."

"In that case, I didn't see a thing."

"No, you're going to talk to him. I don't want him poking around Double Wide any more than necessary."

He ignored me and climbed back onto his barstool. I wrapped my arms around his shoulders and, after a couple of tries, wrestled him out the door and into the Bronco's passenger seat. When he couldn't get comfortable, I took him around to the back, and dropped the tailgate, and he crawled in like he wanted to go to sleep.

Seconds later, he shot up and swung his legs over the bumper to climb out. I leaned down and grabbed his feet and spun him back inside. I'd planned on living the remainder of my life without ever getting up close with Charlie O'Shea's knees.

But there they were. They looked like the elbow joints on a plumber's pipe.

I spread a blanket over him and talked to him for a minute. The only thing I didn't do was read him a story. With his head against the spare tire, he chewed his cheeks and passed out.

TEN

drove downtown. Opal wasn't where she was supposed to be outside the community center. I double parked at her sketch spot and waited.

Without a top on the Bronco, I had nothing to keep the sun off me. In Tucson in the summer, if you stand still, you get baked alive. Keep moving and there's at least the illusion of a breeze, even if it comes out of a pizza oven.

I looped around the block, past Tucson Police headquarters, Saint Augustine's Cathedral, and some of the side streets and couldn't find her. I went back to the same spot and double parked and waited some more.

As I sat there, Fausto Molina called from Monterrey. My ringtone was George Jones singing "He Stopped Loving Her Today," the greatest country song ever recorded.

"Prop, it's me." For some reason, he dropped the "s" in Prospero. "I don't know what's going on. Rolando wouldn't just disappear like this." Fausto had a polite manner and a voice nearly identical to his older brother's.

He last saw Rolando two weeks ago, which was the same time frame Alice had given. "He left the ballpark here saying he had to make a quick business trip and would be back in a couple of days. That was it."

I knew his destination was Arizona. But if I said that, Fausto would ask how I knew, and I'd have to tell him about the hand.

"Did he say anything about gold? Trying to get rich mining for gold?"

"Gold? You mean like Papa? No, I never heard that."

"What about cocaine? Alice said she thought he was doing okay on that."

"I don't know, Prop. Man, really, I don't know about that." He didn't want to talk about cocaine. "He said I was going to be in the big leagues soon."

That left a sour taste. The worst approach for a kid with talent was to tell him about all the great things in his future. Expectation is a beast with no conscience. Given what happened to me, I was surprised Rolando talked that way.

"It's going to happen, Prop. Nobody can hit my pitch."

"Your pitch? What pitch is that?"

"*El Bailador.* I've won thirteen games with it so far."

In Spanish, El *Bailador* means "the dancer."

"You gave this pitch a name? I don't like the advice you're getting, Fausto. That's either confident or really dumb. Did Rolando come up with that?"

"We wanted to give reporters something catchy for their stories. It's a great pitch, Prop. It dives out of the zone."

"Sounds like a split-fingered fastball."

"It's better than a split, much better. The drop is harder and faster." His voice sank. "But Rolando's gone, and pretty soon I won't be able to throw it."

The five o'clock bell had sounded and downtown workers were hustling along the sidewalk to their cars. A TPD squad car pulled alongside the Bronco and the cop waved me out of my spot. I went around the block again, holding the cell to my ear as I drove.

"How old are you, Fausto?"

"I turn eighteen in five months."

"Hey, congratulations."

"I always wanted to be older." He laughed softly. "I guess I'm getting my wish."

"There's a lot out there other than baseball." I talked over the rumble of the Bronco's engine.

"No, no, I can be the best."

"Don't make the world too small, Fausto."

He was young and too wound up to listen. "Prop, I can do this! I can make it to the big leagues! But I need to find Rolando!"

He let out a soft moan. He sounded heartbroken. I had to tell him about his brother. But I needed a place to park. I couldn't spring that news while weaving through traffic, holding the cell with one hand, working the stick shift with the other and steering with my thighs.

Fausto piped up before I could find a spot. He sounded cautious, as though he wasn't sure whether to speak. "You should go see Mr. Danny Wilson."

Wilson was GM of the Tucson Thunder. I knew him from my playing days. He was a bullpen coach in Tacoma when I pitched there. "Why would Wilson know about Rolando?"

"Rolando talked to Mr. Wilson about me." Fausto pushed those words out slowly and said nothing for a long time, as if to gauge my reaction.

I let the silence linger.

"About signing me, Prop. Wilson came to Monterrey to watch me pitch. He was going to give me a big contract with the Thunder."

Fausto had started out saying he had no idea where Rolando might be, but he had a clue after all. Why hold back Rolando's connection to Tucson? He certainly hadn't forgotten. No Mexican seventeen-year-old forgets the interest of an American GM with a checkbook.

Something didn't add up, and I decided to keep my mouth shut. I told Fausto I'd talk to Wilson and get back to him.

ELEVEN

I checked the Thunder's schedule on my phone. They were home against the Sacramento River Cats. I looked up Fausto's record. He was 13–1 with an ERA just below 2.00. A pitcher with those numbers was dealing some pain, no question.

But I wanted to talk to Wilson.

And what happened to Opal?

I had leftover cardboard scraps in the back of the Bronco. When I lifted Charlie's leg to get at one of them, he mumbled the Gettysburg Address but didn't wake up. With a black Sharpie from the glove, I wrote, "Gone to Hi Corbett Field. Meet me there." I leaned it against a tree at Opal's sketch spot and got on Broadway Boulevard heading east.

What could be better than spending a summer night at the ballpark? For me, lots of things. The closer I got to Hi Corbett, the more my stomach knotted up from the memories.

The first time I drove that stretch of Broadway, my sneakers were up on the dash and the radio was blaring some crazy song. The fellow who picked me up at the airport, some front-office box mover, kept eyeing at me as if to say, "This kid's a project. Bitty's gonna have his hands full."

Wilbit Bastion was the Thunder's manager, and if you know baseball, you know Bitty. He was thickly set and mostly bald, and he had a jowly face and a voice full of gravy. His chin dripped spit and he was incapable of speaking an English sentence without cuss words.

Bitty set down lots of rules for players and proceeded to ignore them if your fastball had late movement and hit the catcher's mitt with that sound that caused everyone to turn around and say, "Who *is* that kid?"

We went along Broadway that day, music blaring, my hair going wild from the wind through the window. I was eighteen and sure of everything. Just give me a ball and point out the plate and I'll strike out everybody you send up there. I almost did, too.

And when Bitty told me to get a haircut, I told him I liked my hair just fine. It was so thick my cap flew off every time I lunged into my delivery. That became my trademark. The fans waited for it, cheered at the sight of it. Everyone loved it and loved me.

The Phenom.

The Arizona Diamondbacks called me up to the big club midsummer, and for the remainder of the season, I was the talk of the National League.

Then everything fell apart. My velocity dropped, and the medical people called it a tired arm. They put me on rest, and the rest got longer, and the tired arm became a torn labrum. The surgery went well, and after a long rehab, I came back and tore the labrum again.

Another surgery, more rehab. When I finally got healthy, I still threw a hard fastball. But the physical trouble had migrated into my head, and for a pitcher that's the twilight zone.

Commanding the strike zone starts and ends with a first-pitch fastball. But when I lost that command, I had to pitch from behind in the count, and everything spiraled down.

I kept coming back because the only place I excelled was between the chalk lines. Life baffled me everywhere else. I bounced from club to club, and signed again and again based on what GMs remembered of me, rather than what I could still do.

In my big league career, four seasons, I won a total of twenty-one games, and to the end, my twice-repaired shoulder was more or less fine, my arm fine, my legs fine. But I'd lost the stupid confidence I had as a kid that let me rear back and fire the ball with everything I had, without worry, doubt, or fear.

When you lose that, you can't go to the store and buy more. You can't find it on a headshrinker's couch or on your knees in church. When you lose that, toss your spikes in the closet, because you're done.

TWELVE

Hi Corbett Field is in midtown across from the El Con Mall, part of a multiblock complex with a zoo, a golf course, and multiple ballfields. It's an oasis of green in a city of sand. The road to the park turns south off Broadway and rolls along a pleasant, palm tree–lined lane to the parking lot.

I left Charlie to his gin dreams and jumped a turnstile onto the concourse. The concession people were moving supplies around on dollies as team staffers hustled here and there to get set up in advance of the first pitch.

As soon as I started toward the team offices, I saw Danny Wilson walking toward me. He was a former catcher, an advance scout and bullpen coach for the Diamondbacks. The GM position was his third job with the club, and he was said to be on the way up.

Wilson still looked like an athlete. The walk is a giveaway no matter how old you get. Arms held away from the body, head erect, legs churning forward with that good balance that comes from years of physical confidence.

He was about fifty. His eyes were blue, deep set, and tired looking, but there was still a good bit of the young man in them. He had a mess of sandy hair framing a round face that had spent a lot of time on sunny ballfields.

Spotting me, Wilson clapped his hands. "For a minute there I thought I was seeing a ghost. Whip Stark! Are you kidding me?"

We man-hugged. High hand grip, shoulder bump, back slap. Wilson had on a blue shirt with the Thunder logo on the chest. He wore beige Dockers. If it weren't for Dockers, minor league executives would never wear pants.

"You look fantastic for a retiree. Like you could still heave it."

"I'm only thirty-one, Danny. You bet I can still heave it."

"Where you keeping yourself, Whip? Looking for a job?"

"I'm working on being invisible."

"Well, this isn't the place for you. Have you seen our Heroes' Wall?"

I hadn't seen the Heroes' Wall.

"Right down the concourse, we got us a plaque with your face on it. We tried reaching you for the ceremony. Most strike-outs in nine innings in the ballpark's history." Wilson snapped his fingers. "How about we introduce you to the fans tonight? I'm sure there are lots of people that remember old Whip Stark."

If you run a minor league baseball team, you're thinking about promotion twenty-four hours a day. Wilson would introduce Daffy Duck's long-lost brother, Murray Duck, if it gave the impression the ballpark was the place to be.

Wilson said, "A round of applause, some autographs. We'll have fun with it. Cindy, Cindy?" Wilson flagged a redheaded girl in khaki shorts, white ankle socks, and the same blue Thunder shirt. "Print out some career stats on Prospero Stark. He's in the database. We'll make an on-field introduction tonight."

"Yes, Mr. Wilson," she said and was off.

He turned back to me. "The local ABC affiliate has a crew here somewhere and they're looking for a story. Roxy's the reporter's name. Roxanne Santa Cruz. I'll point you out to her."

"Let's talk about Fausto Molina."

The good-fellow bluster left him entirely. He made a confused face that wanted me to believe he had no idea what I was talking about. He spread his hands to emphasize the point.

"Come on, Danny. You went to Mexico to scout him."

The crowd on the concourse was still thin. He looked past my shoulder, eyes darting. "What else do you know?"

"I talked to Fausto."

His mouth tightened into a scowl. "The kid's not supposed to talk about this."

"Tell me about *El Bailador*. It's a good ball, I hear."

He lowered his voice. "It's filthy, filthy. It's a big league pitch right now."

"Rolando was helping Fausto and now Rolando's missing."

"Missing? I don't know anything about that."

I told him what I knew, leaving out any mention of the hand.

"I know you two were close, Whip. But this is a real tricky topic." Wilson looked around the concourse like a burglar after coming through the window. He was stalling and didn't want to give in, but he was trapped. "Come on." He tilted his head up the tunnel leading to the seats.

We walked to the first row behind the batting cage and sat among a scattering of season-ticket holders. A handful of kids had gathered at the netting to watch batting practice. The ballpark echoed with voices, balls cracking against bats, and the PA system blaring pregame music.

Wilson let out a deep breath and began. "This is tricky, Whip. Honestly, I have no idea what happened to Rolando. But if you want my guess, cocaine. He was all over that stuff."

"When you were there in Monterrey, you met with him, right? Talked to him?"

"Absolutely. We sat together and watched Fausto pitch. Everything seemed fine."

"Fausto thinks he might've come up here to see you."

Wilson looked surprised. "I haven't seen him since Monterrey."

"Okay, what's the tricky part?"

Wilson dropped his head and spat between his legs. He squinted out at the field. "Look, I don't like this secrecy stuff more than you do. But I gave this guy my word that I'd keep his name in my pocket. Fausto's name, too." He jabbed his chest with his thumb. "I keep my word."

That was as indignant as Wilson got. He wasn't the type. On the field he was as tough as they come. But off it, he was a shot-and-beer man who liked to get along.

Wilson watched players running wind sprints in the outfield. The PA system was playing Bruce Springsteen's "Glory Days."

I said, "Nobody will hear anything from me."

"Okay, but I ain't giving up the name." He watched the players for a moment, spat, watched some more, and spat again. "My phone rings out of the blue and it's this guy telling me there's a kid down in Mexico who's a lock to lead a big league rotation, and soon. He wants me to fly down there and see for myself."

"A voice on the phone tells you to scout a seventeen-year-old, and just like, that you go?" The Mexican League is a designated AAA league, but it's actually more of a high double. The competition isn't as good as AAA in the States. Even with Fausto dealing the way he was, it was still Mexican League competition.

"This fellow isn't just anybody," Wilson said. "He's starting to make noise for himself in the game. He's betting big on this kid, and let me tell you, he's crazy, okay? Shit-bottom nuts."

"This is baseball. Could you narrow it down?"

"No, listen to this," Wilson said, warming to the subject. "He has this plan he's trying to orchestrate where I sign Fausto, bring him up, and let him do his thing, build interest, court the media, all that. He wants to market the kid like a rock star. He's got this social media strategy where he puts Fausto in front of teenage girls, does an Instagram campaign, photos, all kinds of shit."

I made a face that said what I thought of the idea.

"I know, crazy," Wilson said. "But have you seen Fausto? I mean, the kid's handsome. My source figures he can work the media pretty good, a town like Tucson. That's why he came up with that name, *El Bailador*, for the Mexican fans. It gives the writers headline material. It's a big part of his marketing scheme. It means 'the dancer.'"

"I know what it means, Danny. I lived in Mexico for five years."

"It's an okay name, but the ball doesn't dance like a knuckleball. It just dives out of the zone. If you think about it, it just might work. We build this bandwagon thing until Fausto's the guy everybody in baseball's talking about."

"That's an agent," I said. "Can't be a scout. Nobody knows scouts' names."

Wilson wouldn't take the bait. He sat watching the players gathered at the batting cage. They were doing what ballplayers do, elbowing, joshing, stretching, and scratching the usual places. Fly balls banged against the outfield wall with a loud *thwack*.

Springsteen wailed.

After a long silence, Wilson said, "This source of mine thinks he's all that. But he's got a vindictive streak like you wouldn't believe."

"That's definitely an agent."

Wilson watched a fly ball sail over the centerfield wall. It took a long time getting out, a white dot against a perfect blue sky. "How about I talk to the ABC gal about doing a spot on you?"

"You haven't told me anything, Danny. Just give me the name."

"If it gets back to this guy, he'll make life miserable for the Diamondbacks, and that'll come back on me. I'll be toast. I can't do it."

Past Wilson's far shoulder, two men walked down the center aisle and settled into the premium box seats on the third base side of home plate. The lead one was young, well dressed, and commanding, and something about him rang a bell. The second one stayed back, about the right distance for a lackey who knows he's a lackey.

A girl in khaki shorts and a Thunder shirt ran between the seats and bent over with her hands between her knees to ask the lead man something. He answered with a wave of his hand, without looking at her. She hurried off, undoubtedly to bring him whatever he'd asked for.

Thwack. I watched another ball sail over the fence.

When you turn your attention away from something you're trying to remember, the answer sometimes pops into your brain.

"You know, Danny, I still read *SI*, watch SportsCenter, the whole bit."

"You still follow the game. That's terrific."

"I'm thinking about a particular agent."

"Forget it, Whipper."

"Read a long piece about him at *Bleacher Report*. Born in New York, a DiMaggio fanatic."

Wilson snapped his head around, worried eyes bearing down.

I said, "They talked about him as the guy no GM wants to see walk into his office."

Suddenly agitated, Wilson twisted in his seat, sighing and fussing. "Promise me, Whip! Really, promise me you won't sell me out to this guy!"

"Keep your voice down."

"Keep my voice down? Why should I keep my voice down!?"

I tapped Wilson on the arm and leaned into his ear and whispered, "Over your left shoulder. Cream pants, black hair. The guy we're talking about is sitting right over there."

Wilson looked and saw Max Mayflower, the man *Bleacher Report* called the hottest young agent in baseball.

"Shit. Shit, shit." Wilson buried his face in his hands. "Look, I didn't tell you squat. You came up with the name on your own, okay?"

"Who's the guy with him?"

Wilson peeked between his fingers. "His assistant, Ed Bolt, a real sleaze hammer. They're both sleaze hammers. Mayflower plays it like he's your best friend, but cross him, and he'll burn you down. I can't lose this job."

He made a pretzel of himself, scrunching toward me to shield his face from Mayflower.

"He hasn't seen you," I said. "I'll take off, and Mayflower will never know I was talking to you. I'll wait until after the game to make the approach."

In a low voice that dribbled out of the corner of his mouth, Wilson said, "Okay, go. Go now! Wait, you'll talk to Roxanne Santa Cruz?"

Even in a time of peril, he couldn't resist making a plug to fill the seats.

"They do live promos in the evening, right?" I said. "Ahead of the ten o'clock?"

"I don't know. Yeah, usually."

"I'll do a promo and then talk to the ABC people for the ten. But only if they agree to the promo first."

"I don't control what they do, Whip."

"Lean on them."

"Swear to God, you're a pain in the ass."

"Have them come by the first base dugout, and I'll say a few words. They'll be unforgettable."

THIRTEEN

Roxanne Santa Cruz was tall, square shouldered, and thin, though not so thin you wanted to feed her a cheeseburger. Everything fit together nicely. She had a wide red mouth and swooping eyebrows that took the long route over eyes that were lively and dark, not quite black, not quite brown. Her tan skin was fine and smooth, and she had long black hair with a strip of purple coloring behind her left ear.

That flourish told me things weren't what they seemed. I assumed that already by the way she carried herself. She had an elegant jaw. She held her head high and had that contained, confident manner that always set me on edge, waiting for the come down.

She spent a lot of time on herself, and that was television. But she would've looked fine without the makeup. She was a stunner. Women like Roxanne Santa Cruz have trouble walking down the street.

It was the middle of the fourth inning. The seat to my left was empty. She sat in it with her cameraman to my right. The crowd around me had dutifully and without complaint cleared away at the sight of the camera and microphone.

Make room, you people. The kings of the culture have arrived. This is television, dammit!

Santa Cruz wasn't like the usual on-air creatures the TV stations sent out. She was intelligent and knowledgeable about baseball. At interview time, she pulled at her hair and shook it out, letting it spread across her shoulders and down her back. She wiggled her neck to loosen up and spat her gum into her palm and stuck it under the seat. I'd never seen anyone do that.

When the camera light blinked on, she mouthed the microphone, and without looking at notes, rattled off the relevant facts of my career, including my twenty-strikeout game. When she asked what it felt like to return to Hi Corbett, I ditched the script she'd written and took off on my own.

"It's bittersweet. The man who made that game possible is missing. His name is Rolando Molina. He was my catcher, and I'm here tonight trying to get answers on his whereabouts. Anyone with information can find me west of the Tucson Mountains at a place called Double Wide. Look for a red Bronco parked outside an Airstream trailer."

Santa Cruz had no idea what I was talking about and hid her confusion like a pro. She looked straight into the camera and said, "The long, strange trip of Prospero Stark, tonight at ten."

When the camera light went off, she barked at me: "What was *that*? Goddamn you, Stark!"

She used words I'd never heard outside a locker room. When she cooled down, I told her more about Rolando, our careers, and our friendship, and said she needed to investigate his disappearance. The more I talked, the calmer she became. She was smart enough to know that a former pitcher looking for his missing catcher was a good story.

"I'll call my assignment editor," she said. "It might take some talking."

"You're kidding, right?"

"He's an idiot."

"I just handed you a potential Murrow Award."

"I said I'd look into it. Don't be a tool."

"A tool? Can you define that for me?"

"No." Santa Cruz had a barrette in her mouth as she pulled the hair off the back of her neck. "Tonight we'll run two minutes on you, and then we'll see if Rolando Molina's a go." She got her hair clip in place. "After you do the on-field thing, meet me by the Heroes' Wall. We'll stand you up there, and no nonsense this time, okay?"

We did the shoot, and it went well. When Santa Cruz was done, her manner changed. Her voice lost the energy of the camera and went back to being a little hard and a little cynical, in that put-on toughness reporters use.

Coolly, she said, "I'll call you about Molina."

"Sounds like I've got a partner. Can I call you Roxy?"

She gave me an icy look and walked off, glancing back over her shoulder at me as she went.

FOURTEEN

I was leaning against Max Mayflower's white Lexus when he emerged from the stadium with his sidekick. I knew it was Mayflower's Lexus because it was the only luxury car in a reserved space with a license plate holder that said, MAX IS HERE. I decided that was a clue.

Ed Bolt hollered at me from twenty feet away. "Nobody leans on Mr. Mayflower's ride. Let's go, mister. Off you go."

When I didn't move, Bolt stepped forward to force the issue. But Mayflower elbowed him and said, "Do you know who that is, Eddie?"

"Somebody that don't hear good," Bolt said.

"That's Whiplash Stark," Mayflower said, pointing at me with admiration. "That man could've made all of us rich, the way he threw a baseball. Unbelievable talent. Once in a generation." Mayflower threw out his hand for me to shake.

"I thought it was time we met," I said. "I'm making my comeback."

Mayflower studied me through a tough-looking face. His eyes angled down in an odd way, the left one lower than the right. His black hair was combed straight back. Some cream must've been holding it down because it glowed under the parking lot lights. He had a swimming pool tan, and wore linen pants, a black belt, and a light-blue short-sleeved shirt with gold trim.

His gold watch blinked under the lights. At what a Gucci watch costs, it should sing Sinatra.

I had no plans to get back in the game. But I didn't want to spook Mayflower by immediately bringing up his connection to Rolando and Fausto, something I wasn't supposed to know. My plan was to engage him in friendly comeback chatter, putting him at ease, and then drop Rolando's name and see what happened.

"If you'd be willing to represent me, I'd love to have you."

"My list is full." Mayflower parked his hands on his hips. "But I might be able to make room for the Phenom. I've always wondered what happened to you."

That question again.

"I've been working out, running to bring my legs back." That part was true, although it had nothing to do with a comeback. I liked to run.

"What about that shoulder? Wasn't it the shoulder that got you?"

"Feels strong. I'm tired of sitting around. Let's make money together."

Bolt drew up close to Mayflower. "I remember this guy, Maxy. He hit ninety-nine on the gun. Regular, he done that." Bolt talked around a lump of tobacco in his cheek.

Mayflower held up his hand to silence Bolt.

But Bolt kept going. "He got pinched in Mexico, a cocaine thing. Remember on the TV all the time? They showed it on the TV."

Slowly, Mayflower turned to glare at Bolt, and Bolt stepped back.

Mayflower looked me over carefully. "America loves a comeback story, and name recognition certainly won't be a problem. Every GM in the game remembers you."

I talked about my repaired shoulder and my desire to pitch again. He bought it, offering to set up a throwing session to see if I still had it.

"I'm free all this week," I said.

Mayflower handed me one of his cards. "Call my secretary, and she'll set it up. We'll do it right here at Hi Corbett."

More fans were leaving the park. Cars crawled past us to the exit lane. Horns sounded. Dads barked at their kids to keep up and watch the traffic.

"One thing, though." Mayflower held up a cautioning finger. "Nobody knows about this, and definitely no media. I work quiet."

The time had come to drop Rolando's name. "First I need to find somebody. Rolando Molina, my old catcher. I can't make a comeback without Rolando."

Mayflower's face got stony. His eyes drew back and became hostile. The smile stayed glued to his face, but everything real had gone out of it.

Bolt's demeanor hardened too. He stepped closer to me. He wasn't an inch above five foot five and looked like a bulldog. Small nose, small eyes, and a shadow of whiskers over a round face pockmarked by acne scars. He glistened with sweat.

"Thing is, I can't find Rolando," I said. "I know he was working with his brother, Fausto, down in Monterrey. But he's gone missing."

"I assure you I have no knowledge of that."

"Sure, you do. You went down there to watch him work."

Mayflower stiffened. The lines around his eyes gathered to spider webs.

I continued. "Fausto last saw Rolando two weeks ago and now he's missing. I have reason to believe he came up here."

Breaking eye contact, Mayflower turned to his car. He looked to be done, conversation over, and then he whirled to face me, his eyes full of anger: "That boy is mine! You stay away, Stark!"

He hit the *doink* button on his key chain, and the Lexus doors unlocked. Bolt shouldered me out of the way and grabbed the passenger door. Mayflower climbed in and Bolt closed the door, giving it a two-handed shove to make sure.

The window inched down and Mayflower angled his hard gray eyes into the crack. He had calmed himself, the voice smooth again. "As I indicated, I try not to make my business public."

I leaned close. "One way or another, I'm going to find out what happened to Rolando."

"Good night, Whip. It was a pleasure meeting you."

He pressed the up button, and the window moved. I grabbed the glass. My fingers were about to get crushed when Bolt's hands clamped down on my shoulders. His mitts were like iron. With sudden violence, he jerked me clear of the car and threw me away like a doll.

Somehow I stayed upright, and when I regained my balance and turned back, Bolt was standing with his legs spread, clenching and unclenching his fists as he snapped his left knee back and forth. Something told me he'd used that pose before.

He glared at me with lifeless eyes. His mouth was a bent nail. Tobacco stains made half moons at the corners of his mouth. "Come on, Stark, you ain't a tough guy."

"All I am is smart. It's my only pitch."

"Smart don't cut it in parking lots."

I was straightening my clothes. "What do you do for Mayflower anyway? Community outreach?"

"You can have that workout now, you want." He leaned over and spat, a brown blob that landed on the pavement with a loud *splat*. Something told me he had done that before too.

"Say, how about a cut of that tobacco?"

He tossed his jaw. "Bounce, Stark."

"Doctors hate chewing tobacco, but it helped me pitch."

"You say so. You're the smart guy, right?" Bolt spoke with barely a twitch of his lips.

I realized something. We were having a conversation from one of my detective stories. In trying to find out what happened to Rolando, I'd become one. Specialty, missing persons. No license, no experience, and no idea what I was doing. Call anytime.

"That's how this is supposed to go," I said. "I say something clever, you say something clever, and we go on like that."

"The heat's got you talking nuts, Stark. Saying stuff you don't know what it means. It causes distractions and so forth."

Bolt walked around the Lexus and opened the driver's door and looked over the roof at me. He made his neck disappear with a hunch of his shoulders. "Whatever happened to your pal, it's got Maxy upset. But he don't know what it is, so don't come around bothering him again. You do and it becomes my business."

Bolt got in. The Lexus started with a mild cough.

I called, "What about my tryout?" but all I got in return was brake lights.

Years ago, I played for a minor league outfit whose owner had a guy walk at his ankles like a kitten. Nobody knew what this fellow did except not talk and look tough.

That taught me that baseball is more than young men gamboling across pretty green fields. The business end of the game is as hard as it gets, and so are the men who run it. Sometimes they need guys like Bolt to stay competitive, and staying competitive means keeping secrets in the courting of big-time prospects.

But whatever was going on with Mayflower went way beyond typical business secrecy.

FIFTEEN

Charlie O'Shea managed to sleep through the clearing of the parking lot. Only now he was covered in popcorn. It looked like some smart aleck leaving the game had dumped a bag on him. I plucked a piece out of his ear and drove toward home, stopping on the way at Opal's sketch spot.

My sign was there but no Opal. I sat in the Bronco for a few minutes waiting and looking around, but that wasn't getting me anywhere.

With Rolando and now Opal, my list of missing persons had doubled.

As I drove west on Speedway toward Gates Pass, I thought about the dead man on the trail. Who was he? A friend of Rolando's. Had to be. Why else leave the hand on my step? He wanted me to know what happened and do something about it.

I drove under the I-10 freeway past the Arizona School for the Deaf and Blind and the entrance to Barrio Hollywood. Right off Speedway, a block south, is Guadalajara Bakery, where I get my beans and tortillas. The building slumps on its foundation and looks like it might collapse in a strong wind, but the Mexican food doesn't get any better.

No rain fell, but the sky was overcast. The clouds threw down occasional bolts of lightning.

What were you involved in, Rolando? Was it gold?

Alice Menendez said Oscar had lost his ranch and now worked as a miner. I should've asked what mineral he was chasing. If it was gold, there might be a connection between Oscar's work and Rolando's hand showing up on my doorstep, two miles south of an old gold mine.

Was there enough color left on Paradise Mountain to justify murder? Tork Mortenson thought so.

It was late, and my foot was heavy, and when you drive a topless Bronco too fast on a summer night, the hot wind drumming against your ears generates all kinds of mad thoughts.

Like something bad happened to Opal.

No, Opal's fine. She stuck her thumb out and hitchhiked home. She made a bundle on the sidewalk, and in a few minutes, I'd see her waiting for me at the entrance to Double Wide, waving a fistful of bills to pay her rent.

Talk about mad thoughts.

After Silverbell, as Speedway begins its ascent into the mountains, the night got blacker with the absence of streetlamps, and the traffic thinned to almost nothing. The key word was "almost." The headlights in my rearview were abnormally bright oblongs. They'd been there since before the freeway, and I was driving too fast for it to be coincidence.

I was being followed.

The rush of sweat came instantly. I goosed the engine and kept it goosed. The two-lane road up to Gates Pass bends around tight curves as it climbs the mountain. At each turn the chasing headlights disappeared for a time and came into view again as the road went back the other way. I drove as fast as I could through switchbacks that got tighter and tighter.

At the peak, there's a parking lot and overlook. I killed my headlights and lurched right onto the long driveway that leads into the lot. But I misjudged my speed, and the Bronco skidded sideways. By the time I stopped moving, the wheels on the passenger side had jumped the curb and slipped into a ditch, the Bronco itself tilting heavily in that direction.

I looked in the back. Charlie O'Shea took the commotion like a pro. Or a corpse. He never budged.

Headlight Man sped past the lot and over the pass. He moved so fast I don't think he saw me. But I couldn't see him either. The car was a white SUV of some unknown make and model, and the driver could've been anyone.

I ran to the cliff at the back of the lot and waited until the SUV cleared the pass and came into view as it descended the other side of the mountain.

From where he was on the flat, he could see a long way across the desert. If he kept going, maybe he wasn't following me after all. But if he realized he'd been hoodwinked and wanted to continue the chase, he'd turn around and drive back up the mountain.

He stopped in the middle of the road and stayed put, not moving, headlights on. I watched and waited for his next move.

The night was lonely, no traffic in either direction.

When he didn't budge, I ran back to the Bronco, slapped it into four-wheel drive, and fought my way out of the ditch. I drove out onto the road, stopped at the top of the mountain facing west, and blinked my beams on and off three times, the way a sailor sends a message by Morse code.

But I didn't need to be rescued. I had nothing to say except, "Here I am! Catch me if you can!" Headlight Man took the bait. He swung the SUV into a U-turn and sped back up the mountain.

The chase was on again.

SIXTEEN

I had a good head start and stretched my lead on the downslope back toward Tucson. Headlight Man still had to climb the mountain and negotiate the pass before he could work up any speed at all. I shot through the Silverbell intersection on a green light and under the freeway on two more greens.

The intersection at Speedway and Stone was brightly lit on its northwest corner by the campus of Pima Community College. My destination was catty corner to the school, a notorious drug-and-homeless park.

I drove straight through the intersection along the park's northern boundary and turned right onto Seventh Avenue. I found a curbside parking spot a short way down, beyond the glow of a streetlamp. The Bronco is a pretty distinct ride, and I needed the cover.

From there I jogged into the park. It was dark under the big trees, and there were groups of homeless men and women gathered on the grass, talking, sleeping, and staring at nothing. I reached a cement picnic table that stood off Speedway, about fifty feet from the pavement.

In the darkness, I sat on the table and watched the intersection for the approach of the white SUV.

Two people lay in the grass at my feet, a man and a woman. The man was enormous, probably three hundred pounds and six foot four. He had a black beard and black hair. He wore tattersall pants and a long tan raincoat against the tremendous heat. He lay on his back, the raincoat open, his button-up shirt untucked and showing a triangle of belly flesh. He wasn't wearing shoes, and the skin on his feet was grotesque, cracked, filthy, caked with blood.

His hands were thrown out at his sides, palms down. The slight up-and-down movement of the raincoat told me he was breathing. But it was noiseless and not too convincing.

A black woman sat beside him. She had a long forehead and dreaded, spiked hair and silver posts jammed through the tops of her ears. With the wide spread of her nose, the high, sloping skull, and high cheekbones, she looked native African.

She was sickly thin. She wore a torn black T-shirt, and her arms hanging out of it looked scabbed from needle tracks. She rocked and mumbled words in a language unknown to me. But they had the rhythm of a plea or a prayer, only the nearly dead giant wasn't listening.

I said, "Is he okay?"

"No man ever loved me the way he did." She had a buttery voice with a British accent. The elegant sound of it was jarring coming from someone so far gone.

"He still loves you."

The woman settled her lost eyes on me, and her mouth fell open. She dragged her right hand slowly down her cheek, the fingertips barely touching flesh. She was especially black to begin with, but her skin had been made blacker by time in the sun and the accumulation of dirt from living on the street.

Her trembling hand stopped at her jaw. "Are you sure?"

"Yes, with all his heart," I said.

She let out a small choking sound, pressed both palms against her face, and cried. She picked up the giant's hand and cupped it tenderly in her lap. He remained corpse-like, seemingly unaware of her ministrations. She went back to rocking.

I watched them a moment longer and didn't want to watch anymore. If I kept at it, I'd invite them out to Double Wide, just for a day or two until they got back on their feet. Before you knew it, they'd be nailing up blanket drapes in my empty trailer and planning other decorative touches, like a door.

Headlight Man pulled up to the red light at Speedway and Stone. From my tabletop seat, the streetlights and the school lights were bright enough for me to see a shape behind the wheel and the color of the driver's hair.

Turned out I had it wrong. Headlight Man was a woman, a blonde with shoulder-length hair. That worked. If I was a detective, she had to be a blonde.

When the light changed, she lurched off the stop line and sped along the park boundary heading east on Speedway. Her passing gave me a side view from forty feet, and it was the same as before. The SUV was traveling too fast to see much detail.

But I saw the blond hair again. Long and snowy white, probably bleached.

I felt triumphant. I'd ditched my first tail.

Something told me not to take the usual route over Gates Pass back to Double Wide. Instead, I drove south, thinking of Mortenson's map, which showed me an alternate route home.

If the map told the truth, it was little more than a fading two-track that would take me past an abandoned gold camp defended by gunmen who may or may not be involved in the assassination-style murder of one man and the brutal dismemberment of my friend.

The way the last twenty-four hours had gone, driving the wagon road made perfect sense. I looked over my shoulder. "How about we take a ride, Charlie?"

No answer. He lay amid the popcorn, snoring like a hog in the garden.

"That's what I like about you, Charlie. You're up for anything."

Nearing midnight, we started the long drive to Paradise.

SEVENTEEN

The trip is a straight shot west of the city on Ajo Way, a two-lane blacktop across open desert, few signs of life anywhere. At that time of night, the traffic is light and at least every other vehicle is Border Patrol.

That part of southern Arizona, from the edge of town out to Three Points and into the vastness of Tohono O'odham Reservation, is among the most smuggled territory in America.

In Mortenson's office, I counted twenty-five miles to the wagon road, and when I reached that point I stopped and scouted around.

A light appeared in the sky to the south. I watched it get bigger and bigger. A Border Patrol rescue helicopter. They regularly flew back and forth from the Mexican line, bringing injured crossers to the hospital. The sound was small and distant, and then all consuming as it roared overhead, heading north.

I went back to business, looking for something resembling a road. I pulled onto the sandy strip beside the asphalt and crawled along until I reached a cut in the four-strand barbwire fence at my passenger door.

Opposite it, on the south side of the pavement, stood two old gas pumps and the shell of an abandoned building with a sign hanging by its last screw over the door. The paint on the sign was chipped and faded and barely readable, except for one word, Glory.

That was all I had to go on. I drove through the fence break into the dark desert.

Mortenson's map said the drive to Paradise was three miles. The road was loose sand in the first portion and hard-packed dirt as the ground rose to meet the mountain. I flipped on the high beams and saw tire tracks—fresh, meaning they were made some time between last night's rain and five minutes ago.

It looked like I might have company on the mountain.

I turned off my cell and headlights and kept going, past clumps of sage and bunchgrass bordering the road. The shrub gave some guidance on a cloudy night, but not much. I alternated between looking at the ground and the way ahead, making sure I didn't drive into a cactus.

As the road climbed, the Bronco had to work harder, and that made it louder. Worried the noise might give me away, I veered into the desert and parked under a cluster of mesquite trees. Charlie was still unconscious in the back. I left him there and jogged up the steep incline.

Good legs are a pitcher's best friend, and I still had mine.

About a mile remained to the peak. I made it easily.

At the top, the road flattened out through the mountain pass that held the remnants of the town. I found cover behind a debris pile on the west side of the road. Four buildings stood on the opposite side, faint halos of light above them, their backs bumping against the mountain.

Crouching and listening, I heard male voices and the rumble of truck engines, which likely explained the light. The men were using headlights to do their business.

I wanted to know what that business was. Honest players don't work in the middle of the night twenty-four hours after police find a murdered man a mile away on the north-facing slope of the same mountain—to say nothing of me finding my friend's severed hand at about the same time. There had to be a connection.

Of the four buildings, three were near ruin. The fourth was a saloon, crumbling but holding on. It had a long porch and windows without glass on either side of batwing doors. A board sidewalk ran the length of the building, and in the street outside, there were hitching rails and horse troughs.

Keeping low, I ran across the street, hopped onto the porch, and stepped inside. Ceiling beams angled down against the floor amid the powerful smell of dust and disuse. The bar and back bar were in a thousand pieces, and broken glass covered much of the floor.

I tip-toed around the shards to the rear window and got on my knees for a better look. Two trucks were parked side by side, their back ends facing me, headlights shining into a drift under the mountain. A third truck faced me, headlights off.

Men were carrying items out of the drift and throwing them into the back of the trucks. The objects were white and bowling ball sized, the exteriors in a checkerboard pattern, like pineapples. They were heavy. The men held them with two hands between their knees, struggling to keep their backs straight.

Others carried something lighter, capable of being handled with one hand.

Over and over, a man growled, "Let's go! Let's go!" He appeared to be the leader. I couldn't see much of him, only his shadow on the wall of the drift.

The building snapped and settled. I wanted to get out of there before it fell on me. I stepped through the saloon onto the porch, and that was as far as I got.

From the corner of my eye, I glimpsed someone at my shoulder and felt cold steel pressing against my cheek. My uncanny powers of deduction said "pistol."

I threw my hands up. "Where can a guy get a glass of milk around here?"

EIGHTEEN

The gunman shoved me around to the back of the saloon and against one of the trucks. With his arm straight out and gripping my shirt at the chest, he yelled into the drift. "*Jefe*! Out here! Found this one sneaking around!"

The leader walked out and faced me. He wore a tactical holster strapped low on his right leg, between thigh and knee. "You're looking for something at my gold mine, friend?"

He was a squat Mexican not long out of his twenties and probably 220 pounds. He had short, wide-hanging arms, a barrel belly, round, pitted cheeks, and a bulb nose. His skin was copper colored and his black hair ran low across his forehead in a straight line, interrupted only by a V in the middle.

"I lost my dog couple days ago," I said. The dog was the first thing that popped into my head. "We were hiking and he got onto a scent, and wouldn't you know it, I couldn't find him again."

"You come here at night to find a dog?" He turned his head as he stared. He asked my name, and I told him. The work went on behind us, the men dropping those bowling balls into the truck bed and hurrying back for more.

Something in the leader's left hand gleamed off the light from the drift. It was a machete held tight against his leg. I thought, "Rolando." I might be standing in front of Rolando's killer.

"You hiked up this mountain, Stark? I don't think so. Where's your truck?"

"I drove and then hiked." I pointed vaguely south. "It's parked down here a ways."

The gunman piped up: "He was spying on us, *jefe*." He pointed to the back of the saloon. "At the window."

"Spying?" Machete's mouth tightened. Muscle packs bulged along his jaw. The smear of tattoos covering his neck and arms spoke of long hours in the prison yard. "No one likes a spy. Is that what you are?"

The gunman nudged closer. "*Jefe*, we have to go—the helicopter."

Machete paid no attention, and said to me, "At night you look for your dog? In the dark? I'm giving you one chance to live. Tell me your business at my gold mine."

"I told you, the dog."

Machete's face wrenched into an ugly knot. His breath hissed, and he drew the machete up and placed the blade on my left shoulder, the cutting edge against my neck. A single downward slash of his arm would do it, and I'd bleed out in a mountain ghost town.

He held the blade steady. Red flecks glowed at the corners of his eyes. "You lie, Stark."

I felt the first surge of panic and fought to hold it back. I tried to stand perfectly still, tried to breathe. But there was no air on that dark mountain. I saw myself falling. I saw a guard walking down the block to Sam's cell and delivering the news through the bars in a cold, flat tone.

"It's your kid," he'd say. Sam would wonder about a town called Paradise. Where is it? On a mountain, you say? What was Prospero doing there? Sam would see the irony of practicing a faith all his life that promised paradise, and this is the paradise he gets.

No, no, don't die this way, Stark. Do something. Fight. Swing at him, go for the machete.

The gunman spoke. "The helicopter will come back, *jefe*. Take the spy with us. We'll find out what he knows."

The blade stayed tight against my neck. Seconds ticked away. I died again and again.

Machete said, "Put him in the truck."

The gunman roped my hands behind my back and shoved me into one of the pickups. Machete sat in the front passenger seat of the lead truck, the gunman beside me in the back. The three trucks rumbled down the road, bumper to bumper, no headlights, a slow, bouncing ride on a moonless night.

The rope squeezed my wrists. The pulsing blood made them feel huge. I worked my hands back and forth to create some give. No one in the truck spoke. The cab smelled like sweat and junk food. The gunman stuck his head between the front seats, watching the road ahead.

I inched closer to the door on my right and stretched my hands close to the handle, fumbling for it. The awkward position cramped the muscles in my shoulders. I relaxed to let the tension ease and tried again.

I found it, slid a finger under the latch, and yanked, but the latch didn't engage. The door was locked.

The unlock button would be slightly forward of the latch. I twisted some more, trying to reach it. If I could get out that door to open ground, I could run. The odds weren't great, but my legs would give me a chance at least.

The truck went along, diving into craters in the road and out again, the four of us bouncing along with it. I worked my hands back and forth, back and forth.

The driver's cell phone trilled. He fetched it from his breast pocket and held it to his ear without speaking. The voice on the other end burped out a string of muffled words. The driver responded by straining to check the rear and side mirrors.

"Behind us, *jefe*! *La migra*! *La migra*!"

The driver opened his door and looked back toward Paradise just as the chopper appeared. Its spotlight arrived first, sweeping the desert at an angle. Then the light beamed down in a blinding circle as the craft drew up and hovered overhead, the whooping blades churning at the ground, whipping dirt, stones, and twigs against the truck.

Amid the distraction, I swung my hands back to the lock, popped it open, shouldered the door wide, and jumped out into a tornado. The powerful wind shoved me back. I thought it would tear the clothes off my body. Debris slapped my face like bee stings.

I knew the general location of the Bronco. The trick was running as fast as I could in the dark with my hands behind my back. I fell twice, rolled to my knees, and got up again. After the second time, I wiggled my hands free and kept running, faster now, knees high, arms pumping.

If any of Machete's men followed, they wouldn't stay with it long. The chopper had made me much less important. With no place to land, the pilot would radio dispatch to send ground agents to check out why three trucks were on a smuggling trail at night with their headlights off, and then fly off to resume its original mission down at the border.

Machete's priority would be getting off that mountain before the agents got there.

I found the Bronco. Charlie was sitting in the passenger seat with a fistful of popcorn and tossing the pieces one at a time into his wide-open mouth. He pointed his thumb over his shoulder. "What's with all the popcorn back there? I'm starved."

I jumped into the passenger seat and started the engine. Charlie chuckled at the sight of me. My clothes were disheveled and filthy, and my hair sweaty and clogged with twigs, and sand stuck to my face. He tugged on the loose rope hanging from my wrist.

"What's going on, Mayor? Did you meet a girl?" He laughed. "I can't believe you're still drunk."

"I'm in the demilitarized zone. Dreadful state. What say we stop on the way back to get a sixer of tall boys?"

He showed no curiosity about where he was or how he got there, and I didn't explain. I drove in the opposite direction from the trucks and the chopper, and after a half mile or so pulled behind a cluster of trees to look back. Nobody rode my back trail and the chopper was speeding south.

Driving east, away from Paradise and the smuggler road, I inched the Bronco through open desert back to Ajo Way.

Charlie yapped about his approaching sobriety until I stopped to let him buy his beer. That kept him quiet until we pulled into Double Wide, and he saw his trailer sitting at a sharp angle, a casualty of the storm winds.

The yapping started again. I promised to help fix it in the morning and he calmed down enough to go to bed.

For me, sleep was impossible. I couldn't shake the feeling of that machete against my neck. On top of that, a coyote had curled up on the front seat of the Bronco and was howling at the stars. He'd become a nighttime regular. I named him Jack, and chasing him off did no good because he came right back. When Jack had to sing, he had to sing.

But my insomnia had a good side. It got me reading my crime novels again, the ones I always carried on road trips. I kept a row of them on the shelf over my bed.

Given how the night had gone, only a Jim Thompson would do. I pulled out a slim volume, filled with his customary double crosses and casual bloodletting, and read along to Jack's high, chasing cries.

NINETEEN

Next morning, I was in middoze with the book open on my chest when Benny Diaz banged on my door. It was still dark outside, not quite sunrise. He couldn't make it a polite Jehovah's Witness knock. No, he was leading a raid on a major terror cell.

After jerking the door open, I spread my hands as if to say, "What the hell?"

Even at that ridiculous hour, every strand of his hair was in place and perfectly trimmed, like the lawn of a funeral home. The connection to my father had gotten us off to a good start, but he was giving me reasons not to like him.

"Did I get you up?" he said.

There was another one.

He wore hiking shorts, fresh-out-of-the-box Timberlands, and a short-sleeved tan bush shirt with at least forty pockets to hold the serious gear he'd need to survive a shift on the mountain. He held a safari hat with a brim so wide that, when properly set on the normal-sized human coconut, it would spread into two counties.

He glanced at the mountain as if it were hell itself. "We're going to canvass the trail from end to end. See if the killer discarded anything."

"Perfect day for a hike. Before long it'll be a hundred and ten degrees up there."

"Thanks for reminding me."

"Out here we call that balmy."

Like it or not, I figured I was up for the day and threw the door open to let Chico hobble-hop down the steps. Bundle arrived to give Diaz his semiferocious greeting. Chico and Bundle were brothers, and even before Chico's shooting, they were completely different.

Bundle was up for anything. He'd chase anything and fight anything, and he gave the *narcos* all they could handle. I named him after his habit of finding their marijuana loads in the desert and tearing off the burlap covers. After exposing them, he'd lift his leg and give it a good hosing. Bundle's indignation was a beautiful thing.

I invited Diaz inside and pushed the button on a pot of Maxwell House. He sat at my kitchen table, folded his hands on top of it, boxed his thumbs, and looked around uncomfortably. "This is where you, ah, live? I mean, all the time?"

"You're inside a classic Airstream, a 1977 Ambassador model. People kill to find one of these. The seller basically let me tow it away, if you can believe that."

"I think I can."

"I've spent a fortune fixing it up."

As I fiddled with the coffee mugs on the counter, I gave Diaz a verbal tour.

Past the kitchen was a couch that folded out into my bed. Opposite the couch was a section of counter space that served as an office. I kept my laptop there. At the back of this room was an accordion door that closed off the bathroom and shower.

The interior measured twenty-eight feet from hitch to rear end, and when people asked if there was enough storage space, I told them I made out just fine. The only thing it couldn't handle was all my books. I stored most of them in boxes in one of the bedrooms in Opal's trailer. The ones I kept on the shelf over my bed were the classics I read over and over.

I said, "There's a whole cult of people who swear by Airstreams and write about them in articles and online. They call it 'rounded living.' No angles."

"It's like being in an airplane fuselage," Diaz said.

"I stand six foot two, and the biggest thing for me was learning when to duck."

"That's a problem I don't have."

I gave Diaz his coffee in a Campbell's Soup mug and sat opposite him. The steaming coffee made it feel more like morning, but it was still dark outside. He said he'd already talked with Charlie and Cash and crossed them off his suspect list.

"I saw your televised plea for information about Rolando Molina. Why didn't you mention that when we talked?"

"Because there's no connection to the body on the mountain," I said, even though I knew there was.

"I'm a cop. We don't close cases believing in coincidences."

I talked for a minute about Rolando helping Fausto in Monterrey. I told him of the Tucson Thunder connection and suggested he call Danny Wilson to confirm. I was in a funny position. I wanted Rolando found but couldn't mention the evidence stashed in my freezer.

Part of me wanted to warn Diaz about Machete. But that would raise questions I didn't want to answer, and he was going up there with plenty of backup.

Diaz sipped from his mug and made a face. "This is truly awful coffee."

"How about a refill?"

Two hours of sack time had made me cranky. Diaz's cologne didn't help. When he left, the Airstream smelled like a Holiday Inn bathroom after the maid finishes.

TWENTY

I stood at my open door and watched him drive off. Morning was breaking. A slash of gray light traced the ragged line of the Tucson Mountains to the east. Their west-facing slopes were still black, but that would change as the sun topped the peaks and slanted down, turning the saguaros to candles as it chased the darkness across the desert.

I whistled for Chico and got no response. I left the front door open to hear the squawk of the cactus wrens and went to the kitchen to cook breakfast. I tossed a few eggs around and made some noise with a frying pan.

The red sun curved into view over the mountains, and when the chorizo started to sizzle in the pan, it became a land rush at my door.

Chorizo does that. Nobody can resist the smell of chorizo.

Charlie came in, then Cash, and I welcomed them both.

Sure, come on in and sit at my public table. What did I care? I never ate breakfast alone, and sometimes space in my trailer got tight, especially when Opal was around. Is that anybody's definition of trouble?

I prefer English muffins to toast, and in either case you can't push down on the toaster until the last minute. Too early and the muffin stiffens up and tastes like a shingle.

No, I had no problems. I owned a little Shangri-La in the middle of nowhere. After I bought Double Wide and before my tenants wandered in, I had the world to myself. It took thirty minutes of driving to see another living thing that didn't crawl, slither, bark, howl, or hoot. At least not sober.

Double Wide was close to exactly nothing, which was a long way from where I used to be. At the top of the world, famous, tossing money around like it was lint from my pocket.

I've been hugged, feted, and toasted by strangers. I've walked into bars and restaurants where I couldn't buy a drink if I begged on my knees. Walked into hospitals to smile in front of sick kids and been treated like I came in on water.

The important part of chorizo, after heating the oil in the skillet, is watching for it to brown. The color has to be just right. You know you've got it when the shade matches a new catcher's mitt. I spooned the cut-up chorizo onto a plate and covered it with a paper towel.

Then, snap of the fingers, my career was over, and I hit the road. Driving nowhere and in a hurry to get there, alone, not hearing jeers I didn't want to hear, not worrying about the next exit, the next, or the one after that.

Just drive, baby.

The farther I went, the better I felt. With every state line crossed, the failure fell off my back, and in the rearview I watched the wind blow it on down the highway. If you could run forever, well, there's your answer.

But at some point, you have to stop and it catches up to you again—the idea that you could've done more, should've done more, and there's no way to go back and get it right. The only thing you've ever done in your life, the thing that defined you and got you up in the morning, is over forever.

Now I lived in a place where having a well-functioning vehicle made me a prince among men.

I scooped the scrambled eggs out of the pan, separating the portions onto three plates. The muffins popped up in the toaster. Perfect timing.

Forget it, Stark. You've got no problems. Dust yourself off and deal with right now, the collection of human strays gathered in your fashionably remodeled trailer.

They're trying to stay out of the line of fire, too. Not bad people, just lost, forgotten, beaten down, unloved, unwashed, and, okay, maybe a little crooked. If copper wiring goes missing from the construction site, hey, everybody has to stay alive, right?

Perspective is everything. My tenants looked at me and thought I had it all, every ounce of hope and grace in the world. Helping them made me think they were right, and maybe that explained everything. Maybe it was just that simple.

The pressing crisis that morning was jacking up Charlie's trailer so he wouldn't have to live uneven.

After breakfast, I went outside to smoke a cigar and called Roxanne Santa Cruz. She'd left two messages while I was on Paradise Mountain. I left her a message of my own, after which Cash, Charlie, and I walked to the trailer next to mine.

The tenants, Gil and Helen Pappas, had left the week before to visit Helen's people in Apache Junction. Gil worked as a handyman and kept every tool and spare part you could think of in his storage shed. I got out his hydraulic jack while Cash and Charlie found two sturdy wood beams, and we carried everything to Charlie's trailer.

The job was to jack it up enough to slip in a replacement block. The jack had a three-ton capacity, the same kind mechanics used to lift cars. I set it up underneath the fallen corner. Charlie and Cash stuck the wood beams under the trailer on both sides of the jack in case it slipped.

I pumped the lever until the lift grabbed the bottom of the frame, the trailer rising slightly with each downward thrust. Charlie and Cash strained with the beams held over their shoulders.

When the trailer got high enough, I locked the jack and grabbed a fresh cinder block.

Before I could slip it into the space, I heard a fast clicking that went faster and faster until the lock gave out, and the trailer crashed down.

The two remaining cinderblocks held. If one or both had shattered, the whole thing might've tumbled over. I told Charlie we couldn't do anything more until I got the jack fixed.

For the remainder of the morning and into early afternoon, I waited to hear from Oscar Molina. Nothing. I called Alice Menendez and left another urgent request for Oscar to call me.

Opal was still missing, and in daylight the problem seemed less sinister. Disappearing wasn't that much out of character for a seventeen-year-old vagabond, someone susceptible to the strongest wind.

But with all that was going on, I thought I'd better look for her just the same, and the best place to start was the last place she'd been.

TWENTY-ONE

Downtown Tucson was busy late in the afternoon. I parked at a meter outside the convention center and walked to Opal's sidewalk spot to canvass passersby. Somebody had to have seen her. Whether she walked away, hopped into someone's car, or boarded a bus, a heavyset Indian girl carrying an easel would be a memorable sight.

Two hours yielded nothing. But I learned that stopping people on a boiling sidewalk in July is seen as a hostile act by an obvious psychopath.

A cop arrived to check me out. He wasn't interested until I told him my name, and then he wanted to help. We were standing in the shadow of TPD headquarters, and he called over there to set me up with a missing-persons detective.

"Whip Stark is coming to see you," the cop said. "Yeah, *that* Whip Stark."

That landed me in a cramped office with a balding officer named Jensen. He pounded the keyboard with two bent fingers. He'd hit a few keys, let five seconds pass as he looked over his glasses at the screen, hit a few more, and look again. After several minutes of that, he sat back to catch his breath.

In a tired drawl, Jensen said, "I'm seeing an Opal Sanchez in the system. We've got two warrants out for shoplifting on the reservation, out at Sells. Is this your friend?"

I dressed up my shocked face. "There must be some mistake. Golly." Now I knew why Opal didn't want me to call the police.

Jensen said, "Looks like multiple DOBs and aliases. Ginger Padilla. Gail Suarez."

To wiggle out of it, I told Jensen I might know where Opal was after all, and as I was talking too much, Roxanne Santa Cruz called. I held the phone up to Jensen, and he nodded okay.

"Been trying to reach you," she said. "I've got news."

"I turned my phone off last night."

"You didn't tell me they found a corpse out your way."

"Somehow you found out anyway."

"When it comes to mayhem, I know all. You have time for a cocktail?"

"A glass of milk maybe."

"We must have a bad connection. Did you say milk?"

We met at the Blue Note. The bar is immediately north of downtown in a part of town built for late-night monkey business. Fourth Avenue is lined with bars, restaurants, tattoo parlors, and other establishments where college kids do things their parents would hate.

The Note has a horseshoe-shaped bar, a few pool tables and a shaded patio out back. A couple of miserable downtown lawyers huddled at tables with their medicated secretaries.

Even though I don't drink much, I like bars and don't ask for a whole lot. The darker the better and there can never be somebody on the next stool singing along with Patsy Cline. If I've got those two things, I'm good.

Roxy wore tight jeans ripped above the knees and a loose-fitting white pullover blouse with three of the five buttons undone, creating a wide and interesting V. She had on ankle boots that were high-heeled and black with silver ankle buckles.

She flattened a twenty on the bar. "The usual for me, Tommy, and whatever for my famous friend here."

Tommy stared at me, the wheels turning as he tried to figure out who I was. He had tortoiseshell glasses and a pug nose over a salt-and-pepper mustache. After a few moments, he gave up and went to work on the drinks.

Roxy whispered, "He has no idea who you are. Must be a foreigner."

Tommy brought vodka neat for Roxy and soda water for me. They didn't have milk.

"Tommy, this is Whip Stark, the baseball player."

He stared again, wide eyed. He thrust his hand over the bar for me to shake. "Sure, sure. I knew I recognized you from somewhere."

Tommy made small talk until he could comfortably leave.

Roxy said, "You realize he's working the tip, right? He's never heard of Whip Stark."

"Once upon a time, everybody knew." I raised my glass. "To once upon a time."

"Look at you, still digging the fame."

"Like a dog digs the dogcatcher."

"I hate to be cruel, but soon it'll only be your mom and your dog who remember anything about you, and dogs can't clap. But it's something, right? Cheers to fame." She raised her shot glass, clicked it against my glass, and said, "Tell me, what's with that cocaine business in Mexico?"

"I take it you Googled me."

"That's what I do at night—drink wine and Google men." She raised a finger to add an activity: "And play SongPop with my nieces."

"I never snorted cocaine, okay."

"The newspaper in Mazatlán sure made it sound like you did."

"That was all Rolando. He couldn't stay away from the stuff. We shared a beach house, and when the cops found his equipment bag stuffed with coke, they grabbed me, too. That's how it works in Mexico. I was a name-brand American they could shake down for a lot of money. They got a suitcase full."

"Wait, did you just say you never did cocaine? Seriously?"

"That's your takeaway?"

Roxy sipped her vodka and swallowed like it hurt. "I don't understand people like you. There's white powder on the table in front of you, you snort it. What's complicated about that?"

"I like to keep my head. That's how I'm made."

Tommy came over to see about another round.

Roxy said, "Tommy, if there's white powder in front of you, what do you do?"

"Easy. Wipe the bar down and grab the tip."

"I'm drinking with the Pope and his accountant." Roxy shook her head. "I knew this day would come."

Two guys came in to play pool. They looked like bums just off the train, which meant they were probably professors. I asked Roxy what she had for me.

"After your promo I got a call at the station. It was a woman, really panicked—said she had information about Paradise Mountain."

That got my attention.

Roxy said, "She talked fast, and there was this music pounding in the background."

"Like a party?"

"Could be. Boom, boom, boom, you know. It wasn't a funeral."

"Name?"

"Didn't say. With the noise and the way she was talking, it was hard to get anything straight. But she identified the dead man on the mountain. Carlos Alvarez. He has a criminal record."

Pool balls clicked. Roxy sipped her vodka and wiggled the shot glass at Tommy. He jumped to her unspoken command.

When her drink came, she said, "The way she talked about Alvarez, it sounded like they knew each other real well. Husband, boyfriend, something close. She was hysterical about him getting shot, and she mentioned you."

One of the pool players bent over the table to make a shot, loudly calling the eight ball. He missed, which I enjoyed. I asked what the tipster had said.

"Something like, 'I need to talk to Stark! The professor says talk to Stark!'"

"Professor? What professor?"

'Beats me. Something about a melody too."

"Melody meaning a song?" I asked.

"Could be. She was raving about Arty's melody. She kept saying the professor told her to talk to you."

The Note's front door swung open, throwing a shaft of street light into the bar. It made shadows of three college girls. Looking wrung out and sweaty, they stagger-stepped to the bar in flip-flops. One of them called out, "Tommy!" and pounded on the top of the bar like she was playing bongos.

Another leaned forward on her elbows and said, "Hurry, Tommy! We need libations! Multiple libations!"

Most students leave town for the summer. The ones who stay spend the days sleeping and nights drinking. After a while they get to know bartenders' names and use them a lot because they think it's what real drinkers do.

Tommy glanced at the girls and went back to cutting limes. He took his time. He dried his hands on a towel, folded it, edges perfect, sighed heavily, and moved toward the girls like he was going to war and might not come back.

"Nice to see you ladies again," he said. "Name your poison and I'll provide it anon."

Roxy grinned at the exchange and sipped her drink. "With this caller, Whip, I know it's frustrating, but that was all I got out of her. Either she passed out from hysteria, or the signal tanked, I don't know. Ooops, my butt's calling."

She jumped off her stool, pulled her phone from her back pocket and looked.

"Really, people? Another bod?" she said. "We're getting them every night now. What a town. Finding a corpse these days is like picking up a penny on the sidewalk and thinking it's your lucky day."

She fingered more text onto the screen. "Well, this helps. Throat slashed, blood all over her blond wig. That's a nice twist. I can lead with that."

"Did you say blond wig?" I thought of the woman tailing me in the white SUV.

"Want to come along?"

"I sure do."

"See, we have something in common, Phenom. You like it when everything goes wrong."

"I've had enough wrong to last a long time."

"There's always room for more. Come on. I'll drive."

Roxy drained the last of her drink with a fast snap of her head. I figured her neck muscles were well accustomed to the task.

Night had fallen over the silent city. The temperature had gone from blazing hot to merely warm, and somehow it felt worse. Roxy drove a black Audi convertible. Had to be a $65,000 ride. She put the top down. I drove all the time with the top down on my Bronco, but that was because it didn't have one. I was working on that.

Roxy drove fast, the wind spraying her hair. She treated red lights as an affront aimed especially at her. She gunned the engine several times, and when the light flipped to green, she squealed off the line, leaving the fellow in the next lane to eat her exhaust. That made her smile.

When we got onto Kino Parkway heading south, she shouted across the seat: "I haven't told Detective Diaz about Alvarez yet."

I said nothing.

Roxy said, "I wanted you to be the first to know."

"Diaz knows by now."

"Still, I should give the man a call. Let him know I'm thinking about him."

"You're thinking about putting another source in your pocket."

She smiled grandly at the windshield. "Isn't journalism an icky little game?"

The airport is on the far south side. The ride from the Blue Note is long, over mostly undeveloped land in a lousy part of town. There's not much traffic, not much street lighting, few businesses, no pedestrians, and no indication that actually people live in the sporadic clusters of earth-colored frame and stucco homes set out in the desert.

The only signs of life were a couple of dangerous drive-up motels with busted neon signs and skeleton dogs darting across our headlights.

TWENTY-TWO

The last half mile of Tucson Boulevard near the airport is lined with hotels and pay parking lots. Police lights blinked at the end of the street. They made a colorful halo in the sky east of the boulevard and the terminals.

Roxy followed a network of side roads to the scene, using the cop lights as a guide. She began to sing. Not a bad voice. She kept singing and motioned to me as though I should recognize the lyrics.

"It's from that song," she said. "'Unchained Melody.'"

"The Righteous Brothers, right? What about them?"

"The caller talked about Arty's melody, and now I've got 'Unchained Melody' stuck in my head. But I don't think she was talking about a song."

"What about art? Put the two together. 'Arty Melody.' Was she talking about an art professor?"

"Let me look." With one eye on the road, Roxy punched at her phone. She couldn't find a University of Arizona art professor with a first or last name of Arthur. She checked for music professors and found nothing.

I suggested looking up the name Melody. Roxy worked her fingers again. "No professor of anything at the school named Melody. What the hell was she talking about?"

The road we were on dead-ended at a pipe fence running along a wash. Two police cruisers were parked against the fence.

A young patrolman waved us to a stop and quick-stepped around to the driver's window like he was on to something big.

When he saw Roxy looking out at him, he stopped short. "Oh, hello there, Miss Santa Cruz."

"Hello, Doug. Nice night."

"We get the bloodiest ones on these hot nights, huh."

"Seems like it."

"Go on ahead. Your cameraman's already there."

"Thanks. Who caught the case?"

"Detective Martin, ma'am. Nice to see you again."

The cop waved Roxy into the desert immediately east of the wash. She parked short of the action, and we walked across bladed ground that had been staked out for a construction job. It looked like the cops had called in an army with orders to stand around. The headlights from a semicircle of squad cars threw a white light over the scene.

I couldn't make out what those lights were illuminating until I reached the yellow tape and peered past it, between parked cars, between cops and crime scene investigators moving in and out of the light. I saw what I expected to see, a white SUV.

Roxy raised the tape and held it high for me. I ducked underneath. The driver's door of the SUV was open. A woman sat with her forehead angled against the steering wheel, her face turned toward us. A long red gash half-mooned across her neck.

The blond wig had shifted back on her head and down onto her left shoulder, and it hung there by its last strand, the shoulder and the hair bright red with blood.

The revealed portion of her skull, immediately back of her forehead, was closely shaved, making her features more prominent. Her upper teeth protruded and a wedge of purple tongue showed between her lips.

Her face was like no color you'd see on any living thing, a sickly gray mask. I turned away. Some sights will burn in your brain a long time.

Roxy talked briefly to Detective Martin and summoned her cameraman. They shot a piece with Roxy standing against the crime tape. It didn't have much meat to it. No name, no possible motive, no mention of evidence found.

Back at the Audi, Roxy said, "Martin asked me to hold off broadcasting the name for a day or two. But the ID says Rosa Lopez. Ring a bell?"

"No, but I'll bet she's your telephone tipster." I explained that I'd been followed the night before by a woman wearing a bleached-blond wig and driving a white SUV.

"Early thirties, manages a strip joint called Skin," Roxy said. "I like that name. It gets to the point."

"That explains the boom-boom music you heard in the background," I said. "She called you from Skin."

"It's up the road here. Shall we have a look?"

On the way out, we passed two SUVs carrying crews from competing TV stations. Roxy wiggled her fingers at them. As she buttoned up the window, she said, "Late again. What losers."

Skin was a mile north, a bleak warehouse-style building set alone on a patch of desert off the boulevard. No sign marked the entrance to the club, either on the street or on the building itself. The exterior was a windowless stone facade. Customers entered through a roll-up delivery door with a red light above it.

Two police cruisers pulled into the parking lot just ahead of us and their lights were still blinking. Strippers leaned against cars talking to cops. Several were barefoot, legs exposed, and had blouses thrown over bare shoulders.

Roxy and I walked between cars and inside the club. The business end of the night had ended with the news of Rosa Lopez's murder. No dancers danced and no customers leered at them. But somebody had forgotten to shut off the music. It pounded up through the floor in that primal beat that made spinning naked on a pole seem perfectly sensible.

A uniformed cop approached with his arms out, intending to sweep us back out the door. "Shut down for the night," he said. "Outside. Let's go. Club's closed."

We turned and ran smack into Detective Martin. He was short and hard looking and not happy to see us. He said to Roxy, "I thought you were going to wait a day?"

"Hello again, Frank. Are you following us, or are we following you?"

"I told you I don't want anything released until we know more. The wrong information goes out, somebody runs, and we never close this."

One of the dancers staggered past us, dollar bills hanging off her G-string. Except for stiletto heels, that was all she had on. She was long legged to begin with, but the heels made her a giant. She was small breasted, and her face was made up to look like a cat's. But she was crying into a handkerchief, and her painted-on whiskers had smeared.

One of the bills floated to the floor in front of Roxy. She grabbed it and showed it to Frank and said, "I came for the ambience."

Martin stood with his hands on his hips. He snapped his chin toward me.

Roxy said, "Detective Frank Martin, this is Whip Stark. We're working together."

Martin gave me a look that said, "Don't get in my way." Switching his eyes slowly to Roxy, he said, "All I can say is it looks like a message killing. Brutal. But they all are." He pointed us toward the front door. "Call me in a couple days. I might have something."

Roxy stuffed the bill into Martin's shirt pocket, and we walked out to the parking lot. The cat stripper was still naked and mewling into her hanky. Two other naked girls stood at her elbows, propping her up.

TWENTY-THREE

We got back to the Blue Note after 2:00 a.m. Roxy suggested a final drink, but Tommy had the front door open and all the inside lights on, and he was sweeping the place out.

"Sorry, we're closed."

"Come on, Tommy," Roxy said. "One little drinky?"

"Forget it, Roxanne. I've been on since this morning, and I have to go home to feed my cats." He shooed us away and slammed the door.

Roxy shivered. "I've never talked to him in proper lighting. Not good."

I offered to walk her back to the car, and she put her arm through mine as we went. Usually at that end of Fourth Avenue, the street and the sidewalks are jumping as the Blue Note and Nutcracker's, a neighboring bar, clear out. But July made for slow Tuesday nights.

Roxy said, "It feels like we're ghosts, out here all alone."

"I don't need the darkness to feel like a ghost."

"We can forget about it for tonight. Let all our stuff go."

"The night's not long enough for that. Here we are."

We stopped beside the Audi. Instead of unlocking the door and getting in, Roxy leaned her back against the driver's door and folded her arms and looked at me through the glow of the streetlamp. "Didn't Skin give you any ideas?" Her tone was full of suggestion.

"I'm out of ideas. Been that way for a couple of years."

"I'm going to have to explain this to the station's accountant. Mr. Beasley smells like an old sofa. He's going to ask if I'm okay. 'Expensing a glass of milk, Miss Santa Cruz?'" She tossed her head and laughed wickedly. After closing time on Fourth Avenue, wicked laughs are the only kind you hear.

She pointed at the slumbering buildings of downtown. "I'm down here along the railroad tracks, behind the blood bank. We can have a nightcap on my porch and watch the trains."

"I've got a long drive in the morning."

"To Phoenix, I know. You go there every week."

On Wednesdays, I drove to the Maricopa County Jail to visit my father. It seemed like everybody knew my schedule. A guard probably snapped a picture of me and sent it out on Twitter or Instagram.

My face must've registered surprise, for Roxy quickly added, "I heard about Sam Houston Stark's loyal son, the famous baseball player, his only visitor. Doing it alone is hard. I take care of my mother."

"Sick?"

"Alzheimer's. But that's just an opinion. She's been off her nugget since I was little and nobody called it anything."

"That's why you're still in Tucson. You strike me as the big-city type."

"I get offers all the time. Good money."

"Sure."

"My sister's busy with her kids and there's nobody else. I'm stuck here."

Roxy unlocked the Audi, got in, and buttoned the window down, resting her slender arm along the door, her long painted fingers gripping the side mirror. For the first time, I saw that she was missing half the pinky finger on her left hand. The sight jarred me, four long, shapely fingers with nails painted blood red, and then a bent stump, like a snuffed-out cigarette.

Something was all wrong about that. It scared me in a way, got my heart racing. She saw me looking at it and jerked her hand inside the car.

Looking straight ahead, she said, "This is the part of the night I don't like. Waiting for dawn, the empty hours."

"Isn't that what vodka's for?"

She sucked in a breath and made a raspberry sound blowing it out. "This town...I don't know. You can't go to the supermarket without running into somebody. You must get that a lot."

"Until this Rolando deal, I've been avoiding town as much as possible."

Roxy looked at her watch, adjusted the rearview mirror. Her movements had become jerky and uncertain. She tapped her index finger on the mirror. "Are you sure I can't talk you into a nightcap? I'll ride up to Phoenix with you in the morning."

"I go there alone to see a man alone."

"Don't get deep. Please. It's too late for deep." She sighed. "So that's it? We're done here?" She pushed her lips out and tilted her head and looked out at me from underneath that waterfall of hair. Her eyes sparkled with invitation, the look every man wants to see.

But I had a lot on my mind. I was busy and exhausted. I was trying to shed every unnecessary thing so I could resurrect myself. It wasn't easy. Desire makes you forget what you want, makes you a fool. I knew all about that from years as a young ballplayer on the road and wanted to leave it there.

With no rancor in her voice, Roxy said, "I can't believe you're going to make me work for this, Phenom. You're quite the bastard."

She started the engine and the stereo came on with it, blasting across the night. The bass reverberated under my feet, the rapper Nelly. She lowered the volume and turned her face up to me with a hard glint in her eyes.

"I know you're holding out on me about Rolando. Tell me everything or I'm out. Nobody plays me."

The Audi shot away from the curb, the bumper brushing my leg. She squealed the tires and pumped the volume again as Nelly shook windows all along Fourth Avenue.

TWENTY-FOUR

Early next morning I drove into Tucson and took I-10 west toward Phoenix, one of the worst drives in the state. Rolling through dark desert, not quite awake, not yet breathing properly, not yet seeing as well as I should, and an hour into the trip, the sun breaks beyond the windshield, and there it is, the boiling brown mess of Phoenix.

Whenever I heard news of a car jumping the median and crashing into an oncoming eighteen-wheeler for no apparent reason, I didn't have to wonder what happened.

The driver saw Phoenix.

Maricopa County's Fourth Avenue Jail didn't open until eight o'clock. I waited in the Bronco listening to ESPN Radio's Mike and Mike talk about the designated hitter, the foulest invention in all of sports.

When it was time, I went inside the Soviet-style brick-and-glass building. The check-in officer's nametag said Rodriguez. She was 250 pounds of woman sweating inside an institutional tan-and-black uniform with a carrying capacity of 150.

She knew who I was from my weekly visits and that sped up the routine. "Sam Houston Stark," Rodriguez said with a grin. "He's been a noisy boy this morning."

"How's that?"

"Talking lines from his plays. He sure attracts attention, that one." She told me to wait while she went to get my father out of his cell.

Attracting attention. Yes. That has always been Sam Houston Stark's special skill.

For twenty-two years, he was a distinguished professor at Arizona State University, brilliant, handsome, a classroom raconteur whose personality drew attention across campus. Students waited in line for a seat in his class. He put on a show using every bit of his energy in every class, and he had the perfect voice for it—a deep, resonant theater voice that sounded like it was echoing even when it wasn't.

His downward spiral came with shocking speed. First alcohol, then whatever drug he could get his hands on, then an affair with a prostitute thirty years his junior, and finally heroin. He fell so deeply into the black pit that he began pulling strong-arm robberies of convenience stores, supermarkets, banks.

The prostitute was with him. Her name was Cristy Carlyle.

The FBI put out grainy security photos of them wearing masks depicting various characters from Shakespeare. They spoke lines from his plays as they pulled their jobs.

An enterprising TV reporter obtained a videotape of one of the robberies. It showed Sam leveling a pistol at terrified bank employees and calling out in that hypnotic voice: "Hell is empty, and all the devils are here!"

That line was from *The Tempest*, spoken by Prospero, my namesake. The video looped endlessly on cable, which wasn't alone in taking up the story. All the media fell hard for the so-called Hamlet Robbers.

But the story didn't go nuts until the cops found Cristy Carlyle dead in her apartment in Tempe, butchered like livestock with what the coroner said was probably a kitchen knife. The knife was never found.

The police located Sam that same night wandering the desert across the street from the apartment, gone on that horrible drug, his clothing splattered with Carlyle's blood. He remembered nothing and still doesn't.

I was watching TV in my Mexican jail cell when a news crawl announced Sam's arrest on a charge of first-degree murder. I thought I was dreaming. Sometimes I still do.

TWENTY-FIVE

A different guard came and got me. I was the only one in the waiting room, but he announced my name like the king's courier. He curled a filthy finger at me and we walked down a long, cold corridor, then another and another, all of them smelling of bleach and whatever the bleach was intended to clean up.

He punched his code into three security pads and shoved open three heavy yellow doors with wired windows. Every sound was unusually loud. Our echoing footsteps, the door locks snapping open with metallic precision, the voices harsh along connecting rooms and corridors.

The door at the end of the fourth corridor opened to the room for contact visits. I took booth number four. Sam sat on the other side of a table, and when he saw me, he brightened and said, "Prospero, you came!"

Every time, Sam spoke those same three words as if he was surprised, as if there were any doubt. His voice was softer than before, back in his throat, chastened, with only a touch of that biblical tone. But enough of the old sound remained, and it was good to hear.

I asked how he was doing. Instead of answering, he got a worried look and said, "Still reading your fedora stories?"

"I keep most of them in storage, Sam."

"Excellent. You need to move on to something more edifying."

"But I did pull one out the other day."

"No! Sweet hour, why?"

"It's a long story. It involves a coyote named Jack."

He stared in professorial horror.

"I don't know, Sam. I guess I miss reading them. Who knows, they might help me figure some things out."

He rose in his chair, his voice loud: "Don't say that! There's no wisdom in those potboilers!"

On Sam's side of the table, a guard stepped to his shoulder and said, "Tame the lips, teach. We don't need no riot this morning."

Sam leaned in and whispered to me: "See. They all talk that way now. Even the constables. Offal. It's American offal!"

"I didn't come all this way to talk about Shakespeare."

Sam's eyes warmed. "The bard is all you need."

It was the same old argument, and I let it go. I watched him. He wavered in his chair as if drunk. Trying to move the conversation along, I said, "I drove as fast as you to get here, Sam." His impressive pile of speeding tickets was a family joke.

The smile vanished. He stretched his neck forward. "They lay out traps on I-10," he said darkly. "Did you know that? The cops do that. Don't think they're not waiting!" His voice rose to a bellow. "They're waiting for you, Prospero!"

The guard stepped forward again and Sam drew back, seeming to shrivel inside his orange jumpsuit. I studied him. He had changed in confinement.

His long, narrow face had turned sallow, his features dulled. Red blotches marred the skin on both sides of his aquiline nose. He still had a full head of hair, but the gray streaking through it had grown prominent. His thin lips were split top and bottom, the bottom cut shining in the fluorescent light.

If he laughed too hard, those splits would open again, and blood would likely run, though I didn't see much chance of that.

He normally smiled as easily as he breathed, giving his face a lively expression through bold blue eyes.

But the old spirit was gone, replaced with a remote, unnatural stare.

"Is everything all right, Sam?"

"I'm writing a treatise on my addiction," he whispered.

"Are you getting enough sleep? You look tired."

"This tainted world needs to know my story. I'm going to see to it that something good comes of what's happened to me."

"You've had enough attention. Let's talk about your trial."

"Heroin addiction is like a train coming. That'll be my thesis."

"Come on, Sam. There's no thesis. Look at me and don't talk like that."

But he wasn't hearing me. He smiled without joy, seemed to look at me without seeing.

He said, "You're miserable where you stand until the spoon is in your mind and then in your hand and then you're breathing it into your lungs. Your lungs welcome the smoke, and you see the first glimpse of the train coming. All you have to do is grab on to that train and ride it. And your troubles ride away with it."

I broke in. "We should talk about your trial."

But he kept going, his voice a homeless-shelter monotone. "Everything inside you knows the truth. You know you shouldn't do it. You know that by grabbing the train, you're entering a darkness you can never leave. But all that matters is the moment. And here it comes, the hard rumble of metal wheels on metal tracks. The squealing, the whistle coming closer, and there's no doubt what you'll do."

"Sam, I don't want to do this. I drove a long way, and it wasn't for this."

His eyes were right on me but still far away. His voice rose: "You reach your hand out as the train nears, and you hate yourself. But there is no 'self' anymore. You take hold of the speeding train, and its power lifts you off your feet, and suddenly you're soaring. Joyous! Full of life as you're pulled along by this power, the instant pure pleasure running through your veins, through your muscles, into your brain!"

"Sam! Stop this, Sam!"

But he was unreachable, gone to me and gone to the world.

He continued: "Anything after that is after that, and to hell with it! Let's ride this beautiful train! But then you don't need the train anymore. You can let go. This is the drug swarming over your brain, drenching it with the excitement, the thrill, the escape, and the wonder of life again. Soon you're parallel to the speeding train, sideways to it. Like Superman!"

He laughed crazily. "The rush is so great you don't have to hold on anymore and so you let go, and you're in the air, and you no longer need its power because you have your own!"

I spun and barked at the guard behind me. "How does he get heroin in this dump?"

Foolishly, the guard said, "It's against regulations."

"Aren't you supposed to stop it?"

Louder, in his guard voice: "Sir, I'm going to have to ask you to calm down."

The guard on Sam's side stalked his shoulder again, taking him by the arm.

Sam jerked away. His voice fell to a dreamlike tone: "Now you're between Earth and the sky, and the thought that the train has to stop, putting you back on the ground—it doesn't exist. It's gone! Do you understand what I'm saying, Prospero? That's a lifetime away. It doesn't matter, for you've departed this realm of lawyers, salesmen, and cesspool merchants. Left its corporeal horrors behind."

The guard pulled Sam to his feet and muscled him out of the room. The visit ended just that way, without ceremony, without good-byes.

I demanded a meeting with somebody in charge. The boss was busy. I cracked my knuckles for an hour in his outer office until my temper boiled up, and I had to get out of there, outside those walls.

TWENTY-SIX

In the parking lot, I leaned against the Bronco to collect myself. The sun-scorched metal nearly melted the skin on my back. A steady wind sent dust clouds marching across the valley.

How does a man with everything anyone could want, a three day-a-week job, nobody looking over his shoulder, steady money, respect, go from that to what sat on the other side of that table?

Sometimes happiness gets to be too much. You become convinced you're bored and look around for something more when there is nothing more. That's when you find a younger woman, in Sam's case, a prostitute who turned him inside out.

Then pile heroin on top of the booze. Why not? Maybe it'll jerk me out of this paradise.

When the sun always shines, you hunt for trouble. That's just how people are.

I checked my phone. No message from Oscar Molina. I called Cash at Double Wide to see if Opal had turned up. No Opal.

Tork Mortenson left a message saying no one from the Rich Hill Gang would talk. Whoever got after them on that mountain really did the job.

I thought about going back inside the jail and tipping over some desks to find out how Sam was scoring heroin. But I couldn't afford to get banned. Sam needed to see me, needed to sit across from someone who believed absolutely in his innocence.

The press and TV people were killing him, and that scared away his friends and colleagues at ASU. They had behaved like cowards, abandoning him. That included my mother, who headed the Western Collection at Arizona State's library. She reacted as if the crime had happened to another family and fled to the safety of her archives.

Sam's lawyer, Micah Alan Gabriel, stayed cool on the question of whether he had carved up Cristy Carlyle. He was a lawyer, and Sam was a client, and that was as far as it went.

A car pulled in next to the Bronco, and there he was, Micah Alan Gabriel.

I didn't like him. He had a long silver ponytail. I was out of touch when my mother hired him, which is a polite way of saying in jail in Mazatlán.

If I'd been involved, the first thing I would've said was no ponytails. Your lawyer in a death penalty case should never have a ponytail. Gabriel's reached the middle of his back. From the front he looked bald. From behind, he looked like he had an aged ferret crawling up his spine with dastardly intent.

He stepped out of his car wearing chino slacks, tan woven-leather slip-on shoes, no socks, and a white guayabera. They're called Mexican wedding shirts, and they make all men look like barbers. They're short sleeved, untucked, have two rows of pleats down the chest and enough pockets to stash your tips, an extra comb, and a straight razor if the haircut goes bad.

He had the look of a man creeping past fifty and tired of it all. He had washed-out eyes, a road map nose and mottled skin. He looked like a bass player. He looked like a twelve-stepper midway through the program who delivers pizzas to pay for his smokes.

But the real reason I didn't like Micah Alan Gabriel was that I was paying him in wheelbarrows of green money, and his investigator still couldn't find the murder weapon, the missing knife that could prove Sam's innocence. Or at least upend the prosecution's theory of the crime.

Two motions to move the trial out of Maricopa County had been denied. Micah Alan Gabriel planned to file a motion to delay the trial based on Sam's drug use and consequent inability to understand the proceedings against him.

Gabriel came around his car to talk to me. "I'm here to see your father a final time before I file. This should be clear cut. He's an addict and needs treatment."

"It needs to begin as soon as possible."

"No question about that. We'll see what the court says."

"He's innocent. Drug or no drug, he'd never do something like this."

I wanted more, some understanding from Gabriel that he was representing a good man. Instead, he assured me of his faith in the system, in a tone that sounded like a speech spoken a hundred times before, and then walked casually into the prison.

TWENTY-SEVEN

On the drive back to Tucson, I jumped off the highway at Tangerine Road in Oro Valley. The Super Walmart had a special on nine-millimeter ammunition. I bought three boxes—brass casings, not aluminum—and some Maxwell House.

At the register, I threw a bag of jellybeans onto the belt for Opal. She went crazy over jellybeans.

From there, I followed Oracle Road along the west end of the Catalinas and down into the rattling city. Most of it was obscured by a cloud of haze suspended over the baking valley. Only the tops of downtown's buildings and the peaks of the mountains pierced the vaguely orange veil.

I thought about Rosa Lopez, her frantic call to Roxy, her desperate attempt to chase me down, and her murky clues. "The professor said to call Stark! Arty's melody!"

Those words had to mean something. She was chasing me to deliver a message. If she knew Carlos Alvarez, maybe she also knew Rolando and what happened to him. Maybe she wanted to tell me where his body was.

Oracle Road was loud and clogged. Late in the day, shadow time. I passed a sales lot brimming with new cars and blowing flags, the Tucson Mall, an endless array of parked cars, cars moving an inch at a time, brake lights shining, horns blaring.

I stopped at a red light and felt myself sticking to the seat. The air-conditioning in the Bronco roared, but without a roof, it only made noise. I've had pitching coaches like that. I'd stick to the seat until I arrived at my destination and then stick to something else.

Summer in Tucson. The key to life here isn't a sun hat or a swimming pool. It isn't a Big Gulp. The only real thing is covered parking.

To drown out the car radios pounding on both sides of me, I turned on my own radio and heard the Righteous Brothers singing "Unchained Melody."

It sparked an idea. Roxy had checked the UA's directory for music or art professors named Arthur or Melody. But she never checked Pima Community College. I got on my phone and checked Pima Community College, and found a plant sciences teacher named Arthur Melody. Had retired from the UA and taught a course at the college.

The light changed. I gassed it while pulling up information on Melody.

He was a genius, highly respected, had published papers and won awards. I found his picture. I knew he'd be bald, and he exceeded expectations. The only hair that remained wrapped around the lower portion of his head like a silver muff. He had wire glasses, a polite mustache, long ears with shovel lobes, and the easy smile and soft, indoor skin of an aging academic.

But why was an unassuming plant sciences professor involved with a strip club manager, dead in a vicious knife attack, and her criminal boyfriend or husband, dead from two bullets to the back of the head?

The Tucson phone book listed Melody's home address. It was time to go ask him.

TWENTY-EIGHT

Melody lived in the Sam Hughes neighborhood immediately east of the university. Known for its Old World elegance, the homes first went up in the 1920s, most in the Spanish Revival style. They were single story, earth-colored or bright white, and they had huge picture windows, sculpted doors, red-tile roofs, and pebbled driveways that circled in from the street.

Professors lived there. PBS, round glasses, white wine at four. Barrio Subaru.

I parked at the curb on Melody's street but down somewhat from his house. Sometimes I get these feelings.

A chest-high wall surrounded the property. Back of it two drooping willow trees shrouded the entryway. The house wasn't kept up and badly needed a new coat of paint. Vines crawled all over the exterior, a clever way to cover the network of cracks.

The doorbell was surprisingly loud. I found out why when no one responded, and I went to knock and saw the door ajar. I pushed it open. The hinges shrieked like a witch in trouble. I called out to Melody, got silence in return, and stepped inside. The house was dark except for a patch of light so far back it only made a faint appearance where I was.

"Arthur Melody!" I called.

No response.

In my stories, the detective never turns and leaves when a door makes that sound. Everyone knows he should run. Everything's going to hell and pretty quick, but the detective never stops, and neither did I.

Brave and clueless. That's me.

I walked toward the light, through a dining room with a long table under a massive chandelier, into a one-window living room, dark with a closed-in feel. The chairs were black and red and way too big for the space. A sword hung on the wall. The white brick around the fireplace was clean. The magazines on the coffee table had been laid out in a perfect fan shape, probably in 1988.

The room wasn't a place someone lived in. It looked as if it had been decorated and forgotten by a bachelor who used it only to pass through on his way to work. The kitchen was the same, sadly clean. The refrigerator door was bare, no family pictures, not even a dog.

But there was a photograph from *Arizona Highways* magazine of a coyote, jaw raised, howling from a mountaintop. What a great idea for a picture. I wished I'd thought of it.

A sign hung on the rounded doorway at the back of the kitchen: "Welcome to Arty's Fabulous Cactus Garden."

The doorway led into an oval-shaped glass walkway wide enough for one person going one way. It went back about forty feet to the light. I heard a sound at the end of the walkway. I called Arthur Melody's name again, got no answer, and kept going.

Farther down, a shadow moved in the light. I heard a loud humming and guessed a window air conditioner.

The walkway opened to a large room full of folding tables, about twenty of them, covered with small cacti in plastic and ceramic pots. There were fledgling saguaros, fishhook barrel cacti, and teddy bear cholla, hundreds of them crowded together on the tabletops.

At the back of the room stood a desk with a laptop on it, an open briefcase, and a paper shredder. Beside the desk was a standup safe, its door wide open. A man was removing the contents and stuffing them into the briefcase.

He looked like his picture. Arthur Melody. I called his name.

Again, nothing. I stood in the doorway and watched him. He had no idea I was there.

He reached into the safe and drew out a silver handgun and a white substance wrapped in cellophane, about the size of a deck of cards. He put both items into a black drawstring bag.

At his desk, he slipped a flash drive into his laptop and typed on the keyboard. He stood, folded his arms on his chest, nervously tapped a finger, and watched the progress bar.

When he realized he had company, it wasn't because he heard me. It was more a feeling. I could see that by way he lurched back as if in danger.

Tall and lanky, he wore brown slacks and an ugly brown pullover shirt that hung loose on his shoulders. His arms were liver spotted, his face pallid.

He fingered through the top pocket of his shirt to retrieve a hearing aid and inserted it. As he stared at me, the expression on his face went from fear and surprise to recognition. "You're Whip Stark, the pitcher."

"That's right."

"It wasn't supposed to go this way, Mr. Stark. It was an intriguing research project, that's all." He stopped talking and went back to stuffing more papers into his briefcase.

But he stopped again as a new thought occurred to him. "I was the last person to see her alive. Except for her killers."

"You're talking about Rosa Lopez."

"I just received word of her death. Someone called from the club. Skin." He pointed to the phone on his desk as if that provided proof. "It's just awful, awful."

I asked who'd called him.

"A female, quite young, I'd guess. She was tipping me off. If I heard her correctly, they're on their way here right now, and I'd better clear out." He looked at the copy bar on the computer screen and made a hurry-up motion with his finger.

He turned to me with his hands on his hips. "Rosa came here two nights ago. The television was on and we saw your appeal for Rolando Molina. I begged her to leave. I told her, 'Go talk to Whip Stark.'"

"Why me?"

"Her boyfriend was killed near Double Wide."

"Carlos Alvarez."

"Yes." Melody looked at me helplessly. "I didn't know what else to tell her. She went on and on about his murder. Raving! In my home yet! You were a way to be rid of her, frankly."

He leafed through a folder and tossed it away. It skidded across his desk onto the floor, the papers scattering. He didn't seem to notice. He rubbed his forehead and said, "I'm very sorry about your missing friend. Truly I am."

"Tell me what's going on."

"Isn't it obvious? I'm leaving before the thugs arrive at my door! Or the police! I'd rather not speak to either one, so I'm destroying evidence!" He leaned forward with his palms flat on the desk and hung his head. "Isn't that what criminals do?"

"Something tells me you're not a criminal, professor. Those papers you're shredding—what are they?"

Melody didn't answer. He jerked open a drawer and tossed more files into his briefcase. "I'm a distinguished botanist!" he said, as if answering voices in his head. "If I'd known these men were gangsters, I never would've agreed to this. You must understand!"

He took a few shaky breaths. "I went along because I was a fool. But I saw it as a fascinating challenge. At my age to have something like this come around, well, I suppose it was thrilling. I won't lie, the money was outstanding."

"Professor, I need you to calm down and tell me what you were hired to do."

"Why, make dreams come true, Mr. Stark. But I'll have nothing more to do with this sordid enterprise. I'll destroy all of my research, and we'll see what they do then. Without their holy grail, we'll just see!"

I repeated my question, and he would've kept talking, but the sound of a car door slamming in the street stopped him. We looked at each other with expectant faces, waiting for some follow-up sound to provide more evidence.

Whispering, Melody said, "Don't the police normally announce themselves?"

The silence thickened as we waited. The next sound was the front door creaking open—those hinges again. Melody's face turned white as a wedding dress. He slammed the lid of his briefcase, snapped the locks, grabbed the drawstring bag, and sprinted out the back door, flipping off the lights as he exited.

The room fell into blind darkness. No time to run.

I would've had to cross the room and get out the door, and that meant navigating the desk and a maze of tables. Hard to do when you can't see. I leaned with my back flat against the wall, the doorway to my left.

Two male voices. Footsteps moving through the house.

They came closer, wasting no time.

I reached onto the table and grabbed the first ceramic pot my hand found. It held a six-inch teddy bear cholla. That was good luck. As cacti go, the teddy bear is the perfect close-contact weapon. The spines grow so densely they obscure the main trunk and branches. They're thin, unyielding, and needle sharp, every one of them capable of slicing human flesh.

When a man appeared in the doorway, I thrust the business end of the teddy bear deep into his neck, right below the ear. He let out a tortured scream, then a series of them, each higher than the one before.

I shouldered him into his partner, and with my eyes now adjusted to the darkness, bolted out the back door.

Forty feet of backyard led to an open gate in the wall at the back of the property and a narrow alley. To my left, the wall broke to make room for a garage. At that moment, Melody's car rocketed out of the garage and slammed into a garbage can, sending it airborne and nearly clocking me. His back bumper stopped inches from my knees.

The professor's left arm, visible only as something white against the night darkness, reached out the driver's window and seemed to arc over the roof, after which the professor spun his tires, tossing dirt and gravel everywhere.

His big white car peeled away. His bumper sticker said, *Saguaro You Today?*

My attention turned to the agonized cries inside the house, made by a man trying to pull cactus needles out of his neck.

If you live in the desert long enough, you've walked unwittingly into one of those ornery specimens. Even when it's an accident, the experience can cause a grown man to wail like a child. Done intentionally, it causes thoughts of bloody revenge.

I ran down the alley to the neighbor's wall, bellied over it, and doubled around to the front. Not bothering to open the door, I hopped into my driver's seat and gassed it.

As I roared away, I checked the rearview and saw nothing. It looked like a clean getaway.

TWENTY-NINE

My heart pounded as I drove home that starless night. Thunderstorms plotted above the solid cover of clouds. Their intrigues produced only a far-off cannonade and scattered raindrops on my windshield. I broke multiple traffic laws rumbling through the populated part of the city.

After the freeway, I broke many more as I barreled into the mountains, thinking about Rolando's hand in my freezer, his body missing, and no clear idea why he was murdered.

Easy does it, Stark. Slow down and let the mind work.

Carlos Alvarez delivered the hand to my door. He wanted me to do something about Rolando's murder, but didn't live long enough to see any result. Moments after driving away, someone caught up to him on that mountain trail and shot him twice in the head.

Rosa Lopez heard of her boyfriend's death, and she, too, tried to reach me.

Same story. Counting Rolando, three killings. Not to mention two strip club mutts bracing a scared-as-hell professor with a revolver in his go bag.

Somebody had a lethal interest in keeping people quiet.

Nearing 11:00 p.m., I arrived at Double Wide. The first thing I did was check Opal's trailer. She was still gone and that didn't help my nerves. Bundle came running, doing his usual coming-home dance. I fed him and Chico and checked on Charlie to make sure everything was fine, and I checked on Cashmere Miller with the same purpose and result.

In the Airstream, I got a water bottle out of the refrigerator and went back to my laptop, sitting open on the counter opposite my bed. A quick Google search told me this would take time. Arthur Melody had a ton of hits.

I learned right away that he had a nickname: Mr. Agave.

Tequila is made from the agave plant. They cut away the plant's swordlike leaves to reach its whitish-yellow heart, the internal crown known as the *cabeza*. Those hearts are fermented to make tequila.

Different species of the plant grow all over southern Arizona and Mexico. But tequila only comes from the blue agave found mainly in the Mexican state of Jalisco.

One of the websites pictured a *cabeza*. Its exterior was white and green in a checkerboard pattern exactly matching the balls Machete's men were loading into trucks.

Well, well. Melody played baseball his freshman year at the University of Texas. That was a surprise. He looked less like a ballplayer than Winston Churchill.

After half an hour, I had the basics.

The agave is quite a versatile plant. The Aztecs used it to make *pulque*, a sacred drink in their rituals, and its components are still used in Mexican folk medicines. Its leaves produce a thick sap that can treat toothaches, snakebites, open wounds, inflammation, and even syphilis.

Drug companies around the world have jumped on the agave and Professor Melody was a leader in that research, his work funded by a German company called A. A. Bildenson.

I found a story saying Melody had traveled to the Mexican Sierra Madre to study how shamans of the ancient Huichol tribe used the agave for its narcotic properties, the feelings of calm and contentment it produced in those about to have their hearts ripped out in ritual sacrifice.

Ah, the old days.

I said to myself, "Contentment similar to a heroin rush." I thought of Melody's last remark, "Making dreams come true," and of the white substance he dropped into the drawstring bag.

A theory formed.

The smugglers hired the professor to make a new drug, possibly a heroin substitute, and that was the connection to Paradise Mountain. They needed the agave that grew on the mountain.

If the substance could be produced in a US lab or even a garage, the cartel wouldn't have to grow and harvest poppies, turn it into a salable product, package the product, and smuggle it across the line. Everything would be easier, and the profit margin would stay the same or increase.

Reading about the agave got me thinking about tequila.

Toward the end of my career, I played winter ball in the little Mexican mountain town of Saltillo, a charming, lost place above the chaos and bloodletting of Coahuila, a drug-trafficking hub. The team was the Saltillo Saraperos—the Serape Makers.

After games, I'd go out with Rolando and a few others. Our favorite spot was a five-table cantina called Mort's, run by a four-hundred-pound American ex-pat from Oakland. He listened to the games on the radio and had tequila shots ready when we came in.

Sitting in the Airstream that night, I thought about those happy nights in Saltillo, and to my surprise, the memory gave me a taste for a shot. In the kitchen, I had a tequila bottle that I'd bought in Jalisco. It survived the cut when I moved into the Airstream. I rinsed the dust out of a shot glass and poured.

Bundle barked, a lone "woof" somewhere way out in the desert. I went to the door and whistled, and in a minute Bundle came to the bottom of the steps.

"It's late for excitement, boy," I said. "Go lie down." Bundle trundled off. He spent the night sleeping on the floor in my empty, doorless trailer.

Up on the mountain, I saw headlights shining through the darkness, a vehicle winding its way down from Gates Pass.

The clouds were breaking up, and a few renegade raindrops had gathered on the hood of the Bronco, where they fetched down the starlight and sparkled. What a sadness when a summer storm fails to deliver and you see it churning away, forever gone.

I threw down the tequila and read more about Professor Melody and his agave research. After ten minutes, I was thirsty again, and for the first time in years, I poured a second shot.

Reading about succulents was ruining me. Happens to everybody.

When I passed the kitchen door this time, the headlights had disappeared behind the mountain dark. I thought nothing of it. The car had fallen into a depression between the hills where the road went to hide, and in a moment, it would straighten out and cough up the car again.

Too tired to read anymore and not ready to sleep, I stepped outside and walked down Main Street, past Charlie's trailer. It felt good to be under the sky, feeling the breeze on my face, feeling the slight numbing action of the tequila on the bottom of my feet.

Chico hopped along at my side. But he kept looking up at me and circling as if in warning. The hair along his spine stood up, a backward-running ridge from head to tail.

"What's going on with you, boy?" I said.

The tequila told me there was nothing to worry about. But tequila always says that.

After a few more steps, I heard a single rifle shot. There was no mistaking it. Knowing that sound too well, Chico squealed in fright and hopped away seeking cover.

I froze where I stood. Tension bolted down my arms and legs. I felt like a paper target at the gun range, waiting for the next round. Unlike a paper target, I didn't have to stand there and get plugged full of holes. I turned and ran back toward the Airstream.

THIRTY

Seconds later I heard three more shots, short, sharp cracking sounds without much staying power. Then the rifle exploded a second time and the mountains tossed the sound around in descending echoes.

The varying tone of the shots meant different guns, and different guns meant a gunfight. I saw muzzle flashes and heard Cashmere Miller shouting.

Running past Charlie O'Shea's trailer, I saw a pickup truck launch out of the wash behind my place, four wheels off the ground, headlights dark. The front end came out so high the driver was looking at the sky before the truck fell to the ground.

It bounced loud and hard on big tires, bounced a second time a little softer, and spun violently in the dirt to swap ends.

In the darkness I saw Cash's distinct form, his bony, crooked, question-mark form, running straight toward the truck. The driver hit the gas, and the engine roared, sending the truck spinning down the exit road.

In a calm, fluid motion, Cash fell to one knee, tucked the rifle against his shoulder, lowered his face to the stock, and wiggled for a comfortable fit as he found the sight. He let several seconds pass before squeezing off three rounds at the bumper.

He lowered the rifle and watched the disappearing truck. "Mama's gonna need bodywork."

I asked what happened.

Cash said, "Heard something and came outside. Seen a guy going through your Bronco and not too gentle." He brushed at his clothes and shifted back and forth on his paddle feet.

Charlie O'Shea ran down the street wearing checked boxer shorts and a T-shirt declaring him the world's best granddad. "Somebody want to tell me what's happening? Sounds like a shooting war going on out here!"

"Hostiles," Cash said. "Two, near as I could see."

"Christ a-mighty. You okay, Cashy?" Charlie said.

"The best," Cash said. "One was poking through the Bronco and the other was tearing apart the Mayor's domicile. I hollered and seen them running. Couple shadows." Cash spat in the dirt. "Couple shadows was all I seen."

The Airstream had been trashed, chairs tipped over, drawers pulled out, cabinets emptied. The contents of the refrigerator and freezer had been tossed around the kitchen. I inspected the Bronco. The glove compartment was empty, the contents scattered, and blood dripped from the door handle on the shotgun side.

"Looks like you got one of them," I said.

Cash smiled through picket-fence teeth.

I didn't call the cops. With Rolando's hand in the freezer, I preferred not to have deputies poking around. It didn't take much to figure out what had happened. The men from Melody's house followed me. I checked the rearview all the way home. Either they were really good at running a tail, or I was in over my head.

My money was on the latter.

They were looking for something they thought I'd taken from the professor. It had to be the contents of his safe, his so-called holy grail.

I got busy cleaning up the Airstream, starting with my refrigerator and freezer. As I worked, I heard a loud truck coming up the entrance road, the engine clicking and knocking the way big diesels do.

The sound stopped, and the door slammed shut as someone stepped out. I heard Cash shouting: "Hold still, and identify yourself!"

I threw open my front door and saw Cash holding a rifle against a man's back. "This fellow got inside the wire, Mayor. Easy does it, partner."

The man looked up at me. Even in the dark from my top step, I could tell who it was.

"I came as soon as I heard," said Oscar Molina. "I came to find my boy."

THIRTY-ONE

Oscar had a broad, friendly face, though it burned with worry over Rolando's disappearance. His hair was wild, growing in every direction, and it bore the outline of the frayed slouch hat he held against his stomach. He had a working man's hands, the fingers filthy and thick as railroad spikes. He stood firm on bowed legs, powerful arms bookending his shoulders.

His eyebrows matched his hair. They belonged on the kitchen floor, scurrying into a corner when the light comes on.

We shook hands. He had a mighty grip. After getting my hand back and checking to make sure he hadn't absconded with a finger, I invited him inside.

"Looks like you had trouble," Oscar said.

"It's over now," I said, feeling awkward. I was a man with a secret about to be revealed. "Would you like a cold beer? I haven't seen you since Las Vegas."

"Rolando doubled twice. Threw out three runners."

"You remember."

"Can't forget. Won't ever forget." His lips shook as the words fell out.

The kitchen felt barren and cold but not empty. It held the strong presence of the man who introduced me to Oscar and Natty Molina years before when we were young ballplayers with nothing much on our minds and nothing to lose. In the mystery of his death, Rolando was bringing us together again.

"Sit down, Oscar. Please, please, sit down."

"I don't want to sit down." Then, regretting his ill temper: "Thank you, Whip. I just need to find Rolando."

The time had come to tell the Molina family what I knew. I got Oscar a beer and set it on the table. Men together always turn to beer, for reasons no one understands.

I stuffed the last of the food into the refrigerator and freezer as Oscar paced, two feet one way and two back the other. Somehow, he didn't knock holes in the walls with his shoulders.

He said, "Fausto says Rolando might've come up here to see Wilson at the Tucson Thunder."

"I talked to Wilson. He never saw him."

"Where is he, then? Somebody has to know something."

I didn't answer. Oscar sensed something in my manner, his eyes coming into sharp focus. "You know something, Whip." When I didn't respond right away, he pressed. "Where's my boy, Whip? Tell me now."

"He's gone, Oscar. Rolando's dead."

"Dead," he repeated. But the word didn't come from his mouth. It came from some place a million miles away. "What do you mean? Where's he at?"

I told him that someone cut off his hand, and I found it in a shoe box on my front steps.

Oscar stared, his mouth open slightly in disbelief. "Do you still have it? His...hand?"

We went out to the freezer. I pulled off the tarp and opened the lid, and Oscar stared down at the plastic bag. He picked it up with two hands and pressed his fingers against the plastic to spread it out and see better.

I held my flashlight against the bag. The letters spelling M-A-R-Y stood out clearly on the backs of the fingers. The silence lingered. It was torture.

I blurted, "I had some extra freezer bags in the house."

Good going, Stark. That was just the thing to say when you're showing a man part of his son's body in your freezer. I don't think my foolish words reached him. Oscar was too far gone. He made a sound in his throat.

"I didn't know what else to do," I said. "I didn't want to hand him over to the cops and I didn't want to bury him until I found the body."

"I have to tell his mother." Oscar's breath exited his mouth in short gusts that chopped the words into small, agonized sounds. "His mother will want me to bring him home. All of him."

"I don't know where he is," I said. "But I promise you I'll find him."

Back in the Airstream, I told Oscar about the gold camp on Paradise Mountain, about the heroin smuggling, about Carlos Alvarez leaving the hand on my stoop, and about the violent deaths of Alvarez and Rosa Lopez.

The names meant nothing to him. I asked if Rolando ever said anything about wanting to mine for gold.

"I asked him to work at my mine, but all he cared about was baseball."

"Something brought him here," I said. "Not just to Arizona but to Paradise Mountain. There's no way he was involved in heroin smuggling."

Oscar lowered his head as if in shame. "I wish I could say that, Whip, but Rolando was snorting that cocaine again, and it changed him. He was different from the boy you knew. Out of his mind. He was far gone on that cocaine! That poison!"

For a long time, he stared at nothing, his eyes hollow and desperate. Without word or warning, he swung his hand violently, scooping the glass off the table and shattering it against the wall.

He leaped to his feet, tipping over his chair. "If my boy is on Paradise Mountain, that's where I'm going!"

Oscar got as far as the open door, saw the darkness, and stopped. He turned back, his face a mask of confusion and embarrassment. In his grief, he'd forgotten that night follows day.

"I'll go in the morning," he said. "It'll be light in the morning."

"You were going to call Natty."

"Natty! My poor Natty!" Oscar set his chair upright and pulled out his phone. He cupped his forehead with his free hand and spoke in a low voice. I heard Natty wailing on her end, and when I couldn't listen anymore, I headed for the door.

The last thing I heard before stepping outside was Oscar saying, "Tell the children…Natty, I know…no, no, Natty, listen to me. It's true, he's gone…God will show us all his mercy…Natty, listen to me. I'm telling you, he's gone."

THIRTY-TWO

B y morning, Oscar had changed his mind about looking for Rolando on Paradise Mountain. He'd spoken to Natty again and decided to go home right away. She didn't believe Rolando was dead, saying her heart would've told her if her boy was gone.

Oscar never mentioned the hand. He couldn't break that news by phone and didn't want to bring the grisly evidence back to Obregon without the body. The hand would stay with me until I located the corpse, which I promised again to do.

There's no manual for how to do these things, and that's what Oscar decided.

After he drove off, I called a woman whose name had turned up in my research on Professor Melody. Annie Patterson, his former assistant. I left her a message to call me and walked down to Cash's place to talk to him about going up to Paradise Mountain to look for Rolando's body.

I told him about Rolando's hand and my encounter with Machete. "Could use an extra set of eyes and a long rifle."

"You're in luck, Mayor. I have both."

I went back to the Airstream and strapped on my hiking boots. I keep my Glock in a clip-on belt holster. It holds the weapon snug without a top strap to undo if you need to pull it out and shoot. I put an extra fifteen-round clip in my pocket.

I filled a cooler with ice and water bottles and carried it out to the Bronco. Bundle knew we were going into the desert and began barking and jumping around crazily. His preparation consisted of peeing on my tire. With that done, he was ready to go.

Before leaving, I called Roxy and left a message inviting her out to Double Wide. I told her I had news and wanted to tell her in person.

Just before 5:30 a.m., the morning still half-dark, half-light, we started out. Cash rode shotgun, his AR-15 standing buttstock down against his leg. Bundle was in back.

I drove on the same bouncing trail that Opal and I had followed the night we found Alvarez. It took work to wrestle the steering wheel around rocks and rain gouges, the Bronco heaving this way and that on its shocks. I couldn't push it past fifteen miles per hour without breaking a rib.

My only plan was to see what there was to see and follow whatever clues came of it. Something might lead to Rolando.

Paradise sat atop the mountain as it had for 130 years. Cash and I walked through the middle of town the way gunfighters do in movies, watching for any sign of Machete. Cash wore a red bandana on his head and held the rifle high across his chest. His eyes stayed on the move, sweeping across the long morning shadows, seeing everything.

If Rolando's body had been left there, my nose would tell me. My nose said nothing.

We walked behind the saloon to the main drift, the one Machete's men had been clearing out.

Two turkey vultures watched from their perch atop the roof, their black forms clear against the blue sky. As we neared, they squalled in annoyance, lifted off the roof, and seemed to suspend for a moment, wings spread in an indignant pose, conquering the air, and then together they dipped their wings and flew away.

Sturdy oak beams framed the drift opening. Bundle ran ahead into the cool dark. I had a flashlight and followed the beam. Bundle sparked on something and ran out with his tail whirling to show me what he'd found.

He had the leaf of an agave plant clamped in his jaws. It was four feet long and green, with sharp teeth running along its edges and a razor tip.

The drift might've been eighty feet long. A tangle of beams and rocks blocked passage beyond that. The remainder of the way, we found nothing, no additional items unusual to a mine drift. The smugglers had cleared out everything except that one leaf.

We departed the drift into painful sunlight and hiked to two tailings piles west of town. They were perfectly symmetrical as they should be. Nothing disturbed.

Far to the west, against the white horizon, stood a low hill that offered the best chance to see any distance. Long before noon and already the sun was a sword in the sky. We hiked through scrub oak and cholla cactus to the hill and climbed it, acquiring thorns and burrs in or socks as we went.

Using eight-power binoculars, I scanned the landscape with no idea what I was looking for. Maybe scavengers, maybe a dark something lying out in the sun. There was nothing out there but shimmering ground that looked wrung out and exhausted and, higher on the slopes, juniper trees climbing to razorback ridges and rock bluffs.

I mopped my neck with a hanky and tried to catch my breath. Bundle sat panting at my feet, his tongue hanging sideways out of his mouth.

"Hot enough for you, boy?" I said. Bundle looked at me like he might attack. Asking that question in Arizona in July should be a felony. I poured cold canteen water into my palm and let him lap it up.

Roxy called. George Jones singing to me in the mountains. Cash sang along to the first few bars, never taking his eyes off the landscape.

Roxy said she was willing to come out to Double Wide tonight, but only if I told her everything. I agreed. Cash and I followed Bundle's lead and hiked back to the silent town of Paradise. Whatever secrets it held, it held them close.

THIRTY-THREE

By late that afternoon, a storm was brewing, and Charlie wanted to right his trailer before it hit. Cash had worked to fix the release lever on the jack and thought it was ready for another go. But the lock gave way entirely and smashed the second cinderblock, leaving Charlie's trailer at an even more severe tilt, only one block holding the whole thing up.

"We have to do something, Mayor," Charlie said. "I can't live at an angle!" When he got worked up, his voice rose higher and higher until it came out of a squeeze toy.

"Why don't you go ahead and take the open trailer."

"It doesn't have a door, and there's a big ol' hole in the kitchen floor. Ain't that where Bundle sleeps, for gosh sakc?"

He kept grousing, and I knew he wouldn't stop. I told him he could sleep on my kitchen foldout until we got his trailer set up, and in return, he had to keep an eye on the place for me.

"Okay, you got yourself a deal," he said.

"Just a couple of nights until we fix this," I said.

Charlie's face got serious. "I won't be a pest. You know me. Soon as Cashy fixes the jack, why, I'll be outta your hair."

We were still talking about it when Roxy drove over the mountain. I introduced her to Charlie and Cash, and she nodded at them with an expression cold enough to keep meat. They gave her shark eyes in return and said nothing, which was the safest move.

She wore black jeans with zipper pockets, a pink T-shirt, and white sneakers with pink laces. Her hair was pulled back in a ponytail, and she wore oversized sunglasses. She glanced around Double Wide and said, "Well, well, Fallujah in the Sonoran Desert."

"It's not that bad," I said.

"Oh, Phenom, it's worse."

The storm winds had begun to blow. She studied the dust devils whirling across the saguaro flats. "Let's go inside. I don't like the wind fooling with my hair."

Without invitation, she walked into the Airstream. She stopped inside the door to adjust to the small space, and walked past the kitchen into the bedroom and office area, pausing to inspect everything before her. She paid special attention to the books on the shelf above my bed.

"All crime titles," she said. "I'm sure that makes your father happy." It surprised me how astute that comment was.

In the kitchen, she ran a palm along the countertop and checked it for dust, turned on the water in the sink and quickly shut it off, and opened and closed cabinet doors. She was like a realtor doing an inspection.

After all that, she sat at the table, exhaled, and said, "All right, take me through what we've got."

I told her about solving the Melody riddle, the trouble at the professor's house, and the shootout with the two bruisers who'd tailed me from Melody's to retrieve what they believed I'd taken from the house.

When I told her my theory that Dr. Melody had been hired by the smugglers to produce a drug made from the agave plant, she showed no disbelief or surprise. "With these cartels, if you can think of it, it won't happen."

She pulled off her sunglasses and dropped them on the table. "Okay, apart from working with Mayflower to get Fausto a contract, where does Rolando fit in? And don't hold anything back."

I shifted around in my chair. Talking about Rolando's hand wasn't easy. I grabbed Roxy's sunglasses and saw the name etched along the temple. Tom Ford. I shoved them back across the table to her.

"That's our world now, isn't it?"

"Something wrong?" she said.

"Some private-jet clown puts out cheesy sunglasses and scribbles his name on the temple like it means something, and people rush out to buy them."

"They go for three hundred dollars a pair."

"How many batters did Tom Ford strike out?"

"He owns the team, genius."

"Another reason not to like him."

The storm had arrived. The rain drummed on the roof.

Roxy said, "I get a kick out of it when millionaires fuss at one another."

"Everybody thinks I'm rich."

"I read about your contracts."

"They don't write about how fast you spend it," I said. "Right now I'm looking for a deal on a new roof for my Bronco, if you know anybody good."

"You're a working-class guy fighting to stay afloat, is that it? Like your tenants?"

I pointed outside. "This country's filling up with people like them and nobody notices."

"Everybody's busy. I see what's out there."

"No, you don't and neither did I, until I hit bottom. And there they were, all over the place."

"Maybe they should try working. A wild idea, right?"

"The jobs that pay are all gone," I said. "If you walk around with a bunch of keys on your belt, this country's got no use for you anymore."

"I feel like I'm at a boring meeting in somebody's basement," Roxy said and sighed to the bottom of her feet. "Do you have news for me or not?"

I came right out with it, told her about Rolando's severed hand and my encounter with Machete on Paradise Mountain.

She was shocked. "You met Rolando's killer?"

"That's my guess."

"The stakes are definitely rising. You're lucky to be alive, Prospero."

"Yeah."

"Who is this cat? What do you know about him?"

"Nothing. He's fat, wears a sidearm, and carries a machete."

Her eyes were bright. She gave me a level look. "It's time for a story. A maniac in the mountains is good, but it's only half a story. I need a visual for the other half and a hand in a freezer is a visual times ten. I could take this national."

"We wait. You and Cashmere Miller are the only ones who know about it."

"A story can protect you. It might get more law enforcement out here."

"You need to listen to me, Roxy. I'm telling you we wait."

She stood up, cracking her knuckles, moving up one hand and down the other. "I need to look in that freezer."

I gave her my red hoodie to wear against the rain, and told her to go out to the freezer herself. At that moment I didn't like her much, didn't like her attitude or her expensive sunglasses. She pulled the hood over her head, tugged the drawstrings tight, and went.

I didn't want to be standing at the freezer when she looked down at Rolando's hand and had no reaction at all, or said something that masked what was hidden inside. Or worse, said something that confirmed there was nothing inside to hide.

Roxanne Santa Cruz was like the women in my books, the way they all are, the way they have to be. Beautiful for sure. Eyeshadow too heavy, lipstick too red. That worked. She had luxurious hair and the striding, all-in walk that gave men water legs. That worked, too.

And she had the right job, working people for information, manipulating them to get the best stories. All that was supposed to be a blind. Underneath, she was supposed to believe in people and that basic goodness should reveal itself in moments like this.

Somebody once said I have a heart-of-gold problem, and maybe so. But I wanted her to come back feeling the awful weight of Rolando's death, the darkness of it. Put a hand on my shoulder and tell me how sorry she was, maybe fight back a tear.

Instead, she looked as if she'd seen nothing more upsetting than roadkill. At least she wasn't whistling. I'll give her that much.

She flipped the hood back off her head and wiped rainwater from her face with her sleeve. She wiggled her shoulders out of the jacket and shook it like a bullfighter's cape. "Wooo! It's a wet one out there!"

On light feet, she bounced to the refrigerator, bent down, grabbed a candy, bar and inspected the label. "I can't believe you buy candy bars with nuts in them," she said.

"You like your chocolate straight, huh?" My mind was in a hundred places and that's just what came out.

"The nuts just get in the way," she said, using her fingernails to pick the nuts out of the chocolate.

THIRTY-FOUR

The next two mornings, Cash and I drove up the mountain to search for Rolando's remains. As much as possible, we stayed on open ground, keeping a long view of the surrounding terrain and bypassing canyons and rock formations where Machete's men could hide.

On returning to the Airstream, I sat at my kitchen table and spread out my map and marked in red the routes we'd taken, to avoid doubling up the next day. I marked in green the routes I still needed to check.

Oscar called. He said Fausto had taken Rolando's death hard, Natty was still a mess, and he wasn't able to leave either of them to return to Double Wide. He asked me to call Fausto and try to calm him down.

After a pause, Oscar said, "Any luck finding my boy?" His voice was weak and unsure.

"I'm looking every day."

"Be sure to keep an eye on him. I mean...out back."

"You know I will."

I called Fausto, got his message, and asked him to call me. Later on the second day, Detective Diaz drove up my entrance road. I stood with my shoulder against the doorjamb and offered a pleasant greeting. If I didn't have Charlie, I would've invited him in.

Diaz might've been the only man in Tucson outside of the downtown courthouses to wear Oxford shoes. Two-toned with brogue detailing. He had on a red pullover shirt two sizes too small, highlighting his nautilus arms.

Someone had ironed his pleated chinos. My guess was him. While listening to a self-improvement tape in a spotless white T-shirt.

"Carlos Alvarez," he said, without any throat clearing. "He's been arrested twice for assault and twice for drug possession with intent to sell. One of the assaults was with a dangerous weapon."

"Roxanne Santa Cruz said he had a sheet."

"Were you aware that Alvarez and Rolando Molina were friends?"

I had no idea and said so.

Diaz said, "On a hunch, I checked the Monterrey Sultans roster from two years ago. Turns out they played for the club at the same time."

"Plenty of guys play on the same team for years and can't stand each other."

"You're saying they weren't friends?"

"I'm saying I had no idea. Rolando never mentioned Alvarez to me."

Diaz stood with one shoe resting on my bottom step, arms across his thighs. All I could think about was Rolando's hand. Did he suspect I was up to something? Was he going to ask if he could have a look around?

A morning breeze blew, not charging but steady. It whistled like the mailman through the junked cars stacked up behind Opal's trailer.

We listened to it together, until Diaz said, "My vic is found on a drug trail, he and Rolando Molina were friends and both had a drug history. Then Rolando turns up missing. When your job is making connections, I'd say we hit the jackpot here."

I nodded in agreement, because that's what you do when you're withholding evidence in the form of a human hand twenty feet away in your freezer. Diaz let the silence run on, staring right into my eyes.

"I hope you find Rolando, Detective. I really miss him."

I spent the afternoon watching TV with Charlie and fighting off thoughts of Rolando, and the grinding sadness of his murder. I wondered about Opal. Still gone. She goes to town for some sidewalk sketching and poof, four days missing.

In the kitchen I made tuna sandwiches with cut-up celery, lemon pepper, and minced onion flakes. Charlie and I ate our sandwiches under the TV and drank Tecate from wet cans while watching old movies and listening to the incessant *hoo-hoo, hoo-hoo-hooooo* of the mourning doves.

They make that call every ten seconds or so in the summer, hour after hour throughout the day. You hear it, wait for the next *hoo-hoo*, the one after that, and on it goes until you're paralyzed by it.

At 4:00 p.m., Opal called. She was fine. She'd been at the Arizona Inn, the guest of a New York couple she'd met downtown. Hearing that, I launched and hollered at her for disappearing.

"I don't believe this. You're safe in town? Why the hell didn't you call?"

"I don't have a phone."

"What do you mean? You just called me. Borrow one."

"The people here are crazy rich, Mr. Whip. Not like you. Range Rover rich."

"I was afraid something happened to you."

Her voice fell. She sounded like she was cupping a hand over the receiver. "The Gelmans paid me a bunch of money. I'm not kidding."

"What's going on? Where are you?"

"The lobby." Whispering now: "The people look at me funny."

I kept hollering until Charlie gave me a stare that said, "Do you mind? I can't hear the TV." Opal whispered some more before asking if I'd come pick her up, and I jumped into the Bronco and went.

THIRTY-FIVE

The Arizona Inn is old Arizona, an elegant, casita-style hotel set in the middle of a residential neighborhood near the university. It has lush flowerbeds, a beautiful swimming pool, and manicured grass over multiple acres and buildings. The color motif is sandstone pink, and it applies to the aging clientele as well.

You see them tapping arthritic toes in the piano lounge. The women wear lots of turquoise and full moons of cheek rouge. The men are hairless cadavers with too-long fingernails and exploding bourbon faces.

Opal was standing on the sidewalk outside the main building when I drove up. She held her easel and sketch gear under her arm.

"Mr. and Mrs. Gelman are super rich," she said, tossing her gear into the backseat. She climbed in front and jitterbugged around. "They wanted me to do sketches and paintings and liked them so much they took me all around to paint landscapes and stuff. They picked me up at the community center."

"I don't care where they picked you up."

She was hard to reach in her excitement. "Are you still mad at me?"

The driver behind me leaned on his horn. I waved and pulled out and went north on Campbell Avenue up to Speedway. The gunplay at Double Wide had me on edge. I kept checking the rear and side mirrors and drivers on both sides of me.

I noticed a price tag clipped to Opal's pant leg. The pants were red with a yellow dot pattern, loose fitting and down to her shins.

"Ooops, forgot." She yanked it off. "The Gelmans thought I could use some new clothes and took me to Target."

She pronounced it "Tar-jey."

"I'm styling now. They said I could get whatever I wanted. I found this cool blouse too." From her pocket she pulled a wad of bills that practically overflowed her palm. "Look at this, just for painting lightning!"

She bit her lip, stretched out her Jell-O arms, and chair danced.

"Look, you want to disappear, go ahead and disappear," I said. "I don't know why I should care. Can you tell me why I should care?"

Opal made a pouty face and tilted her head toward me. "Because you wuv me?"

"Don't push it."

"You're a good white man, Mr. Whip."

"I'll print that on T-shirts. Whip Stark, a helluva white man."

As we neared the Silverbell intersection, the last one before climbing the mountain, Opal said, "Let's stop at Albertson's. I want to spend my money."

"How about saving some? You owe me two months' rent, remember."

"I'm gonna buy a case of Pepsi and all the imitation crab I can carry."

We shopped. I pushed the damn cart. I kept thinking I could be watching TV. I could be at the dentist. Hadn't been bowling in a while.

Opal walked down the aisles, stopping to give every item close inspection. The smallest ones went into her pocket instead of the cart. Each time I made her take it out of her pocket and put it in the cart. In her pocket, she had a small screwdriver she'd snatched from Target. I dropped that off in frozen foods.

I said, "What's wrong with you? You know the cops got warrants out for you."

She paid no attention. The sketch money had her skipping down the aisles like a kid on Halloween.

That night at my place, I made imitation crab cakes with brown rice and salad. Dessert was orange sherbet with plastic spoons. Opal gripped the spoon in her fist and stabbed at the sherbet like she was trying to kill it. She broke three spoons.

After eating, she peeled some bills off her stash and paid her rent. I almost fell over.

On the way back to her trailer, she said, "I was too scared to ask the Gelmans to use their phone. That's how come I didn't call you."

Charlie got himself set up to sleep on my foldout. He flipped on the overhead TV and worked hard to position his gin bottle on the floor just so, allowing him to reach for it without leaning over too much and refill his paper cup.

I went back to my bed and tried to sleep. Every time I got close, I heard Charlie's exploding laugh, which started with three quick door slams, became a partially clogged drain, and finished up with the whine of a bad radiator.

He fell asleep with the TV on. I went out and turned it off, thought about pressing a pillow over his face, and went back to reading my book instead.

Next morning, Cash and I prowled Paradise Mountain again. If sweat were a clue, we had a bucketful. But nothing else. I was beginning to think Rolando wasn't on that mountain.

At the Airstream, I updated my maps and left another message for Annie Patterson.

Roxy called after supper. "Hey, Phenom, do you know where the Humane Society is?"

"Sure, out near the end of the Country Club Road."

"When can you get here? I have a lead on the good Dr. Melody."

THIRTY-SIX

The Humane Society sits in the middle of a residential neighborhood that might've been the place to be in the 1950s. Now it just looked run down and neglected. No sidewalks because the city forgot to build them, and no lawns because the water bills would crush the mailboxes.

I got there at 7:00 p.m. Roxy pulled up behind me a minute later. She had a photograph showing Professor Melody and a blond woman with massive hair canoodling at a cocktail table.

She looked topless, although it was hard to tell. The photograph couldn't contain her breasts. They started under her chin and plunged down through the remainder of the shot in an impressive topple of flesh.

Melody and the woman had their cheeks pressed together. He was smiling like he'd won the lottery. She was smiling like the boss had gotten off a groaner at the morning meeting.

Roxy said, "I swiped this off a bulletin board at Skin. She performs there from time to time, the biggest draw they have."

"Melody's girlfriend?" I said.

Roxy pointed. "See that house down the street? All lit up? That's hers."

The house was painted purple and yellow and had a two-pillar front porch with bright red lights on both sides of the door. There was a red Cadillac in the carport, maybe ten years old.

But what caught my eye was the large flag flying over the roof. It had a pink rabbit on it.

Roxy saw me looking at it. "That's her logo. Her name is Bunny Slippers."

"You're kidding, right?" I said.

"She markets herself under the Bunny brand. She's a legend in the trade. A girl at Skin tells me Dr. Melody moved in with her three days ago."

"He flees his house and runs into the arms of his stripper girlfriend, Bunny Slippers."

"It never gets too weird," Roxy said, as we approached the house. Lights shaped like pink rabbits lined the brick walkway. I thought I should hop.

Roxy said, "All these dancers dream about being actresses. They love the camera. Let me do the talking."

In response to our knock, the front door opened a tiny crack, and cigarette smoke rushed out. In the space, I saw one big, tired blue eye and crow's feet that had walked a long, long way.

"Hello, Miss Slippers," Roxy said. "Would it be possible to get a few minutes of your time to talk?"

"Well, I don't know. Can you tell me what this is about?"

"Arthur Melody. We're researching Professor Melody's groundbreaking work."

She hesitated. "Well, Arthur *is* very famous."

The door stayed in the same position, not an inch wider. Bunny's eye studied us. "Can you tell me who you are?"

"I'm terribly sorry. I'm Roxanne Santa Cruz, *Channel 7 News*. This is my intern, Mr. Stark. It's his first day."

"Howdy," I said, and finger waved.

The door opened a little wider. That put two eyes before us, along with greasepaint eyebrows, puffy cheeks, and deep slashes around her mouth. Her lips had been done and the work left them preposterously thick.

But the hair was the thing. It went straight up, consuming a dangerous amount of airspace. The color wasn't natural, more bedsheet white than actual blond. Standing atop her head in a stiff, excited, frizzed-out pile, it looked like a wildland creature that died scared.

Bunny stayed stingy with the door until Roxy held out her ID on a lanyard, the station logo prominently displayed. The door opened a bit wider.

Roxy said, "We were hoping you'd go on camera to talk about him. We'd need to hear from people who know Arthur well."

A hurricane wind practically tore the door off its hinges, and Bunny thrust a hand out for Roxy to shake. Her eyes searched past our shoulders. "I don't see a cameraman."

"This would be a preliminary interview," Roxy said. "We'd give you time to prepare for the real thing, of course."

"I always freshen up before seeing my public," she said.

"Absolutely," Roxy said.

The living room was cramped, with a couch taking up most of the wall under the front windows. A coffee table stood in front of it and a big-screen TV in front of that. A foldout table bumped against the far wall. On top of it were five Styrofoam heads with different colored wigs on them, a makeup mirror, and various small bottles, lipsticks, creams, and lotions.

Bunny motioned for us to sit on the couch before realizing the seats were filled with assorted clothes and work papers. The papers were piled atop a tan briefcase that looked like the same one I'd seen at Melody's house.

"Glory be, don't look at the mess. I've had Arthur three days." She moved the papers and the briefcase onto the floor to make room. "I'm telling you, that man."

"We've been trying to reach him," Roxy said. "Do you know where he went?"

"Yes, I do. Walgreens."

"Walgreens?"

"He went to Walgreen's yesterday and didn't come back. There's a bad situation at his work." Bunny showed us her palms as if to remove herself from the matter. "He doesn't want me to know about it, no matter how many times I ask. All I know is that some men are very eager to talk to Arthur, only he don't want anything to do with them."

Roxy put on her innocent voice. "Do you know what it's about?"

"Arthur thought it was smart I didn't hear about it, and Arthur knows best," she said. "The poor man, he was so nervous. I told him, 'Arthur, you have to relax, hon. You don't have to talk to nobody you don't want to.'"

Bunny had on white pants that stopped just below the knees, drawstrings dangling lower from there. The pants were so tight they showed her shape in unobstructed outline. She wore a half top that stopped midway down her stomach. For breathing room, she'd left the top button of her pants undone, and her gaping bellybutton filled the V. It looked like an infant yawning.

The bra beneath the loose pullover worked hard to contain her breasts. They heaved this way and that as she scavenged for cigarettes.

"Out of sorts about what?" Roxy asked.

"Rosa Lopez, for one thing," Bunny said. "She was a living doll, that one. Arthur was crazy about her, too." She stopped and pointed at me. "Do I know you from somewhere?"

"Heavens, no," I said. "I'm an intern."

She stared a moment longer before resuming her hunt for cigarettes. She bent over to pick up a pillow, and the sound was long and tight, like a geezer having a good laugh. Her pants had split in the rear, right down the middle seam. The sight confirmed why there were no visible panty lines beneath those white pants.

Bunny spun around and sharp-eyed me as if I were responsible for what I'd seen. She had that exactly wrong. I was responsible for forgetting what I'd seen. Roxy jumped in with a cover remark, and Bunny's attitude went away. She must've remembered what she did for a living.

Roxy kept smiling with everything she had. "Can you tell us what Arthur was working on?"

"Something doggone important. Arthur's a genius." She put a finger to her lips to help with her search. "I had those cigarettes five minutes ago."

She disappeared into the kitchen and came back with a fresh pack of Camels. She peeled off the wrapper and knocked the pack against the heel of her hand to bring one out. She stuck it between her expensive lips. With the same hand, she produced a lighter and a flame, and stood before us drawing hard on the cigarette, grimacing, pulling her lips back against her teeth as she inhaled, her face tilted toward the ceiling.

Roxy said, "Did he ever mention the agave plant?"

Bunny gave an obvious shrug. "Everything with him was the agave. He got up in the morning thinking about the agave." She puffed and blew and looked at us sideways. "But he went to bed at night thinking about me."

"Dear me," Roxy said, and pretended embarrassment.

Bunny waved blue smoke from her face. "But like I say, I stay out of his work."

"What about heroin?" Roxy said.

"Arthur?" Bunny thought that was funny. The cigarettes had given her a lawnmower laugh, residual smoke shooting out her nostrils. "His idea of a wild time is having Dr Pepper with his Subway footlong. He's a darling man, but heroin?"

She folded her arm under her elbow and held the cigarette up near her ear, letting the tips of her thumb and pinky finger play with one another. Beside the couch sat two Nordstrom bags bulging with new clothes. The TV was a huge cinema-screen job. The shipping box was beside it, along with some plastic packing material.

Roxy said, "If we could find him, we could fast-track this segment. Do you think he went back to his house?"

"He's scared to go back," she said. "The other thing, he don't look the same." She grabbed the hair dye bottle off the table and held it out. "I dyed his hair black, what there is of it anyhow, and taught him how to put on makeup. A little concealer can work wonders, hon."

"I am aware," Roxy said.

"That's why he left this morning," Bunny said. "He was going to Walgreen's to buy a new pair of glasses. Those magnifying glasses, for his disguise."

"Disguise?"

"He's not wearing the wire rims anymore," she said. "I helped him put on makeup, too, and told him to buy black glasses that matched his new hair. Don't you think they should match his new hair?"

"It'll sell the whole darn outfit," said the cheery intern.

Bunny put the hair dye back on the table and stared at it with a wistful look. "He walked out of here looking like William Holden. Whatever it is, I'm sure this trouble will work itself out." Her thick shoulders went up and down in a shrug. "He don't have a lot of friends. My Arthur was all work."

"If he comes back, you need to call us right away," Roxy said.

"What about my interview?" Bunny said. "I'd like to time it to my upcoming shows. Do you think we can do that?"

"For sure," Roxy said, and gave Bunny her card.

Bunny went to the kitchen and came back with a card of her own. On it was picture of a pink rabbit and the words "Everybody Loves Bunny Slippers—the Comfiest Fit in Town."

THIRTY-SEVEN

We walked down the street to the cars. Darkness had fallen. I felt out of sorts. July nights in Tucson will do that. The streets are empty and everything feels dead.

Anybody with sense is in San Diego with their toes in the ocean, trying to stay cool, and the people left behind are in no mood. They're stuck making sandwiches because the boss won't let them go.

I leaned against the Bronco. Roxy stood in the street opposite me.

I said, "She knows where he is and exactly what the trouble is. She's lying her ass off."

"She's protecting her man. I admire that."

"Her man or her meal ticket?"

"Same thing."

"She acted like Melody's in charge, and she does what 'my Arthur' wants. Did you see that two-thousand-dollar big screen and those bags filled with clothes? She's big time into his bank account."

"Don't get righteous. She's a stripper, and strippers are users."

"If you asked him, he'd say he loves her. The other way around? No way."

Roxy rocked her head with a maybe, maybe-not expression. "Love is a high bar. Melody's having the time of his life. Whether it's real or not isn't important, whether it lasts or not isn't important."

Roxy stood with her hands in her back pockets. She looked down one end of the street, and then the other. Her expression became thoughtful.

"I've seen it before," she said. "An older man with money who never had a family or luck with women starts going to a club and, for the first time in his life, gets female attention. Now he's feeling things he's never felt before. His whole world is new."

She took another random look around. "Confidence is quite a thing. So what if he's paying for it. Let him have it."

"They both get what they want—is that the idea?"

"There's no 'forever' in strip clubs. All those dancers have is tonight."

"You seem to know a lot about this."

Roxy grinned like she had a secret.

I caught on. "Don't tell me. You?"

"I climbed the pole way back when."

"You stripped?"

She held up an indignant hand. "Don't be a beast. I danced."

"I'm impressed. The change you made getting into TV must've been huge."

"Not really. Stripping and TV have a lot in common. I still manipulate people to get a rise out of them." Roxy rocked her head. "Only in TV the lighting is better."

I asked if she had a stage name, and she said yes, the coolest stage name ever. She invited me to guess what it was, but I didn't get the chance.

From down the street came the sound of a truck's engine rumbling to a stop. I saw a black pickup pull in front of Bunny's and thought little of it. But Roxy kept looking toward the truck. The more she stared, the more tense her manner became.

The truck door slammed shut as someone got out. That made me look again, but I didn't get far. Roxy stepped forward, setting her feet outside mine and leaning full against me with her palms flat against the Bronco.

She covered my body with hers and pressed her lips to mine. She held that position and said, "Keep kissing me."

"Do I have a choice?" With my mouth otherwise occupied, my voice sounded like it came through a pillow.

"Don't stop," she said.

I hadn't had a fresh idea all day, couldn't get my mind to dredge one up. I had plenty of ideas now. The kiss went on, until, without taking her lips from mine, Roxy turned her head slightly and looked over her outstretched arm down the street again.

She said, "I'll bet that's the guy."

"What guy?"

The question hung there as Roxy bought her eyes to mine and stared, holding the pose for a full half minute. She kissed me on the lips again, this one a slow, tender kiss, not a mash job. She pulled away reluctantly and stared some more with a look of pure surprise. "I didn't mean to be so forward," she said.

"Not you. You've never been forward in your life."

"But I'm all right with it. And you—you're alive after all. I can feel it, Prospero Stark." She looked down the street again, seemed reassured, and lowered her arms. "I don't think he recognized you."

"Do you mind telling me who we're talking about?"

"You described Mayflower's sidekick. Little fire hydrant guy with a crewcut."

"Ed Bolt."

"I think he just went into Bunny's house."

When my head stopped spinning from the blood rush, the first sensible notion I had said that Mayflower and Bolt were trying to find Melody too, and that meant Bolt was likely one of the men at Melody's house the night I was there.

And these same two, when they couldn't find whatever they were looking for, drove out to Double Wide and trashed the Airstream and the Bronco.

Roxy and I walked down the street through the glow of one streetlamp and into the darkness beyond it to Bolt's truck, a black Chevy Silverado. In the tailgate were three holes, dead center and in tight grouping, bull's-eyes on a truck fleeing in the dark.

Cashmere Miller, protector of Double Wide, dangerous man, dead shot.

"I don't think the guy saw us," I said. "Let's pull behind the Silverado and wait for him to come out."

"All right, a tail job. I had a feeling this was going to be a fun night."

Roxy positioned the Audi well behind the black Silverado and we sat watching Bunny's front door. The silence dragged on, full of thought and calculation, each of us measuring the new information and coming to our own conclusions.

Roxy was the first to speak. "I have a suggestion. How about we drive up to Sullivan's, get a steak and a nice dessert, and forget about this business. To spice things up, I might even tell you my stage name."

"Not a chance."

She looked away, and said quickly, "It's obvious Max Mayflower's on the same trail we are. He's trying to find Dr. Melody and the contents of his safe, which he and Ed Bolt presume you possess, correct?"

"It's a misconception."

"A lot of people get hurt because of misconceptions." She tapped her fingers anxiously on the dash. "All I'm saying is this thing is looking bigger than you know. And more dangerous. I don't think you've accepted the idea that your friend was smack in the middle of it."

"We don't know that yet."

"Okay, say it's legit that Rolando Molina was helping Fausto get to the big leagues," she said. "What's he doing mixed up with guys like Carlos Alvarez and Max Mayflower? Unless he was part of the smuggling operation on that mountain."

"Mayflower's on his way to becoming one of baseball's top agents," I said. "Does it make sense he'd jeopardize that by smuggling heroin? He's too smart for that."

"Smart jumps out the window when the money's right. Thinking of your theory, if they can manufacture some drug without the trouble of moving it across the border, why not? And your pal—let's face it. You can't trust an addict."

She was making sense, and it ticked me off.

"Listen, Phenom. You stuck with Rolando through his cocaine trouble. You paid for his rehab, and now he's back jamming up his life again, and you're back sticking up for him. Sometimes you reach a point with people where you cut your losses and walk away."

"Rolando was my friend."

"I knew you'd say that. You never do anything easy, do you?"

"Not if there's another way."

Roxy let out a breathy sigh. "Don't get me wrong, I'm all for fucked up. That's my life story. And this thing is majorly fucked up. I mean, Machete nearly chopped your head off. These are seriously bad people and the chances of it turning out good for either of us are miniscule, especially you. At least I get a story out of it. You get worked over again by your best friend and maybe shot at by Ed Bolt."

"Stop talking, will you. We're doing this."

"Goddamn, I think I'm falling for you."

THIRTY-EIGHT

We sat in Roxanne Santa Cruz's Audi and waited. The night inched along, a slow plodding in the warm darkness. From inside the Humane Society, we heard desperate dogs howling in their pens. They couldn't afford San Diego either.

Half an hour later, a man walked out of Bunny's house. I squinted through the windshield. "It's Ed Bolt, all right."

Moments later, we were two cars behind the Silverado and following it up Campbell Avenue into the Catalina foothills. The road bends back and forth through a luxury neighborhood with plenty of saguaros, ironwood trees, and mesquites sheltering big homes set back along poorly lit side roads.

About three-quarters of the way to the top, Bolt turned west onto a gravel path. Roxy let him go and drove on past. We couldn't follow him onto a ten-miles-per-hour road and not be spotted. She continued to the next street and waited, taking a guess at how much time Bolt would need to park and enter whatever house he was looking for.

We doubled back, turned onto the gravel, and followed it for a dark, twisting mile back into the desert, checking driveways on both sides. We couldn't find the Silverado. The driveways all made long circles back to mysterious homes. The Silverado could've been on the far side of one of those driveways, invisible in the darkness.

On our second trip along the road, I spotted something on my side that Roxy had missed the first time through. It was a mailbox in the shape of a baseball cap.

I said, "Here, here. Stop here."

Roxy pulled up short of it. Without prompting, she saw what I was talking about and laughed. "I'd say we found Max Mayflower's house," she said. "What, is he ten years old?"

"I don't see Bolt's Silverado."

"What's that car beside the house, the white convertible?"

"Chrysler LeBaron. My agent owned one. Nice ride."

She stared. "Looks like there's a road looping around behind the house."

"Got it. Okay. Through that gate."

"Bolt probably lives in a guest house back there."

She killed the headlights and we sat looking at the house, as much of it as we could see behind two sheltering Aleppo pines. It was single story, not new, probably built in the 1970s. It was made of sturdy brick—red brick, not adobe.

From one side to the other, it rambled a long way over what had to be fifteen rooms, probably five baths, a nice fireplace, and a newly remodeled kitchen with black-granite countertops.

Anchoring the west end of the property was a three-car garage separate from the house. On the east, there were two tennis courts set on ground much lower than the house itself. A bright light glowed in an arched picture window left of the front door.

Roxy said, "That's good living right there. What's the plan?"

"We knock on the door and see what happens."

"You think Mayflower will talk?"

"He didn't when I hit him up outside the ballpark."

"A bold and pointless exercise, I like it. I'll need makeup." Roxy bent the mirror and leaned into it for a full facial inspection.

"You do the talking this time," I said. "I have an idea how to make the approach."

She looked across at me, her expression hard. "Don't tell me how to ask questions. I've been doing this a long time."

She groped in the backseat for her purse, set it down in her lap, zipped it open, thrust her hand inside, and fished around to retrieve something. It sounded like varmints in a cereal box. The hand came out with lipstick that she applied in slow swipes at pushed-out lips. After each pass, she checked the mirror to assess the success of the effort and, finally satisfied, dropped the lipstick back into the purse.

I thought she was done, but no.

Next, she groped for her hairbrush, and for a full minute fought to yank the brush down through the tangles in her hair, prompting an impressive cussing spree with damnation of monsoon humidity and uncooperative hair in general.

Done with that, she returned the brush to her purse and did a final mirror check that included running the tip of her little finger over her roller coaster lips.

A second time I thought she was ready to go. Not yet.

She loosed the purse varmints again to retrieve a package of wipes. She grabbed one from the pack with her fingertips, gave her hands the once-over, and returned the package to her purse. No one has ever conducted an interview without disinfecting their hands.

She zipped the purse shut, returned it to the backseat, opened the driver's door, put a foot out, looked back at me with supreme annoyance, and said, "Are you ready or what?"

Walking toward the house, I said, "Hang on. I want to see who owns this LeBaron."

"Is that really important right now?"

"I don't like loose ends." The car was unlocked. I found the registration slip in the glove. "Lily Lee Summers. Age twenty-eight. Lives right up the hill here."

I read the address to Roxy, she scribbled it in her notebook, and we proceeded to Mayflower's front door.

I said, "Okay, how're we going to do this?"

She threw me another hot look. "You mean how am I going to do it?"

"I'm not a traffic cone. I'm in this, too."

"If it's all right with you, I'm going to jump right in, okay? Tell Mayflower I'm doing a story, and I suspect Rolando's disappearance is connected to the murders of Rosa Lopez and Carlos Alvarez. See what shakes loose."

"Are you sure that's the way to go?"

"What the hell, are you getting cold feet?"

"We're talking about a guy who might be involved in heroin smuggling."

She stopped. Her face was flushed. "I know exactly what we're talking about. Don't tell me what to do. I've interviewed bigger jackoffs than Mayflower and come out of it just fine."

She'd gone nuclear in a blink. I began to think the idea of confronting Mayflower wasn't so smart after all. But trying to get Roxy to back away at that point seemed frankly dangerous.

Sweeping my hands forward, I said, "I'm the intern here."

With a last iron look, she walked to the front doors, and I followed.

THIRTY-NINE

The elaborately carved black double doors were set into a deep alcove lit by an orange bulb. The doorbell played a recording of Lou Gehrig at his final game as a New York Yankee in 1939: "Today I consider myself the luckiest man on the face of the earth."

Hearing that, Roxy flattened her palm to her chest and gasped. "That is such incredibly bad taste."

Just as she spoke, the door opened, and Mayflower was there. He wore a chestnut bathrobe with black velour striping along the edges and a black velour sash dangling at the waist. The robe looked expensive, probably lambskin.

Six inches of hairy legs showed at the bottom, a horrible sight.

He saw Roxy first, and his eyes stayed put. His expression started out hostile at the interruption and changed into a high-eyebrow ogle.

He said, "Talking to yourself?"

Roxy tilted her head in that way that causes men to lose their mud. "Your chime is so darn original."

"I grew up in Brooklyn. Sometimes I think I was at that game."

"You weren't."

"Is that so? Are you sure?"

"Don't be a fool."

"I'm trying very hard."

"You can try harder, Mr. Mayflower."

His eyes roamed over her with oily intensity. After a while, he smiled, showing pampered teeth. He followed that with an approving nod, eyes still fixed on Roxy with an expression of wonder usually reserved for the Grand Canyon.

When he noticed me, it seemed to come as a surprise. The smile vanished, and his eyes became small and black. He looked back at Roxy and said, "Can I ask what this is about?"

Roxy impressed me. She'd pulled back on her anger. But the suddenness of her recovery was as troubling as the outburst. She flamed and cooled in a breath, and when you see that in a person one time, you never forget. It's always there, and you wait for it to happen again.

In spite of her forced calm, there was still an edge to her voice, a cannon ready to fire, and it wouldn't take much.

"I'm from *Channel 7 News*," she said, holding out her hand. "I'm doing a story on the disappearance of Rolando Molina."

Mayflower looked at me for a long time, then at Roxy, and then past her at the empty street. He was stalling to get his bearings.

Smoothly, he said, "I believe I've seen you on television. Very flattered to have you at my door. I'm sorry, but I'm afraid I don't know anything." He nodded in my direction. "I already explained this to Mr. Stark."

Roxy said, "How about the murders of Rosa Lopez and Carlos Alvarez?"

"You think I know something about murders?" He chuckled at the foolishness of it. "You're aware I work in baseball?"

Firm, steady, confident, Roxy said, "We suspect a connection to the heroin smuggling in that area."

"I'm an agent. I represent talent." He stared, bug eyed. A triangle of black hair showed in the V of his robe. His wrists were matted with a fine layering of hair as well. The diamond in his left ear twinkled in the orange light.

"I'm not sure what else I can tell you," Mayflower said. "We're all hoping Rolando turns up and I'm happy to help any way I can. But I simply don't know anything. May I suggest calling the police?"

A female voice called to Mayflower from inside the house. It was a young voice, whiny, unhappy with the interruption, the kind of voice that goes with a lambskin robe.

Mayflower said, "I'm getting ready to sit down to dinner, so if you'll excuse me," and started to close the door.

Roxy stopped it with a firm hand. "Rolando's not going to be turning up anymore. He was murdered."

Mayflower blinked. "Murder? What makes you think he was murdered?"

"I've been out to Double Wide," Roxy said. "I've seen the evidence myself."

It was my turn to change colors. I coughed and shuffled my feet. Mayflower noticed my unease and said, "What're we talking about here? What evidence?"

I coughed again to signal Roxy to quiet down, but she kept going.

"Let's just say it's being properly preserved," she said. "Can we come inside and talk?"

Mayflower clamped his hand around the door again and used it to shield his body. He poked his head around it and said, "You need to speak with the authorities. It's beyond my ability to help you this evening."

He shut the door and bolted it, and we walked out to the street.

I said, "Jesus Christ, you just drew a roadmap to Rolando's hand. The police don't know I have it—I told you that."

"Mayflower's not going to the police."

"How do you know that?"

"He won't call attention to himself that way."

"You better be right."

"I'm always right." Roxy pointed back at the house. "Everything about that guy is sour apples."

FORTY

Roxy tore down the gravel access road to Campbell Avenue. She flipped open the console between the seats and pulled out a half-pint bottle of Chivas Regal scotch and offered me a sip.

"You're not supposed to drink and drive," I said. "They have commercials."

"Everybody needs a hobby." She sipped and stood the bottle between her legs. "Are you just being difficult or is something on your mind?"

"The tan briefcase at Bunny's house. Those papers on top. Did you see it?"

"I was busy checking out the Nordstrom collection."

"I think it's the same one I saw at Melody's the night of his getaway."

"You want to go back for it?"

"There might be something in it that answers some questions."

Roxy sipped some scotch. It sent her voice down to the basement and put gravel in it. "Okay, let's go steal a briefcase. How do we do that?"

"Distract her somehow. Get her to go out to the kitchen. Hide her cigarettes, and when she goes to look for them, I'll grab it."

"I'll ask about her hair. Seriously, did you see that monster do? What *was* that?"

The turns on Campbell Avenue are tight, and Roxy didn't slow down for any of them. She peeled through the night traffic and pulled up outside Bunny's house in no time. The Cadillac was gone from the carport. The front door was ajar and lights shone inside.

Roxy and I saw the door at the same time and gave each other worried looks.

Without a word, we jumped from the Audi and trotted across the street and onto the porch. I rapped on the door and pressed the bell and got no answer. The curtains at the front window had been shorn nearly off the rod.

Roxy cupped her hands at her eyes and peered through the window into the living room. "Oh, man. It looks like Bolt tore the place to hell."

"Any sign of Bunny?"

"Don't see her. I got a bad feeling about this."

I pushed the door all the way open. "Bunny! Bunny Slippers! Are you all right?" No answer. "Bunny! We're coming in!"

The living room smelled of baby powder and cigarette smoke, and looked like it'd been dynamited. Nothing was where it should've been. Wall hangings had been ripped down and chairs lay on their sides. The briefcase sat open and empty on the floor, papers of various kinds scattered around it.

"Bunny! It's Roxanne Santa Cruz! From *Channel 7*!"

Roxy went to search the remainder of the house. I got on my knees and looked under the couch, and through the debris pile on the floor. I thought back to that night at Melody's house when he took a gun from his safe, along with a white brick in cellophane wrapping, and put both into a black cloth bag.

That's what Bolt was looking for, the white brick.

Mixed with the papers, there was unopened mail, bills of various kinds, and what looked to be random pages from one of Melody's research papers. I counted six pages in all. They consisted mostly of charts, graphs, and equations.

Taking up one whole page was an abstract illustration of an agave plant, identified as the Palmer agave. Arrows pointed to parts of the plant with identifying information and brief paragraphs explaining its life span, growth patterns, location, water and climate needs, and other scientific information.

Roxy returned to the living room. "Bunny's not here. No blood and no body, thank heavens. What do you got?"

I was picking through the stack. "Stuff. Mail. Melody's papers."

"Bolt wrecked the whole house. Everything's tipped over."

"I hope he didn't hurt her."

Roxy peered around the room, making thinking sounds with her tongue. "He didn't. I'm sure he didn't."

"How do you figure?"

Roxy picked up the Nordstrom bags and turned them upside down to show me they were empty. She kicked some couch cushions out of the way and motioned with her hands to prove there was nothing underneath them.

"Look around. No Nordstrom clothes anywhere in here, and we know Bolt didn't take them."

"Good point."

"After he left, I'll bet Bunny wanted to get out of here fast and grabbed her new clothes. I'd do the same thing. I'm thinking she kept her cool and went to be with her man."

Figuring to inspect the pages more closely later, I swept up the whole lot and dumped them into the briefcase and snapped it shut. We turned off all the lights and walked out to the street. I tossed the briefcase into the passenger seat of the Bronco and started the engine.

It was nearing midnight. A hot wind blew down the street carrying the scent of water from the nearby Rillito River.

Roxy leaned in the driver's window. "I'm going to Skin to poke around. Bunny might've wanted to be with friends."

"Be careful in that place."

"Are you kidding? It's like going home." She gripped my arm and squeezed as a way of saying good night, and walked toward the Audi. I watched her go. Aware of the attention, she put her saloon legs to work, and that reminded me of something.

I leaned out the window. "Was it alliteration?"

Roxy gave me a puzzled look. "Huh?"

"Your stage name? I'm a fan of alliteration. Was it Mindy Moonlight?"

She made a sour face.

"Come on, alliteration's good. How about Barbie Biscuit?"

Roxy pondered that seriously for a moment. "Barbie Biscuit. That's not bad. I'll call you in the morning."

FORTY-ONE

I got onto Speedway Boulevard heading west toward the Tucson Mountains. I was hungry. Fast food signs turn Speedway into a neon fireball after dark. They run one after another until the city gives up and runs out of pavement.

Mexican sounded good. I swung into the next available place, the drive-thru at Tom's Tacos. The name screamed caution. How good could it be if the guy didn't even have the initiative to come up with a decent name?

If I'm a gringo opening a taco joint, I'm styling it up. Tacos by Tomás.

My phone rang when I got back on the road. I grunted hello around a bite of supper. Annie Patterson, Dr. Arthur Melody's former assistant, apologized for not calling back sooner, said she didn't do phones very well, and no, she didn't know where Melody was, although a man had visited her asking questions about him.

When I described Ed Bolt, she said that was him. I told her as little as I could to get her talking, and then said: "It's crucial that I find Arthur."

"Well, there's a woman who knows him as well as anyone. I hesitate to give you her name because she's such a private person and, if you'll pardon me, a little off."

"In my world, a little off makes her a stellar citizen." I stopped at a red light. "Hold on, Ms. Patterson."

I leaned out the window and spat out a mouthful of Tom's so-called food. It took three hocks and a yack to get the awful taste out of my mouth. The guy in the next car saw me and pretended to fiddle with his radio.

Pulling my head back inside, I said, "Have you ever had a taco that tasted like a slipper filled with grass?"

Annie Patterson wisely let that go.

"Anyway, you were saying, Ms. Patterson?"

"Elizabeth Bonheimer is the name. Arthur studied under her in Germany."

"You mean at A. A. Bildenson?"

"Correct. She's got to be in her eighties now, and she's a chemist, not a botanist. They call her Aunt Izzy, and she's a peculiar one. Brilliant, eccentric, has a reputation for being attracted to risky projects."

"Like what?"

"When she came to this country, she worked with our special forces on chemical enhancements, interrogation drugs, things of that sort. Very hush-hush. You can find her outside Oracle on the north side of the Catalinas, a ranch called Blue Lonesome. Nobody goes out there, and just so you know, she might take a shot at you."

That sounded like the perfect hideout. Before hanging up, I asked Patterson if Melody had been researching the Palmer agave.

"Yes, he'd taken great interest in the Palmer. In scientific circles they call it the *Palmeri*, for the legendary botanist Edward Palmer."

"Of course, old Ed Palmer." Never heard of him. "What was Melody's angle?"

"I'm sure I don't know. Ask Aunt Izzy. Bildenson sent her to this country specifically to study the Palmer. It's quite an exciting plant."

An exciting plant. I stayed calm.

Patterson went on: "We're learning that agaves have interesting chemical properties with multiple real-world uses."

"Narcotic properties?"

"Very much so. It has several pharmacological applications. The leaves contain a steroid-like compound that can be squeezed out and modified to make birth control pills. That's one example."

"Did you say steroid-like?"

"They're called saponins." She paused. "Wait, you're a baseball player. I hadn't thought of that."

"Let's say a kid wanted to juice up, get stronger. Could these…saponins do that?"

"I've never heard of it, but I suppose so. They're certainly available. Saponins are phytochemicals that occur naturally in lots of plants, soybeans, herbs, yucca. But the Palmer is loaded with them."

Back at Double Wide, I hurried behind the Airstream to check the freezer. Roxy had basically told Mayflower that we had evidence of Rolando's death, and that could only mean one thing. If Mayflower was involved, retrieving that evidence would be crucial.

I threw open the lid, and the hand was there. Seeing it again sent my stomach leaping into my mouth.

Charlie was asleep on my foldout. Trying to be quiet, I poured a glass of milk and carried Melody's briefcase back to my bedroom. Chico limped after me to give the situation a thorough sniffing. When he saw that the briefcase held papers and not T-bone steaks, he looked heartbroken and flopped onto his side for a recovery nap.

I sat on the edge of the bed and read Melody's work. I was more confused than when I started. Much of it was chemistry with Latin phrases tossed in. It might as well have been Sanskrit.

In high school, I took a chemistry test and got 26 out of 100. The teacher allowed a retake and I scored 19.

Maybe Bonheimer could tell me what it meant.

Bunny's phone bill looked interesting. She'd made eighteen local calls and another fourteen to the same number in Las Vegas, Nevada. I sat at my laptop and signed on. Google told me that nine of the local calls went to Skin, and the remainder to everyday locales, a beauty salon, a credit union, and other such places.

I typed in the Vegas number and it came up as a private cell. With that many calls, it had to be somebody she knew well, someone who might know where she was. I dialed the number, got a zombie message, and hung up.

Then I flipped open my laptop and read about steroidal saponins. They're not an anabolic steroid but a precursor that helps the body increase testosterone and build muscle on its own.

When I was playing, the guys who juiced kept it quiet, even in late-night conversation. But when a player showed up at spring training with a head the size of a dumpster, you knew it wasn't spinach and yoga.

Would I have used saponins to gain an edge on the field?

Did Babe Ruth enjoy happy hour?

FORTY-TWO

The next day was like all the others, the monotony of harsh sunlight broken only by a few impertinent white clouds and a blowtorch breeze.

I followed my routine. I showered and made a breakfast of oatmeal and eggs with english muffins and grape jelly for Charlie and myself. In keeping with our deal, he folded up his bed and stacked the linens neatly on the bench.

We finished eating and were still sitting at the table when Cash came in, and then Opal. She poured herself orange juice and sat. CNN was running a story about a woman's 105th birthday. They asked the secret to a long life, and she said, "Stay away from men!"

"Got that right," Cash said, and let out his squeaky-gate laugh.

After breakfast, I tried the Vegas number again, got the same message, and went outside to smoke a cigar. Chico hobbled down the steps after me and sat at my feet. Every cigar I smoked made me think of my grandfather.

He was a big, fat incorruptible man, a railroad brakeman who, on Sundays, dressed in a vest and watch fob. Barely literate himself, he demanded to the point of physical threat that his children finish school.

He could light a stick match with one long, elegant swipe along his pant leg. Watching him as a kid, I thought that was the coolest thing I'd ever seen.

I was still smoking when Roxy called. I told her about the call from Patterson and the tip about Elizabeth Bonheimer. "As soon as I can, I'm heading up to Oracle."

"Where have you gone, Arthur Melody?"

"He's either dead or in hiding."

"Yeah, and either one makes him hard to quote."

My goal was getting Charlie off my couch and back to his own trailer. He kept saying, "I can't sleep at an angle. It upsets my molecules."

Opal cleared the table and washed the kitchen dishes, after which I insisted we try again. I cranked the lever and got the trailer up high enough for him to slip two fresh cinderblocks underneath.

But the jack gave way again and crushed the last good block. I was surprised the whole trailer didn't tip over.

As it was, we heard Charlie's wall hangings crashing around in there and a cat screeching. Charlie and his molecules were going to be with me awhile.

I didn't get out of Double Wide until late afternoon, and on the way I stopped at a midtown garage. Pete, the nervous ninety-pound body man, offered to put a new roof on the Bronco for $900. I said I'd call back to make an appointment, and right away dreaded having to wait three hours while he did the work.

Waiting rooms bother me. They're filthy, the coffee is foul, and I can't read three-year-old magazines. They say I'm particular, but I don't see it.

FORTY-THREE

At 6:30 p.m. I left Pete's and drove west on Grant Road, braving Tucson's new Wild West. It takes place on streets that are uncared for and unmanaged by any recognizable authority. Frantic drivers rush to the next red light so they can crawl into your trunk and look around.

The potholes are so deep and numerous they've become tourist attractions. See our urban caves. See how many you can leap without snapping an axle.

At the intersection of Grant and Oracle Roads, I waited in the boiling heat through three lights, experiencing the standard hallucinations of the non-air-conditioned. At the fourth turn to green, I abused the accelerator to get as far from that light as I could.

The wind smoked through my hair. My phone rang. I listened to George Jones for a spell. The man broke my heart every time.

"Hellooo."

"We got us a new resident, Mayor," Cash said. "He made his way into the open trailer and went to sleep."

"Does he have a name?"

"Won't say. Some kid. Should I run him off?"

"Let him be until I get back. I want to talk to him."

My goal was making the forty-mile drive to the Blue Lonesome before nightfall. Sunset was at 7:30 p.m. I didn't want to be on mountain roads in a monsoon, and so far, the sky looked cooperative.

I drove north on Oracle Road into the Catalina foothills and kept going above the clamor of the city until human habitation thinned to not much at all.

At Oracle Junction, I turned right onto Highway 77 and rolled through empty desert for eleven miles into the town of Oracle. It consists of tin-roofed miners' shacks, gray adobes, some trailers, and a few modern two-story stucco homes spread willy-nilly over the hills fronting the north face of the Catalina Mountains.

Downtown isn't much: a gas station, a market, a few store-fronts where artists go and don't make money, and a boarded-up steak house and lounge where Dean and the Destroyers killed it on Thursday nights.

Oracle definitely didn't bustle. More like a wheeze.

Three blinks after downtown, the road split. I took the right fork into the Coronado National Forest and the Blue Lonesome turnoff, three miles along.

The dirt road snaked up the mountain at a steep climb. Every half mile or so, there were bullet-riddled No Trespassing signs. They should come out of the factory that way. It'd save the locals time and a bundle on ammunition. I passed oak trees and tall yucca plants that looked like warriors' lances emerging from blossoming stands.

The switchbacks kept switching until I reached a meadow overlooking a huge expanse of the San Manuel Valley. The hills were burned and brown where the meadow fell off, and they flowed steadily down to deep canyons that made the ground disappear and towering stone ridges that brought it back again.

Far below, blackening clouds made a patchwork of shadows on the valley floor. A storm was building out there and blowing my way.

Another turn after the meadow, I came to a stone ranch house, headquarters of the Blue Lonesome. The bottom was long and low in the traditional ranch style. The windows were

LEO W. BANKS

partially below ground level and the overhanging log roof only a few feet above it. A dome-shaped addition on top had a glass front affording a view across the great valley.

A massive Emory oak shaded the back of the house, and back of these was a corral.

The entrance gate was a metal bar controlled by a punch pad. I ducked under the bar and walked toward the house.

A female voice called out, "A locked gate means stay out! Declare yourself, sir!"

I couldn't see the speaker. I shaded my eyes and said, "Are you Elizabeth Bonheimer? I'm looking for the famous chemist. My name is Whip Stark."

The voice again: "Whatever news you bring today, Mr. Whip Stark, you best deliver it from behind my gate."

Scanning the house and the area around it, I couldn't locate her in the glow of sunset. I said, "I assume you're not going to shoot me."

"You assume too much, Mr. Whip Stark."

My eyes followed the sound of the corral gate squealing open, and there was Bonheimer.

She had snow-white hair cut in a nun's bowl. She wore a rust-colored buckskin shirt straight out of a Wild West show. It had long sleeves, buttons up the front, white stitching over both pockets in eagle-wing design, and black horsehair tassels hanging from those designs. The horsehair was woven with turquoise beading.

She was way too thin for it, and it certainly wasn't a summer shirt. But if you had no blood in your veins, I suppose you could wear it comfortably in the heat.

Bonheimer stepped toward me and snarled. "I don't talk to men with the manners of a goddamned goat."

Close up, she had the finely lined face you see a lot in Arizona's backcountry. The sun is youth's second-story man, its silent thief.

176

But her voice had depth and hung on to the end notes longer than necessary. It sounded vaguely like yodeling.

"Are you the one they call Aunt Izzy?" I tried to sound friendly and came across like the guy who goes door to door offering to fix leaking roofs after causing them.

Unmoved, she wiped her mouth with her hand and stared. The veins on the back of it were cornflower blue.

Thinking quickly, I threw out another name, hoping it might earn me some credit. "Annie Patterson sent me."

Bonheimer wasn't impressed with that either. She tucked two fingers behind her teeth and whistled like a traffic cop. Three German shepherds darted around the house at attack speed.

Without turning, Bonheimer held up a hand to stop them, and they obeyed, pulling up in the dirt right beside her. They stood stiffly, poised on low-slung hips, teeth showing. They had unusually thick fur around their necks and hungry eyes.

I said, "I would've called first, but Annie didn't have your number."

Bonheimer stared without speaking. I was getting nowhere. Thunder shook the valley. The storm I feared was coming.

Saying nothing, I held up both hands and backpedaled toward the gate. Moving as deliberately as I could, I ducked under the gate, nearly brushing the dirt with my lips. I straightened up and took a few extra steps back, putting me within scampering distance of the Bronco if she decided to release the hounds.

"Talk," said Bonheimer.

"I'm looking for Arthur Melody. It's urgent."

"Arthur?" Bonheimer's face softened. "I don't know where he is or where he might've gone."

Not exactly a firm denial of having seen him.

More thunder boomed and the storm winds swirled. The twilight was uncertain. It made patches of darkness on the plateau and patches of radiant noon, as the last of the sunlight streamed through the clouds in shower-like formation.

Three vehicles were parked at the edge of the plateau facing the valley, a white pickup truck, a red jeep, and a white Lincoln Continental, maybe twenty-five years old.

I thought of the night of Melody's frantic escape from the alley behind his house, his white car shooting out of the garage. I didn't catch the make. But it was huge and old, so different from sleek modern models.

It could've been a Lincoln, the same one parked thirty feet in front of me. Then again, the Lincoln worked as well for Bonheimer as it did for Melody. It was the perfect old-lady car.

"It's urgent," I said. "It could be a matter of life and death."

"Yeah, whose?" She wasn't buying it.

"The doctor's on the run, and his life's in danger."

Bonheimer cocked her head. "On the run from what?"

"Drug smugglers."

"Arthur Melody involved with drugs?" She cackled from the mountaintop.

"I have some of his research papers in my car. He was into something pretty deep. If you could just take a look at them."

"I recommend you leave while I still have my patience and you still have your scalp."

I pointed to the Lincoln. "That's a nice ride you have there. How'd you get a car like that up this mountain?"

"Drove it on the road, Mr. Whip Stark. The road you came in on and the same one that's going to haul your disagreeable self out."

I tried a couple more approaches and nothing worked. When the dogs picked up Bonheimer's hostility and showed more teeth, I got the message and retreated down the road. A blustery wind shoved the Bronco around, but the storm failed to deliver any rain, and I made it out of there, dry and alive.

FORTY-FOUR

On the drive home, I kept thinking about the look on Bonheimer's face when I mentioned Melody's name. It sparked something—a memory, anxiety, possibly guilt.

I wished I'd gotten a closer look at the back bumper of that big white car. If it was Melody's, he might've peeled off the identifying saguaro sticker, leaving a glue outline that would still show. It was impossible to tell from the gate.

Charlie was talking in his sleep when I stepped inside the Airstream. Best I could tell, he was eating carrots while being chased by a panther. I listened some more. No, it wasn't a panther but the Seventh Cavalry led by George Armstrong Custer.

Back in my bedroom, I grabbed a blanket and made a door of it, held up by books stacked on the shelving on either side of the entrance. Not much of a sound barrier against Charlie's battle cries, but it provided at least some privacy.

I couldn't get over Bonheimer's shirt. You expect to see that attire on actors and models smiling for the camera in glossy western magazines. They see the West mainly through the tinted windows of SUVs trolling the paved roads around Santa Fe.

If by some misadventure said SUV happened to depart said pavement, encountering actual western dirt, their first reaction is to call the police.

Dear Aunt Izzy, a real specimen. But she didn't bother me. I had a weakness for outliers, and her hostility wasn't a surprise. Mountain people are different. They've chosen to shun the world.

Mountain people typically don't greet you with a welcoming smile and a steaming bowl of raccoon soup.

Next morning, I made scrambled eggs sprinkled with cut-up steak. I sliced a cantaloupe into squares and put them on a plate alongside a bowl of grapes. It started out being just Charlie and me, but Cash came in after a while.

We ate together, and afterward I got out a sheet of paper and made a list of groceries and supplies we needed in town. We usually made one run a week and split up the chore. It was Cash's turn.

But Charlie volunteered to make the drive for him, saying he was low on propane. When Charlie said propane, he meant gin.

He grabbed the keys to Cash's Dodge Dart and threw up smoke signals all the way over the mountain. Roxy came to Double Wide about noon, and when Charlie returned, we divvied up the supplies and put everything away, Roxy helping out with my end of it.

Cash hauled out the jack, which he swore was finally fixed, and rousted our surprise visitor out of the open trailer. I'd forgotten about him. His name was Angel.

He wore a filthy black Oakland Raiders T-shirt, untucked and way oversized. He had on Levis that were just as dirty and also oversized. It looked like he'd found them, and he probably had. The desert is an outdoor JCPenney of clothes discarded by illegal crossers.

The toes of his sneakers pointed up, like clown shoes. He had a long knotted black hair down to his shoulders. I put him at fourteen.

Charlie said, "You want to go to work, Angel? We could use some young muscle."

"I can do lots of work for you." The kid took a deep breath and held it, ballooning his cheeks and curling his arms over his head to show muscles he didn't have. Everybody laughed.

Charlie said, "Okay, okay. Take it easy or you'll hurt yourself. I'd be much obliged."

Just as before, I placed the jack underneath the corner of Charlie's trailer and cranked the lift to the ready position. Charlie and Cash each placed one of the wood beams under the trailer on either side of the jack, splayed their legs, and gripped the beams above their shoulders.

I cranked the lever, and the trailer went up. I kept cranking. Every four or five tries, I stopped and waited to hear the fast clicking and didn't. The jack held every time. When I got it all the way up, I set the lock and stepped back and waited for the crash.

Just in case, Angel grabbed the bottom of the trailer and lifted with everything he had, his face turning crimson in the effort. Roxy grabbed a fresh cinderblock and slipped it into the space, and then another. I cranked the trailer down onto the top block as gently as I could and it held.

The job was finally done.

We shook hands all around, after which Roxy turned to Angel, eyeing him with keen interest. She took him by the shoulders, and leaning down to take a close look, inspected the back of his T-shirt.

"Check this out," she said, pulling on the shirt. "Is this blood? How'd you get blood all over yourself, kid?"

The back of the T-shirt was a darker shade of black than the front. The bloodstain went all the way down to the top of his Levis. As Roxy looked, she caught my eye and pointed to the name etched in the leather along the back of Angel's belt.

Carlos Alvarez.

FORTY-FIVE

We brought Angel into the Airstream and sat him down. He smelled like a carful of wet dogs, only not as good. Roxy pulled off his T-shirt. The kid might've weighed ninety pounds. He had buggy-whip arms, and his torso was nothing but sharp bones jabbing at mocha skin.

I tossed his T-shirt into the trash and got out one of my own and threw it over a chair. I soaked a washcloth and gave it to Roxy to wipe the blood off his back.

"Wait a minute. He's been shot," she said. "Get a load of this. It looks like a bullet grazed him. What happened here?"

I looked as Roxy washed off the blood. The kid had a gash to the right of his spine. From under the sink, I got out my first aid kit. Roxy took out the small alcohol bottle and cotton swabs, wet one of the swabs, and dabbed at the wound.

Roxy said, "We've got a lucky boy here. Another inch or so left and he's a goner. Who shot you, Angel?"

"Roscoe Rincon."

"Roscoe Rincon," Roxy repeated. "Who's that?"

"He *jefes* the *chivastas* out here," Angel said, using slang for the heroin smugglers. "He guards the smuggler trail from Mexico all the way up here."

Roxy looked at me, eyebrows raised. I knew what she was thinking. Machete. I asked Angel to describe him.

"Sinaloan dude, big, ugly. They call him *Rojo*." Rojo is Spanish for "red." "He'll kill anybody." Angel snapped his fingers. "Like that. He likes his machete. Chop, chop, chop. Don't matter to *Rojo*."

That confirmed it. Roscoe Rincon was the man who threatened to murder me on Paradise Mountain.

Roxy said, "He sounds like a *sicario*, an assassin. They keep everybody in line on the routes they own. Anybody steps off, Rincon handles it."

As Roxy dabbed at his back, Angel's eyes moved around the Airstream, taking it all in. His left eye was black, deep set, alert, and suspicious. Something was wrong with the right one. It looked like he was rolling his eyes, and it got stuck in the up position. It was mostly white with a quarter moon of black showing under the lid.

It made me think of *The Tempest*. By the time I was nine, Sam made sure I knew the play by heart. The character Caliban was called a mooncalf, someone born with a deformity, which in those times was thought to be caused by the machinations of the moon.

Roxy asked why Rincon had shot him, and again the kid didn't answer.

"I'm hungry," he said.

I poured a glass of milk. He sucked it down in a swallow and wiped the residue off his mouth with his forearm. Getting the hint, I broke four eggs into a frying pan, got out a second pan, filled it with sausages, pulled out a roll of biscuits, and put them into the microwave.

Roxy said, "Tell me, Angel. How do you know Roscoe Rincon?"

"I work for him in Phoenix, Tucson, all over. I met him in the Sierra Madre. That's where I was born."

The drug cartels control the Sierra Madre mountain range in northwest Mexico. It's an impenetrable stronghold where they can do their business unbothered by any law but their own.

The microwave beeped. I put the steaming biscuits on a plate and carried them to the table with butter. Angel grabbed a knife, sliced off a two-inch wedge of butter, and popped it into his mouth. He stuffed a biscuit into his mouth, cut another butter wedge, and ate that too.

All I had was duct tape. Roxy bit off a portion and pressed it against a bandage on the kid's back. As she smoothed it, she said, "Tell me about Roscoe Rincon."

"I was loyal to him. I did what he wanted. I worked for him a long time."

Roxy said, "On Paradise Mountain?"

Angel nodded. I was standing at the oven working the scrambled eggs with a spatula. "Did you live in one of the buildings up there?"

Angel turned toward the kitchen. His good eye found me. The black moon eye journeyed around in its socket, taking a while to settle on its target.

"I live with the animals," he said. "All the animals on the mountain know me."

I scooped the eggs onto a plate and did the same with the sausages. Angel watched my every move. I poured orange juice and brought it to the table with the food. He pounced before I drew my hand away. He ate like a Doberman.

Roxy said, "Why'd Roscoe Rincon want to kill you?"

Angel had a fork in one hand and a biscuit in the other. He used the biscuit to roll bits of egg onto the fork. "I seen things."

Roxy asked what things, and he didn't respond. She nodded to get my attention and then motioned with her hands for me to hold Angel down by the shoulders. As soon as I had him in my grip, she reached down, unbuckled his belt, and slipped it off.

The kid had no time to resist. He lunged for the belt. "That's mine! I found it! Give it back!"

"It's not yours," I said. "It's ten sizes too big for you."

The angry twisting of his mouth showed a gap where several teeth had been. He lunged for it again. Roxy shoved him back into the chair.

"You saw what happened to Carlos Alvarez, didn't you?" I said.

The kid held his hands a few inches apart. "That's how close I was. Roscoe Rincon killed him real quick." Angel made a gun of his fingers, put it behind his ear, and dropped his thumb, making a wet gunshot sound.

I remembered something Opal had said the night we found Alvarez's body. She saw a dark object in the passenger seat of his truck, possibly a jacket on a hook. She said if it was a person, he was small. Angel.

I pulled out an apple pie out of the refrigerator, cut a slice, and put it on a plate. I held back, making no move to hand it to him. Angel's attention fixed on the pie.

He said, "I know about your friend."

The muscles in my shoulders turned to iron. "Do we have a deal?"

He nodded. When I put the pie in front of him, he grabbed it with his bare hands and devoured it. Never looking up, he said, "I know where your friend's hand's at."

He had barely gotten the sentence out when I bolted out the door to the freezer.

FORTY-SIX

Returning to the Airstream and feeling a grinding anger, I grabbed a magazine off the counter and whipped it across the room. Loose pages flew everywhere.

Roxy said, "The hand's gone?"

"We know one thing for sure. Mayflower's connected to the heroin smuggling over this mountain."

"Dammit. That's on me, Prospero. I'm sorry."

I leaned across the table close to Angel. My pulse punched hard against my neck. "I want it straight, kid. No bullshit now. What happened to Rolando Molina? Where is he?"

Angel shrugged. I pounded my fist on the table so hard it sounded like a dynamite blast in the tight space. I reached across to grab him, and Roxy's hands clamped down on my shoulders.

She edged me aside. "You're going to talk to me, right, Angel?"

He stared at her with his good eye. The half-moon eye was off in some other dimension.

"Let's start with the hand," she said. "What happened to it?"

Angel looked mesmerized. She saw that and leaned closer. "Talk to me, kiddo."

Still staring, Angel said, "Roscoe Rincon told me to steal it, and when I brought it to him, he tried to kill me. He smiled like he was happy, and that's when I knew he was going to kill me. He reached for the gun on his leg, and I pushed him away and ran. He fired at me and kept firing. When I couldn't run anymore, I hid in the bushes."

"What'd you do with the hand?" she said.

"I dropped it when I was running. I dropped it in a well."

I spoke up. "You're going to take me to that well."

With his eyes firmly set on Roxy, he nodded.

"First thing tomorrow morning," I said, and poked the kid on the chest to get his attention. "You and me, we're going up the mountain."

"You have to protect me," he said. "Rincon wants to kill me. He'll try to kill me again."

"I'll protect you."

A few hours later, I whipped up more eggs and sausages and fed Angel again. I threw him in the shower, gave him my Adidas T-shirt, washed his Levis, and gave him a belt to keep them up.

The kid sat in front of the kitchen TV for several hours. With night coming on, I sent him back to the open trailer and told him to be ready at first light. Roxy spent the remainder of the afternoon working sources to get more information on Rincon and I mulled over what I knew for certain.

Roxy had let it slip to Mayflower that there was evidence of Rolando Molina's murder at Double Wide. That meant the hand. And the next day someone came and stole that evidence. It seemed clear Mayflower told Roscoe Rincon of the problem and sent Angel to steal it.

Then he shot Angel because he knew too much.

Angel was the passenger in Carlos Alvarez's truck when that murder happened, meaning he was probably working with Rincon to set up Alvarez, and Rincon betrayed him.

Roscoe Rincon killed Carlos Alvarez and probably killed Rolando before that. Now he was trying to eliminate evidence of both crimes, and it just might work.

In Rolando's case, no hand meant no evidence. As far as anyone knew, he'd never been anywhere near Paradise Mountain or

Double Wide. He simply said good-bye to Fausto in Monterrey, Mexico, and disappeared.

No trace anywhere. At least until I located the body.

The remainder of the night was quiet except for Roxy's voice outside on the phone. She was calling cop sources to dredge up information on Roscoe Rincon, but nobody was calling back. After an hour she came inside and found my tequila bottle and held it up to read the label.

"Gran Patron Platinum. This is like three hundred dollars a bottle. Did you buy this?"

"Yeah, I used to be that guy."

"No wonder you're broke."

I was sitting at the kitchen table. The weather report was on TV. Hot tonight, hot tomorrow, and hot the next day. The weather tart had to act like she'd just found that out, and it was big news.

Roxy poured herself a shot and threw it down like water. She leaned against the counter and stared into the empty shot glass like it was telling her a fascinating story. "How do you read this kid, Prospero? You believe him?"

"What choice do I have? He knows where Rolando's hand is."

"So he says."

"I'll do anything to avoid telling Oscar Molina I lost his son's hand."

"Isn't it obvious? Rincon's working with Angel to set you up. He steals Rolando's hand and comes back and tells you, 'I know where it is, follow me.' He'll be waiting for you up there."

"It's a chance I've got to take."

A moment passed. Silence.

"It sounds like you're worried about me, Rox."

"This kid's like nothing I've seen before—part animal, part human, and I don't trust either part. He's something awful this border created. You can't feed him because he'll keep coming around like a nasty cat until he feeds on you. He's no good."

She pointed the shot glass at me. "At least tell me you're not going up that mountain alone."

"Cashmere Miller will come with me."

She threw her head at the ceiling in frustration. "The Skipper and Gilligan. This gets better all the time."

She washed out the shot glass, dried it and put it back in the cabinet. She made me promise to call her as soon as I returned from the mountain, and then she grabbed her keys and drove off.

FORTY-SEVEN

The morning sky looked the way the afternoon looks when a storm is coming. The clouds were dark and swirling. The rain, if it came, would make passage difficult on slick roads. But there would be no harsh sun, and that was good.

I filled Charlie in on the plan and told him to keep an eye on Opal. Make sure she didn't wander off. Make sure to watch for anybody coming around who didn't belong.

Angel sat next to me on the front seat wearing my Adidas T-shirt. He moved well, showing scant ill effects from the wound. Cash sat in back like he was going to a picnic.

He wore an Arizona Feeds ball cap and a sleeveless blue muscle shirt that showed off his spare torso. He was as lean as a teenage boy, sinewy, not weak. He smelled like he lived under a tree. He wore cargo shorts with dirty socks that bunched around his hiking boots and leather gloves with the fingertips cut off. He carried his AR-15.

I trusted Cash completely and don't know why.

We reached the top of the mountain about 7:00 a.m. At the outskirts of Paradise, I stopped to look for anything out of the ordinary. I saw nothing, and neither did Cash. Angel urged me forward. I drove quickly between the buildings, shifting my gaze from one side of the street to the other, listening for sounds, looking for movement, alert for anything out of place.

If gunmen were waiting, this was as good a place as any.

When we were clear of town, Angel pointed me to the west onto a secondary road leading to a higher set of mountains about a mile away. The road rolled out under black clouds along ground that monsoon storms had dotted with patches of green.

About halfway there we heard the first boom of thunder. No rain yet, but it was coming. The air pulsed with the smell of it.

Cash chuckled in the backseat. "Weren't you going to put a roof on this rig, Mayor?"

The road split the mountains and turned south. I followed it up the rocky slope. The wind picked up. I went a short distance and stopped. I didn't like what I was seeing. The way ahead narrowed, with tall ridges looming on both sides of the road approaching the mouth of the canyon.

"Keep going," Angel said. "Why are you stopping?"

"Getting in is the easy part," I said. "I'm worried about getting out."

"It's right up here. Not far."

I pulled a map from the glove and unfolded it against the steering wheel. Another cannon blast of thunder. I traced our course from Paradise to our present location, and saw we were entering a place called Crooked Canyon.

The name seemed just right. I put the map away and kept going.

After another half mile, Angel shouted, "There it is!" and jumped out of the Bronco and ran ahead. I braked and watched him go.

He came to a set of stone ruins on a gentle rise at the mouth of Crooked Canyon. They were the remains of an old house with the well beside it. The cement housing stood intact, as did the wood frame that held the crank for the rope and bucket.

When Angel got to the housing, he spread his hands on the lip and leaned over to look inside. He held that position for a few seconds and ran around to the other side and dropped his head inside to look from there.

I said to Cash, "What do you think?"

"Remember your training."

"We never did anything like this in spring training."

"That's the only thing our CO said worth a shit."

"Did it work?"

"Until he got himself blowed up."

I left the engine running and stepped out. Cash did the same. The wind blew stronger, and the air was much cooler, the temperature falling with the coming storm. Angel was fifty yards ahead of us, still peering into the well. I studied the ridge tops, and so did Cash.

The kid probably couldn't see more than fifteen feet into that well, and the bottom had to be far deeper than that. I grabbed my flashlight. Angel swung his arm to wave us forward, and we started walking. I couldn't have gone much farther in the Bronco anyway. The road had been made impassable by huge boulders carried by rainwater through the narrow canyon.

Cash held the AR-15 in front of him with two hands, the barrel angled down. The first raindrops hit, followed almost immediately by another crash of thunder that obscured the gunshots, three in quick succession.

Angel ducked for cover. Three more shots. A chunk of cement flew off the well housing. The gunshots jumped atop the wind and rode it through the canyon.

Cash stood in a crouch, eyes raised to the ridge tops. "He's up high, Mayor," he said coolly. "When he fires again, I'll have him."

I ran behind the nearest boulder. I had the Glock in my left hand and don't remember drawing it. "Cash! Over here! Get over here!"

That was it for talk. The morning exploded in gunfire. It came first from the ridge, and then from Cash returning fire.

The echoes made it sound like a hundred guns going at once. The sound reverberated in my chest.

I saw where Cash was aiming and fired four times in the same direction. With a nine millimeter, I couldn't hit anything at that distance. But I wanted the gunman to know that I was armed too.

Cash ran for my position behind the boulder. A man was running along the ridge, bent at the waist and moving quickly, a rifle in hand. He had dark hair and dark clothing and lumbered along, running in a heavy-footed side-to-side gait. It was Rincon.

He dropped out of sight. Ten seconds passed. He popped up in a spot farther down the ridge and sent multiple rounds at our position, the bullets slapping against the boulder. Cash returned fire, but Rincon dropped out of sight again.

When I looked again, Angel was out in the open now, running away from the well. I yelled for him to stay put, but he couldn't hear me over the driving rain and the shooting.

"He's going to get himself killed!" I said. "Cover him!"

Cash put the AR-15 atop the boulder and fired round after round. I emptied the first clip, shoved in a fresh one, and kept firing. Angel ran in a zigzag, Rincon's bullets digging at the ground around him. He was trying to make it into the mouth of the canyon and cover.

"Come on, kid!" I said. "Run! You can make it! Run!"

I watched until the rain enveloped him. Cash stopped firing, and so did I. There was no point anymore. The ridge had disappeared behind the downpour.

"Let's get outta here!" I was two feet from Cash, but I had to yell to be heard as the rain pounded down.

"You know what, I think I'm shot, Mayor," he said, and laughed. "Look at this here!" There was blood on his fingertips. "I'm over there in I-raq and nothing and here I get myself shot up. Baby, that's rare."

He sat with his back against the boulder holding his hand to his forehead.

"We have to move," I said. "There's a flash flood coming."

In a storm like that, in a narrow canyon like that, the rushing water comes with incredible force and little warning. Cash held his hand out and looked at it. It dripped with a thin mixture of rainwater and blood. The bullet had left a gash on the side of his forehead.

"Funny, I don't feel nothing," he said. "I seen plenty of guys shot. Screaming, man."

"Can you run?"

"Man, all day long. This ain't no thing."

"Let's get outta here."

We ran to the Bronco and sped out of Crooked Canyon in reverse. I spun the wheel in a wild U-turn and glanced over at Cash. He had pulled off his muscle shirt, and rolled it up and was pressing it against the wound.

"We might not be done yet," I said. "Keep that peashooter handy."

It took fifteen minutes of hard driving through mud and running water to get to the other side of the mountain and find the trail up to the gunman's ridge. Even in four-wheel drive, I couldn't make it all the way to the top. I had to walk the last few hundred feet.

The storm had already done its work and moved on, leaving behind billows of cool, ground-hugging mist. When a desert storm almost kills you, it leaves a parting gift. I walked through the mist with the Glock in my hand.

No sign of Rincon and no way to track him on rain-washed trails.

I heard the rushing water before I saw it. At the peak, I looked down at the brown, wall-to-wall mass roaring through the canyon.

FORTY-EIGHT

Opal bandaged Cash and spent the remainder of the day resting. His mind seemed fine, although that gets into definitions. He wanted to go back to find his Arizona Feeds hat. I told him we wouldn't be returning to the mountain until the roads dried out.

Besides, I knew one of the company executives and could get him a brand new hat. Any color he wanted, snap-back or fitted. I have connections where it counts.

I called Roxy and told her what had happened. She crowed, telling me I needed to listen to her next time. I said I didn't think Angel could've survived the flood, and as close as the gunman's bullets came to killing him, it didn't look like a setup.

Then I made the call I dreaded making. Oscar Molina.

When I told him Rolando's hand was missing, there was a long silence on his end, and then, in a bitter, accusing voice: "You promised to take care of him."

It was his turn to listen to a long silence. I had no idea what to say except that I'd get it back. I repeated my promise to find Rolando's body. It was a difficult conversation.

I punched off on the call and felt lousy. I'd let him down, let happen the one thing I vowed wouldn't happen. If I were a serious drinker, that would've been the time to hit it. But I lacked the constitution for boozing. Always had.

I poured myself a glass of milk and waited for it to calm my stomach. It didn't work. Misery had found a home in my gut, and seemed to like it there. I took a shower. I cleaned the kitchen until the smell of bleach made me sick and went outside and paced around.

It was sunset time, and the sky was dressed up in all the colors you can imagine, putting on another of its shows. This one was a full Broadway extravaganza, with a long-legged chorus line and a pale-faced orchestra in pearls and tuxedos squeezing out that knife-in-the-neck sound of too much cello.

A lot of people go crazy over Arizona's sunsets. They travel from around the world to see them, fumble around with a camera, and gurgle on about this or that aspect of the beautiful natural world.

Like the next fellow, I can see a splashy sunset and be reminded of eternity or someone who died too soon. But it's different when you live with it every day. It gets exhausting. After a while, you want to be left alone, without all that Jackson Pollock business.

That was one of those nights. I looked up and said, "Okay, I see you. But right now I could use a little honest darkness, so go ahead and set already."

FORTY-NINE

Two days passed with Opal glued to my hip. She was afraid Angel would return and do something terrible to us. She didn't spell out what that was. When I told her he was probably dead, she said, "You can't kill a thing like that."

Not even a boy. A "thing."

Over and over, I ran the facts through my mind, trying to find what I was missing. I kept going back to that night at Melody's house, his car screeching down the alley, Ed Bolt and his partner following me to Double Wide thinking I'd taken something important from the house.

That something was the key to Mayflower's side of the conspiracy. The holy grail, Melody called it. Mayflower and Bolt desperately wanted it back. They researched Melody the same way I did—online—and found Annie Patterson, and Bolt beat me to her with questions on the professor's whereabouts.

On the second night after the flood, I was lying in bed with Melody's alley getaway looping through my head. Because of Angel, Opal was afraid to stay at her place, so I set her up on the foldout. She was asleep.

Chico lay on the floor beside my bed, close enough so I could reach over and scratch his ear. I'd scratch, he'd settle into a snooze, and then he'd whimper until I scratched again. The only way to stop the cycle was to lift him into the bed with me, which I did.

He curled up with his chin on my knee, looking up at me with great satisfaction.

"You're shameless, Chico," I said. "Go to sleep."

I went back to thinking about Arthur Melody's alley. In my mind, I saw his hand reaching out the driver's window of his big white boat of a car, the white of his arm flashing in the darkness as the hand arced over the roof.

That hand must've held something.

In the house, he'd said he was going to rid himself of the contents of that black bag and maybe that's what he did. The darkness hid its flight, and the grinding of his tires on the dirt muffled the sound of its landing.

It could still be there in the brush along the road or in the backyard on the other side of the chain-link fence.

The next morning, I shook Opal awake and told her I was going to look for Dr. Melody's black bag. Not wanting to stay at Double Wide with Angel, she was dressed and in the Bronco before I could ask if she wanted to come.

FIFTY

At 8:00 a.m., we pulled into the twelve-foot-wide alley that separated Melody's backyard from his neighbor's. A high chain-link fence bordered the neighbor's property, with shrubbery at the bottom growing to the knees.

Opal and I started at different ends of the alley and walked toward one another, kicking through the weeds as we went. No black bag. We peered through the chain-link fence to see if the bag might've landed in the neighbor's yard and stayed hidden under a bush or a tree.

After half an hour, we returned to the Bronco and sat for a minute. The scene played again in my head. Melody's car shooting out of the garage and stopping an inch from my leg, the arm reaching out the window and heaving the black bag over the roof.

From the location of Melody's car, the landing spot could've been the flat roof of the metal storage shed at the back of the neighbor's yard. It bumped right against the alley fence and stood about ten feet high.

I pulled the Bronco tight against the fence, jumped onto the hood, stepped onto the Bronco's windshield frame, double gripped the edge of the shed roof, and climbed up.

The black bag was there. "Got it!" I hollered down to Opal. "I've got it!"

I loosened the drawstrings and pulled out a silver .38-caliber Smith & Wesson. Also in the bag was a soft white substance wrapped in cellophane, about the size of a bar of soap.

A voice called, "Hey, over there! What all you doing on my roof, partner?"

The speaker was invisible, hidden by the four Arizona cypress trees shading the rear of the house that belonged with the shed. A few seconds later, a man walked between the trees. He wore a white T-shirt, blue sweatpants, black socks, and black slippers. He was gangly, bald, unshaven. His narrow face looked like a long crack in a crumbling adobe wall.

"Gathering up my belongings is all," I said.

"Something fall out the sky, did it? Land on my roof?"

I didn't see the rifle until he came closer. That changed everything. Rifles usually do. I had the pistol in one hand and the black bag in the other, and from his perspective, I can see where the rifle might've seemed essential.

"Hold on," I said. "I know what this looks like. But I left my bag up here, and that's all there is to this." That made no sense, of course. How do you leave a bag on a roof? But I was stalling for time and thought it'd be nice if he didn't shoot me.

He stepped closer and squinted up at me. "You a Red Sox fan?"

"No, I'm not a Red Sox fan."

He pointed with the rifle. "You got on that there Red Sox T-shirt."

"Oh." I'd forgotten I had it on. "It was in my drawer, that's all. I pitched a season for their AAA club in Pawtucket, Rhode Island."

"What a coincidence. Me too." He turned his head and squinted, watching me carefully. "My wife's inside on her laptop. You think I should have her call the police? Figure they might want to talk to a Red Sox fan with a gun standing on my roof for no good reason."

It had to be 130 degrees on that roof. The sweat ran down my back like a waterfall.

"First off, don't call me a fan," I said. "I don't like that word. I quit being a fan of any sports team a long time ago. I've seen too much."

"Right, when you were pitching in Pawtucket."

"Pawtucket and a lot of other places. I'm Whip Stark." There it was—the name bomb. If the planets were aligned, everything would click in his brain, and the problem would be solved.

"Very glad to know you, Whip Stark. I'm Walter Howell Pinckney, and I'm telling you not to move one inch too awful quick until I figure out what you're doing on my roof with a pistol. Who in the hell is Whip Stark?"

"I pitched in the big leagues. I pitched for the Tucson Thunder."

"I drove a truck cross-country. Got disability for my back. Thirty-one years."

"Will you put that gun down? You look twitchy."

"Not until you tell me why you're on my roof." Pinckney shouted to his wife. "Honey, we got Whip Stark on our roof! Says he's famous. What should I do?" She shouted something that I didn't hear and Pinckney said, "She don't know you either. The police are on the way."

That wasn't good. I was standing on a roof with a gun and what looked like a bag of drugs. "Why don't you tell your wife to type my name into her computer? Plenty of information will come up, pictures and everything. You'll see who I am."

The wife must've heard me. Before he could respond, she said something, and Pinckney said, "Mama's gonna look you up on the Google."

Sirens wailed in the distance and I realized I'd made a big mistake. She'd see the cocaine stories, and here I was on a roof with a suspicious white substance and a gun.

"We don't need the police," I said. "If you let me, I'll get off this roof and we can talk. I'll put this gun back in this bag, and we can meet properly. Like gentlemen."

Holding the gun by my fingertips, I dropped it into the bag and held my hands wide and backed away slowly. "Now take it easy, Mr. Pinckney," I said, and inched back to the edge of the roof. "You're not going to shoot me, are you?"

"I'm pondering that with all my mental faculties." He spoke over his shoulder to his wife again. "Honey, should I shoot this Red Sox fan?"

The wife shrieked a response that indicated she wasn't necessarily opposed to the idea.

Right then I heard a loud wolf whistle. It was Opal. She had raised her Tweety Bird T-shirt and pressed her big floppy breasts against the chain-link fence.

Walter Howell Pinkney's eyes popped, his face dissolving in shock. He looked like a man riding a high roller coaster in a lightning storm. Turning, he bellowed over his shoulder: "Better get out here, Mama!"

With his attention focused entirely on Opal, he couldn't have squeezed the trigger with the finger of Hercules. I could've line danced away and he wouldn't have noticed.

I jumped onto the hood of the Bronco, scrambled into the driver's seat, and fishtailed back to Opal, dragging a pile of dust with me. She was stuck to the fence showing Pinkney the goods and didn't look to be in any hurry to stop.

Leaning across the seat, I shoved open the passenger door. "Opal! Let's go!"

I whistled again and hit the horn. She stayed put. Another long horn blast got her away from the fence, and she jumped in. I booked it down the alley with Opal shrieking like a kid on a wild ride at Disneyland.

"Yeeee-hahhh! Did you see that? I bamboozled him good! I saved you!" She bounced in the seat. "Did you see that, Mr. Whip! Yeeee-hahhh!"

I tried to keep to the speed limit, and it wasn't easy with Opal having a seizure beside me. I got off the side streets and onto Speedway Boulevard and blended into the solid line of traffic.

"I can't catch my breath!" Opal said, fanning herself. She corkscrewed her shoulders, looked quickly behind us and back again. She buried her face in her hands. "I can't believe what just happened!"

"I can't either," I said. "That was fast thinking."

"I did good, didn't I, Mr. Whip?"

"You sure did."

"I saved you, didn't I?"

"Yes, yes, you saved me. Yes, you did."

FIFTY-ONE

I drove along, checking my mirrors to make sure we were clear of Walter Howell Pinckney and the police. Opal began to cry. I thought I should say something but couldn't think of anything. She reached over and grabbed my hand.

I said, "Why are you crying? I don't like it when a girl cries."

"I'm happy. I'm really happy."

"Well, then, you should be smiling. You're all mixed up." I squeezed her hand. "Come on, knock it off, okay? I've got to drive here. This traffic."

At that, her cry became a shoulder-shaking sob. I supposed they were tears of joy. She'd jumped into hot water to rescue me. She'd pulled one over on a world that didn't have much use for her, and that small triumph set off powerful emotions.

I pulled into the parking lot of a Taco Bell and waited, remembering the number of times I'd been in a Taco Bell parking lot with a woman crying in the seat beside me. I counted three.

Opal said, "I know I should've called you, but I just didn't. I don't know why!"

"Called me? What are you talking about?"

Two cop cars whizzed by, sirens wailing.

"When I went with the Gelmans."

"I don't care about that. Forget about that. Just quit blubbering."

Opal kept a tight grip on my hand. After a minute I said, "Okay, are we done now?"

She sniffed and wiped away tears. "I'm soaking wet. I'm drenched. I'm a girl all wet and crying in your car. I'm sorry. Do you have, like, a towel?" She snorted and laughed.

"Can I have my hand back?"

"Sorry, I forget stuff sometimes. I'm goofy today, Mr. Whip."

I grabbed the black bag out of the backseat and opened it. I peeled the cellophane off the white bar and manipulated it with my fingers. Breaking off a small piece, I could tell right away it wasn't cocaine. Being around Rolando had made me something of an expert.

I held the piece under my nose. No smell. Opal smelled it, too, and pressed it against her tongue, immediately pulling away.

"Tastes like cough medicine," she said, wrinkling her face. "We drank that stuff at school." She caught herself. "Some of my friends did anyways. Crazy, huh? What is it?"

"Dr. Melody's holy grail," I said, "I know a chemist who might be able to tell us exactly what this is. How about we go for a ride?"

We ate Taco Bell takeout as we went, and an hour later we were at Izzy Bonheimer's ranch on the backside of the Catalinas.

The sound of the Bronco nearing Bonheimer's electronic gate brought her hounds running. Opal spotted them and said, "Look at the beautiful animals!"

She was out of the Bronco and throwing a leg over the gate before I could stop her. The dogs growled and bared their teeth as Opal walked toward them. She didn't hesitate or show any fear, and when she got to them, she leaned down and petted them.

"Nice pooches!" she said. "Hello there, pooches! Nice pooches!"

The dogs danced at her feet, tails wagging. Opal sat on the ground, folded her legs underneath her, and played with them.

"Never seen that before."

The voice belonged to Bonheimer. She came around the side of the house wearing a blue railroad shirt that snapped up the front and had embroidered red roses above the chest pockets. She wore brown leather gloves and carried a gardening trowel.

"Did I tell you not to come back here?" She wiped her brow with her sleeve. "If I didn't, I have a feeling it was a mistake I'll regret the rest of my life."

I had the brick in my pocket. I peeled away the cellophane and took the portion I'd already broken off and held it up to her. "I'll pay you good money to tell me what this is." In my other hand, I held Melody's paper from Bunny's house. "And this. It's one of Dr. Melody's research papers. It might help you."

"You want to hire me?"

"That's right."

Opal and the dogs were cooing. Bonheimer looked at them with annoyance, pulled off her gloves and tucked them under her arm, and let out a shrill, two-fingered whistle. The dogs tucked their tails and ran back inside.

"Dr. Melody invented this, and he's on the run because of it," I said, and handed her the substance.

She made no move to take it. "Arthur referred to a gum he was working on, but that's the limit of my knowledge. As I said, he didn't discuss his project with me, and I had no part in creating it."

"It might have to do with steroids, something to juice up an athlete. Do you know about steroidal saponins?"

She looked at me with perfect disgust. "I know about everything, Whip Stark."

Holding the substance close to her, I said, "Please. Dr. Melody's life could depend on it."

Sighing, Bonheimer grabbed it and inspected it with genuine curiosity, as if seeing it for the first time. She rubbed the tips of her fingers over the smooth white surface and sniffed them, rubbed again, and touched her fingertips to her tongue.

As she did that, I checked the back bumper of the white Lincoln for a glue outline. Nothing. Clean as could be. It looked like the car belonged to her, not Melody.

I handed her the six pages of Melody's research and she took it. All I had in my wallet was sixty dollars. I should've stopped on the way to get more cash. I handed her the money anyway.

"You've already taken up more than sixty dollars of my time," Bonheimer said.

With her newfound confidence, Opal stepped forward. "What about this?" She pulled the Gelman roll from her pocket and handed it to Bonheimer. "Is this enough?"

Bonheimer snatched it away. Her fingers did a dance number with the bills as her eyes ballooned.

"Wait a minute," I said. "That has to be a thousand dollars. We should negotiate a price."

"We just did," Bonheimer said, flipping through the bills. "What a coincidence. This is the exact amount I had in mind."

Opal put her hands in her pockets and beamed. She'd rescued me again.

I said to Bonheimer, "I need this as soon as you can do it."

"It'll take several days at least."

"How about tomorrow?"

Bonheimer let out a cackling laugh that sounded like fine crystal shattering. "I've got to clear brush out of the creek or the next rain will wash me away. Four days."

"Dangerous men are hunting that stuff," I said. "You need to keep your wits."

She gazed at the solitude of the mountains, unbroken in every direction. "Who the hell's going to bother me out here, the birdies?" She turned and walked back to the house, wiggling four bony fingers over her shoulder.

"Four days, Whip Stark."

FIFTY-TWO

Monsoon storms stayed away the next two days, enough time for the ground to dry out on Paradise Mountain. I drove back up there to look for Rolando's hand, and Cash came too. He was still wobbly from his wound but tired of sitting around. He had a white bandage around his head and looked like the flute player from the famous Revolutionary War painting.

Even if Angel had tossed the hand into the well as he claimed, Roscoe Rincon had likely removed it by now. But I had to check for myself. And I wanted to look for Angel or his remains, if it worked out that way.

If he had somehow made it through the flood, he was my best chance of finding Rolando.

But the flood had boosted the water level to almost overflowing, and there was nothing to see but floating debris.

We drove into Crooked Canyon, both of us hanging out the windows for any sign of Angel. Not far along, the road disappeared, replaced by tossed boulders, tree branches sticking out of the ground, and sand berms sloping against the rock walls on either side.

We got out and walked another half mile or so. Cash kept his eyes mostly on the top of the canyon. But when he spotted something colorful in the debris, he kicked at the ground, thinking it might be his lost hat.

"You're making me crazy with this hat business," I said.

"My mom told me when you find a hat that fits good, you're living life."

"Your mom said that? Well, okay, then. Why didn't you say so?"

"She stood six foot four. Could clean out the gutters with just a folding chair."

"She sounds like a wonderful woman."

Cash bent over to pull at a debris pile. "Weighed ninety-seven pounds with Johnnie Walker in one pocket and Smith & Wesson in the other."

"I know a bigwig at Arizona Feeds," I said. "I'll get you a brand-new hat. How's that?"

"For real? Man, that pleases my heart."

Looking for human remains was a grim business, and nothing came of it. That was the way the whole case was going. Rolando's hand was gone, Angel was gone, and when we got back to Double Wide and I called Roxy for a morning update, she still had nothing to report on Roscoe Rincon.

This was my day to visit Sam and after that, I had a meeting with Micah Alan Gabriel. Before Roxy and I finished up, she said her time at Skin had produced a lead, and she wanted me to meet her there on the way home from the jail. We set a time.

I ate lunch, tuna on toast with an apple and lemonade, and I could barely finish. I lit a cigar and stepped outside with Chico bouncing at my heels.

My mind kept circling through the case and stopping on Detective Benny Diaz.

With Rolando's hand in my freezer, I had good reason to keep him at bay. But why now? Rolando's hand was gone, and with Angel talking, I knew who killed Carlos Alvarez and probably Rolando. If I brought Diaz in on the Alvarez murder, he might turn up something on Rolando's whereabouts.

I called him and got his message. "I've got a name for you. Roscoe Rincon. He killed Carlos Alvarez. Call me back."

My cigar was still burning when George Jones sang "He Stopped Loving Her Today." Diaz didn't bother with hello. "I looked up this Rincon. He's in the system. How do you know he killed Alvarez?"

"I'll give you the information, but I can't tell you my informant's name. It has to be confidential." The odds told me that Angel was likely dead. But if he turned up alive, I didn't want him and Diaz connecting in any way. I couldn't trust the kid to keep his mouth shut about the hand.

"Fine. Everybody has confidential informants these days." He cleared his throat. "Let's see. Rincon's with the Sinaloa Cartel. On the heroin side, a serious player. Thirty-one years of age, five foot six, two hundred and twenty-five pounds. Born, Culiacan, Sinaloa, Mexico."

He read the information in rote tones, sipping a drink between starts.

"Arrested multiple times. A DUI, two ag assaults in Phoenix. Sat for eight months on the first one, four years on the second. The guy's painted like a peacock. Tats on his neck and arms. He's got these weird eyes. Like a cat's."

"Color?"

"It says here brown, but there's a note about them maybe being red. I'm not sure what that means. Nickname *Rojo*."

"Send me the booking mug." I knew it was Rincon, but I wanted to see his face.

"It's law enforcement sensitive, Whip."

"Don't bust on me, Detective. You wouldn't have the name at all if I hadn't told you."

"Okay, but only because of your father. By the way, I need to talk to you about that. Hang on." For a full minute, I listened to rustling sounds, Diaz breathing, items being moved around. "By the way, did I ever tell you that your dad tried to convince me to get a PhD instead of going to the academy?"

"Sounds like him."

"He almost had me. It's hard to say no to your dad."

Another silence. Diaz hummed a number from the musical *La La Land*. Something tells me he would've been well suited to Shakespeare work.

I heard computer keys clicking and then: "There you go, Whip. Mug's on the way."

A few seconds later, my phone chirped. The sound made my nerves sizzle as I remembered that night on Paradise Mountain. Even under the glare of the photographer's light, Rincon's face was dark and bleak. There was no mercy in that face, only a savage glare in those strange eyes.

"Whip, are you there?"

"Yeah, yeah, I'm here. You were going to say something about Sam?"

"Get yourself another lawyer," Diaz said. "That fellow you hired isn't up to the job, Micah Alan Gabriel. Cops know the best defense lawyers, and Gabriel's not one of them. He used to be a trip-and-fall guy and decided he wanted to be a top-notch defense attorney."

"You're trying to help me out now?"

"Like I said, your father was special to me."

FIFTY-THREE

I left for Phoenix at nine o'clock in the morning. The Gelmans wanted Opal to sketch for them for a few days, so I dropped her at the Arizona Inn and got to the jail at eleven o'clock. They brought me into the same depressing room, and I talked to Sam across the same depressing table.

He was restless—kept looking over his shoulder at the guard and rubbing his calves—and when I asked how he was doing, he wouldn't answer.

"They're watching me, Prospero."

"Who's watching you?"

"The guards."

"This is a jail, Sam."

He sat forward, hunched and whispering: "They've taken everything away from me. My toothbrush." His eyes rounded in outrage. "My books! I've never lived without books! Prospero, I'm half a man!"

"That's crap. I'll talk to somebody."

Sam ran his finger back and forth under his nose, and dried it on his pant leg. He rubbed his calves again and turned and eyeballed the guard and wiped his running nose again.

"Sam, Sam, look at me. How many no-hitters did I throw? Do you remember?"

He once told me that watching me play ball as a kid was the happiest time of his life. He liked talking about it, liked the warm memories of those nights at the ballpark. I thought if I could tap into that feeling, it might bring him back, if only for a moment.

"Sam! Sam! Don't you remember?"

He stared right through me.

"Do you still have all my game balls at home? In your sock drawer? The coach signed every one of them. Remember that, Sam?"

His eyes were frozen and impenetrable, and I knew why. Rubbing his calves and the runny nose were symptoms of withdrawal. They'd blocked his access to heroin and that was good, but taking away his books was like depriving him of oxygen.

The meeting was short. I was the one who cut it off. I couldn't stand what I was seeing, this man who'd been so engaged and lively reduced to a semihuman emptiness in an orange jumpsuit.

On the way out, I said to the guard, "Why'd you people take away his books?"

The guard looked startled. "They do different things around here. You want I should ask somebody?"

I decided to take the matter up with Gabriel and found him at Nora's, a breakfast and lunch spot around the corner from the jail. The floor was uneven, the linoleum rotting. He sat with his chair against the wall. I was surprised that my legs carried me over to him. I wanted to see him as much as I wanted to set foot in that jail again.

He didn't get up, didn't shake hands. He wore a blue checked shirt. Under the table, I saw a white linen pant leg and one shoe, a suede loafer.

"I'm getting the chicken-fried steak," he said. "I highly recommend it." He had a superior attitude. He was slumming and wanted to make sure I knew it.

He ordered the chicken-fried steak. I got the same and couldn't eat. The waitress had cherry-red lipstick and called us "boys." Her nametag said Bree. She had a swaying walk that used every part of her body and very much interested Gabriel. His eyes tracked her around the room. She wasn't particularly attractive, but waitresses don't need to be.

"I just came from Sam," I said. "He needs his books back. The withdrawal's killing him."

"I know. I'm monitoring it."

"Monitoring it? What about treatment? You asked the court about getting him treatment."

"I'm expecting a ruling any day. These things take time, Stark."

That felt like a brushoff, and I considered firing him right there. He wouldn't have cared, and that was the main reason I didn't. He showed a confidence I hadn't seen before, and I liked that.

"You're going to win this thing, right?" I said.

"I never predict juries, but I like the way this sets up."

"You still can't find the murder weapon?"

"Gone." Gabriel was leaning forward holding the chicken-fried steak with two hands, chewing. "If my guy can't find it, it's gone. Forget the knife. My strategy is one juror."

The ceiling fan over our table hung loose in its housing, turning with a rhythmic *fahtink-wump, fahtink-wump, fahtink-wump.* Gabriel saw me looking at it and said, "That thing comes down, it's a hell of a tort," and laughed out of the side of his mouth.

Bree caught the exchange. It reminded her she was hot. She stuck out her bottom lip and blew the bangs off her forehead.

With his eyes set on her, Gabriel wiped his mouth with a napkin and said, "There's not one shred of evidence proving that Sam Houston Stark committed that violent act. If he murdered her in that apartment, his blood, his DNA, would be everywhere in there. You know what police found? A couple fingerprints. Nothing more."

Hunched forward, still staring at Bree: "But there was a second blood type found in the apartment. Whose was it? I'll tell you whose, the killer's." He slurped his drink through the straw and held up a lone finger. "One juror. That's my strategy."

It sounded like Gabriel had worked on his closing. I didn't know much about the law, but his legal reasoning made sense to me.

"Okay, let's do this," I said.

"I have a good feeling." He eyed my chicken-fried steak. "Are you going to eat that?" He held up his glass and shook the ice. "More Coke, Bree, darling?"

FIFTY-FOUR

Back in town, I stopped at the Arizona Feeds store off Interstate 10 and picked up a new hat for Cash. It was green with a white square on the front, with the word "Arizona" in the square and "Feeds" in green. Spiffy, with that out-of-the box smell.

I met Roxy at Skin at 3:50 p.m., ten minutes early. She was parked back from the front door between two other cars. I pulled up next to her and got into the Audi. She looked awful and knew it. Hangover.

I said, "You look radiant today."

She gave me a sneering look. She pointed out the windshield toward the club. "I want you to get a look at somebody. Name is Mace Finch. His shift starts at four."

"What's he do?"

"You might say he's in human resources."

"Bouncer?"

"Correct. He keeps the drunks off the girls."

A red Jeep Cherokee rolled into the lot and parked outside Skin. A man stepped out and Roxy pointed. "He's early."

The man probably stood six foot five. He had a crew cut, a drill instructor's block face, a bandage on his left bicep, and legs from the elephant enclosure. He yawned, closed the Cherokee door with his knee, and walked with his head down into the club. Definitely on his way to work.

"Recognize him?" Roxy said.

"Should I?"

"See the bandage on his arm? He's got scars on his neck too. I'm thinking this is the guy you maliciously attacked with one of our protected native plants."

"It was clever. MacGyver did stuff like that."

"Great show. Great show."

We sat quietly, staring out the windshield at Skin's front door.

Roxy said, "After you jabbed Finch in the neck at Melody's, he went to Double Wide and got himself shot by your inscrutable sidekick, Cashmere Miller. What do you think—same guy?"

"I can't tell. Happened fast."

A car arrived, and two girls hopped out and went inside the club. They had ponytails and wore sneakers and sweatpants and carried gear bags. Dancers.

"Tamara and Lily," Roxy said. "I've been spending time here, keeping my eyes open. I hope Lily's mom's out of the hospital."

I looked over at Roxy. She shrugged. "What? It's hard to go to work without a sitter."

She surprised me again. Maybe there was a human heart beating in there after all.

I said, "Let's go inside and have a look at this guy. It might jog my memory."

"That's the thing—it's tricky. It's dark in there, and you'd have to get real close. You might not remember him, but he'll remember you. How he reacts will answer the question, but how he reacts also might require police protection."

"You mean if he wants to beat the crap out of me?"

"Like I said, tricky."

The afternoon shadows crawled across the parking lot. The day was ending, but the heat still rose off the hot top in violent waves. We sat thinking things over as the Audi's air conditioner blew a gale.

After a moment, Skin's front door opened, and Mace Finch walked out with a man trailing him.

"Wait a minute," Roxy said. "What have we here?"

The second man was Ed Bolt. I asked Roxy if she'd seen Bolt at Skin before. She hadn't.

I said, "First we find out Mayflower's connected to the smugglers on Paradise Mountain, and now we learn he's connected to Skin too. What does it mean?"

"Don't know." Seconds later: "Money laundering?"

"Did you find out who owns this place?"

"It's under a corporate shell to hide the real owner. The name is 56 Enterprises."

I smacked the dashboard in excitement. "That's Mayflower. Mayflower owns this place."

"How do you figure?"

"Joe DiMaggio. Mayflower's a DiMaggio freak. His fifty-six-game hitting streak is the longest in major league history."

Roxy nodded. "Not bad, Phenom. I might have to rethink my opinion of you as a detective."

FIFTY-FIVE

Finch and Bolt drove off in the red Cherokee, and we followed. They headed north on Kino Boulevard through the center of town, past the sprawling red-brick sameness of the university. We made our way to Oracle Road and north on Oracle past the strip-mall glitter.

The late-day traffic was thick, which should make it easier to run a tail—unless the subject gets through an intersection and you get the red light. That changes the game.

Roxy stayed two cars back as we neared the Tucson Mall. But at times we got caught in the flow, moved to where we didn't want to be, and landed right on the Cherokee's bumper. That's another problem.

"You're making me nervous," I said. "Do you even know how to tail people?"

At a red light, with the Cherokee right in front of us, I put Cash's hat on and lowered it to shield my face. "Fall back a few cars, will you."

Roxy looked over at me. "That's the stupidest hat ever. Arizona Feeds?"

"They're running a special on goose pellets."

We began the climb into the foothills. Finch was really pushing it, jumping in and out of lanes to get ahead. Roxy stayed with him until she got caught behind a furniture truck struggling to make the grade. By then, the Cherokee was well ahead of the truck and zipping out of sight.

"Hop around him," I said. "Come on—go around."

"Take it easy, will you? Finch isn't going anywhere."

"You have no idea what you're doing. Go around him."

"Jesus Christ!" Roxy zipped into the right lane and was blocked again, this time by a passenger van with disabled plates. She gave a hearty laugh. "See those plates? Those plates aren't going anywhere."

"Hit the horn. He'll speed up."

"Disabled plates slow down when you beep. He's already had the big one and ain't gonna chance another."

A car pulled up behind the moving truck and boxed us.

"We're losing him!" I said. "You don't know what you're doing!"

"Hey, I've followed more men in my dating life than most cops do in a career. Watch and see how this is done."

She jerked the wheel left, shooting the Audi into the space between the truck and the van. It was a video game move. She might've had enough room left over to fit a dollar bill front and back. Gunning it, she roared ahead and cut off two more cars to bring us within sight of the Cherokee again.

We stayed on him north of the city. It wasn't hard to figure out that Finch was going to Izzy Bonheimer's ranch. I'd been to Aunt Izzy's twice, once already that day, and wasn't followed either time.

How'd Bolt find out about her?

Easy. He visited Annie Patterson again and wasn't polite this time. He probably threatened her, saying he wasn't going to leave until she gave him something. She told him of my visit and about Melody's mentor, the famous chemist living in the remote mountains at Blue Lonesome Ranch.

I told Roxy what we were driving into and she suggested calling the Pinal County Sheriff to have a deputy meet us there, which I did. I wished I had my Glock. On a hunch, I opened Roxy's glove box and found a Colt .380 Mustang with a pink grip.

"How'd I know you'd have a piece in your glove?" I said.

"This is Arizona. It's required by law."

The Audi banged and bottomed through the forest. A hundred yards short of the ranch house, with the road worsening and the car sounding like it was on its last axle, Roxy had had enough and pulled over.

I handed her the Colt. She ejected the clip to make sure it was loaded and expertly palmed it back in as two gunshots sounded up ahead, shattering the mountain quiet.

We jumped out and ran toward the house.

FIFTY-SIX

We hadn't gone far when Ed Bolt turned a bend in the road and ran toward us on his cartoon legs. He had to have seen me, but he didn't slow down or alter his course in the slightest. At the last second, I stepped aside and landed a hard left on the point of his chin and knocked him down.

But Bolt could take a punch. He was almost on his feet again as the momentum of my shoulders spun me all the way around, and on the return pass, I rammed my elbow into his nose.

He went down a second time, the back of his head banging against the ground. He shook his head to shoo away the hornets, but that forced blood from his nostrils. He rolled onto his side, choking and spitting.

"Get up, munchkin," I said. "We're going to have a conversation."

Bolt's eyes looked like they wanted out of their sockets. Blood pooled over his acne scars and sweat leaked everywhere. His face was a landfill. He could barely speak loud enough to be heard, but he managed to throat out his most articulate objection: "Fuck you, meat!"

Roxy stuck the Colt against his neck. "Your language is atrocious." She grabbed him by the shoulder. "Up you go, hard case. We're going to go talk to the nice lady."

At the ranch we found Aunt Izzy standing by the big oak tree at the back of her house. She had a revolver in one hand and a garden spade in the other. Mace Finch sat on the ground at her feet. A welt blossomed on his left hand and another bled on his cheek. We sat Bolt down next to Finch.

"They busted my kitchen door," Bonheimer said. "Won't do that again. Two warning shots and a swing of my trusty shovel, two burglars down." She pointed beyond the house and said to Roxy, "I've got rope in my shed back there. Would you mind tying these two clowns to my tree?"

Roxy fetched the rope and got to work. Bonheimer stood over her, breathing rapidly and holding the pistol in her still-shaking hand. She pointed with it as she gave directions. "A little tighter in the chest. Good and tight now. There you go."

The gun had Roxy's attention. She said to Bonheimer, "It sure looks like you know how to take care of yourself. Would you mind showing me what you did?"

Bonheimer beamed at the idea of recounting her heroism. She walked us to the open kitchen door. The small windowpane nearest the doorknob had been shattered. Bonheimer stood up straight and paused to ensure that our attention was only on her as she regaled us with the details of her brave stand.

She gave her rendition all the theater she could muster, waving the pistol around like a stage prop. "I keep my gardening tools and handgun right by my door here. As you can see, it was bad news for those buzzards."

"They're lucky to be alive," Roxy said, and carefully took the pistol from Bonheimer's hand. She didn't seem to notice. A holster and cartridge belt hung on a hook behind the door. Roxy returned the gun to the holster and asked for a glass of water.

That pulled Bonheimer farther from the gun. At the sink she drew a glass of water for Roxy, and another for herself and sat at the table.

"I presume those fellows were here about Dr. Melody's work," Bonheimer said. "My protégé seems to have generated quite a bit of interest, although I can't understand why."

She sipped her water. Blotches of red returned to her face and her hand had steadied. "That paper Arthur wrote about the Palmer agave is pure hooey. Not one thing in there makes sense chemically and Arthur had to know it. I taught him too well to make those mistakes."

"What about the gum? Did you study the gum?"

Without a word, she got up and walked into an adjoining room and returned with a piece of the gum in a circular glass container. It looked about half the size of the piece I'd given her. She unscrewed the top and removed the gum with two fingers. "Chew this."

I hesitated.

"Go on. Unless today's my lucky day, it won't kill you."

I popped the gum into my mouth and chewed like it was a piece of Wrigley's spearmint. Immediately, I felt the weight of the released liquid. Extremely thick, bitter, almost metallic.

Bonheimer said, "That taste you're getting is from the agave— the leaf sap, to be precise. The dosage has to be tiny or you'd be retching. Lovely, isn't it? Rather like ass after a day at the beach."

I could've asked, but I'm not a fool. "Can you make a performance-enhancing drug out of this stuff?"

She twisted her mouth in thought. "In a gum? I wouldn't think so." She held out her palm for me to spit the gum into it. I hesitated again and she grew impatient. "I haven't got forever."

I spat.

Bonheimer held the gleaming wet blob in front of her face, examining it with one eye closed like a jeweler with a rare diamond. "I can't rule anything out, steroid or otherwise. Whatever its purpose, finding the Palmer was Arthur's first challenge. It requires specific conditions to thrive, the most prominent being elevation. We only find it at a set elevation."

"I'm guessing right around forty-eight hundred feet?" That was the elevation atop Paradise Mountain. I told her about seeing men hauling agave leaves and hearts out of the mine drift.

"I'd say they had a harvesting operation going on," Bonheimer said. "To create what, I can't say. All I can tell you is don't confine your thinking. The chemicals we're extracting from the agave can have a range of impacts, some quite profound."

"Profound how? Psychedelic?"

She threw me a surprised glance. "I see you're familiar with my work. Yes, psychedelic is one possibility. You also have industrialists looking for a next-generation superlubricant using this very same Palmer sap. Some of the world's biggest corporations are chasing that particular Bigfoot and the winner promises to reap a fortune.

"My point is, Whip Stark, the Palmer is a powerhouse, a true force of nature. But I'll need more time to understand exactly what Arthur was up to."

FIFTY-SEVEN

I didn't want to leave Bolt and Finch alone for long and started back outside. At the kitchen door, I heard Finch speaking to Bolt and stopped to listen.

Finch said, "You say the Mexicans are gonna handle this on their end, right, Eddie?"

Bolt said, "The job might already be done. Keep your voice down."

Finch said, "Okay, then, what're we doing breaking windows in Timbuktu for?"

Bolt said, "We do what Maxy tells us. Keep your mouth shut anyways, you want a job."

But Mace Finch wasn't done: "I'm tired of doing Max Mayflower's dirty work. I got shot, stabbed, and hit with a garden tool! I'm tired of it, Eddie!"

"You're not tired of nothing. Shut up!"

"I'm done with you and Max Mayflower. I quit. Jesus has other plans for me."

"Jesus? Jesus don't care one shit for you!" Bolt's voice was a growling whisper.

"I quit drinking," Finch said. "You didn't know that, did you, Eddie? I'm taking a Bible class. I'm studying the Bible."

"An old lady hit you with a tiny shovel. How about you start drinking again?"

"Two nights a week. We say our prayers, have donuts."

"Shut the fuck up!"

I grabbed Roxy. We left Bonheimer in the kitchen and Roxy untied Finch except for his wrists. She handed me the Colt, and I held the gun against his spine and walked him away from the house and down the road a short way.

With his hands tied and his back against the tree, Bolt screamed: "Shut up, Macey! Don't say nothing! Don't you dare!"

I had half of the white brick in my pocket. As soon as we got out of sight, I stepped close to Finch and held it to his face. "You're here because of this, right, Mace? I need to know what it is. You help me out and I'll talk to the old lady about easing up on the burglary charges."

"I ain't supposed to talk. Eddie Bolt said so and he's my master, my wonderful counselor." His face twisted in revulsion. "Screw Eddie Bolt."

I stand six foot two and had to look up at Finch. He had a wide flat face and small eyes without much in them.

"Does the name Rolando Molina mean anything to you, Mace? He's dead, killed because of Dr. Melody's invention. He was my friend."

Finch looked away. Blood ran down his cheek from where Bonheimer had thumped it.

"I knew his family and his parents, and his body's missing," I said. "I need to find him and see that he gets a decent burial. You can understand that, can't you, Mace?"

Finch shrugged his enormous shoulders. He couldn't look at me.

I moved so close to him that the brim of my Arizona Feeds hat practically touched his chin. "You've fallen off the path of righteousness, Mace. I know what that's like. There's only one way to get back on and that's to tell the truth."

He stared as if seeing me for the first time, a softness entering his voice: "You read the good book?"

"Every night."

"I like Corinthians best of all."

"It shows me the path, brother." Truth was, I was reading James M. Cain. His path led to an entirely different place.

Finch studied the mountains, a large, confused, bleeding man with breath like a Teamster. He sniffed hard. "Cartel business is cartel business, and they don't tell me nothing."

"But like you say, you hear things."

"What I hear is there's nothing to find. Okay? That Mexican, the one honchos the trade down there, he chops up his enemies and burns up what's left. That's what he done to your friend, made little pieces of him. Sorry, man, but the wind's got him."

Made little pieces out of him.

Roscoe Rincon. An icy hand crept through my body.

"You got a name?"

"I don't know no names. But *Rojo's* what they call him. For his eyes."

"I promised Rolando's father I'd find his body, Mace. His family's heartbroken."

"Man," Finch said, dragging out the word. "I don't know where all he's at. That's their business and I stay out." He rolled his head, the neck bones crunching like a bag of chips. His face told me he wanted to say more.

"It's just me, you, and the sky, Mace. You know something."

"There's more killing coming and I can't be part of it. You need to do something, Stark. It's gonna happen. Down in Mexico, they're gonna kill somebody, and you don't have a lot of time. I swear on the Holy Bible, Stark, that's all I know."

A sheriff's cruiser arrived. Bonheimer wanted to press charges, and the deputy cuffed Bolt and Finch and took our statements.

The Mexican had to be Fausto Molina. I broke away and called him, but the call didn't go through. Roxy and I ran back to the Audi. The whole way I kept punching redial, desperate to get a signal.

FIFTY-EIGHT

As Roxy rolled down the mountain on that terrible road, the Audi made noises normally associated with tank warfare. The call finally connected and Fausto's cell jumped to voice mail. I called the office of the Monterrey Sultans and got their recorded message. The team was playing at home against the Mexico City Reds and was on the field. Walk-up tickets still available.

The Mexicans are going to handle this on their end.

Roscoe Rincon's crew was getting rid of any evidence that could hang them. They killed Rolando. They stole the hand. They killed Carlos Alvarez and Rosa Lopez. Anyone who got out of line was dead.

Mayflower's job was to retrieve Dr. Melody's gum, whatever it was. That's what brought Bolt to Bunny's house, and it brought Bolt and Finch to Double Wide and the Blue Lonesome.

The job might already be done.

For Mayflower and Rincon, Fausto was a key tentacle.

I called the team office again and someone picked up. I said I needed to talk to Fausto Molina. The man said he was in the dugout and couldn't be reached until after the game. He was about to hang up when I said, "I'm Max Mayflower, and this is urgent."

"Mr. Mayflower, I didn't know it was you, sir. I'm so sorry. How can I help, sir?"

I told him to give me the number of the clubhouse and bring Fausto in from the dugout and that I'd call back in five minutes.

Roxy retrieved her bottle of Chivas out of the console and sipped it as we drove through the sleeping town of Oracle.

"They kill baseball players, don't they?" she said. "Wasn't that a song?"

"I think it was piano players."

"Piano players, ballplayers, they kill 'em all."

I called the Monterrey clubhouse and Fausto picked up. He spoke rapidly: "Mr. Mayflower, I didn't tell anybody, I swear."

"Tell anybody what, Fausto?"

Slowly, his voice full of suspicion: "Who...who is this?"

"You'll talk to Max Mayflower but not me?" I said. "I've called you five times and you haven't called back. What's going on?"

"I can't talk now, Prop. I should be out in the dugout."

"What haven't you told anybody?"

"All I know is *El Bailador*'s dead and I can't get anybody out." Ever since Rolando left, Fausto's performance had tanked. He'd lost the strike zone and was constantly pitching from behind, giving up home runs in bunches.

"There are things you don't understand, Prop."

"What don't I understand? Tell me what I don't understand."

"I need Rolando. What he brought. The help he gave me."

"That doesn't matter now," I said. "It looks like Rolando was involved in a smuggling operation up here involving this gum Dr. Arthur Melody made. What do you know about that?"

He didn't answer.

"Fausto?"

"I'm not even supposed to talk to you."

My voice shot out fast and angry. "You listen to me. Your big brother's dead and Mayflower's part of the conspiracy that killed him. Do you understand that? Who the hell are you loyal to anyway?"

"I don't know. I don't *know!*"

"Look, some men are coming to see you and not to talk. They're Sinaloa people. You know the name Roscoe Rincon? They call him *Rojo*."

Fausto gasped.

"Yeah, that's right," I said. "It looks like he killed Rolando and he's coming your way. You need to get out of there right now. Is there any place you can hide out?"

I waited. The silence persisted until I realized there was nothing connecting us but dead air. Fausto had hung up. I punched in the clubhouse number again, and it rang and rang.

It was just after 8:40 p.m. Roxy drove along Highway 77. We were quiet. Only the rumble of the Audi's engine broke the night silence.

The darkness was complete until we came even with Biosphere II, set off in the desert to the south—and how perfect was that. A bazillion-dollar monument to getting out of town for a few days. Way out.

The Biosphere was built by a moon-bat with a portfolio who thought the planet was washed up and it was time to put on spacesuits and go populate a new one. That was what I wanted right then, a long trip in a crash-proof helmet. To a destination untraceable, and far, far away.

The unconscious mind works in strange ways, entirely independent of the conscious mind. It grinds away and delivers its conclusions at unpredictable times.

Into my mind popped something Aunt Izzy had said.

A next-generation superlubricant.

Made from the Palmer agave.

Her words skipped past me at the time, but as I stared out the window at the lights of the Biosphere, I knew.

"Shit, Rox! Goddamn, that's it! Son of a bitch!"

She gave me an amused look. "You explain things with such precision."

"Hold on," I said and grabbed my phone and called Oscar Molina in Obregon. He answered on the first ring. I told him to drop whatever he was doing, drive to Monterrey, get Fausto, and bring him to Tucson. And I told him why, leaving nothing out.

Roxy overheard and pounded the steering wheel. "Are you kidding me? That's the holy grail! Are you kidding me?"

I said to Oscar, "If you have to hit him on the head and toss him into your truck, he has to get out of Monterrey tonight."

Oscar didn't hesitate or ask any questions. He said he was on his way, but the drive was more than six hundred miles and would take time. He promised to keep in contact, and we broke off.

"Change in plans, Rox. We're going to Hi Corbett Field. Step on it."

"I'm going as fast as I can. What a story!"

"I can't believe I didn't see this earlier. Every pitcher in history has tried this."

I checked my watch—8:57 p.m. "If we hurry, Danny Wilson should still be there."

The Audi's high beams sliced through the darkness as Roxy sped around the end of the Catalina Mountains and down into the valley.

FIFTY-NINE

The game was over by the time we got to the ballpark. The parking lot was nearly empty, but Wilson was still in his office. He sat behind his desk looking over the night's gate receipts. He didn't look happy. Then again, if you see an ex-ballplayer looking happy behind a desk, he was never any good in the first place.

He glanced up without expression as Roxy and I walked in and motioned with a tired hand to his chewing-out chairs.

"I hear Fausto's gone in the tank," I said.

"His ball has completely flattened out. Looks like the dancer has quit dancing."

"Any idea why?"

"The kid was riding a hot streak." Wilson rocked his head. "Hot streaks end."

On the wall behind the desk was a picture of a young Danny Wilson in a mound conference with Hall of Fame pitcher Greg Maddox. Another showed him in civilian clothes, sitting in an empty stadium next to Hank Aaron.

"How about handing over your scouting video of Fausto. I'm going down to Mexico to help him out."

If my request produced any shock or panic, Wilson didn't show it. He leaned back and parked his boat shoes on the corner of his desk. "You're too late, Whip. Mayflower came and took it. Yeah, he bailed on Fausto. He's walking away from his hot prospect."

"Let me see the video, Danny. Maybe I can spot something."

"I told you, Mayflower took it."

"You didn't keep a copy?"

"Mayflower came here six days ago demanding I delete it from my computer. And any copies. He was waiting for me first thing in the morning. He's freaking out over Fausto's collapse. All that money he planned on making, forget it."

Six days ago. That made it the day after Roxy and I confronted Max Mayflower at his front door. It looked like we'd sent him into a panic, after which he squealed to Roscoe Rincon about the hand and threatened Fausto to keep his mouth shut.

Wilson said, "He stood over me and watched as I deleted it. Can you believe that jerk?"

"I take it you did what you were told," I said, "like a good boy?"

Wilson swung his legs off the desk and leaned forward, face flushed. "Fuck Max Mayflower. That's the first thing. Second, I already had it copied on a flash." Wilson reached into his pocket and held up a flash drive. "I'll show it to you or anybody wants to see it. Rox, you want to put it on TV tonight? Go ahead. I'm done doing what Max Mayflower wants."

"It's easy now, Danny," I said. "With the Fausto project falling apart, you have nothing to lose anymore."

Wilson popped the flash into his computer and glared at me. "I'm showing you the video, Whip. Just what the fuck is it you want me to do?"

He breathed heavily and said, "I'm working my tail off to keep the lights on here. We drew one thousand, seven hundred, and twenty-three people tonight. Is HBO running some hot new series on girls in jail? Who doesn't want to come to the ballpark? Dollar beer night and we pull in one thousand, seven hundred, and twenty-three people. Tell me what I'm supposed to do, give it away? Let people belly up to the taps for free? Swear to God, this country is done!"

He went back to looking at his computer screen. "You want a drink while you watch?"

Roxy got herself a Snapple from Wilson's minifridge. He began the video. I watched it carefully, Wilson less so. He'd probably seen it a thousand times already.

Fausto was a tall righty with long legs, strong thighs, and a lean build. He had a straight-out front-leg kick that almost put his knee in his mouth and brought the leg down in a long, falling stride driven mainly by his thighs.

The delivery ended with his weight carrying him toward the plate, the fingers of his right hand nearly touching the ground and his rear leg bent at the knee and high in the air. He threw a first-pitch strike for the setup.

Then he delivered one inside and one outside to establish both sides of the plate, and with two strikes he dropped the bomb, *El Bailador.*

After that Gumby windup, the ball stayed hidden for a long time, making it hard for the batter to pick up before it exploded out of his hand. It looked like a fastball until it was too late. The batter got steak-dinner eyes before the pitch dropped like a stone.

"I understand why you love this kid," I said. "Tell me what you see, Danny?"

"Asses in the seats."

"I mean from Fausto."

"What I'm saying. A dominating seventeen-year-old with that stuff, a handsome kid—you kidding me? He'd sell lots of tickets."

"Steps off the mound a lot, right? Licks his fingers?"

Wilson gave me a fast look. "What of it? It's legal."

"Have you ever seen a baseball move like *El Bailador*?"

"Pedro Martinez. His slider was lights out." Wilson wrinkled his face to help round up more names. "Today you've got Clayton Kershaw. Kershaw's an animal. I could see this kid right up there with Kershaw and so could Mayflower. That's why he was all over him."

"That's one reason."

Wilson folded his hands in his lap. He knew I knew El *Bailador* was a spitball, a doctored pitch. But he was going to string out the revelation, I suppose out of self-respect or simple stubbornness. Knowing Danny, I voted for the latter.

He climbed slowly out of his chair and went to his little refrigerator and pulled out a can of Diet Coke. He splashed it open, hurried to suck up the volcano of foam, took a long sip as he stood beside his desk, let out an equally long "Ahhhh," and sat down again.

Wilson put his fist against his lips, burped silently and said, "I get the distinct impression something's on your mind, Whip. Let's get to it."

SIXTY

I pulled Dr. Melody's gum out of my pocket and dropped it on his desk. Wilson stared at it, his face smoothing and relaxing as the tension ran out of it. He looked happy that the project was exposed. He sat with his palms flat on his desk for a moment, and then grabbed the brick.

"This the stuff Fausto was using?" Wilson snorted, frowned, and shook his head.

"Danny, man, how could you not suspect something?"

He put the brick down and sipped his Coke. "I knew they had a project going. Mayflower kept coming here wanting to use the field. Had a pitcher with him, a Golden League washout named Will Evers."

"What about a guy in his sixties, looks like he should be loading up at the buffet at Furr's?"

"Him too."

"That's Dr. Arthur Melody, the inventor. You never asked what they were doing?"

"Not one time," Wilson said, and stared into space.

"How about when you watched Fausto pitch in Mexico? Didn't you pick up anything?"

"Mayflower told me to forget it. I had my suspicions—don't think I didn't have my suspicions, Whip. But I can look the other way when I need to. Nothing's obvious on that tape. That tape's from Mexico when I was there. Can you tell he's throwing a spitter? I can't."

He had a point. Even knowing what he was doing, it was almost impossible to pick up.

"I watched it again and again," he said. "Fausto's chewing gum, and before he throws *El Bailador*, he steps off the mound and licks his fingers three times, wipes them on his pants and throws. The ball's falling out of the sky. That's the only thing funny, the way it moves."

I said, "The gum's got a sap in it that makes the ball drop like that. I just talked to a chemist."

Wilson stared at the brick on the table. "Long as he wipes his fingers after licking them, it's legal. Beautiful, beautiful." He pronounced it "beauty-full." "The umps go out and practically undress him and can't find a thing. They can't see it, I can't see it, so why make an issue out of it? I'm not the kid's rabbi."

He wiped his mouth with the back of his hand, like a man fresh out of the desert and badly in need of water. "Do you know how many pitchers I've seen try stuff with the baseball? Over thirty-odd years? I'll tell you how many, every single one."

He pointed at me accusingly. "You did it too, Whip. I know you did, you and Rolando."

"Pine tar at first."

"It worked, right?"

"A dab on the middle finger, and my breaking ball had a twelve-six bite."

"You did more than that. You worked on a spitter of your own."

"At the end when I was trying to hang on," I said. "Rolando taught me how to throw it with Vaseline. He kept it on his shin guard and swiped a little off throwing the ball back to me. I got real good at it. I might've made it back if Mazatlán didn't happen."

Wilson said, "I knew a guy had a thumbtack in his glove and he'd cut the ball to get extra run on it. You can't rely on that trick today because the umps toss out balls all the time. Like every five seconds. It'd be like doing carpentry out there."

"I saw a guy use sandpaper taped to the heel of his hand."

"Same problem," he said. "They toss out the ball and you do it all over again. I've seen baby oil, turpentine, shaving cream. I know a guy used vaginal cream. Called him Dr. Johnson. Swore by it."

Wilson laughed quietly to himself and looked past me, lost in thought. "I want to make one point here," he said slowly. "The spitball's been dead in the big leagues for, what, three decades? Too many cameras seeing every damn thing, from every angle. No place to hide nothing. Plus, why get suspended for a spitball when the split-fingered fastball has almost the same action? But still. But still."

Wilson stopped. His eyes became intense, and his breathing quickened. I knew the look. For athletes, the love of competition never wanes. It's a drug.

"I'm telling you, Whip, this kid was going to bring the spitball back single handed. Fausto was going to change the game the way steroids changed the game. He was masterful using this stuff. Never seen it done better. Ask Rolando what this kid could've done."

Roxy threw me a side look, eyes full of surprise. Wilson had no idea Rolando was dead.

I said, "But sooner or later, you knew this scheme had to go public."

"Even if it did and I looked stupid to the brass, the whole world, I didn't care."

Wilson was excited, gathering himself in his chair to mount his argument. "You understand what I'm saying, Whip. Every pitcher wants to do this. Guys like Gaylord Perry? Gaylord Perry couldn't match Fausto Molina using this stuff, and I wasn't going to stop him. No, sir. I had to see how far he could push it."

Wilson had unloaded everything, put it all on the record, and there was relief on his face. "What went wrong, anyways? All of a sudden Fausto can't get anybody out."

"He ran out of his holy grail," I said, and told him the story.

"You mean people got killed over this?"

I sat there and said nothing.

He said, "Wait a minute. Last time you said Rolando was missing." The realization hit him, and he looked at us with dread on his face.

"He's not missing, Danny," I said. "He's dead."

"Whip, man, I'm so sorry. I had no idea. I know how close you guys were. Goddamn. What happened?"

I told him we'd get into details later.

Roxy spoke up. "I'm going to need you to go on camera, Daniel. We're going to take down Max Mayflower and get the man who killed Rolando Molina."

"On air? Talking about this?" Wilson exhaled, flapping his lips. "I'll look like a fool."

"Not if you tell the truth," Roxy said. "But if you 'no comment' me, I'll chase you around the parking lot with a camera. Remember, Daniel—I always get the story."

Wilson looked across the desk at Roxy. For a second I thought he might get up and run away. But gradually his manner eased, and he nodded. "Okay, I'll do it. But only if you've got Fausto too, both of us on camera together."

"He's on his way to Tucson as we speak," Roxy said.

"Taking down Max Mayflower…it'll be my pleasure," Wilson said.

We didn't get out of his office until after midnight. Roxy was on fire thinking she'd nailed down the piece. Fausto was the indispensable part, but Wilson added the weight of a respected GM. She wanted them in front of the camera as soon as he arrived in Tucson.

With Fausto and Wilson on the record, and Arthur Melody if we could find him, all the "no comments" in the world from Mayflower's side wouldn't make any difference.

SIXTY-ONE

When I arrived home, Opal was standing in the open front door of the Airstream. Charlie had picked her up at the Arizona Inn. Her face had that familiar look of trouble.

"Charlie found him outside his trailer," she said. "He was almost dead."

"Almost dead. Who's almost dead?"

"Somebody's hunting him. They're going to murder him!" Opal's face had lost its color, and her voice was filled with air.

I walked past her into the Airstream. "Who's going to get murdered?"

She craned her neck out the door and peered down the street. "Cash is keeping watch in case he tries any funny business." She closed the door and turned to face me. "He's back!"

"Opal, it's late, and I don't want to play guessing games. Who's back?"

"Angel. He ain't dead, just like I told you. What do you think about that, Mr. Whip?" She folded her arms on her chest and stared at me as if we both had ten minutes to live.

I was shocked but tried not to show it. Opal's panic didn't need encouragement. I spent the next half hour trying to get her calm as we went through a normal night's routine. She brushed her teeth and got the foldout ready.

After feeding Chico, I went through a box of mementos and retrieved a small tobacco tin that had belonged to my grandfather.

It was blue and had on it the logo of Dexter Cigars. I put the tequila gum inside, snapped it shut, and stuck it in my pocket.

I sat with Opal and talked to her about small matters until she fell asleep and then grabbed my flashlight and walked down to Cashmere Miller's trailer. He sat on the front porch with his dirty bare feet up on the railing. Beside him on the table was a .45-caliber Ruger automatic.

"It's after midnight, Cash."

"I don't sleep good. Night's my time to ponder and such." He sipped from a can of Red Bull. "The kid's in the open trailer. I'm keeping an eye on him."

"Opal says he's in bad shape."

"He was beat to hell when Charlie found him drinking at his garden hose. Doctored him up." Cash held up the can for me to see. "I got extras Bulls in the fridge."

"No, thanks. I can't believe he lived through that flood."

"Says he grabbed a cottonwood branch and held on." Cash leaned over and spat and rubbed his palm over his face. "He's got hair coming back here after leading us into that canyon the way he done. Says he knew nothing about what was going down."

"You believe him?"

"I got a hole in my head answers that question. He says he's waiting for his friend."

"What friend?"

"Search me. Says he's going hunting rabbits to feed his friend. Meantime, he wants us to protect him here at Double Wide." Cash snorted. "Know what I say? Run his ass off. Let Roscoe Rincon have him."

"Until the kid tells me where Rolando is, he stays."

Cash bunched his lips and sniffed the night air. "The way it dopes out, you're betting the whole pot of beans on the kid knowing stuff maybe he don't know."

"He knows."

The open trailer sat on Opal's side of Main Street. No lights were on inside, and without a door the entrance was a black hole. I stepped into the living room, a large, stifling space with nothing in it except a torn-up couch with springs showing.

Angel slept on newspapers spread out over the orange carpet. He lay with his hands between his thighs, his knees by his chin. He wore only one shoe and a pair of white briefs. The shoeless foot was filthy, the ankle swollen to twice its size.

The bandage had come off the bullet wound in his back, the scar black and ugly. Charlie had put new bandages on his ankle, his thigh, and both arms. A black bruise covered his cheek below his right eye.

If the flood had killed him, it couldn't have done much worse.

I went back to the Airstream, and six hours later, I was lying in bed staring at the ceiling when Oscar called. The phone woke Chico, who bent his neck to look up at me. He didn't like anything interrupting his sleep, even George Jones.

My phone said it was 4:32 a.m.

"Fausto's gone, Whip. Gone. He's gone."

I sat up and spoke in a tight whisper. I didn't want to wake up Opal sleeping out on the foldout. "What do you mean? Gone where?"

"He wasn't at his apartment, and I banged on the Sultans' door until the clubhouse boy opened up. He didn't know anything."

"Nobody was hanging around the parking lot, guys that might've grabbed him?"

"The boy didn't see anything," Oscar said. "All of Fausto's stuff was still in his locker, his phone, too. He wouldn't leave his cell behind. He sleeps with that thing."

I listened to my own breathing as I tried to think. Chico stared up at me, tail wagging.

Oscar said, "I've got a bad feeling, Whip."

I said maybe Fausto was being smart. He knew the cartel could trace him if he used the cell, so he left it in his locker, hung up from me, and went on the run. Not sure I believed that myself, but best keep it positive. I asked if he had any idea where Fausto might go.

"We got family in Mexico City. I'm headed there now. Do you think he's all right, Whip?" Then desperate, scared, pleading: "I can't lose another boy!"

SIXTY-TWO

I started moving around at sunrise, though at reduced speed. I felt as if I'd pitched nine innings and got the loss on a bases-loaded walk. There was nothing to do about it but pour a pot of coffee down my throat and hope it passed.

After breakfast, I told Charlie to roust Angel and bring him to the Airstream for a talk. Charlie cleaned him up and dressed him in one of his palm tree shirts. It hung to the kid's knees. The uncovered parts of Angel's body showed ugly bruises and puncture wounds.

He had information about Rolando, I was sure of that. But he wouldn't say much. He mumbled disjointed phrases and bobbed his head, his good eye glassy and half-closed above that ugly blue bruise on his cheek.

The only thing he said with certainty was that Rincon was coming to kill him, and he needed protection. I wasn't going to get any more out of him and let it go for the time being.

Charlie kept an eye on Angel the rest of the day, bringing him food and an ice pack for his wounds. I called Roxy at the station and gave her the bad news about Fausto. Her reaction was succinct and well-reasoned.

"Shit!" she screamed, and said she'd call back.

Without Fausto to go on camera, she had nothing. Rolando was dead. Carlos Alvarez and Rosa Lopez were dead. Dr. Arthur Melody was missing and unavailable to talk about his gum, and Roxy had no clue to his whereabouts.

Danny Wilson? Fine, but all he could speak to were suspicions that he kept to himself. Not exactly a source to run to the bank with.

Roxy had information that baseball's hottest young agent owned a strip club that laundered heroin money—surely a story. But the corporate setup gave Mayflower room to deny knowing about it, and that would leave viewers with no clear idea whom to believe.

Without Fausto, she had to fight for some weaker version of the story and I could imagine the screaming, the running of the midmanagement weevils into dark corners where responsibility would never find them.

At a small station, a big story like that can break careers. The decision would go all the way up to the general manager, a fellow with friends at the chamber who got to be GM precisely by killing stories like this.

The big secret is that good journalism brings as much trouble as prestige, especially when the subject is an operator like Mayflower. He wouldn't bother calling the station bosses to complain. He'd go straight to corporate and let the boulders rain down from there, and that's even before the story aired.

I knew the GM's answer before Roxy did. When it comes to their stories, reporters always hold on to foolish hope.

She called two hours later and let loose an avalanche of invective that involved, among other things, the GM's relationship with his mother and his dog, which was apparently furry. Roxy mentioned his bald head, no longer furry, his journalistic bravery or lack thereof, and of course the size of his "nozzle."

Her word. I could infer where he landed on that crucial scale.

"I take it the story's dead?" I said.

She made a variety of jungle noises and asked me to meet her at the TV station in the morning and bring Dr. Melody's gum.

Next day, 10:00 a.m., Charlie drove Cash's Dodge Dart to the Goodwill store to buy clothes for Angel. Opal went with him. With Cash staying at Double Wide on Angel watch, I followed them over the mountain and tried not to choke to death on the black smoke pouring from the Dodge.

SIXTY-THREE

The day was blindingly bright and dead, one of those summer Saturdays in Tucson when only the homeless are out. Roxy met me in the parking lot with her bearded, surly, disheveled cameraman. His name was Ralph.

At introduction, Ralph gave me a grudging nod and went back to loading his gear into the back of a KPIN van. He and his sourpuss got behind the wheel and waited, his tattooed arm holding up the roof. TV cameramen don't have last names or personalities.

Roxy and I pulled away in the Audi, Ralph following. She drove in bare feet, her high heels tossed into the backseat. She wore a black-and-white-pinstriped pantsuit, square in the shoulders, tapered at the waist, the jacket double breasted with a narrow and low V-neck.

She looked like a cold-blooded banker who couldn't wait to line out her next foreclosure before luncheon at a place with cloth napkins.

The TV station was on the west side of Tucson near the freeway. As Roxy drove east from there along Grant Road, she said, "I've been thinking about Fausto. Let's assume Rincon didn't get his mitts on him and the kid made it out of Monterrey. He's on the run, and we don't know where he is."

"Optimistic, but okay."

"If that's true, Mayflower doesn't know either," Roxy said. "All right, we go to Mayflower and say we've got Fausto and he's spilled everything about Melody and the gum."

"We already tried the ambush approach."

"Yeah, and it worked in a way," she said. "He called Rincon about Rolando's hand and made sure it disappeared from Double Wide. That wasn't what you wanted, but it told us a lot."

"How's this going to change your GM's mind?"

"Forget him. He's planning his next vacation. When in doubt, stick a camera in your source's face and see what he says. You never know."

When we got to Campbell Avenue, she turned north and drove up the winding road toward Mayflower's house.

"Waiting around for something to break is torture, and I hate being bored," Roxy said.

"You're bringing me along to show off your new outfit?"

"Neiman Marcus." She jiggled in her seat. "Hoo-hoo! No, you're protection for both of us. I want to make sure Mayflower knows you're still with me. Two is better than one. Last night they found Mace Finch dead in the Pinal County Jail. Somebody cut his throat."

That familiar cold hand crept through my gut. "For talking to me?"

"You're a dangerous man to hang with, Prospero. That's why you need me."

Roxy stopped outside Mayflower's house. Ralph pulled in behind us. When the maid opened the front door, Roxy asked in Spanish where Mayflower was. The maid stared at Roxy and then at Ralph, who had the camera balanced on his shoulder.

Without a word, she stepped aside, gestured toward the pool, and the three of us walked through the house and out the sliding glass door.

Mayflower sat under a white umbrella at a pebbled glass table. His chair was white bamboo, and he wore a white robe over blue swim trunks. His feet were bare, and a pair of dark sunglasses sat atop his head. He used the corners of his eyes on us. His mouth twitched.

"Roxanne Santa Cruz. Don't you know you shouldn't wear black in the heat?" he said, and turned back to the plate of fruit on the table in front of him.

The yard was a paradise. Lush grass, tall palm trees ringing a flagstone patio, a hot tub. White-flowering oleanders hovered over the perimeter fence, except where there was a good-sized gazebo. The sun made the swimming pool sparkle.

A shirtless black man stood over the water working the net pole. He had granite abs, muscle lines on his thighs, arms like railroad ties, and a white Speedo with a sack of summer berries stuffed inside. His hair was cut into lightning bolts above his ears.

He dropped the pole and started toward us. Mayflower stopped him with a raised hand. "It's all right, Reggie."

Roxy knew how to make an appearance. She strode across the cool deck straight to Mayflower's side using her bouncy walk—long steps, shoulders high, elbows high, hips swaying, her face sculpted and resolute. Her high heels hitting the cool deck sounded like small arms fire.

The creator of the pantsuit doesn't get enough credit. Properly worn, it's a diabolical thing. Its power rests almost entirely on mystery. But still, lean over slightly to pick up an orange slice, letting the V of the jacket billow out just enough, and a man can forget his name.

Then let some of the orange juice dribble down the chin, with a sweeping tongue in pursuit, and the pantsuit is suddenly more effective than a bikini. Throw in the heels and somebody better call the cops.

Mayflower did a poor job pretending his brunch was more interesting.

Roxy said, "I'm producing a story, and I'm going to tell you what I know."

Without looking up, Mayflower raised an indifferent hand as a go-ahead.

"To succeed at your job, you needed to find an edge and in the service of that idea, you hired the genius botanist Dr. Arthur Melody," she said, and pulled the gum out of her pocket. "He came up with this."

Mayflower gave as little effort as he could to looking at it, just a fast back-and-forth glance. "What exactly is that, please?"

"I don't know what to call it," Roxy said. "What do you think, Prospero? Let's try Dr. Melody's fabulous tequila gum. It has nothing to do with tequila, but what the hell. I like the name."

Mayflower dabbed at his mouth with a napkin. "Sounds impressive. Please, go on."

"You needed access to the agave on Paradise Mountain and that brought you to Roscoe Rincon, who owns that mountain as part of his smuggling operation," she said. "The two of you made a deal. He gives you the access in return for laundering his heroin money through Skin."

She leaned forward, turning her head. "Skin is your company, correct, Mr. Mayflower?"

He said nothing and glanced at Ralph as if seeing him for the first time. A good cameraman masters the art of not being there. The camera is there, changing everything in the most fundamental way. But the man behind it is a ghost.

Roxy continued: "Everything is going peaches. Fausto is burning it up in Mexico and the plan's working. *El Bailador* is the next big thing in the game. But Roscoe Rincon makes the terrible mistake of killing Rolando Molina, and that brings this dogged character onto the scene."

She motioned to me. I gave Mayflower a goofy smile.

"Now," Roxy said, "Fausto has run out of his gum and your whole scam has fallen apart. I'm sure you know Ed Bolt is in jail on burglary charges for trying to retrieve it and his partner has been murdered. You and Roscoe Rincon can't kill enough to keep this quiet anymore."

She grabbed another orange slice from Mayflower's plate and popped it into her mouth. She used her index finger to collect the excess juice from her chin and sucked it clean.

She said, "Before you comment, I should mention that I have Fausto Molina in a secure location in Tucson. And that young man is talking like crazy."

The red in Mayflower's face turned a sickly white, the first crack in the facade. He dabbed his lips with a napkin again and put it down. He stared at his plate, stood up, and fought with his robe before pulling it tight and pointing at Ralph.

He said, "I want you to come in tight. The frame should have my face only. This side, please." He raised his jaw and patted his left cheek with his palm. "Are you ready, sir?"

Ralph pointed at Mayflower like a director beginning a scene.

"I have no idea what you're talking about," Mayflower said, in a robotic voice. "I've never heard of this Dr. Arthur Melody. As for heroin smuggling—preposterous. I'm a baseball man. But if one of my companies has fallen off the straight and true, I will of course cooperate with authorities in correcting it and telling them everything I know."

He smiled without a hint of pleasure. "I'll have no more to say this afternoon. Reggie, can you show our visitors out?"

As if on a spring, Reggie lunged toward the camera. I got there first and hip-checked him into the pool. He departed the cool deck in a spasm of gorgeous limbs, and thrashed around in the water until he could pull himself out.

Mayflower jumped up and blocked Reggie from getting to me. He was hot, jumping around in his Speedo. Holding Reggie back, Mayflower said, "I won't have that in my house, Reggie. I'll show our guests to the door."

Mayflower followed us through the house. He waited until Ralph and his camera were far ahead, and then he called Roxy and me back.

"Don't make a mistake here. A deadly mistake."

He paused to let that sink in.

"You have one source, a seventeen-year-old Mexican boy, and what is he saying? That I hired a mad scientist to produce a heretofore unknown serum with properties never before seen outside an H. G. Wells story? And these properties cause a baseball to move in an unhittable manner? A pitcher whose record these past weeks is quite pathetic?"

He plunged his hands into the pockets of his robe. "Is anyone going to believe that? Or do you think they'll laugh until they cry?"

SIXTY-FOUR

Roxy tossed her high heels into the backseat of the Audi and sat behind the wheel huffing in frustration. "I thought I'd enjoy that more," she said. "I half expected Mayflower to break down and admit everything."

"Did you catch the mistake he made at the end?" I said.

"He didn't dispute that we have Fausto."

"Right. He wouldn't do that if Roscoe Rincon had found him."

"Okay, we know Fausto's alive," Roxy said. "But we don't have him and when I don't air this story, Mayflower will know we don't have him. And I can't find Arthur Melody."

"If we find Bunny Slippers, we'll find Melody."

"Don't you think I know that? I've been back to her house three times, and it looks exactly like we left it. What about that Vegas number she was calling?"

"Tried it fifteen times. No answer, no call back."

"She's a ghost, Prospero. Gone. Before long, Mayflower will know I don't have jack. The cover-up is going to work."

After that, we didn't talk much on the ride back to the station. We pulled into the back parking lot. The rear of the building was a solid block wall broken only by a high strip of blurred windows and a single gray door.

It was the middle of the afternoon, and one of the male on-airs was tossing a football to his female desk mate. She made sure to drop it, and then giggled, chased it, and threw it back to him, and he made sure to catch it.

Roxy pulled up beside the Bronco, and we sat watching the footballers. They were the weekend team, brand new to the job, still happy, not yet ready to go at each other with ball-peen hammers, and by their faces, fresh out of eighth grade.

They saw Roxy and waved, though you might describe it as more of a salute. Roxy didn't wave back.

She said, "If you stay past thirty in this market, you're a legend."

We stepped out of the car, and Roxy walked toward the station. As I reached the Bronco to leave, the football rolled to my feet, and the female anchor bounded over in her pink go-to-work sneakers to retrieve it. I ignored her and whipped it across the parking lot.

Instead of trying to catch it, the man ducked to avoid certain decapitation. He survived with his hair in place. He probably used prime product. All the best ones do. Roxy opened the gray door and held it wide. She gave the two young anchors an exhausted wave meant to summon them in out of the heat. They obeyed at once.

I got into the Bronco and started the engine. As I drove toward the street, I heard a loud bang. In the rearview I saw that Roxy had thrown open the station door, thumping it against the wall, and she was running after the Bronco in bare feet. I braked and poked my head out the window.

"Wait up! Wait a minute!" she called. "I said we've got nothing and Mayflower knows it, right? But that's wrong. We have Dr. Melody's fabulous tequila gum."

"You want to put the gum on camera?"

"No, I want to put you on camera. I saw the way you threw that football." Breathing hard, Roxy tucked a wild strand of purple hair behind her ear. "That's the most powerful evidence we have. All we have to do is show people how it works. That's your job, Prospero. Show them!"

"You want me to pitch again?"

"We wouldn't be telling people what this stuff does to a baseball—we'd show them!"

"That's crazy."

"It isn't crazy at all," she said. "Think about it. We can make this into an event. Everybody loves a comeback story, right? This could be the greatest comeback of all time. It could be huge!"

"I haven't picked up a baseball in two years."

"Isn't this exactly what Mayflower was trying to do with Fausto? Create a circus atmosphere around this young guy and his fabulous pitch? Everybody still knows your name, and I can guarantee serious publicity. The national boys will turn out big time for this."

Roxy was gleeful. She dragged her hand over her head to make an air headline: "Come watch Whiplash Stark's return to the mound! The Phenom is back!"

"You're forgetting something, Rox. I don't have a team."

"Yes, you do. The Tucson Thunder."

"You think Danny Wilson would go for something like this?"

"Wilson lies in bed dreaming of drawing fans to the ballpark," she said. "Show him how this stuff works, and he'll sign you in a heartbeat. Whiplash Stark is back. Are you kidding me?"

I started to speak, but she interrupted.

"After the game, we hold a press conference and spill everything. We'll screw Max Mayflower to the wall—tell how *El Bailador* is a doctored pitch, how he hired Melody to create this stuff using the sap from the Palmer agave, laundering drug money through his club, the whole bit."

"He'll deny everything."

"So what? A million eyes have just seen proof. If you pitch well, hold the gum up for the cameras, say what it is, how it came to be, it'll be riveting. Who knows, maybe we'll have found Melody by then."

"Roxy, I don't even know if this stuff works."

She wasn't listening. She snapped her fingers as she bounced from foot to foot on the hot pavement. "This is epic! This is huge! Wait, where's your mitt? You kept your mitt, right?"

"Of course. I'm not a barbarian."

"How about I call Danny Wilson right now? Set something up at Hi Corbett? If the stuff works, we're in business."

Roxy already had her cell out. She was so excited I didn't think she'd be able to hit the numbers. As she waited for Wilson to pick up, she leaned in the driver's window and kissed me, a real smooch.

"Daniel," she said, and gave me a confident nod. "Roxanne Santa Cruz here. Clear your schedule for tomorrow morning."

SIXTY-FIVE

The next day, Saturday, we pulled into the parking lot at Hi Corbett at 9:00 a.m. It was me, Roxy, and Opal, and when we walked into Wilson's office, he fixed on Opal. "You brought your maid? Are you trying to tell me something?"

"She's my friend, Danny," I said, and tossed my glove onto his desk and sat down.

He caught my irritation and gave a "surrender" nod.

Opal paid no attention. She had her hair in a ponytail and wore a loose, yellow-and-blue tie-dyed shirt. Her legs were dimpled behind the knees and stuffed into spandex denim shorts. Her feet were bare, the toenails painted black.

With her flips-flops hooked under one finger, she strolled barefoot around the office looking at the pictures on the walls and examining various exotic office items, like the stapler.

Roxy and I laid out the plan. As we talked, Wilson's eyes bounced between us. He listened carefully with a wry look on his face, nodding from time to time.

I explained that nothing would be off limits. At the postgame press conference, I'd produce the gum for the cameras and tell everything I knew about *El Bailador* and how it came to be. I'd talk about Dr. Melody and Roscoe Rincon and the heroin connection. I'd describe my background with Rolando and how he tried to help Fausto reach the big leagues.

The off-limits part wasn't entirely true. I said nothing about Rolando's hand or my decision to withhold it from the cops.

The only time Wilson blanched was when I said he'd be sitting at my side to tell the press he knew that I was going to use an illegal substance. But he could say he did so to expose what he considered a serious threat to the integrity of the game, in the person of Max Mayflower.

"The integrity of the game," he said. "That's true. I have thought about that." He bunched his lips and made a thinking face. "You're sure you can make this pitch dance like the name? If you can't, the whole thing falls apart, and we look like fools."

"Come on," I said, and grabbed my glove off the desk.

Wilson changed into sweats and met us on the field. It was empty and silent under a cloudless blue sky. Our voices echoed in the empty stadium. The air smelled of wet grass from the groundskeeper's morning work.

Roxy sat cross-legged in the dugout. She wore those tight-fitting shredded jeans that showed patches of leg through gaping, white-fringed holes. Opal tripped through the moist grass barefoot, whirling her arms like a bird trying to fly. She returned to earth in centerfield and sat on the wet grass to watch me work.

I wound up and threw a pitch, the first since I'd walked off the field in Mazatlán. I threw a second and a third, all from flat ground in front of the mound. It was blazing hot. I threw for five minutes with undoctored baseballs.

When the sweat cleared away the initial lethargy and I began to feel loose, I moved back onto the rubber.

I broke off a small section of the gum and stuffed it against my cheek. I didn't bite into it. I threw several pitches from the mound, all of them clean. But before each one I licked my fingers as a diversion. I didn't want Wilson to know which balls were doctored and which weren't.

At first I stayed with my two-seam fastball, thrown at three-quarter speed. On days when I was clicking, my two-seamer was a dandy pitch. I'm left handed, and it had a natural run that moved outside to a right-handed hitter and jammed a lefty. The run was still there and that was good to see.

After fifteen or so balls, I bit into the gum, releasing the thick liquid and that sour taste. It was like having a mouthful of Pennzoil. I wondered if Dr. Melody could enhance the flavor. If we found him alive, I'd be sure to mention that. Dark chocolate was my choice.

My first doctored pitches went wild, but soon I zeroed in. The dive at the end of its ride was sharp, not lazy, the same dramatic movement I got on my Vaseline spitter in Mexico.

I threw *El Bailador* again and again to get the right rhythm fixed in my head. Step off the mound and lick the fingers and dry them on the pant leg. Most of the drying pressure had to be on the last two fingers, with less on the thumb, index, and middle fingers.

That kept just enough of the saliva-sap mix in place. Step back onto the mound and throw before the ball dries. Several pitches nearly bounced in the dirt in front of Wilson and on every one of those, he nodded at me to indicate, "Yes, that's the one we want."

I began mixing my pitches, some doctored and some not. I threw my spitball only ten or twelve times a game. After the first one, the opposing dugout knew the pitch was there.

If I was doing my job, it stood out in their minds like a pimple on prom night. The psychology of the spitball, the choreography of deception that I went through in the mound, was as powerful as the pitch itself.

After five minutes, my fastball was hitting Wilson's glove with a solid *pop*, the sound echoing around the empty ballpark.

I felt good, confident and clearheaded. It had been a long time, and I wasn't sure I could throw the strikes consistently. But the basic skill never goes away and the muscles remember, making the routine movements automatic. The key was going to be getting my mechanics right. If I could find my arm slot, every-thing else would follow.

From the dugout, Roxy mimicked the hum-baby cheers of excited Little Leaguers. "Way to go, Prospero!"

From centerfield, Opal gave a piercing, two-fingered whistle and shouted, "Mr. Whip, he's our man! If he can't do it, nobody can!" and gave a cheerleader fist pump.

Wilson hollered out a caution not to overthrow, saying I'd been out of the game two years and should take it easy. But I couldn't stop. The harder I threw, the better I felt, and the more Wilson liked it.

He bounced on his haunches like a young man. He hid his free hand behind his thigh, as if protecting it from a foul tip. He was fiercely alive and all business.

When I threw a hard strike, he called out, "That's the one, Whiplash!" and pointed his catcher's mitt at me before firing the ball back.

When I threw another, he hollered, "Ninety located. Say good night, Audrey!"

I threw *El Bailador* just as Rolando had taught me to throw a Vaseline spitter. I gripped the ball with my fingers on the hide, not the stitches, to reduce rotation. With a tiny amount of that thick sap on my fingertips, combined with the hide-only grip, the ball slicked out of my hand in a squirting action.

When I used Vaseline, the balls I got back had a slight sheen on them. If the umpire caught on, or the opposing manager got suspicious, they could sometimes see it. But the balls Wilson returned were dry. None of the Palmer sap remained.

No discoloration, no soft spot on the hide, no odor, no moisture.

Fausto won fifteen games with *El Bailador* and not a single umpire figured it out, though a lot tried. It was a desert plant, after all, and the substance evaporated on the way to the plate.

Sixty feet, six inches, evidence gone.

When Wilson stopped the session, he looked like he'd stepped out of the shower. His sweats were drenched. He used his forearm to dry his face. "What's in that stuff again?"

"A sap from the agave plant."

Wilson's face wrinkled in confusion. "Like tequila?"

"It's a different agave, but yeah. The ball sure likes it."

"Hell, yes. Yes, it does. My word, what a pitch."

Roxy whistled and stood up in the dugout and waved us over. We listened as she spoke on the phone. She said, "Okay, George, sounds good. Right. It'll be a sweet piece."

Wilson mopped the back of his neck with a hanky as he listened.

Roxy said, "Sure, George. I'll let you know as soon as we have a date. I can't wait, George. Okay. Will do. Take care, my friend."

She ended the call and said, "That was a guy I used to work with. He's an ESPN producer for *Baseball Tonight*. If we can give him a date certain, he'll have a crew here to cover Whip Stark's return."

Wilson's jaw departed his face. ESPN showing up at a minor league ballpark was a blizzard in July. It just didn't happen.

"That's one phone call, Daniel," Roxy said. "I've got a million contacts. You want me to start calling around? The gate will make your whole summer."

Wilson pondered, drawing excited breaths. He whipped out his cell, called his on-field manager, and walked in circles as he spoke. Slipping the phone back into his pocket, he said, "We're home in thirteen days, and you're on the hill two days later, Sunday afternoon, July 20."

Roxy piped up: "We'll call it Tequila Sunday." She pressed her lips together and nodded, impressed with herself. "They call that marketing, Daniel. Pretty good, don't you think?"

"It's brilliant," Wilson said, and looked at me. "Can you be ready, Whip?"

"I'll be ready."

"Two years is a long time. You're sure you can throw that ball in front of ten thousand people and all those cameras?"

"I'm the Phenom, Danny."

He studied me, eyes burning. "Yes, you are. Roxanne, start making calls."

We went into Wilson's office. I signed a single-game contract for a dollar, and then Danny had to ruin it by joking that I was worth twice that much. Like every other joke a general manager ever told, I didn't think it was funny.

SIXTY-SIX

Roxy summoned her crew to Hi Corbett and her piece aired that night. She filmed me sitting on the dugout bench wearing a Thunder jersey and cap, and split that with B-roll of my twenty-strikeout game. I couldn't believe how young I looked.

I watched the 5:00 p.m. show on my kitchen TV, Charlie and Opal there with me.

"The excitement builds at Hi Corbett Field tonight with General Manager Danny Wilson promising major surprises for the big game. That's in addition to the drama of watching Whiplash Stark return to the same mound where he won fame as a teenage superstar. On Sunday, July 20, Tucson and the nation will learn if the Phenom can recapture that faded glory.

"Live on KPIN with the real story, this is Roxanne Santa Cruz reporting."

Soon as I flipped off the TV, Opal said, "I didn't know you were so big."

"Gargantuan," I said.

She sipped her Pepsi. "Cool beans."

Charlie pointed at me. "This man struck out A-Rod. Jeter, too. In the same inning!"

Opal tried to look impressed, but it was obvious she had no idea who they were.

"Easy, Charlie," I said. "A-Rod got me three innings later—a four-hundred-fifty-foot bomb."

Roxy called wanting to know what I thought. I scolded her for not mentioning that even though I was far from a teenager, I was still devastatingly handsome. And the "faded glory" line was a lamentable cliché. She agreed but said anything original would've confused her boss and sent her to the editing room to cut it from the piece.

"I've already had two texts from New York media looking for you," Roxy said. "They'll come in bunches now."

"I've been through the frenzy before."

"I have something to say, and it's important, Prospero. As of tonight, Mayflower and Rincon know if this game goes ahead, all the dirty laundry's coming out. About *El Bailador*, heroin, the murders, Dr. Melody's fabulous tequila gum, all of it. They know this isn't about Whip Stark's comeback."

"They'll be ticked off. I get it."

"They can't let this game happen. And with Wilson committed, he can't back out. That leaves you a sitting duck at Double Wide."

"Kill me and the trouble goes away—is that it?"

We both knew that was it exactly. Stop me from taking the mound and using the gum. Stop me from broadcasting the conspiracy to the world.

Cash stepped into the Airstream.

"Don't worry," I said to Roxy. "My security chief's on hand, and he's a crackerjack."

Cash scratched his stomach and saluted. He stood his AR against the wall and sat at the table.

I said, "I talked to Benny Diaz an hour ago about getting the county to patrol out here. He's going to make it happen."

"What you need is a babe with a gun at your side."

"I've been thinking you should come out and talk to Angel. I've tried three times to get him to tell me more about Rolando and can't get anywhere."

"I've got a couple of stories to edit before I go anywhere. Let's see…how about Saturday?"

"Laura Lace."

"Laura…what?" Roxy said. "What're you talking about?"

"Your dancing name. I'm stuck on the alliteration thing."

"Not even close."

"I'm coming to the end of the alphabet. Sapphire, Scarlett, Sierra. At least tell me if I'm in the ballpark."

"Saturday."

"If you want to use a day, Tuesday's better. Remember Tuesday Weld?"

"No, no, no. I'm coming Saturday for dinner. Do you like crab tacos?"

SIXTY-SEVEN

The next day, Sunday, I was national news. The local paper followed up on Roxy's piece, added more detail and it moved on the AP wire. Within an hour ESPN put up a crawl announcing Whip Stark's return to baseball.

Roxy threw up a Facebook page touting the upcoming game and got twelve messages from reporters trying to track me down. Wilson had his own stack. They came from as far away as Mexico City and London.

But I had plenty of time to talk to the media. My priority was defending Double Wide against Roscoe Rincon.

I went through Gil Pappas's storage shed and found two portable stanchion-mount spotlights. Charlie and I rigged one of them to the corner of his trailer. The light shone down Main Street, bright at Charlie's end, diminishing at mine, but it was something at least.

We set up the other light out by my entrance sign. It threw a glow over the county road, not much beyond, and served as more of a decoy. I was fine with a decoy if it made that part of my perimeter less appealing to intruders.

The work was hot and took all of Sunday, Monday and Tuesday. But the hammering was comforting, evidence of a plan rather than just sitting around waiting for Rincon to act.

I called Oscar Molina. He should've arrived in Mexico City by now. No answer. I left a message.

Over those three days, I followed the same routine. Up early, Maxwell House, shower, shave, breakfast for me and Opal, and then, with Cash on guard duty at Double Wide, we drove over the mountain to Hi Corbett.

Even early in the morning, satellite vans waited in the parking lot. Wilson served coffee and Krispy Kreme donuts to the news crews. He walked around with the satisfied smile of a man in the middle of something exciting and loving the attention.

From his office, I did phoners with a Mexico City paper, the *LA Times*, *Yahoo Sports,* and *DeadSpin*, and sit-down interviews with *Fox Sports* and ESPN *Deportes.*

The national correspondents made assurances about how they'd handle the story of my cocaine arrest in Mazatlán and the sensitivity they'd show in talking about my father's situation. But as soon as it was wheels up, they'd toss the promises and do what they needed to do to make the piece work.

Nothing is more dangerous than an out-of-town reporter.

After the interviews, I worked out with Danny again, until the Thunder's regular catcher flew back to town from the road trip. Danny wanted the two of us to spend as much time as possible together before the game.

Rodrigo Peña was a black Cuban with a shaved head. After our first session, I told him about *El Bailador*, explaining that a scientist had created the gum with a sap from the agave plant. He gave me a shocked face, as if I might be joking.

He said, "This is how we make our living now? With a forbidden substance?" After more of the somber routine, he broke into a huge grin, his face full of larceny and gold-capped teeth. "Whatever it takes, baby."

His attitude reminded me of Rolando, and that made me feel good.

I returned from those workouts around lunchtime. Over the remainder of the afternoon and into the evenings, Cash and Charlie and I worked to clear brush from between the trailers and along the entrance road. The less cover Rincon had, the better our chances to react.

Angel's health had improved and he was eager to help. He made quite a sight, lurching down Main Street on that bandaged ankle, taking a long step and a short one, jerking his arms up and down to generate momentum.

He wore Charlie's Goodwill clothes: a blue railroad shirt, long sleeved with flap pockets, and dark-blue work pants with the cuffs rolled up several times. The pants and shirt were so baggy he practically disappeared inside them.

Cash said, "He's been going into the desert to hunt for food for his mysterious friend. But he won't tell me who it is."

"That kid hasn't got a friend in the world."

"He makes spears out of saguaro ribs and stalks through the brush. When the critters come by, he pounces. He's like a Injun out there."

"Keep your eyes on him."

"He don't go nowhere without I'm watching."

SIXTY-EIGHT

I caught a break in the search for Bunny Slippers. On Saturday, I got a call from the same Las Vegas number that showed up repeatedly on Bunny's bill. A grouchy female said, "How come you keep calling this number?"

I said I wanted to hire Bunny for a gig. The caller said she was Bunny's sister and vamped around for a few minutes while deciding whether to tell me where she was. "Well, Bunny needs the money for sure. Try the Mustache Room on the Strip. She's doing two nights a week over there."

Within minutes I was looking at the Mustache Room's website. No mention of Bunny Slippers. I called the place and got stuck in phone jail until I pushed the right button, and a girl picked up and said, "Dressing room."

I didn't ask for Bunny. The clubs work hard to shield the dancers from troublesome men, which would make the direct approach tricky. Still working on the theory that she and Melody were together, I asked for Arthur instead.

The girl said, "Who?"

"Arthur Melody. Bald, big ears."

"Oh, the professor. He comes in with Bunny and sits around. He ain't here. Try tonight. Bunny works tonight."

Bingo. I'd found Arthur Melody.

Roxy rolled into Double Wide at seven thirty.

Opal, Cash, and Charlie were just leaving the Airstream when she stepped from the Audi. All eyes settled on her. She wore skinny black jeans, the legs stopping high enough to show six inches of sculpted ankle. Below that she had on bright-red shoes that looked like ballet flats.

Her shirt was white lace and almost sheer, revealing the faintest outline of the black bra underneath. Her hair looked blacker than normal as though newly colored. She had added a blond splash to the streak of purple behind her left ear.

She wore only a silver-band thumb ring on her left hand, the one with the half pinky. All the attention went to her right hand. A ring decorated every finger. The stones were all coral and not small. The color matched the ballet flats.

Roxy came around the Audi and posed for me, stretching her arms out and pointing with both hands back to her body. "What do you think? Is this gonna get Angel talking or what?"

"The kid doesn't stand a chance."

"That's the idea. What about you, Prospero? Anything?"

I let the question slide and told her about finding Bunny and Melody. She was surprised and impressed. "You're getting to be like Sam Spade or somebody."

"Now we've got to figure a way to get him back from Vegas for the press conference."

"Simple. We call him up and say if he comes back, he gets to shape the story of his involvement. First time the public hears about this is key. It can go good or bad, depending on how he handles it."

"I haven't decided what to do yet," I said. "The last thing I want to do is spook him."

"While you're thinking, give me a hand with the groceries."

She popped the trunk, and we each grabbed a bag. I caught a whiff of Roxy's perfume. Flowery, but too discreet to stand out above Double Wide's beguiling aroma of motor oil and decay.

As Roxy passed Cash and Charlie, she nodded, and they seemed to nod back, although the mechanical up-and-down movement of their heads might've been involuntary man tics.

Roxy stepped into the Airstream and began fixing dinner. I showered, dressed in clean clothes, and sat at the table while she worked in the kitchen. Roxy uncorked a bottle of red wine and brought me a glass. I left it alone. My stomach still had me on milk.

She poured a glass for herself and put it next to her on the counter. She sipped as she cut and seeded the jalapeno peppers and described the difficulty of finding kosher salt in Tucson.

But the remainder of the ingredients had made it safely to my kitchen. She had minced garlic, Roma tomatoes, cilantro leaves, iceberg lettuce, chopped onions, and shredded jack cheese. She brought the cooked crab in a cellophane-covered bowl.

"I cooked the crab at home before coming over," she said.

"You didn't have to go to that trouble."

On the way back to the kitchen, she stopped behind me and put her hands on my shoulders. "Let's see—what else? Wait, taco shells! Einstein here! I must be working too hard."

She poured herself another glass of wine and brought a plate of hard-shell tacos to the table and set them down and pulled her chair forward. "Dig in. This is a build-your-own feast. I love to eat, so there's no guarantee they'll be any left if you're not fast."

I said it looked delicious. We ate as a night wind swirled outside. Chico lay beside my chair, his eyes raised and watching my every bite with primal interest. That was a message that his dinnertime had arrived as well.

Afterward, Charlie came to the door to say that Angel had fallen asleep in his trailer. That was phase one of our plan. After that, Roxy was to go into his trailer unannounced, wake him up, and start in with questions about Rolando.

Our theory was that the surprise and Roxy's wiles might shake something loose. Before leaving, she went to the refrigerator and pulled out a loaf of bread to make him a sandwich.

She said, "The real key to this plot is peanut butter and jelly. I mean, he's a kid, right? To a kid, a PB and J is better than money."

SIXTY-NINE

We walked down to the open trailer. Roxy went in first and turned the light on over the stove. That was my signal to step into the kitchen. Charlie was right about the rotted hole in the floor. A Sumo wrestler and his family could've disappeared inside it.

I stayed out of sight with a view of Roxy and Angel through the doorway.

The living room was dark. Angel slept in his underwear on his newspaper bed. With a glass of water from the kitchen, Roxy sat beside him, legs folded. Angel didn't budge until she shook him by the shoulder, and he sat up quickly, the newspapers crinkling underneath him.

He rubbed his eyes and yawned. "I know you. You're pretty."

"You bet your life. I'm Roxy, remember. You can call me that."

He yawned again. "Okay."

"I have something important to ask you."

"Okay."

"I need to know everything you remember about Rolando Molina."

Peering around the door frame, I could see Angel from the side, his arms on his folded legs. Clumps of dirt made elaborate hair castles on his head. The T-shirt I'd given him was torn every way a shirt could be torn. He yawned again and didn't move or speak.

"No one's going to make you leave here if you talk to me," Roxy said. "You understand that, right? You'll be safe here as long as you want to stay."

The kid still didn't speak. The air in the room was stagnant and hot.

Roxy waited a long time and said, "You know, my real name isn't Roxy. It's Roxanne. I've never liked Roxy. Do you like it?"

Angel nodded. Roxy smiled and said, "I'm glad you like it, because I never know. Are you sure you like it?"

"It's a cool name," Angel said. "I like it. Honest."

"I'm glad. Here, I forgot about this." She handed him the peanut butter and jelly sandwich wrapped in a paper towel. He grabbed a half and shoved it against the back of his throat.

He chewed and said, "My mother was Magda and my sister was Trini. They're dead."

"Do you miss them?" she asked.

"Sometimes I can't remember them too good. But sometimes I do."

"Somebody buried them, right?" Roxy said. "Made a sacred place where they can rest forever? Everybody needs a place in the ground. You understand that, don't you?"

Angel shrugged and ate more. Outside, the wind surged and whined and surged again. The trailer creaked on its blocks.

"I watched your friend die," he said. "Roscoe Rincon did it with his machete."

Roxy cocked her head in a listening posture.

"The men were screaming. Rincon's men," Angel continued, his voice a child's whisper. "They were scared because Rincon was crazy, swinging his machete. The blood was going everywhere, like a hose. And Carlos Alvarez tried to stop him, but it was too late. Everybody was running away."

Roxy and Angel sat close together in the empty room, two shadows in faint light, two soft voices sharing the same breath. Roxy asked what they were fighting about.

"Roscoe Rincon was breaking the deal," Angel said. "He was opening a new trail and didn't want nobody using his land up there." He pointed toward the mountain and Paradise. "He owned it. Rincon owned it."

That sounded right. When smugglers bleed and fight their rivals to "own" a trail, they don't give it up, even if they're moving to a new location.

Angel continued, "Rincon wasn't giving out no more of that plant and Rolando was mad. He needed it. He come all the way up from Monterrey with Carlos and said, 'You give me more. I have to have more!' Like that. That's what started the fight. Roscoe Rincon wouldn't let nobody tell him what to do on his trail."

"What'd they do with the body?" Roxy said.

"Rincon told Carlos to put the pieces into bags or he was going to kill him too."

"He obeyed, right? I sure would, a guy like that."

"He hid the hand," Angel said. "He covered it with brush and got it later."

"After that, you and Carlos delivered the hand to Whip, here at Double Wide?"

"Uh-huh. Carlos was going back to Paradise to kill Roscoe Rincon, but Roscoe Rincon was waiting for him on the trail."

Now I knew. Finally and irretrievably I knew. The truth closed in on my throat, making it hard to breathe. I already had a good idea how Rolando had died. But Angel had watched it unfold, had seen the blood and the wild swings of the machete and his unadorned account had a powerful finality to it.

Roxy said, "This is important, Angel. Tell me what happened to the body."

"Roscoe Rincon told one of his men to put the bags into Rolando's truck and drive it far away so nobody would see the smoke. He burned up the truck with your friend inside. Rincon don't want his enemies on Earth no more, so he burns them. He likes fire."

"Where'd they take the body?" Roxy said. "I need to know."

Angel kept eating the sandwich. When he was done, Roxy handed him the glass of water. He drank it and wiped his mouth with his arm.

"I should've made two sandwiches," Roxy said. "How about I make you another one when we're done here?"

The kid didn't respond. Roxy reached through the darkness and put her hand on his shoulder. "Angel, you need to tell me where they took the body. Rolando needs his sacred place. Just like Magda and Trini."

"Somewhere. I don't know," he said. "They threw the bags in a truck and drove off. Everybody else was leaving too. Leaving that mountain altogether."

"In Rolando's truck?"

He nodded. "Yes, a red pickup. But I don't know where they went to. Honest. Somewhere far away so nobody could see the smoke. That's what Roscoe Rincon said." He sat motionless, seemingly awaiting some sign that he'd upheld his end of the bargain. "I told you what you wanted. I can't leave here. Roscoe Rincon will kill me for sure."

"That's all you know?"

Angel nodded.

Roxy considered for a moment and nodded back. "Okay, I guess that's a yes." She got up and started for the door.

"Wait—you're not going to make me leave, right? I can stay?"

"Yeah, you're good. As long as you've told me everything."

"That's it. I swear."

She looked at him for a long time. "Hang here, and I'll get you that sandwich, kiddo."

SEVENTY

Roxy made a second PB and J and brought it to Angel. She came back to the Airstream, got out my expensive tequila bottle and a shot glass, and sat with me at the kitchen table.

She said, "Well, you think he told the truth?"

"Not everything. He knows where Rolando is. I'm sure of it."

"The kid's cunning, Prospero. Really hard to read. Sorry. I did the best I could."

"I promised Oscar I'd find him, and I will."

Roxy poured herself a shot and held it high. "I like your optimism." She drank it down and made a tequila face. "I've never understood the fascination with this stuff. With tequila, you go along, and all of a sudden it's four in the morning, you're missing a shoe, and you have no idea what went wrong. That doesn't happen with a civilized drink like Chivas."

"Civilized," I said. "There's a disappearing concept."

"I know that was brutal, what you just heard about Rolando. But now we know what happened."

"We're looking for a torched red truck somewhere in the badlands of southern Arizona with a body inside. How many of those do you suppose there are?"

"With the drug war the way it is, dozens," Roxy said. "But we have a lead—a red truck, maybe an F-350."

"I can verify the make easy enough."

Roxy grabbed the tequila bottle and was about to pour another shot and stopped. "Why am I drinking this? I've got Chivas in the Audi. Silly girl." She went out to her car, got the Chivas, poured two inches, and sat down again.

She held the glass with two hands at her mouth and tipped it back for a sip. "What about Dr. Melody? Let's call him at the Mustache Room and talk him into coming back."

"Won't work. He's too scared. He's got some explaining to do about what he was up to. Bonheimer said that paper he wrote was baloney."

"You think he was scamming the scammer?"

"He was up to something."

I went to the door and looked out, which I did about every half hour. Storm clouds had tracked in on the wind, and a light rain was falling. In the kitchen I poured a glass of milk and stood with my back against the counter, sipping and thinking.

Roxy watched, nursing her drink at the table.

I said, "The only way we get Melody back here is if Bunny talks him into it. The bait is the publicity."

"We get to him through her?"

"If she knows cameras will beam her face all over the country, she'll convince Arthur that talking to the media is the right thing to do."

Roxy nodded in agreement. "She'll stand right up there with him."

"But we can't do it over the phone. It's got to be in person. They can't avoid you if you're standing there."

"Me? You want me to go to Las Vegas? Mr. Beasley in accounting will love that."

"I can't leave here. It's too risky. You're good at working people. You're hard to say no to, Rox."

She raised her shot glass. "To my special talent."

She sipped. I drank some milk. The wind bumped around outside, and the rain made a faint whispering sound.

"I have a question, Prospero." Roxy swept her hair off her face and turned sideways, one leg stretched all the way out along the bench seat. She held the glass along the top of her thigh and gave me a playful look.

"Why does my special talent work on everybody but you?" She wiggled her foot, the red shoe half-on, half-off, and barely clinging to her toes.

Before I could answer, the door opened without a knock, and Charlie O'Shea stepped inside, Cash right behind him. Charlie smelled like a distillery. He sat at the table next to Roxy. Cash pulled out a loaf of bread, made himself a peanut butter sandwich, and stood next to me at the counter.

He stared at the floor and made smacking noises as he chewed.

Roxy looked like she couldn't believe what was happening.

"Thought I'd take a walk," Charlie said. "Yes, sir, see what the mayor of Double Wide's up to this rainy night."

He spotted Roxy's Chivas bottle on the table. "What have we here?" He picked it up and inspected the label. His eyelids weighed a thousand pounds. "A fine beverage indeed, and that's no fooling. Cashy, grab me a glass, by gub."

Charlie opened a cabinet door and moused around inside. "Glass or mug? We got both."

"I like my beer in a mug. Not scotch. Scotch I want to see through the glass." He seemed quite certain of that.

"He's got plastic cups," Cash said. "How about a plastic cup?"

"Red or blue?"

"You got a choice there too. He's got red, he's got blue. Wait, there's Dixie cups."

"Dixie cups! Impossible!" Charlie evidently found Dixie cups unacceptable.

Cash said, "You throw 'em away when you're done. You don't have to clean nothing."

"Like you ever cleaned anything in your life. I've seen your place."

Roxy tapped an annoyed finger on the table. They settled on a glass. Charlie poured himself an inch, drank it in a swallow, poured another, and the conversation moved along in the same general way, the topic switching to baseball and whether Mike Trout or Mickey Mantle would win a footrace.

After his second scotch, Charlie banged the glass down on the table and stood up. "Time for *Matlock*." He threw open the door, raised a hand over his head, and gave a loose-armed wave. "Nighty-night, you people."

Cash finished his peanut butter sandwich and made another. When Roxy saw that, she fingered the loose shoe back onto her foot, grabbed her Chivas bottle, and walked out. I followed her down the steps.

At the Audi, she said, "Life doesn't have to be as cold as you make it, Prospero. When you figure out what you're running from, let me know."

Surprised and unsure what to say, I stumbled through a few beginnings. Then: "I never know what I'm going to have company."

She gave me a frustrated look. "I'll talk to my boss about Vegas and let you know."

Roxy got behind the wheel and gave the engine a triple revving that sounded like a lion roaring, and then she was gone in a hurry. That's how a romantic night at Double Wide ends, with brake lights escaping up a mountain road.

I went inside, got my phone, and dialed her number. It rang and rang.

"Come on, pick up! Pick *up*!"

I stood in the rain and the darkness thinking that Roxy was a situation I was going to have to handle. And I had no idea how to do that, any more than I knew what I would've said if she'd answered the phone.

The easiest choice, ballplayer preferred, would have been to scatter the Airstream with torn clothes, scare the hell out of the birds with the standard cries, and see what the morning brought. The dangling shoe almost sealed it for me.

But something happens to a man after thirty. A certain caution takes over. Her drinking factored into my thinking, mainly for what it said about the demons she was escaping. They must've been something. I have a few of my own and no reason to believe that hers and mine would play well together.

Just from a practical standpoint, it never works when side of a relationship likes to put it away, and the other has two drinks and next morning he's a corpse, walking around trying to find his keys. There's nothing to talk about and the jokes don't translate.

Not loving liquor is a gift. It keeps you out of bad situations on dark sidewalks after midnight. When you're young and not part of the action, you wonder what you're missing. After thirty, you realize you're not missing anything.

It helps you relax and makes the nights shorter, with fewer black eyes. What I had left inside, the part that was still whole and functioning, was hardly enough for me, and I couldn't see how it would be enough for someone else.

That was the scoreboard. Roxy was smart, lovely, and weak, and I was empty. Not a combination to ensure happiness, even for a couple of weeks.

But something surprised me. I cared for her and didn't see that coming.

SEVENTY-ONE

Game week dawned. To keep my legs strong, I got up each morning and put on my Red Sox T-shirt and jogged Double Wide's perimeter, Bundle beside me and the Glock on my hip.

I thought a lot about Sam. I'd asked Micah Alan Gabriel if he could arrange for Sam to listen to the radio broadcast of the game at the jail. I thought it would boost his spirits to remember better times, for him and for me.

Maybe he could listen and believe there was still hope. Gabriel said he'd get it done.

The cicadas screamed all week long. Whatever problem you have, cicadas make it worse.

Roxy finally called on Friday night.

"I'm in the parking lot at the Mustache Room," she said. "I worked this place when I was seventeen. I forgot all about it until I walked in the door."

"Seventeen? That can't be legal."

"I started earlier than that. I basically went from homeroom to the pole. They're gonna do a movie about me someday."

Sirens blared in the background, the mood music of the Strip. The pounding beat from inside the club sounded like distant artillery.

Roxy said, "Arthur's inside. He says his reputation will be ruined if he talks."

"It's the only way to save it. Maybe his life too."

"Bunny's working him hard like we figured. But this is going to be tough."

"We need him at that press conference, Rox."

"Doing my best. Hey, speaking of comebacks, if the Moustache Room offers me a job, you think I should take it?" She gave a Chivas laugh. "Ciao, baby."

Two hours before sunset on Saturday night, Diaz rolled into Double Wide with two cruisers trailing him. One of them kept going down Main Street behind Charlie's trailer and parked a few hundred yards up the mountain road.

He gave a couple of whoops on his siren to signal that he was in position. After conferring with Diaz, the second deputy drove out the entrance road and parked on the county road next to my Double Wide sign. He whooped his siren too.

That blocked two of the main entry points, and Cash had the wash covered.

After a final walking tour of the premises, Diaz said, "They'll stay through the night and I'll have another crew out here in the morning."

"I thought you'd be here a week and a half ago."

He bristled. "You think this was easy to get done? Do you know how many deputies we have to cover a nine-thousand-square-mile county? You're lucky the sheriff's a baseball fan."

"What about tomorrow morning?"

"I'll come back and we'll escort you into town. But I need to be clear, this is a one-time thing. After this game, you're on your own."

The night was full of sounds and sleepless, and in the morning Diaz returned with his relief deputies. Opal watched *Channel 7 News* on my kitchen TV. The game dominated the coverage. A young reporter did a live standup from outside Hi Corbett at 7:00 a.m., and the place already bustled with activity.

I couldn't watch, couldn't sit still.

Roxy hadn't called back with any more news about Melody. Every call I made to Oscar Molina went straight to voice mail. Same with Fausto.

Why is nobody calling back? Something must've happened in Mexico.

At 8:00 a.m., it was time to go. I loaded my gear into the Bronco. I kept Dr. Melody's gum in my pocket, in the Dexter tobacco tin. Cash and Charlie went ahead in the Dodge Dart and parked at the top of the mountains. Charlie stood by the car while Cash scouted the slopes sheltering Gates Pass.

From below, we could see him topping out on one hill, disappearing for a time and emerging on an adjoining one. He waved a red bandana over his head to signal all clear, and Diaz led the caravan out of Double Wide.

Opal and I followed in the Bronco, and a cruiser trailed us, roof lights spinning. The paved road, one lane each way, twisted through the saguaro and creosote flats. The thick brush on both sides offered good cover. Anyone could've stepped out of the desert and riddled us with bullets.

Diaz drove as fast as he could. But as the road climbed, the turns got tighter and the incline made speed impossible. The higher we went, the closer the mountains came to the road, until the black rock cliffs were hugging the pavement.

We inched along. There was stillness in the air, an odd calm. I looked out the window.

Boulder sat atop boulder on the mountain slopes. The saguaros seemed to grow out of the jutting bighorn cliffs. Higher up, amid clusters of prickly pear, the slopes became steeper with more cliffs that split into caves, and then came the peaks, jagged and crazy looking against the sky.

The danger made no impact on Opal. She sat next to me humming a song and eating jelly beans.

Another deputy waited at the top. Diaz stopped. The deputy approached Diaz's window, and the two spoke. Charlie used the break in the procession to join us in the Bronco for the ride to the ballpark.

I'd ordered Cash to stay behind and watch Angel: "Don't let him leave your side. If he goes to the bathroom, you go with him."

The deputy had stopped five cars coming from the opposite direction. He held them back with one arm and waved Diaz around the last elbow turn with the other, then waved the Bronco through, and there was the city spread out below, looking peaceful under a cover of Sunday-morning clouds.

That was good. No hot sun to sap my strength. Maybe I could go the full nine, and when it was over, tip my cap to the cheers of a standing crowd. I felt better than I had in a long time, as if some seed from my early days had sprouted again.

But there was anger, too. At the way my career had gone, how it ended, how the stories of my father's trial and my cocaine arrest dominated Google. They led the list for anyone who typed in my name.

Whip Stark, crook.

That was my legacy in black and white unless I could replace it with a competing story, something better, and that was the promise of the game. If I pitched well, I could banish Mazatlán, at least partially, and fill Google with accounts of the second great game Whip Stark pitched at Hi Corbett Field.

Life doesn't offer many chances at redemption, but this was mine, even if it was achieved with an illegal substance. Rolando would've loved that part.

Nearing the ballpark, I felt the old rush, the wicked burn of competition massing at my shoulders and spreading down my arms and legs. I couldn't wait to get back on the mound.

SEVENTY-TWO

The high temperature on Tequila Sunday only reached ninety-three degrees, not enough to cook a grilled cheese sandwich on the hood of your car. Late July is normally reliable grilled cheese weather. A drizzle helped. It fell on and off in the two hours before game time.

The circus was well underway when we pulled into the parking lot. Reporters rushed me as I stepped from the Bronco, shoving one another and barking out questions.

The clamor frightened Opal. She stayed behind me, one hand gripping the back of my shirt. Charlie walked ahead as a bulwark. He had on pink shorts, and his shirt sported the usual palm trees, only this version had gorillas on lawn chairs eating Doritos. By their expressions, they were having a wonderful time.

Charlie's belly stuck out, the gorillas helping him push through the crowd.

He said, "Whip Stark here, folks! Let's not crowd him! Whip Stark coming through!"

He struck out A-Rod and Jeter in the same inning! Move aside, you mortals!

As I passed a concession booth by the front gate, the salesman spotted me and held up one of his T-shirts. The front had P-H-E-N-O-M printed on it, above my image.

I stopped at the locker room door to remind the reporters to stick around for the postgame press conference. "You won't be disappointed," I said and ducked inside.

Danny Wilson came in with a quart of milk and a red Solo cup. A high-dollar talent like me gets to make certain demands, and that was mine, milk in the clubhouse. I felt fine until Danny started in.

"You've got to bring it today, Whip," he said. "Everything's riding on *El Bailador*."

"I know that."

"Where's Roxanne?" He smacked his palm with the back of his other hand. "We need Dr. Melody at this press conference. Where the hell is she?"

"She said he'd be here."

Wilson sat on a bench across from my locker, his hands folded between his knees. "If you get chased in the second inning, we'll both look like knuckleheads."

"I'm not going to get chased in the second inning."

"Third, fourth—that isn't so good either."

My stomach tightened. Messing with a pitcher before his start is like poking a tiger.

"I need you still throwing into the seventh inning," he said.

"Danny?"

"Yeah? What is it, Whipper? What is it, big guy?"

Softly, I said, "Get out of my face or I'll break both your arms."

Now I needed milk and plenty of it. I poured myself a tall cool one.

Two players in shower togs came over and shook my hand and said nice things about my career. They had faces like Little Leaguers. Others made cracks about the old man drinking milk in his underwear. I told them to go take a look at the Wall of Heroes.

If your teammates ignore you, you're cooked. If they ride you, you're in. Locker rooms never change.

The clubhouse buzzed. Thunder employees came in periodically to describe the wild scene outside, the traffic on Broadway and Twenty-Second Street, the fight for parking, the fight for tickets.

Whenever the clubhouse door opened, we heard the excited voices of fans streaming in, the shouts of vendors, and Springsteen wailing over the stadium's speakers. We also got a heavy whiff of diesel exhaust as charter buses from the foothills and the east side pulled up to unload fans, who promptly bolted for the ticket booths.

Wilson ordered that every ticket, except for those that season-ticket holders already held, would be a walk-up, with prices roughly doubled. He knew nobody was going to turn around and go home once they got there. The publicity had been consistent and fevered for that entire week, the anticipation just too high.

The players soaked up the boisterous energy. No one dragged around. No one moaned about a hangover or a nagging injury.

I got the day's first sighting of Rod Peña when he bounced out of the shower to the emotional wail of Mexican music. The song was the usual bloodbath, a smashed-up *corazon* here, another over there, and all of it accompanied by sobbing trumpets.

He was short, thick, black as coal, and well put together, the muscle all natural. No weight rooms for Rod Peña. He had a rising mound of muscle from his shoulders to his neck and prominent pecs. He wore only a white towel around his middle and shower flip-flops.

Shaving cream covered his entire head, except for a half-moon razor swipe over his left ear. It looked like the path the first snowplow makes after a storm.

He danced around with one hand flat to his belly, the other raised to accommodate the imaginary woman he was holding. She must've been a beauty, for his eyes were clamped shut and his face scrambled with passion as he gave it every bit of his lungs.

Several players sang along, and when the song ended, they clapped and hooted.

Peña somehow disposed of his woman without a scene, took a deep bow complete with a dramatic hand sweep, righted himself and belted out a series of high-pitched cries, like he'd dropped a rock on his foot.

With his face suddenly severe, he leaned close to me, and in heavily accented English, said, "We go dancing this day, my friend?"

"Yes, we're going dancing!"

"*El Bailador!*" He screamed the words and danced away.

SEVENTY-THREE

The stadium's capacity is ten thousand, but Wilson had removed the outfield fences and stretched yellow police tape from foul pole to foul pole around the warning track. Fans covered every inch of ground behind the tape. They sat on blankets, captain's chairs, ice chests, the grass itself, and on each other. There had to be four thousand more people back there.

On the waist-high wall along the first base line, someone had attached twenty blank cardboard squares. At each of my strikeouts, they'd fill a square with a K, the expectation being that I could reach twenty again.

I took my warm-up throws, and when it came time for the first pitch, Rod ran out to the mound and pulled off his catcher's mask and leaned over with his newly shaved head almost in my face.

The crowd response told me they knew what was going on. But I didn't. It seemed that Rod's pregame ritual involved shaving his head to bowling ball purity and letting the starting pitcher give it a public rubbing for good luck. The crowd clapped in rhythm until I caught on and rubbed his head, and they clapped even more.

The first inning didn't go well. I walked the second batter on four pitches. In my eagerness to fill up the strike zone, I hung a curve to the cleanup hitter, and he launched it over the tape in centerfield, giving the Stars a 2–0 lead.

In the second inning, I lost the jitters and threw *El Bailador* for the first time. With two strikes on a batter, I let it fly. The ball moved like a dream. It would've been called a ball if the batter hadn't gone for it, but he took a lunging swing more suited to a nine iron, and missed by two feet.

Walking away, he gave me the bitter eye, and in the dugout I saw him making a dive-bomb motion with his hand. That put the hitters on alert.

Every one of them would be waiting for *El Bailador*.

I threw it several more times in the second and third innings, probably more than I should have. But it thrilled me to see the baffled reaction of the batters. After the third inning, Rod told me to slow it down, and he was on to something.

After the first few pitches of the fourth inning, the Stars' manager asked the umpire to inspect the ball. He found nothing and threw it back into play. The manager stormed out and demanded the umpire inspect my glove and clothing.

The manager shouted, "Nobody can make a ball move like that!"

The umpire ran a finger under the wrist strap on my glove and along the bottom of the pocket. He looked at my pant leg and cap for illegal substances. He felt along my forearms for the same thing.

I stood on the mound chewing Melody's gum the whole time. The crowd stomped and screamed through the delay. The umpire declared me clean. Rod smiled with his gold teeth and trotted back to the plate.

The fourth inning ended with the Thunder still trailing 2–0. But by then I'd fallen into that cocoon of concentration in which sounds disappear, distractions disappear, and the world empties except for the ball and the catcher's glove.

We tied the game in the sixth on a two-run homer and went ahead 3–2 on four straight hits in the seventh. We held that lead into the top of the ninth.

I got the first batter on a called third strike and walked the second batter. The one after that hit a line single to centerfield, the Stars holding the lead runner at third. That put runners on second and third with one out.

I was at ninety-eight pitches and feeling an energy dump. Rod sprang to his feet and ran to the mound, all the while looking over to see what the manager wanted. The manager stood on the top step of the dugout. He knew it wasn't his game and wasn't his call, but he'd pull me if that's what I wanted. I held my hand up to him. He nodded. I was staying in.

The strikeout wall showed eight red Ks in eight-and-a-third innings, a long way from twenty, but that was a lifetime ago. Nobody would fault me for letting a relief pitcher try to get the final two outs.

But I wanted to finish it, for myself and for my father listening from his cell. With the crowd cheering, I wanted him to hear the announcer say that Whip Stark, in his return to baseball, had pitched a complete game.

I got the first batter on a bit of luck. He went for a pitch out of the zone and rolled a topper back to the mound. I looked the runner back to third and threw the batter out at first.

One out remained.

The first pitch I threw split the middle of the plate. I was lucky. The batter was way ahead of it. He fouled off the next pitch, leaving a no-ball-and-two-strikes count. Three times in a row Rod signaled for *El Bailador*, and I threw it three times into the dirt in front of the plate.

But the batter wouldn't bite.

That left a three-and-two count. Rod came out again to talk to me. "Throw the pitch. Throw it again. I know he'll bite!"

I threw the dancer one more time, and the batter lunged.

I had summoned all my reserves to throw that pitch. No muscle in my body went unused. Even my hat had taken part. It went flying just like in the old days. I made no effort to pick it up and couldn't if I wanted to. I had nothing left. My mind and my body were cold chicken soup.

Swing and a miss. Game over.

With the crowd roaring, I bent over and put my hands on my knees. Next thing I knew, Rod had me in his grip as our teammates swarmed us, jumping and screaming in unison.

In the melee, I glimpsed a woman in a white shirt jumping the wall onto the field. Two cops grabbed for her, but she was a firecracker with the tossed elbows and flying black hair.

That was all I saw before the throng closed around me again, cameras clicking, players grabbing my hand and leaning in for a shoulder bump.

Someone smeared my face with a towel full of shaving cream. I was wiping it away when a pair of arms went around my neck and locked there. I felt a soft cheek against mine, smelled sweet perfume.

"You did it!" Roxy exclaimed. "You did it, Prospero! I'm so proud of you!"

"You made it back. Is Melody here?"

"Don't I always get the story? Isn't that what I told you?"

The two cops she'd evaded came to nab their fugitive. When they saw who it was, one of them said, "You're Roxanne Santa Cruz! The reporter lady!"

"At your service, officer," she said, and smiled through the smear of shaving cream.

"But you're with the TV," he said. "You didn't have to jump the wall."

"I was too excited to wait," she said.

As they walked away, one of them looked back and said, "Beautiful game, Whip."

With her face beaming, Roxy threw her arms around my neck again. "It was a beautiful game, the most beautiful baseball game ever. Now let's go piss in Max Mayflower's lunch box."

SEVENTY-FOUR

The press conference was in a small meeting room under the stadium. It held maybe forty folding chairs.

Danny Wilson waited for me while I showered and got an ice bag taped to my shoulder. He was a wreck. He kept checking his watch and snapping his fingers into his palm. A door in the locker room led to the back of the pressroom, which was packed and smelled like cheese nachos.

We sat behind a table covered with tape recorders and microphones. I scanned the crowd to find Roxy and Dr. Melody, but the TV lights blurred everything beyond the first few rows.

Someone shouted, "Tell us, Whip, how were you able to strike out nine batters after a two-year absence from the game?"

Wilson held his hand up. "We're not having an ordinary press conference today. If you'll stay with me, I'd like to make a few remarks about how important it is to play honestly and fairly and, most of all, by the established rules of the game of baseball."

He pulled out a piece of paper and made a Cecil B. DeMille scene out of spreading it out on the table, squeaking his chair, coughing, adjusting the microphone, coughing again.

His voice started uneven but smoothed out as he explained his decision to allow me to pitch the game and how he thought it was the best way to expose a serious threat to the integrity of baseball.

He hadn't gone far when a voice called out, "Come on, Danny, we didn't come here for you to read to us. What's this about?"

Departing his script, Wilson said, "You asked how Whip here was able to strike out nine batters. Well, I'll tell you how. That gum he was chewing—that's a special gum made out of the agave plant that grows right out here in our Sonoran Desert."

The reporters traded puzzled looks.

The same voice said, "You mean Whip Stark was hammered on tequila?"

Everyone laughed.

Wilson said, "What I mean is, he was throwing a spitball, an old-fashioned shine ball, ladies and gentlemen."

The room rumbled with shocked voices. The noise grew as the back door swung open. Wilson shielded his eyes and squinted into the TV lights as Bunny Slippers emerged from the glare. She made a stage of the center aisle, striding along, heels tapping.

She was heavily made up with blue eyeshadow and dark-blue lipstick. She wore tight jeans and an even tighter leopard print shirt. Her big arms made it out of the short sleeves, but barely. If she took a deep breath, a button might fly off and hurt somebody.

Near the tables, she looked back as if surprised that no one had followed her. She waved like a mom hurrying a child, and along came Arthur Melody. He made no sound but for the *swish* of his corduroy slacks. He walked on his turned-in toes, careful not to break any eggs.

He had on a paisley shirt and his William Holden glasses from Walgreens.

Wilson piped up: "Why don't I forgo the remainder of my statement and throw this over to Whip. He can talk on this matter some more."

I pulled out the Dexter tobacco tin, took out the remaining gum, and held it up for everyone to see.

"Like Danny said, my pitch out there today that tied up those guys—that was a spitball, a doctored pitch using this gum right here. The inventor, the brilliant botanist Dr. Arthur Melody, is standing to my right."

The reporters shouted questions. I shut them down to finish my statement.

"People have been killed over this, and the men responsible need to pay," I said. "The first is the agent Max Mayflower. He hired Dr. Melody to create this gum using the sap from the Palmer agave.

"The agreement involved the vicious cartel enforcer Roscoe Rincon. He allowed access to the agave plants on Paradise Mountain to keep producing it, and in return was allowed to launder his drug money through a club owned by Mr. Mayflower. Men have been murdered as a result, and Rincon and Max Mayflower need to answer for those deaths."

Reporters scribbled into their skinny notebooks. Cameras whirred. There was nothing to do then but keep talking. The hardest part was talking about Rolando's involvement in the conspiracy, but I had to do it.

When I was done, Melody sat behind the microphones and read from a prepared statement detailing his dealings with Mayflower.

He began with a lot of trench coat talk about their first meeting. Mayflower's demand for secrecy. An initial public meeting place where a different man showed up, and that man driving Melody to a hotel room on the freeway.

I wondered if the driver had been Ed Bolt. Mayflower paid Melody his up-front fee in cash, in a plain paper bag.

The initial deal called for Melody to deliver a usable PED made from steroidal saponins. When that didn't work, Melody engaged Mayflower in offhand conversation about his favorite subject, the sap from the Palmer agave and his decades-long work with A. A. Bildenson to use it in a lubricant.

More as a lark than anything, Melody remarked that if he could develop a way to apply a substance of that viscosity to a pitcher's fingers, the result would be an unhittable spitball. But it had to be concealable and leave behind a clean ball.

Mayflower jumped at the idea. Melody got another bag of cash and went to work searching for a workable delivery system.

He settled on gum, ordinary chewing gum with a small but precise amount of Palmer sap added, along with "a few modest chemical enhancements" to maintain its integrity and remove its toxic properties.

He declined to document exactly how much of the sap he used or say anything about his enhancements. He kept the information secret from Mayflower as well, which explained the false research he'd created.

Melody said he did so because he no longer trusted Mayflower and had begun to fear him. He wanted to delay turning over the formula as long as possible while he tried to extricate himself from the deal.

"When I came to suspect that serious crimes might be involved, I hired a lawyer to help me do the right thing," Melody said. "To me, the project was a work of science using skills I'd developed over a lifetime. My mistake from the beginning was trusting Max Mayflower."

Maybe that was plausible for an innocent professor lost in his work. But trusting a man who worked with paper bags full of cash should've been a tipoff.

I suspected there might've been more to Melody's motives. In withholding the formula from Mayflower, he might've been plotting a shakedown of his own, demanding more money in exchange for the real formula.

At the end of Melody's speech, Bunny Slippers got up and stood behind him, placing her hand lovingly on his shoulder.

That's when it became clear this was a performance, and Bunny was the master director. She'd schooled Melody on how to put on a show, ensuring his name and his invention would be known around the country, even as he distanced himself from the resulting crimes.

He concluded, saying, "I deeply regret the terrible things that happened, the lives lost as a result of my work. If I'd known that was even possible, I never would've accepted Mr. Mayflower's offer."

Reporters shouted questions, but Melody didn't respond. He fell back into dazed-professor mode. Bunny leaned into a microphone. "I want to say that I insisted that Arthur accompany me to Las Vegas, Nevada, where I had a long-standing commitment to perform at a club called the Mustache Room."

A voice shouted, "Never heard of it!" His tone meant the opposite.

Everyone laughed. Bunny said, "Two nights a week, sugar. Stop on by."

More laughter. Bunny raised her hands to bring quiet. "I want you to know Arthur Melody didn't run from nobody. That's not what happened."

She paused to emphasize the importance of what she was about to say. "As soon as Arthur found out these were evil men, he wanted out. But when they threatened to kill him, I made him come to Vegas to save his life. That's as true as I can make it."

SEVENTY-FIVE

The press conference lasted ninety minutes. As I exited, I saw Roxy and Benny Diaz standing against the back wall. Diaz asked us to join him in Wilson's office.

I knew something important was happening when he cop-marched around Wilson's desk and sat erect in the chair. That caused Wilson to pull up and stand there looking puzzled. Charlie and Opal stood at the back of the room. Roxy and I sat opposite the desk.

Diaz folded his hands on the desktop and said, "I noticed in your little speech you didn't mention anything about Rolando Molina's severed hand."

My stomach flipped. I tried to stay stone faced, but I don't think it worked.

Diaz said, "Right hand, Virgin Mary tattoo between the thumb and forefinger? You must remember that tattoo, Whip?"

"Rolando had one just like it."

"A hiker found a hand matching that description in a wash on Paradise Mountain." Diaz shook his head as if he couldn't believe it either. "How about that? Your friend's hand in a plastic freezer bag, half-buried under a rock. Reasonably well preserved."

The floodwaters must've washed it out of the well and carried it off. I sat motionless and said nothing. Wilson stood with his hands in his pockets. He knew nothing of the hand or my involvement in hiding it, but he knew enough to keep his mouth shut.

"We tried pulling prints but no luck," Diaz said. "I'd love to know how it got there."

I didn't move or speak. Roxy jiggled her foot.

Diaz said, "I don't see Roscoe Rincon killing your friend and putting the hand in a plastic bag. Somebody who cared for him did that, somebody who cared a great deal."

Roxy jiggled some more. My stomach turned right side up, only now it was full of ants.

Diaz said, "Words are easy, like the wind. But faithful friends are hard to find."

"Shakespeare," I said. "I'm blanking on the play."

"*The Passionate Pilgrim*," Diaz said, and his eyes held mine. They weren't angry or searching. They looked peaceful in a way. For a full minute, he stared through the unbearable silence. Four people breathing in an office can sound like a jet plane in a janitor's closet.

"I've placed a call to the Molina family in Mexico," Diaz said. "If you've got any ideas where to look for Rolando's body, I'm interested."

He slapped his palms down on the desk, stood up, and walked out of the room. Roxy and I went out too. Just as we stepped onto the concourse, her phone rang with a loud rendition of "The Bitch Is Back," the Elton John song.

Two seconds later, Diaz's phone played the theme from *Hawaii Five-O*.

As he read his message, Diaz turned and walked back to us looking at his screen, his face taut in concentration. "There's been a shooting at the residence of Mr. Max Mayflower. Black male dead by the front door, one bullet hole in his forehead, another through the heart."

Not looking up from her phone, Roxy jumped in: "Deceased white female in back. Floater. Well, well."

"It looks like Roscoe Rincon's going after his partner now," Diaz said. "I guess I'm working late." He turned and walked quickly down the concourse toward the exit.

Roxy and I followed. As she walked, she fingered more text onto her screen. "No sign of Mayflower. Uniforms searching the neighborhood." She slipped the phone into her back pocket and quickened her stride. "We can get there in twenty."

Annoyed, Diaz said, "You receive the same alert seconds before me. That's just wrong."

"It should've been sooner. I'll have to straighten some people out."

"Would I be wasting my time if I told you to stay away?"

"Come on, Benny. I'll get the information anyway, so it might as well come from you. Besides, Prospero and I have been there and can help ID the bods."

"No cameras at my crime scene. Just you and Whip under the tape. And do me a favor, Roxanne?"

"Of course."

"Let me get there first."

SEVENTY-SIX

It was 7:15 p.m., not quite dark. The day's last light glowed behind the mountains. Driving the Audi, Roxy did her best to stay on Benny Diaz's bumper, using his spinning roof light as a guide as we raced through the city at twilight.

But he gunned it to beat a red light and disappeared. Roxy pounded the steering wheel. "Did you see that! He did that on purpose! That prissy jerk!"

I choked down a laugh. Cops and reporters.

She slapped the Audi into reverse, swung into the space between the lanes, and inched forward, biting her lip to keep from pin-striping adjoining cars. At the front of the line, she gunned it without waiting for the light to flip.

Ten minutes later, we pulled up to Mayflower's ranch house off Campbell Avenue, halfway up the foothills. Diaz stood outside with three uniforms. Cop headlights from the driveway lit the place like an amusement park. The front door was wide open and it looked as if every inside light had been turned on as well. Crime scene techs bustled around.

The first victim lay flat on his back in the doorway. He was barefoot and bare chested, wearing only lime-green shorts. His mouth and eyes were open, his lips stretched wide over prominent teeth.

The expression of shock was probably the same one he had right after he opened the door, looked down the dark gun barrel—the instrument of his death—and thought, "Oh, shit."

Diaz got as close as he could without stepping in the ocean of blood. Down on his haunches, hands folded between his knees, he said, "One in the chest when he opens the door, one in the head to make sure. Professional job. Tentative ID is Reggie Lake."

Roxy looked over Diaz's shoulder. "That's him. Worked for Mayflower."

"We found his ID in the guest house in back," Diaz said. "It's the other one we need help with. Follow me, if you would."

We jump-stepped around the blood and went through the kitchen and out the sliding glass door to the backyard. The second victim floated face down in the pool, the water a sickly yellow with the mix of her blood. She was tanned and blond and had on a white bikini bottom, no top. A tattoo of a fire-breathing dragon decorated most of her back.

Two men from the Pima County Coroner's Office laid out a black body bag on the deck beside the pool. As Diaz approached, one of them straightened up and said, "Detective," and they both stepped aside.

Diaz said, "It looks like the killer shot Mr. Lake at the door and chased this victim through the house, caught up to her here. Pop, pop, two in the back of the head."

He nodded to the coroner's men, and they lifted her out of the water. She couldn't have weighed more than a hundred pounds, but she made them struggle to get her laid out on her back on the zipper bag. The dead always make a last effort to matter.

"We're not finding a purse, a car, nothing to identify her," Diaz said, and leaned down to finger a chunk of wet hair off her face. Her right eye was open and frozen and blue as the sky. A bullet had passed through the left eye, leaving a round black hole.

Roxy looked. "Sorry, Benny. I don't have a name on this one."

Diaz tilted his head at me.

"Never saw her before," I said.

Diaz stripped off his crime scene gloves and handed them to one of the workers. He put his hands on his hips, eyes roaming the scene, thinking. Probably twenty cops and other officials stalked the backyard, not talking much, each doing separate jobs with grim efficiency.

Diaz said, "Mayflower's out here enjoying himself by the pool. He hears the shots at the door, knows he's got a few seconds at best, and takes off running."

"Leaves the girl to fend for herself out here," Roxy said. "What a guy."

"It was business. No witnesses." Diaz motioned to the back of the property. "Mayflower jumps the fence and escapes ahead of the gunman. Won't get far. We'll have him before the night's out."

I noticed something. The gate at the west side of the house was wide open. I remembered our first trip to Mayflower's house, when I checked the registration on the Chrysler LeBaron in the driveway. Apart from Reggie Lake, only one other person had been at Mayflower's house that night, his girlfriend.

I gave Roxy the high sign. We finished with Diaz and left through the open gate.

In the front yard, I said to Roxy, "Mayflower didn't go over that fence."

"I'm thinking the same thing."

"They can't find the victim's car because Mayflower bolted through the open gate and beat it in his girlfriend's Chrysler LeBaron."

"What was her name? Lily Lee something."

"Summers. You wrote down the address."

"I should have it here somewhere."

Roxy threw open the back door of the Audi and leaned in. Her backseat looked like a homeless camp. She sorted through piles of newspapers, food wrappers, beer cans, multiple pairs of shoes, some pantyhose, fast-food bags, and half-eaten boxes of jujubes.

She went through some old notebooks to find the one she wanted and flipped to the correct page. "Lily Lee Summers. Lives right up the hill here, unit 51A, Copper Queen Apartments."

I said, "Want to bet that's where Mayflower went?"

"Let's go."

"Should we tell Diaz?"

Roxy glared at me. "I'll pretend you didn't say that."

SEVENTY-SEVEN

Roxy hit the accelerator so hard it launched her back in the seat, arms straight out, hands squeezing the wheel. Campbell Avenue winds high into the Catalina foothills. With no moon on a black night and no streetlights, only the Audi's streaking high beams lit the way.

The darkness hid the fine pueblo-style homes in the desert beyond the road, an occasional window light winking through the tangle of brush.

Over the roar of the engine, I said, "Lily Lee woke up happy this morning because she had a date with her boyfriend."

Roxy said nothing, her face mangled in concentration as she darted in and out of traffic, the descending whine of angry horns all around us.

The Copper Queen Apartments consisted of three buildings set in the mouth of a canyon on the north side of Skyline Drive, a main east-west thoroughfare. The place looked well tended and elegant. The location high above the city probably added $300 a month to the rent.

The buildings were painted white, the apartment doors red, and the roofs covered in copper-colored sheeting. The main office looked like a country club with putting-green grass all around it, a glass front, and chandeliers throwing off bright light inside.

We drove down to Building A. The LeBaron was parked right outside unit 51. No lights shone in the apartment.

Roxy said, "Mayflower's hiding under his bed. How do we get him out of there?"

"Pound on his door. Don't identify yourself, don't say anything. He'll think it's Rincon and take off out the back."

"How much time you need to get back there?"

"Count to fifty," I said.

"You can move faster than that. You're a jock. Make it thirty."

The night was silent. No cars moving. No people walking. I raced to the back of the building on spaghetti legs. Nine tough innings will do that. Sweat beaded out on my forehead.

I turned the corner and hustled along the sidewalk between the swimming pool and the back of the apartments. The pool sat above flagstone steps leading to a shelf higher than the apartments, on the first rise of the Catalinas.

The water slightly cooled the night air. Add another $300 to the rent.

Lily Lee's apartment was the fifth in from the end of the building. At exactly thirty seconds, I pushed open the wrought-iron gate leading to the back of the fifth apartment.

A short porch led to a sliding glass door, the curtain half-open. A jumble of sounds came from inside the apartment, of the kind made by confusion, chaos, someone stumbling, knocking into furniture in the dark.

Then the sound took the shape of a vague figure, arms and legs flailing as he ran toward me. Mayflower rolled open the rear door and shot onto the porch. His journey stretched to three feet and ended when I kicked a lounge chair into his path.

His legs got tangled and he showed the sky his heels before landing with a thud on the cement. He lay on his back moaning, eyes spinning. When he recognized me and realized he was alive and would stay that way, he growled for an ambulance, a doctor, a lawyer, and the police. He left his Pilates instructor out of it.

"Someone tried to murder me! I've committed no crime!"

I broke up laughing, and when Roxy ran through the gate, she did too. Mayflower wore the same lambskin robe he had on the first time we'd met at his backyard pool. Chestnut colored and the length of a miniskirt, it stopped above his knees with his hairy pipe-stem legs swinging out the bottom.

"That robe should be ten years minimum," I said, and shoved him into a porch chair. The effort caused the robe to fall open.

Roxy said, "It ain't Christmas, Max." She shielded her eyes. "Hide the package, please."

"He invaded my home! He tried to murder me!"

I tied his hands behind his back with the robe's sash.

"Who are we talking about, Max?"

"I didn't see anybody. I saw nothing. I didn't have to. It was Roscoe Rincon."

"That's some partner you've got there."

"He's crazy! He killed Alvarez and Rolando Molina. I had nothing to do with any of that. That was all Rincon. I wanted Rolando's brother in the big leagues—that's all."

Hearing him say Rolando's name spun me up. Rioting blood made my face hot. I squeezed his jaw and leaned down. "What you need to do right now, Max, is shut the hell up. I don't want to hear that name coming out of your mouth again."

I pulled out my phone to call Diaz and tell him we'd found Mayflower.

Roxy stopped me. "I didn't drive up here for the scenery. Let me." She was smiling as she punched in his number.

SEVENTY-EIGHT

R oxy had to do some talking when Diaz arrived. He was mad, which must've explained his shirttail hanging out in back—a rare sartorial imperfection.

He directed most of his ire at Roxy, saying she'd withheld Lily Lee Summers's name at Mayflower's house. Roxy explained that she had to fetch her notebook out of the car first, and even then, it was only a hunch that Mayflower had gone to Lily's.

"We lucked out and found him, and now he's yours," Roxy said. "So what's the problem exactly?"

Eventually, Diaz let it go. Every cop in town knew they had more to lose than gain from a fight with Roxanne Santa Cruz.

She and I waited in the front parking lot of the apartment complex watching Diaz do his business. There must've been fifteen squad cars standing by, all of them angle parked the way they teach it at the academy.

Diaz put Mayflower into the back of one of the cars and walked over to us.

"Mayflower says we'll find Rolando Molina's body on Paradise Mountain. You two crackerjack amateur sleuths know nothing about that?"

"Nope," Roxy said.

"Not a thing," I said. "Haven't you searched up there a dozen times already?"

"At least. He's probably lying, but we have to look again. We'll send some deputies up there in the morning."

Copper Queen residents had gathered on the sidewalk to watch, some of them in nightclothes. Cop radios let out staggered burps and beeps. The proximity of the big mountains made the sounds bigger and more dramatic.

Diaz watched the squad car carrying Mayflower roll out of the lot. He said, "It's all about Roscoe Rincon now, Whip. My advice is to pack up your desert circus out at their Double Wide and drive away."

"I'd miss the views. You know how I feel about the views."

"Buy a picture book."

"What about the people that live out there, Benny? They count on me."

"They're drifters. They'll find a new place."

"Get lost, move it along. That's all they ever hear."

"But now they've got a home, is that it? That makes you what, landlord, parole officer, case manager?"

Roxy scoffed in agreement. "You got that right."

"Don't forget chef," I said. "I run a pretty fair greasy spoon."

The lines in Diaz's face tightened. "For a guy like Rincon, revenge is food, and after you fingered him to the whole world tonight, I guarantee you he's hungry."

"I've been running since Mazatlán, Benny. No more."

"You're a baseball player. Rincon's a cold killer. You don't know what you're facing."

"One way or another, we're going to meet. Nothing I say or do can change that."

"Just leave Double Wide and it's over." He stopped to gather himself and then continued in his reasonable tone: "Take a trip for yourself, give us time. Every free hand we've got will be looking for Rincon. If we find him, this goes away and you can concentrate on Sam."

"Can't do it, Benny."

He nodded with resignation. "I figured."

SEVENTY-NINE

I got up the next morning and peered out the door. The early sun painted the sky in a dramatic blue-gray light.

Opal was spread out corpse-like on the foldout, one arm and one leg hanging off the mattress, her head nearly off, that long hair obscuring her face and tumbling all the way to the floor. It shook in and out as she breathed.

I made coffee and let it perk while I went outside. Cash sat on his front porch watching Angel's trailer. If Cash ever slept, I was unaware of it. Vampire blood.

He hollered to me down the street, "Cops," and pointed toward Paradise Mountain.

Up on the slope, the sun gleamed off a car as it bounced down the road toward Double Wide. Two other cars were farther up on the peak. Diaz had made good on his promise to search for Rolando. They wouldn't find a thing.

The breeze felt nice. The birds sang behind the pure light of the morning.

I called out to Cash, "I feel like cooking this morning. You in?"

"Be down in a minute. I'll roust Charlie."

I went back into the Airstream and made breakfast. Opal sat up in bed in her Spiderman pajamas. "Mr. Whip, can I just say something. Oh, my God! Like, what time is it even? I couldn't sleep at all."

"Yeah, I could tell."

I rolled up a scrambled egg burrito with bacon bits and handed it to her. She made *mmm-mmm* noises as she ate. She sounded like one of Gladys Knight's Pips.

Roxy called. She'd spent the night at the station working on her stories.

"Have you turned on the TV? It's all you, Prospero. They're saying you could write your ticket back into the game, gum or no gum."

"I put my soul through that wood chipper once. I'm not doing it again."

I motioned for Opal to turn on the TV. She fumbled for the remote, broke off a yawn that ended with a resounding elk bugle, and flipped on CNN. My face filled the screen. The story was a morning show extravaganza.

"The legendary left hander, reportedly in seclusion at his remote desert outpost..."

"Murders at the luxurious home of Max Mayflower, one of the game's hottest young agents, now in custody..."

"A secret formula derived from the agave and invented by a botany professor..."

"A pitch called *El Bailador*, the dancer..."

Roxy said, "Have you read my stories at the KPIN site? I posted three of them and beat everybody." She was running on no sleep and sounded frazzled.

I wasn't interested in reading about Mayflower's arrest, the press conference, none of it. And I had no interest in what CNN said about the game and what it meant for my prospects. My career was over. I knew what I'd done in my final game and couldn't have been prouder, especially for what it meant to Sam.

Roxy said, "Has Angel told you anything more about Rolando?"

"Not a word. He spends all his time hunting rabbits and burying them."

"You need to think about what Diaz said. He's right, you know."

I talked with my phone on the counter, set on speaker. I was making blueberry waffles. Cooking gave me something to do while I noodled things out. The egg whites have to be beaten until they're stiff. Anything but real butter is cheating.

"There might be a solution to this," Roxy said.

I added a few drops of vanilla to the batter for the aroma.

Roxy said, "If you threaten to run Angel off, he might talk. Think about it. His chances of surviving Rincon on his own are zero. How many murders has Angel seen him commit?"

I poured the batter into the waffle maker, sprinkled the blueberries on top, and closed the lid. "If Angel's gone or dead, I'll never find out what he knows about Rolando."

"The kid knows that too. And he knows you won't play hardball."

When I didn't dispute that, Roxy breathed a sigh. "Okay, have it your way. But I'm going to call every morning and again at dinner to make sure you're all right."

"You don't have to do that."

"If you don't pick up, I'm calling 911 and coming out there myself. That's a promise."

Cash and Charlie came. I fixed plates for them and one for Opal, her second breakfast. She had a healthy appetite. Roxy was right about a lot of things, the most obvious being that by the time she got to Double Wide, everything would be over. But I kept that to myself.

We broke off the call, and I spent the remainder of the day indoors. Late the next afternoon, Oscar and Fausto Molina drove down my entrance road.

EIGHTY

I'd had no contact with Oscar since our last phone call, when he told me he was going to Mexico City to search for Fausto. He'd failed to return multiple calls. I brought them inside, closed and locked my door, and poured them lemonade, and we sat at my kitchen table.

"You've made a ghost of yourself, Oscar," I said. "I thought something bad happened."

"I didn't call you because they listen in. You know they do that, Whip. These cartel men, they have ways of finding out what they need to know."

He was right about that, and I said so.

He gave me a fierce look. "I wasn't going to lose another boy."

There was nothing I could say to that.

He invented the story of going to Mexico City, and made sure to say so in his last phone call to me—an effort to throw off the men hunting Fausto. Instead, the Molinas had holed up at Oscar's gold camp in the mountains until Diaz called asking Fausto to testify against Mayflower.

When it was Fausto's turn to talk, he could barely raise his eyes to look at me. I remembered Wilson describing Mayflower's plan to market the boy as much as *El Bailador* and turn him into a teenage celebrity.

Seeing Fausto for the first time, I thought it might've worked.

He was lean and muscular with soft, almost feminine features. His hair was light, more like gringo hair. His eyes were a rich brown with long lashes and thick, swooping eyebrows much darker than his hair. He had a goatee that tried valiantly to make something of itself, but it needed more years.

Oscar told Fausto to go ahead and talk. He said he knew nothing about how the gum was made, the connection to drug smuggling and heroin, none of it. All he knew was that Rolando had given it to him and taught him how to use it, and it worked.

Rolando's instructions were to keep quiet about it no matter what.

"Even after he went missing?" I said. "You didn't think he might be in trouble?"

Fausto's eyes begged forgiveness. I thought he might cry.

"He was out of his mind on cocaine, Whip," he said. "I thought that's what he was off doing and didn't want to get him in trouble." He was almost pleading. "Mayflower told me not to talk to anybody. He threatened to kill me."

No doubt he did. But I also knew that Fausto was winning games with that gum, and I remembered what it felt like to be young and on top and willing to do anything to stay there. If he'd spoken up, it might not have saved Rolando's life, but he'd never know for sure, and the question would likely haunt him forever.

Based on Diaz's offer of protection, the rest of the Molina family planned to come to Tucson as soon possible. Oscar had an appointment with Diaz later that evening.

"He wants me to make an identification," Oscar said, and his voice fell. "Of the hand."

Fausto heard that and whimpered. Oscar put his hand on his son's shoulder. "Go get something to eat, *mijo*. I'm sure Whip has food."

There was cold pizza in the fridge and Fausto went.

"I won't say anything to Diaz about you having the hand, Whip," Oscar said. "We know how much you loved our boy." He lost his voice to grief, and when he could speak again, the sound was small and hushed. "All we want now is a proper burial."

"I'll find Rolando. I made a promise and plan to keep it."

Oscar nodded in acknowledgment. "I have something that might help. It's not much."

"Please, anything."

He leaned across the table. "There's a fellow works for me that got run out of the Sierra Madre by one of the *narcos* up there, by one man in particular. Roscoe Rincon. Everyone knows him in that region. He owns mines there, and the ones he couldn't buy, he murdered to get."

"Gold mines."

"He loves gold. Talks about gold all the time." Oscar spread his hands. "Does that help?"

Maybe it did. I had a hunch—a long shot but worth a try.

When Rincon told his men to dispose of Rolando's body, what if they drove to a place they knew, another remote gold mine Rincon had found on the Arizona border? With Paradise Mountain in the police spotlight, Rincon was relocating his heroin operation. He needed a new trail, and to indulge his obsession, he might've chosen one with a gold mine nearby.

After Oscar and Fausto left, I called Tork Mortenson, the historical society curator who first alerted me to gunmen threatening visitors on Paradise Mountain. At the time, he'd said members of the Rich Hill Gang had been concentrating on border-area mines.

In Mortenson's book I found five possibilities, gold mines that had thrived and died in the mountains along the Mexican line. If the Rich Hill Gang visited those mines, they might've seen something suspicious, some sign of renewed activity.

Mortenson said they'd visited two of the five mines but encountered nothing interesting. "Next weekend we're traveling to Oro Grande in the Patagonia Mountains, and I'm leading the group," he said. "It seems you've inspired me to get back into it."

I cautioned him to be careful.

"I'm way ahead of you," he said. "The marshal in Patagonia's a dear friend, and he's agreed to escort us. He came on board when I informed him of our exhaustive food preparations." He chuckled. "Lots of iced tea and exotic cheeses."

EIGHTY-ONE

The next few days were hot and slow moving. Opal and Charlie spent most of the time in the Airstream, the door closed and locked. Cash came in at odd intervals to eat standing up and then hurry back outside on patrol.

I strapped the Glock to my hip in the morning, and it stayed there all day. The gun weighs a little less than two pounds. I felt it at first, the burden of it. After a few days, I couldn't feel anything. But when I took it off to go to bed, I didn't feel right. Something was missing.

The shootists of the Old West must've felt the same way.

There had been a change in everyone's attitude. The tension was there from the beginning, but as the days passed, it intensified, and the conversations got shorter.

Charlie played solitaire and chattered on about anything that came to mind. It was all nervous talk. He told jokes only he understood and laughed alone. Opal passed the time cooking.

Exactly a week after Tequila Sunday, we were sitting at my kitchen table when a late-night thunderstorm blew in, the first in days. The sounds of it knocking around outside rattled Opal, and got her talking about Gila monsters.

"They come out of their burrows at night to look for food." She chewed on a strand of her hair and stared across the table as she spoke. "The closer they get to you, the more the ground shakes. He's probably out there right now."

Charlie wasn't much better off. His eyes were puffy and restless. I poured him a Coke. He splashed it with gin from his pocket flask and got up to return to his trailer for the night.

Before walking out, he said, "Doesn't it wear you down, Mayor? Thinking he's coming all the time and nothing?"

"Hang in there," I said. "Rincon wants us to drop our guard."

"Wish he'd get it over with." Charlie stood at the door watching the rain. Chico came out from under the table and hobbled down the steps. Charlie watched him go. "Where's Jack the coyote at, anyhow? He's usually out there giving us the business."

"Go home, Charlie. Cash has us covered."

"You're right, Mayor. Cashy's good. Old Cashy'll watch over us."

Opal got her foldout ready for the night. Before going back to my own bed, I opened the door one last time and whistled for Chico. Sometimes he explored for a while and barked when it was time to come inside.

The rain poured down. Chico never lingered in bad weather.

As I walked back to my bedroom, the wind rocked the Airstream the way turbulence rocks an airplane. I got a book from my shelf and tried to read. Couldn't concentrate with the noise of the hoist chains banging against the flagpoles.

Across from the bed behind my laptop, there's a small window. I leaned over and pushed aside the little curtain and peered out through the half light thrown by the spotlight on Charlie's roof. But it wasn't bright enough to see much.

I went out to the kitchen and opened the door and whistled as loud as I could for Chico. No response. I shut and locked the door. Opal lay there with a pillow clutched to her stomach.

The TV was still on. Thinking she needed the voices, I left it on.

Back in the bedroom, I took the Glock from the holster and checked the magazine. Fifteen rounds. Should I keep one in the pipe? Or is it a waste of time to fret over the two seconds it takes to rack a round?

Two seconds is a long time if you need it to stay alive.

I racked one into the pipe.

The light in the laptop window changed, meaning one of my outside spotlights had blown. I heard Chico's rapid-fire barking in the silence between gusts. I went to the kitchen and opened the door and saw that Charlie's roof light had blinked off.

"Chico! Come on, boy! Where are you?" Whistle, whistle.

As I stood there, the half-moon glow in the sky over the county road disappeared, which meant my second spotlight, the one illuminating my entrance sign, had gone out too. I heard a sound above the rain, a short, high-pitched yelp—then nothing.

The Glock filled my hand.

I flipped on the main kitchen light and threw the door open all the way to send more light outside. "Chico! Come on, boy! Chico!"

A shape moved in the darkness. As I struggled to see through the sheeting rain, a lightning flash threw down a split second of daylight. Someone stood on my entrance road, shoulders hunched, knees bent, arms extended in the shooting position.

The figure fired several shots in rapid succession. Three hit the body of the Airstream, back to back *thumps* into metal. A fourth ripped through the air just beyond my ear, close enough for me to feel the breeze. It struck the Airstream's back wall.

I jumped for cover to my left. While moving, I squeezed off four shots as fast as I could jerk the trigger, aiming where I thought the running figure would be. The Glock threw up a storm of spent shells.

I flipped off the overhead light and waited with my back pressed against the wall, gulping air and holding the gun with two hands between my legs.

A bottomless silence descended. It lasted until Opal started screaming.

EIGHTY-TWO

Opal rolled off the bed. With the remote still in her hand, she pancaked her face to the floor and screamed like somebody had gone to work on her leg with a hacksaw. The TV played on above the foldout, the light flickering on the walls. The wind grabbed the open door and banged it against the side of the trailer, again and again with each gust.

My heart roared in my ears and maybe I wasn't thinking clearly. But I couldn't just stay put and take cover, leaving the gunman in control. He could sit back and riddle the Airstream with bullets until Cash stopped him, if Cash was still alive to stop him.

The backlight from the TV would make me an easy target. I pried the remote out of Opal's hands and turned it off.

Complete darkness.

"Stay inside, Opal! Don't you move outside this trailer, or you will be shot!"

I jumped out of the Airstream and crouched behind the Bronco and waited, letting my eyes adjust to the darkness and the rain. From behind came a sharp whistle, and the white portion of Cash's Arizona Feeds hat appeared.

"Don't shoot. I'm coming over there," Cash said, and ran to my side.

"I saw one guy, that's it. I couldn't tell if it was Rincon."

"He's here and he ain't alone. Count on it."

"We need light. Cover me."

From the passenger side of the Bronco, I crawled in and started the engine. Bending low in the driver's seat, I got the Bronco turned to shine its headlights down the entrance road. The rain blinked through the beams.

Someone was crawling through the brush beside the road. He moved with difficulty, using his elbows to pull himself along. My wild firing must've scored. He pulled up behind a rotting saguaro, twisted his arm around the spines, and snapped off two shots.

He didn't bother to look. Only the arm swung out and it wasn't bad work. The bullets whizzed overhead.

The wind howled and that old saguaro swayed in the gusts.

Squirming out from under the dashboard, I rose and fired twice. The bullets hit the saguaro with a heavy thump, like someone whacking a blanket with a broom. The gunman fired again. My left headlight shattered.

I dove across the seat and belly-flopped out the passenger door into a puddle and sat with my back against the front tire, gulping air.

"He ain't giving up," I said. "That was close."

Cash squinted over the hood of the Bronco at the gunman's position. "Sit tight, Mayor. I got this peckerneck right where I want 'im."

With the AR up at his shoulder, Cash stepped around the Bronco into the open. The gunman fired again, but that was his last go. Cash fired, stepped forward, fired again, stepped, fired again, and kept walking.

He was collected and exact in his aim, the sound deafening. Nine shots, the spacing precise. The saguaro visibly wavered and seemed to steady as the wind eased. But in the next second, another gust came and the giant began a slow, backward fall.

The gunman screamed a long, "Noooooooo!" and then another and another.

Cash hollered, "She's a going! Yeee-haaaa!"

The gunman's cries became a continuous bawling as the saguaro crashed to the ground, the desert exploding with mud and stones. Cash ran forward and picked up the gunman's pistol and stuffed it under his belt.

He said, "Get a look at this. Never touched him!"

The saguaro landed on one of its bent arms. The gunman lay in the small opening between the elbow and the main column, perfectly protected.

"I call that luck right there," Cash said.

The gunman had been hit above the knee. His eyes were the size of dinner plates as he screamed his face red. Only after he ran out of breath and his facial features returned to their normal locations did I recognize Ed Bolt.

I said, "You get bailed out and run to Rincon? Not smart, Eddie. You'd have been better off staying in the cage. Where's Rincon?"

Bolt gasped and pressed a hand over the hole in his leg. "You shot me, Stark!"

A bloody knife lay on the ground beside him, a foldout with a four-inch blade and thumb stud release. I wiped the blade on my pants, folded it into the hilt, and dropped the knife into my pocket.

Bolt said, "You're going to die tonight, Stark! You shot me!"

A tremendous explosion split the night. It left Cash and I sprawled over the wet ground, covering our heads against falling debris. When the earth stopped shaking, I pulled myself out of the mud and looked.

The blast came from Angel's trailer.

Cash rose to his knees and spat. "What the hell?" He wiped mud from his face with his arm. He stood up awkwardly, unwinding his long body and setting his big feet wide for balance as he straightened his wire legs beneath him.

"That's Rincon," I said. "He's going after Angel."

"Looks that way."

"We've gotta get the kid out of that trailer. He gonna burn alive in there."

"Easy does it, Mayor. Rincon wants us to come running down the street like chickens." Cash ran his tongue along his bottom lip as he looked down the entrance road and then toward the wash and the fire, assessing his options.

When he made up his mind, he nodded and said, "Got me an idea, Mayor. Follow my lead." As he moved out, he mumbled, "Too many sons of bitches in this world."

EIGHTY-THREE

We ducked behind the Airstream and ran south on the narrow strip of ground between the back of the trailer and the lip of the wash. The Airstream provided cover and so did Gil Pappas's trailer next door.

From the narrow space between the two, we had a straight-on view across Main Street to Angel's trailer. The flames thumped like horses on a dirt track as they spread across the roof, devouring it. The back portion by the propane tanks had already collapsed.

"If he's alive in there, he doesn't have much time," I said.

"Big if."

"Where the hell's Rincon?"

"Watching. Itching to take a shot."

A window to the left of Angel's front door exploded, throwing out a thick plume of smoke. A few seconds later, the window on the right blew, the heat rolling over us in a wave.

"I can't just watch this," I said. "We need to get to that trailer."

Cash said, "I got an idea. I'll double back and cross the street down by your place. If I can get behind the trailers on the other side, we might shake him loose. You okay by yourself?"

"Go, go, go!"

He went back the way we'd come, emerging on the far side of the Airstream. He barely made two steps across Main Street when three shots ripped through the rain.

Bap! Bap! Bap!

They came from somewhere to my right. Close by, same side of the street.

Past Pappas's trailer stood a cluster of paloverde trees. I leaned out and looked in that direction and saw nothing. Cash hollered for me to get back and cooked off four rounds toward the trees, the white lick of his muzzle flashing in the dark.

When I looked again, Rincon was sprinting across the south end of Main Street. He disappeared into the desert behind Charlie O'Shea's trailer.

Cash ran down the street in pursuit. "Let's get him!"

"We have to get Angel!"

"He's dead in there! We go in there and we're dead too!"

Cash was right. The trailer was fully involved.

We ran into the desert where we last saw Rincon. Beyond the glow of the flames, it was too dark to see much, and the rain made it hard to hear. Cash held a closed fist over his shoulder recon style and dropped to his haunches behind some brush.

He whispered, "We're close behind. If we keep going, we walk right into him."

"What's the plan?"

"Force multiply. You move left, I move right, and we flank him. If I hear shooting, I'll come running, and you do the same."

Cash ran into the soggy gloom, darting from saguaro to saguaro, shrub to shrub, and I did the same.

EIGHTY-FOUR

Twenty minutes of scouting the desert yielded nothing. The rain had eased considerably, making it easier to see and maneuver. But I had no contact with Rincon, and based on the silence from Cash's AR, neither did he.

Rincon might've heard Bolt screaming and, calculating the odds against two guns, took off to plan another run later.

Sloshing through water and mud, I made it out to the county road. At my Double Wide sign, I turned down the entrance road, and halfway along, near where Bolt lay, I spotted something black on the ground.

Closer in, I saw Chico. He wasn't moving, and his red tongue curled out the corner of his mouth, bunching grotesquely in the dirt. Feeling the fur along his ribs, my hand came back bloody. A wound in his side had penetrated his heart, killing him.

That explained the yelp I'd heard when I opened the Airstream door, and the blood on Bolt's knife.

Rincon's plan was to blow up Angel's trailer. The explosion would draw me out of the Airstream, and with Bolt on my left and Rincon on my right, they'd shoot me down. Chico's barking alerted me to the trouble and forced Bolt to act early to shut him up, saving my life.

I marched over to Bolt, still moaning under the fallen cactus.

"You killed my dog, Eddie! Tell me you killed my dog!"

"What do I care about a dog? I'm bleeding to death, Stark! You shot me!"

I pressed the Glock against his temple. "Tell me what you did to my dog!"

"It's a dog! I'm shot!"

"Tell me what you did!"

The fire continued to burn. The desert glowed red all around it. Gunshots echoed far out in the desert. I recognized the sound of Cash's AR, and then three quick reports from Rincon's pistol: *Bap! Bap! Bap!*

Then the AR returning fire, a deeper, more powerful sound: *Boom! Boom! Boom! Boom!*

Bolt said, "Your friend's all alone, Stark! And he ain't coming back! And you're next! Today's the day you die!"

I pushed the Glock harder against his temple, my finger tight around the trigger. A hiccup and he was lion food.

"I'm telling you to shoot!" Bolt gritted his teeth and blew snot. "Go ahead and shoot! You ain't got the hair!"

From Angel's trailer came a piercing metallic screech, like a castle door opening after a thousand years. Flames painted the sky above it amid the sounds of wood and metal straining and twisting as one corner of the trailer collapsed.

The sudden weight shift sent the whole thing thudding to the ground. Sparks mushroomed, met the rain, and became smoke.

"Shoot me, Stark!" Bolt yelled. "Go ahead!"

I thought of Sam in his cell, waiting, praying for help in his trial, wasting from that murderous drug. He needed me. I couldn't do it.

I stood up and, not wanting to be provoked by Ed Bolt's face, turned away. But he blabbered on about his bleeding leg until I couldn't stand it any longer. I drove my foot down on his knee with everything I had.

It made the same loud snapping sound a turkey leg makes when you break it in half. It was the least I could do. Bolt's leg looked like it was on backward. He cranked his mouth wide open and wailed.

The gunfire in the desert had stopped, which meant either Cash or Rincon had prevailed. I ran down the entrance road in the direction of their gunfight. A few steps along, I pulled up short. Just ahead, Roscoe Rincon was dragging Opal down the steps of the Airstream, his left arm wrapped around her neck, the machete in hand.

He walked toward me. I pulled the Glock from the holster, held it wide of my hip, and walked toward him. He was smiling.

EIGHTY-FIVE

Rincon stopped ten feet from me. "You have a gun, friend. You think you can shoot me?" He grinned and cackled. "Here I am!"

His head loomed over Opal's right shoulder. He fought to hold her up as she struggled beneath him. The kicking looked to be reflex. Fear had stolen her senses, turned her legs to rubber. Her mouth hung open in a silent scream.

Angel's trailer smoked over my shoulder. A few fire pockets crackled and snapped, and those sounds worked in concert with Bolt's operatic moaning.

"She's got nothing to do with this, Rincon. Let her go."

"Throw the gun away, Stark."

"She's done nothing to you."

Rincon's black hair lay flat from the rain. Tattoos covered his left arm. He wore a black T-shirt and baggy jeans, both drenched. He had a pistol strapped to his left hip, the same rig he wore the night of our encounter on Paradise Mountain.

He gave me more of his grim smile. "Throw the gun away or watch her die. Do it now!"

If I tossed the gun, he could kill Opal with the machete and draw his pistol and kill me before I could retrieve the Glock. I had Bolt's knife in my pocket, but that required a few extra seconds and closer proximity.

"She has nothing to do with this, Rincon. What do you want with her?"

"I want you, Stark. You have a bill to pay."

I stepped closer to him. The moment became crystalline and slow moving. My mouth was dry, and I couldn't swallow. I felt cold.

I said, "Let her go and it'll be just the two of us, you and me. We'll settle this."

He grinned and glared over Opal's shoulder. "I'll let you go down like a man. Rolando Molina died like a man. You'll be reunited with your friend, Stark. Isn't that what you want?"

"You murdered him. You're a coward, Rincon."

"All you can do is save this girl, Stark. That's the only honor you'll have tonight. Angel's dead and your gunhand's dead in the desert. There's nothing else for you."

Cash was dead. Hearing that was like getting hit with a hammer. No, no, no, no, no. I felt sick, the bile rising into my throat. I swallowed it back and anger took over.

I took another step forward. "Let her go, you goddamned coward."

Rincon's grin vanished and his face became a stone. Those red flecks gleamed like embers in the corner of his eyes. His arm tightened under Opal's chin, and with his free hand, he grabbed her hair and jerked her head back to expose her throat.

"Don't! Don't! Don't do it! I'm tossing the gun! Look!" I threw it away. "I've done what you asked. Now let her go."

"You're a fool, Stark. What do you care about a damned Indian for?"

"She's a teenager, Rincon. Her name is Opal Sanchez. Don't hurt her."

The sound of her name seemed to jolt Opal. She stopped struggling under Rincon's arm and looked at me, recognition coming into her face. "Mr. Whip?" The voice was pleading and childlike. She said nothing more.

"I don't care what her name is," Rincon said. "She's going to die with you, Stark." His face twisted. The muscles in his forearms tightened as he hardened his grip on the machete.

A rifle shot boomed, and a bullet struck Rincon in the right thigh. He bellowed. His body jerked and his leg buckled, his torso bending in the same direction.

I looked to my left, and there was Cashmere Miller, fifty feet away, on his knees in the firing position. Blood soaked his muscle shirt. He dropped the AR and collapsed in the mud.

Opal had crumpled to her knees with her face in her hands. Rincon cried in agony as he groped at the ground for balance with his right hand, the machete still in his left.

Putting most of his weight on his good leg, he pulled himself up and raised the machete behind his head, his face knotted with rage. With an open-mouthed roar, he took three lurching steps toward me.

I drew Ed Bolt's knife from my pocket, flicked the thumb stud to release the blade, and threw it with all the strength I had. It stuck in the center of Rincon's chest, a perfect strike. His face contorted and he sagged, dropping the machete.

He looked down in shock, groping for the knife with both hands. But his hands only found the blood trickling down his chest. He looked at his smeared fingers and then at me, curious, seemingly baffled.

His strength gone, he sat down with his legs stretched out in front of him.

I kicked the machete away and grabbed his pistol out of its holster. Rincon didn't speak or try to interfere, but his eyes tracked me in slow, mechanical movements.

Quiet now, he looked down at the knife in his chest and the blood spreading across his shirt and smiled. "I'm surprised."

Rincon's face emptied, becoming flat and distant. He fell back, dead.

Opal lay with her face in the dirt, whimpering. When I put my hands on her shoulders, she turned, startled, her eyes huge. "All of a sudden he was just there! That bad man!"

Cash wasn't moving when I got to him, but he was alive. He groaned when I rolled him over and pulled up his muscle shirt. Rincon's bullet had struck his stomach right of center and passed clear through. That was good, but he was losing a lot of blood.

"Cash, look at me. Open your eyes."

I gripped his chin and shook it. He opened his eyes halfway. They were a mile deep. He let out another aboriginal groan.

"Stay with me, Cash. Stay with me."

"Rincon. You get him?" His voice was weak, barely a voice at all.

"I got him."

"Let the river run, baby."

He nodded and closed his eyes. I talked to him until they opened.

He said, "Where's my hat at?"

"You're wearing it. Arizona Feeds."

"Sweet." He closed his eyes again.

EIGHTY-SIX

I kept pressure on Cash's wound until the Rural Metro ambulance screeched and flashed over the mountain. Opal helped out, dabbing at his forehead with a wet cloth. Diaz came and saw Bolt wounded under the cactus, Rincon dead with a knife in his chest, and Angel's trailer a pile of smoldering ash.

"I'm impressed," he said. "I think. Are you all right?"

Better than all right. I felt an unexpected righteousness and a dangerous joy. Roscoe Rincon was dead. I'd killed the man who killed Rolando Molina, and not a glimmer of guilt clouded my heart.

The ambulance took Cash first. I insisted on that. Ed Bolt couldn't stop yelling about his leg. The EMTs gave him a shot of something to quiet him until another ambulance showed up and they shoved him in the back and took off.

The next morning, the fire captain returned to Double Wide to kick through the debris again in daylight. He confirmed the fire was arson caused by ignition of the propane tanks.

The only mystery was Angel. Cash said he was in the trailer when the shooting started and when the explosion and fire happened. But they found no remains in the ashes, no wounded or burned Angel wandering the nearby desert, no Angel anywhere.

The only possible way out of that inferno was the hole in the kitchen floor.

By then, my mind was on a grim task.

The night before, I'd wrapped Chico in a blanket and placed him in the backseat of the Bronco. Now it was time for burial. With my dead dog in my arms and Opal beside me, we hiked into the wash.

Mesquite trees clustered along the chest-high banks, their gnarled branches overhanging the rocky sand. Chico would need shade in his last resting place, and I could use some for the digging. I needed to go deep to keep rushing water from dredging him up and giving the coyotes and javelina a feast.

Opal watched. She wore her straw hat with the plastic rose on top. The skin on her face was pale and tight, making the bones more prominent. She chewed her bottom lip. I didn't ask what troubled her, figuring she'd tell me on her own when she was ready, which she did.

"The fire guy is wrong," she said. "That fire wasn't on account of propane."

"Those investigators are pretty good."

"Angel's friend did it. Angel's friend was fighting that bad man. That's how the fire started."

"We're back to the mysterious friend," I said, and kept digging.

"That's why Angel was hunting. He was getting food and burying it to leave a trail so his friend could find his way down here. He wanted his friend to protect him."

"There is no friend, Opal."

"The breath of the Gila monster started that fire!" Her words sputtered out on a rush of emotion.

I straightened up and stood leaning on my shovel like a dumb man, no idea what to say. Opal gave me wondering eyes as if she couldn't believe how I was missing the obvious.

"The Gila monster came and warned Angel to get away! He's here! The bad man is here! Angel escaped and the Gila monster fought that bad man with his breath. That's how the fire started! I know you don't believe me, but that's the truth."

I started to say something about superstition, science, the twenty-first century, and other ideas that wouldn't mean a thing to Opal Sanchez. People believe what they believe, and beliefs are hard set. Any time spent trying to talk someone out of an article of faith they've held since childhood is time wasted.

The digging done, I lowered Chico into the hole. Opal folded her hands on her stomach, closed her eyes, bowed her head, and recited a Catholic prayer.

Blessing herself, she said, "Chico was like us, Mr. Whip. He was a good old dog, but he didn't have no easy life in this place."

EIGHTY-SEVEN

O ver the remainder of that week, I checked out two of the border gold mines on my list, hoping for some clue to Rolando's whereabouts. I saw no sign of renewed activity, and that Sunday night Tork Mortenson called to report on his trip to the Oro Grande. His news mirrored mine.

He rattled on about the mine's history, and I was about to hang up when he said, "The only thing interesting out there was a Mexican boy. He wouldn't talk to us and that was that."

The blood raced up my neck. "He had a bad eye, right?"

"Why, yes. He looked rather like a lad from Dickens. How'd you know?"

Next morning, I picked up Roxy in Tucson and we drove sixty miles to Patagonia, an old cattle and mining town of nine hundred people southeast of Tucson.

The mountains swell up behind it through thick oak and manzanita forest all the way to the Mexican border, eighteen miles away. The trees made shadows on the switchback road. We blinked over twelve empty miles, nothing but white dirt ahead of us and dust devils behind.

My map placed the Oro Grande in Crying Times Gulch, a deep gash of rock, scrub, and barrel cactus accessed by a road jammed against the hillside and too treacherous to drive. I spied down with binoculars on three clapboard buildings and scattered pieces of mining gear.

No sign of habitation. I scanned the empty countryside waiting for an idea to pop into my head. Frustrated, I reached into the Bronco and leaned on the horn and shouted, "Come on, Rolando! Where are you, Rolando?"

The shrill sound probably split boulders as it echoed through the gulch.

With the racket still going on, Roxy put a hand on my shoulder and pointed to the ridge at the gulch's southern end. A figure stood against the sunlight. I wasn't sure it was Angel until I fixed him in my binoculars.

"That's him," I said. "I'd recognize those Goodwill clothes anywhere."

He gave me his two-fingered whistle and motioned toward the southwest. He made a steering wheel of his hands and an air map, telling me where I should drive. He made a cross of his arms for an intersection, held his hands apart to indicate a short trip, made an X of his fingers to mark the spot, and then vanished from the ridge.

I found the spur road he indicated and inched the Bronco along for a back-jarring half a mile before stopping at the edge of a deep, east-to-west drainage. A truck lay on its side at the bottom, burned to rust brown and half-covered with dirt carried by monsoon waters.

It looked like someone had set it on fire and rolled it off the edge. Not a bad way to dispose of a vehicle and human remains. The flames had scorched away the metal's original color, but I had a good idea it was red.

Roxy said, "You sure you want to do this?"

"Yes."

"I'd go with you, but these are brand-new shoes. Nike Flyknits."

"I can do it myself."

"It's too naturey down there. Why don't you stay up here? We can call the marshal."

"I owe it to Rolando."

"You're like a dog with a piece of meat," Roxy said. "If I wind up dead in the mountains, you're the one I want looking for me."

I hiked down the steep slope, my heels sliding on the rocky ground. I turned sideways for balance. Avalanching pebbles rolled into my shoes. With my hands, with rocks, and a loose tree branch, I dug at the dirt.

It didn't take long. The skull staring out at me could've been anyone who'd died badly. A skull is a skull. But I knew in my heart it was Rolando.

EIGHTY-EIGHT

Oscar and Natty Molina got the burial they so desperately wanted, and sometime later, Roxy and I sat in on Max Mayflower's sentencing in Pima County Superior Court.

He started his legal battle playing it tough, until Ed Bolt cut a deal with prosecutors and rolled on him. Mayflower pleaded guilty and got twelve years for money laundering and conspiracy to smuggle heroin.

A few days later, Roxy and I went to Costco to load up on supplies. Pete, the nervous ninety-pound body man, had installed the new roof on the Bronco and this was the inaugural trip. But it didn't sit evenly. The whole apparatus shook at any speed above forty miles per hour.

We were driving west on Speedway. It was late in the afternoon and the sky was pale and ordinary, with none of the customary sunset shenanigans. That was good.

"You need to take this back and get it fixed," Roxy said.

"I went by the garage the other day. It's boarded up and Pete has disappeared."

"Natch."

Roxy had on tight jeans and a form-fitting T-shirt with a crochet pattern at the chest. She wore a straw sun hat with a wide, waving brim. It had a burgundy ribbon around the crown and an oversized bow of the same color over the right ear. She had on those huge Tom Ford shades and dollar sign earrings. She called it her Costco outfit.

"How do you stand it?" she said. "Nothing works in your life. Everything's stolen, broken, or about to break."

I grinned and pointed out the windshield. "Double Wide's just over the mountain."

"My point exactly."

The rattling roof sounded like a blackout drunk trying to break down a door with a poleaxe.

Roxy said, "Next time we go to Phoenix, we're taking the Audi. This is ridiculous."

I'd been going to the Maricopa County Jail every week to visit Sam. Most days Roxy came too. It had become a regular thing and would continue. The judge had granted Micah Alan Gabriel's request to investigate Sam's drug use and assess his ability to stand trial. Gabriel had no idea how long that would take or when the trial might start.

"I never thanked you for coming with me," I said. "Sam lights up when he sees you."

"He's a sweetie, but it's all about you. He knows you'll be there, same time every week. Never a doubt."

"Everybody needs somebody to look after them that way. If that's not written down somewhere, it should be. That's something I've learned."

"You're pushing self-improvement now?" She snickered. "My idea of self-improvement is buying clothes, maybe making a deadline now and then." For a long time Roxy said nothing. "Who do you need, Prospero?"

"I've been thinking a lot about that. Maybe I need you."

She burst out laughing, a long, rolling laugh with much more in it than humor. "Let's review, shall we? You came to the desert thinking you could help your father and clear your head, find something decent in your life because yours had gone to hell. And that's me? *I'm* what you're looking for? That's crazy. I can't be anybody's dream."

"I'm not saying I know what's going on here," I said. "But I don't want to see you walk away. That's all I know for sure."

I drove along. It takes concentration to negotiate the switchbacks through Gates Pass. Miss one and the trip to the bottom ends with a very loud noise. I reached the saguaro forest with that familiar feeling of entering an alien world.

Roxy said, "You're interested, but you don't know why?"

"Something like that."

"What every girl wants to hear." She didn't move a muscle as she stared out the window. Then: "A door slammed on it."

"Huh?"

"My imperfection, my pinky." She held out her hand to show me her half finger. "I was a little girl, four years old, and my stupid brother slammed the door on it. But that's not what I tell people. No, sirree. I say it happened on a story, and there were bad guys and gunshots and all that. I tell a different story every time."

"You're protecting your brother."

"Oh, Prospero, that's what I love about you. I do it for me, not him." She made a gesture of conclusion. "There you go. No secrets. You wanted to know and now you do."

The shadows had grown long on a hot day. A roadrunner darted in front of the Bronco, head angled forward, feet a blur as it zipped into the desert.

Roxy perked up and said, "Wait—there's something else. It's important. If we're going to do this, you have to guess my dancing name."

"Miss Honey Jones."

She bumped her shoulder against mine. "How'd you know?"

"Asked around, simple detective work. I like it."

"The 'miss' part cinches it," Roxy said. "It means she's important and available. And it's simple. Simplicity's the key with men."

I bounced along the county road past the skulled fence line to my painted Double Wide sign and turned onto the entrance road. The Airstream faced us. Ed Bolt had shot holes in my trailer and I hadn't repaired them yet.

They looked like stars shining in the dull twilight.

"I don't know what you're talking about," I said. "Everything in my life works fine."

Roxanne Santa Cruz rolled her eyes.

ABOUT THE AUTHOR

In high school, Leo W. Banks worked loading delivery trucks with the Sunday edition of the *Boston Globe*. In those days the Sunday paper was really heavy, so he switched from lifting to writing. He graduated from Boston College and earned a master's degree from the University of Arizona. He has been a correspondent for the *Los Angeles Times* and the *Boston Globe*. His articles have appeared in the *USA Today, National Review, Los Angeles Times Magazine, Sports Illustrated, Wall Street Journal*, and many others. He has written four books of Old West history for *Arizona Highways'* publishing imprint, and his book about the saguaro cactus won't stop selling.

He has won thirty-eight statewide, regional, and national journalism awards. Today, he writes a column for *True West* magazine. *Double Wide* is his first novel.

Made in the USA
Lexington, KY
05 November 2017